COMPARTMENT EAST

La vie d'Adréan Putney poète
La Table Ronde

ESSAYS

La mort de Floria Tosca
Mercure de France

Callas, une vie
Ramsey

Si j'étais romancier
Garnier

Chine, une itinéraire
Orban

POETRY

Urbanisme
NRF

UNDER THE PSEUDONYM RAYMOND MORLOT
Gaugins à Gogo
Denoël

Les suicides du printemps
Denoël

COMPARTMENT EAST

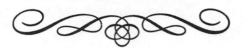

Love and Adventure
on the Orient Express

Pierre-Jean Remy

translated by St. John Field

WILLIAM MORROW AND COMPANY, INC.
New York   1980

Library of Congress Cataloging in Publication Data

Remy, Pierre-Jean.
    Compartment east.

    Translation of Orient-express.
    I. Title.
PQ2678.E420713   843'.914   80-23875
ISBN 0-688-03739-9

Printed in the United States of America

First U.S. Edition

1 2 3 4 5 6 7 8 9 10

BOOK DESIGN BY MICHAEL MAUCERI

For Antoine, and for Claude Barma, who first had the idea of putting this Orient Express back on the tracks . . .

CONTENTS

Above all, this is a book of adventure. A novel of love and adventure in the oldest sense of the French word *roman,* meaning "novel," for truly it is a sort of epic romance. It is a nostalgic novel too. How few can now remember those great old trains that once made their way across Europe; they have long since been replaced by a faceless gray express. It is an old-fashioned novel, weaving a story of human lives into the vast tapestry of history. The characters, naturally, are all imaginary and have nothing in common with any real person. Or, as the old formula goes, "Any resemblance to any person, living or dead, is purely coincidental," etc. History furnishes the framework, the realistic background for the book, but from time to time some liberties have been taken and a few adjustments made. No one should dream of assuming that the various details which add up so nicely to make the story can be taken as actual history; it would be absurd to think that Germany left the League of Nations because Helene Petresco happened to be riding the train from Bucharest one evening in 1933. Our world is one where trains are still allowed to fall behind schedule, where railway time-tables, with their pages of perfect columns, are never so sacredly inviolable as they seem. But then really, isn't everything very much a matter of appearances?

PROLOGUE

The girl looked at her watch: it was 7:12. She stood at the entrance to the international departure platform in the Gare de Lyon, holding an overnight case; she was waiting for someone. It was beginning to seem that she was waiting in vain.

"He doesn't give a damn about anyone!"

She had spoken out loud, to herself, and a passenger walking by turned to look at her. He might have been around forty, perhaps a journalist or traveling diplomat—a type fairly common on airplanes, ships, trains—and he was unable to catch a glimpse of her face through the thick lock of hair that had fallen across it. He could see only her mouth, full, generous, fashionable. There was, after all, nothing very unusual in a girl standing on a train platform and talking to herself. . . . The passenger hurried on, telling himself that since she was standing on the platform, it was likely that he would see her again on the train.

Had he stopped to look at her more carefully, he would have seen that Lise Bergaud was pretty—more than that: she was one of those girls a man sees from his train window just as the train is about to pull out of the station, a girl he will remember the rest of his life . . . or for days, at least; he will regret not having spoken to her. So Lise

Bergaud was pretty, and she was alone; it was now 7:15, and the train was scheduled to depart in exactly seven minutes. She muttered something under her breath, not loudly, although any passerby could have overheard—something that sounded like an oath. She picked up her leather traveling case and walked swiftly down the platform to the Simplon Express—to what is left of the Simplon Express in this day and age—where the last passengers were boarding.

What an idiot he was. So she was to travel to Venice alone; the photographer who had been supposed to accompany her hadn't shown up . . . but what she felt, suddenly, was something like relief. After all, why not? Why not enjoy a long trip in solitude, falling asleep in Paris and awaking to see the blue mists of the lingering summer beginning to clear. . . . She pushed her hair back and looked around.

There were only two sleeping cars. One of them was the old-fashioned kind with large compartments, commodious; the other, two cars further along, was modern, streamlined, the compartments staggered one into the other by some economy-minded designer in order to make use of every inch of available space.

"And they call that a 'special'!"

The conductor who took Lise Bergaud's ticket grumbled to her over what had been done to his train; he was to be the first of many. Later, at dinner, the passenger across from her would do the same, as would the chef who had been reduced to serving up cold platters in the "express grill." Each would reminisce about the old days, the old trains, but Lise Bergaud was blithely unaware of any change. This was the first time she had made this trip. She was delighted to be going . . . and she was looking forward to meeting the old diplomat she was on her way to interview, who lived in one of the most beautiful of the country villas outside Venice, in that countryside she imagined as still looking something like an engraving by Tiepolo or Canaletto. Above all, she wasn't going to miss anything she was leaving behind her in Paris.

Men were such idiots. This time the words were spoken silently, in her mind, but no less deeply felt for that. Yet as she opened her toilet case, took out a brush and carefully repaired the line of her eyebrows, glancing at herself in the mirror, she felt surprisingly free. Almost happy . . . happy at again being free, happy that the fool of a photographer had missed the train, happy that Michel X or Daniel Y—or whoever—had made up his mind to leave her for another girl, happy at the way she looked in the mirror, at being twenty-three years old with a great idea for a book and a tidy advance from an interested publisher.

Of course, the dining car she entered a few minutes later was not one of the old-fashioned restaurant cars, with glass-shaded Gallé lamps and panels of cut glass, but what difference did that make? Lise Bergaud was oblivious to the luxuries she was missing, and she sat down quite contentedly to her ragout of veal or mutton or whatever, facing an elderly dowager dripping with pearls and with a voice like a parrot. She was fat and voluble, she wore a great many gold rings and a vast expanse of purple silk and she went on about the trains in the old days; her penetrating voice grew more insistent as she noted that their fellow passengers looked more like Italian waiters or Yugoslav laborers returning home, not at all like the passengers one had found on luxury trains in the past. Then there had been Brazilian millionaires ostentatiously traveling in their own private cars, brought with them to Europe from Manaus; there had been elegant women of—the expression was— "easy virtue," women who took a single compartment at the end of the train and sold what little modesty they had for a thousand francs a client!

"Yes, they probably are Yugoslav laborers . . . what difference does it make?"

Lise Bergaud's disinterest eventually silenced the woman with the pearls, but not before she had managed to mention that she would be staying at the Gritti in Venice . . . at the Danieli these days, you didn't really know what kind of person you might run into! When the journalist or diplomat who had turned to look at Lise on the platform slipped into the seat across from her, vacated by the dowager, she answered his probing, indirect questions evasively, making it obvious she wanted to be alone. When he invited her to have another glass of wine with him—the train had just passed Joigny—she refused bluntly and returned to her compartment. She felt that she had come to a moment in her life when she suddenly never wanted to look at another man. Such idiots men were.

And true enough, Michel X, who had thrown her over for some common little fool, was an idiot. As Paul de Morlay, the old man she was going to interview at his villa in Castelfranco, near Venice, would one day remark, Lise Bergaud was the very image of the girl anyone would be lucky to meet, regardless of age, regardless of time.

Lise Bergaud extinguished the blue night-light glowing in the ceiling and fell asleep, repeating to herself calmly that men were such idiots. Shortly before the train reached Mestre, the porter brought her a plastic cup of boiling hot instant coffee which she found excellent, and when the chauffeur Paul de Morlay had sent to meet her at the Santa Lucia station—Venice, at last, in the early morning—turned out to have the dark eyes of a mysterious young highwayman, she began to think that perhaps men weren't all idiots, that sometimes they were terribly handsome. . . . And she felt a surge of excitement.

Fifty years ago, the countryside around Venice was one of the love-liest in the world. The Brenta, the long and serene river that traverses the Veneto from the Adriatic, shelters in its bends and curves villas, follies, little palaces built to provide asylums from the summer heat to the patrician families of the Most Serene Republic. Fifty years ago, the entire area—that landscape of green plain and copses stretching away to the northern hills with the Villa Maser on the slopes and the village of Asolo perched at the summit—was filled with such villas, such miniature palaces that caught the eye everywhere.

These villas of the Veneto, so closely united with the landscape of which they are a part—like the palazzos of Venice along the Grand Canal—are perhaps some of the architectural masterpieces of all time. The great Andrea Palladio, the architect who created Vicenza and who invented the style that bears his name, designed the most glorious of them in the sixteenth century. The most beautiful is the Villa Ro-tonda, a circular structure open on all four sides to the winds of the Mind, a building imitated by Lord Burlington when he came to build Chiswick House near London. There is the Villa Barbaro in Maser, where the frescoes of Veronese—women on balconies, girls, maid-servants, peering through half-opened doors, a green-clad huntsman at the end of a corridor—create false perspectives in a dizzying display of *trompe l'oeil*. And there is the Villa Emo, the Caldogno, and all the rest. . . . Palladio, however, was not the only one to build classical pediments, columns, porticos: all through the seventeenth and eigh-teenth centuries, such superb summer houses continued to be con-structed, the paragon among them probably the Malcontenta—circular and square at one and the same time—standing beneath the shadows of the Brenta willows. The light there in the summertime—the trees and columns, the green lawn, the flowing river—cannot be found any-where else.

All that remains today of the nostalgic countryside are these villas. They stand there separated from the landscape, out of context. The countryside has become an eerie universe of high-tension wires, a vast expanse of factories and warehouses, poles and wooden shacks—and the Brenta is polluted with empty bottles, plastic bags, dead dogs and rats; it gives off the nauseating smell of ammonia and rotten eggs. Thus would Paul de Morlay have described it to his visitor had he been seated beside her in the white Bentley as it made its way out of Venice and Mestre along the road to Castelfranco. However, Lise Bergaud—just as she had not minded that the train that had borne her here, had not really noticed that the Simplon Express was only an ordinary fast train furnishing transportation to migrant workers from France to southern Europe, enjoying the solitude she was savoring like a drug—was now oblivious to the high-tension wires, the twisted poles and the grotesque factory smokestacks. . . . They were simply there. And with them, for one brief, dazzling moment, there was also the noble perspective of an avenue of trees leading up to a baroque facade with pediment and columns, a vision that sped by before she fully saw it, but which helped her to overlook the shantytowns in the green fields.

Besides, she was thinking of the task that lay ahead of her. Her great idea had been a simple one: Paul de Morlay, a long-retired French ambassador, had, over the past fifty years, known all the great of this world. He had moved from post to post throughout Europe, and his life had been closely linked to historical events spanning half a century. It was obvious that this old man—who was said to be charming—would have a thousand tales to recount, anecdotes, recollections, and she would turn them into a book. That was what readers wanted nowadays: true stories, first-person memoires, as-told-to biography. It was her good fortune that no one had had the idea of Paul de Morlay before, that she had been the first to think of sitting him down before a tape recorder . . . even though everyone else, from country shepherd to second-rate athlete, had been subjected to that ritual. Lise Bergaud was not merely pretty (although only from the age of twelve—prior to that, she had looked more like a tiny monkey); she was not merely unattached (for forty-eight hours now—prior to that, she had relied on X or Y). Lise Bergaud was also ambitious. She had always been ambitious. And since her ambition focused on writing, what better introduction to publishing than the collected reminiscences of an elderly man concerning his rich past? At least, it was a realistic way to begin her career . . . "literature" could come later.

But as she caught sight of the Villa Manni, de Morlay's home, her heart began to pound. The house, which had been built in the early eighteenth century, spread a charm that was almost nostalgic: sheltered beneath immense trees like the Villa Malatesta, it stood in the midst of vast, overgrown lawns that were populated by glistening white statues —nude women, supple and graceful—which, she would learn, Morlay had carefully selected himself. There was a broad staircase leading up to the entrance, its low, wide steps designed by the mad first owner of the villa in order that he might bring his horses into the house. The entire landscape was bathed in a clear yellow light that filtered through the leaves and over the wicker chairs set upon a broad gallery opening onto gardens with orange trees in tubs and beds of flowers. Like some antique and beloved engraving brought to life, the Villa Manni—its inhabitant an elderly man in love with love itself, a love she would soon discover—seemed like some enchanted dwelling floating in time between the century of its construction and this moment when Lise discovered it.

"You have no idea how happy your visit makes me!"

Lise Bergaud was sitting in one of the wicker armchairs, having been led to the gallery by a maid wearing a voluminous white skirt. At the sound of the voice, she started. Paul de Morlay stood before her.

He was old, very old; yet his tanned face, the fine longish white hair, his solid, square hands, everything about him suggested youth, vivacity, a kind of strength that belied his eighty-nine years—he had been born in 1890. Lise Bergaud was at once aware of his eyes—his luminous gaze. His eyes were pale blue; perhaps age had drained their color, made them paler, but they were still as lively and sparkling as those of a boy in his teens. She noticed especially the aged ambassador's way of looking at her. It was that of any man at a woman . . . it had nothing to do with age or years; it was totally straightforward. At nearly ninety, Paul de Morlay looked at Lise Bergaud, sixty-some years his junior, with the frank candor of a man looking at a woman he finds beautiful and who is not shy at showing it.

Perhaps more surprising, Lise did not feel ill at ease or uncomfortable beneath his gaze: a kind of complicity had immediately sprung up between them, the young woman and the aged man who had always naturally—it was obvious—loved women and would continue to love them.

"You have no idea how happy your visit makes me!"

Lise Bergaud knew at once that de Morlay was speaking the truth and that he *was* happy at seeing her; she was glad she had given rise to his happiness. He clapped his hands, and a girl wearing a white apron and a tiny cap perched on her black hair, a girl who looked like a maid in a play, appeared from nowhere bearing a tray with coffee, cups. . . .

"Or perhaps you would rather have chocolate? Because we have delicious chocolate, too, do we not, Despinetta?"

The little maid clapped her hands with pleasure when Lise, already caught up in the spell cast by the bond she sensed between these people in this place, accepted the offer. Chocolate—why not?

"Fetch us some chocolate."

"You'll find my chocolate is delicious!"

Despinetta disappeared, and Paul de Morlay drew an armchair closer to Lise and into the sun, which was now casting broad, warm shadows onto the black and white tiles of the gallery floor. He lit a cigarette.

"My first and only cigarette for the day! I've given up many things, even smoking . . . but not my first morning cigarette. . . ."

And by the time Despinetta had returned bearing the steaming chocolate (it was very good—she had taken a sip, of course, on her way from the kitchen to the gallery overlooking the garden), Lise Bergaud and Paul de Morlay had become friends; they had already begun to discuss the work they were to undertake together. But the elderly diplomat's suggestion was far from what Lise had expected.

"Tell about my life? Why not? But do you really believe my life would be so interesting? To whom? I knew Aristide Briand and General de Gaulle, Pétain, Laval, Colonel Passy, Mussolini, old Victor Emmanuel. . . . I sat down to dinner with Chiang Kai-shek, had breakfast with Mao—but what's interesting about that? Many other men have done the same things, and—more important—many other men have recounted their experiences, and much better than I could, even with your assistance. . . . Just another memory cocktail—do you really believe anyone needs it? The few state secrets I chanced to be privy to—for in my life, everything has depended upon chance—those I intend to keep to myself. They are all laid away in the archives in the Quai d'Orsay, and when the gentlemen in the 'Department'—that seems to be what they're calling it these days—see fit to release the files, they will all come out anyway. And there will be a lot of surprises! But I was never much amused by embassy gossip, and as for the rest . . ."

Lise Bergau sensed that she must play this game in which the old ambassador obviously took so much pleasure . . . and she seized upon his last words.

"That's just it—the rest! Let's talk about that."

Paul de Morlay's eyes twinkled.

"Ah . . . the rest!"

The "rest" was his own life, real life. Traveling across the face of Europe in the course of his career for over fifty years, seeing everything there was to be seen, grasping at all life had offered him . . . "the rest" consisted of faces, of women, of departing trains and trains arriving. . . .

"Ah, the rest!"

The sun was now shining directly into the ambassador's eyes, but unlike most elderly people, he seemed to relish the light as it touched his forehead, his mouth, just as he was obviously enjoying the girl's presence at his side, this girl who was about to draw up out of the depths of his memory so many souvenirs . . . his buried youth.

"Yes, after all, it is about the rest that I'd like to tell you. . . ."

He laid his hand on Lise's: the firm hand of a firm man.

"And perhaps I should enjoy telling you about a few women . . . women I have met. . . . Or at least about some of them. For, you see, as time goes by I have come to the realization that they—and they alone—were what mattered to me."

History with its capital letter had been unrolled before him; he had lived intensely, he had fought against every kind of tyranny, he had loathed war, he had believed with all his heart in a kind of peace. "The League of Nations—yes, I believed in that, too. For six months. I believed deeply." But History was available to anyone, and it was his own history he wanted to talk about.

"Does that suit you? I promise to try not to bore you."

As though he were an adolescent eager to please, de Morlay turned on all his persuasive charm—and it worked. Lise was listening to him with an attention that was amused, but also suddenly touched.

"Bore me? I'm sure . . ."

"You are a very sweet young woman. . . ."

He had let go her hand, and Lise realized in that second that Paul de Morlay at age eighty-nine was an accomplished master of seduction. Like a devil—a beneficent devil—he seemed to be acting his age, calling her "a very sweet young woman" and talking to her like a grandfather, yet at the same time his eyes were those of a young man attempting—and he would continue to attempt—to conquer her. And a mere twelve hours ago, she had been telling herself that all men were idiots!

"You shall tell me whatever you want."

The air was warm. The autumn day glowed with the glorious colors of long-forgotten end-of-summer vacations. . . .

Luncheon was served in a dining room, awnings drawn down over the windows by Despinetta and Barberina, who was an equally sprightly girl. The walls were covered with frescoes in blue and pink showing clouds and sky, in which Rinaldos and bare-bosomed Armidas exchanged embraces, where Cleopatras gave way before the conquering gaze of Antonys and victorious Caesars. The menu had been chosen with care and taste, and the sunlight filtering through the awnings lent to everything—to the silver and crystal on the table—its gold and blue reflections; and Lise listened to de Morlay speak. She listened intently. And then, once more, there was coffee, this time in a conservatory that was also a cage for a thousand multicolored birds—birds that sang softly, chosen one by one like the lovely naked statues in the gardens by the ambassador himself. Lise spoke first. She talked about herself, about her pleasure at having traveled alone, of her pleasure at being solitary in her train compartment the evening before, of the night just passed.

"Ah, train journeys," de Morlay murmured, also remembering.

After a moment, he rose.

"One of the many ways I deal with my age is to allow it a half-hour siesta each day."

Alone, Lise Bergaud thought—as she had on the previous evening—that it had been the lucky chance of a lifetime—or of the past year, at least—that that stupid photographer had missed the train. From that moment on, the days she was to spend in Paul de Morlay's company were imbued with a strange kind of grace.

"My child," the ambassador began when they met again in the open gallery overlooking the gardens, where the colors of the day were reflected, one after the other, "my child, I sense we are in agreement. I shall not tell you things about war or peace or treaties or secret agreements . . . even though such matters are, of course, woven through everything I am about to say. Instead, I shall speak of the things closest to my heart. You already know what those are."

Women. The faces of some of the women who had made Paul de Morlay's life what it was: moments filled with happiness and with heartache.

"However, I won't tell only about women I have possessed. First, it would be indiscreet, and that is the worst kind of tactlessness. For that matter, the adventures I remember most clearly are not necessarily those in which I was most involved. Quite the contrary: I shall tell you about some women I never met, perhaps, or about women I merely encountered. Yet each one illustrates something, I believe. Because in each of these women there was something that helped me to become what I am. Each of us is born—in the deepest sense . . . I don't mean merely being brought into the world by our mothers—of woman. In my case, I know that in one way or another, I have been in love with every woman who has touched upon my life."

Evening fell: without Lise Bergaud's awareness, the day had flown by. The gallery was now bathed in pink and ochre—the sun was setting across the garden and the vast baroque fountain—and Paul de Morlay's voice was soft.

"In sum, my life has really been made up of nothing but women's faces, and it has passed in traveling . . ."

He chuckled.

"That's it: travels! You told me of your journey here on the train. But you have to realize that trains—the great trains of the past and, above all, the most famous train of all, the Orient Express—have played a starring role in my life. What a pleasure it was to fall asleep in Ostend and awaken in Cologne or Frankfurt, the long, varied spell of the Istanbul Express—stations, vast plains, the first sight of the Caspian, and all the women . . . sometimes nothing but a glance exchanged between Ruschuk and Varna. A gesture, a touch in passing as we went through the long tunnel just before Linz."

He laughed again, a short laugh.

"But I wouldn't want you to think of me as a horrid, aged libertine filled with nostalgia at his former conquests. I can assure you, that's not the case. I am old, yes, but as for the rest . . ."

Despinetta and Barberina arrived with a plaid shawl which they placed about his shoulders with tender care. Despinetta's bosom was as white as a dove's beneath her beribboned bodice, and saucy Barberina wore white stockings and a skirt made to be tucked up. Lise, seeing this elderly man so delightfully surrounded by such attractive young women, felt a new kind of emotion.

"I assure you, I'm not as awful as I may appear," de Morlay went on. She quickly laid her hand on his.

"I understand completely; you had no need to tell me."

As the lamps were being lit—the afternoon, the evening, had flown by—Paul de Morlay asked: "It's decided, then? I shall tell you about these women?"

"It's decided. A woman is as good as a treaty."

To think that she, Lise Bergaud, filled with notions of female freedom and independence, had come out with such a male chauvinist reply. . . .

But de Morlay continued: "And about my trains? I am allowed to tell you about my women and about my trains?"

She laughed aloud. "It's a bargain!"

Thus, beginning the following morning, Paul de Morlay, retired ambassador, began to tell about the women who had crossed his path . . . and about the trains he had taken. . . .

"First, you should know a bit about my background," he began. "I was born nearly ninety years ago, at a time when diplomacy was a way of life as much as it was a vocation—barely a profession—and when politics, excepting for men who were naive enough to be pure in heart, was a pastime for tired stock market gamblers, men bored with gaming tables and racecourses. There was the fire at the Bazaar de la Charité, there was Eiffel and his engineering feat, just to set the scene, and, of course, there was Dreyfus, who was about to become such an overriding subject of conversation.

"My father was a diplomat because his father had been a diplomat before him, and his grandfather before him. Two generations before that, my family had been Breton royalists. On my mother's side, Protestant banking money had been injected into the de Morlays' somewhat weakened blue blood. Neither my mother nor my father played any very great part in my life—he was always pressed for time, she was resigned to her lot. . . . A quick embrace before dinner, the theater, a party, my father's formal dress and my mother's boas, her evening dresses that were always a bit provincial—she had been born in Metz— even in the heart of Paris. Aside from one or two posts abroad, my father's entire career was confined to Paris. Following the prescribed pattern, I attended the Lycée Fenélon, Condorcet, and then on to the College of Political Science, preparing myself year after year for what was known in those days as the '*Grand concours.*' At the time, of course, there were other exams for entry into the French civil service, and those for the Conseil d'État and Treasury were nothing to be sneezed at, but *the Grand concours* was for entry into the Foreign Office: you know the myths about that as well as I—with Claudel's massive, lyric figure looming above it. . . .

"Like Claudel, I too wanted to be a writer. I dreamed of a life filled with travel and meditation; of the serenity of embassies in Prague or Vienna, baroque buildings with silent, carpeted corridors—and of adventure, too, of the exotic life in Fu Chow or Peking, the other side of the coin. And in the meanwhile, there would be quiet, book-lined rooms with a fire burning in the marble fireplace, and I too would write my few great books. Paul Claudel, St. John Perse—who was simply Alexis Saint-Léger Léger in those days—and so on . . . Old men, ghosts: my life could so easily have been like theirs. . . . But I discovered that life, my life, could be lived in the world as easily as it could among books, and I spent so much time in living that I had no leisure to write about it. I have waited for nearly ninety years—and now it is because you have wanted me to. If you knew how idle I was at twenty . . . how idle I still am. So I put my budding novel and the few short stories I had perpetrated into a secret drawer in my most secret desk, and I embroidered the style of my dispatches as only a foreign officer of those days could decorate austere administrative reports.

"And then, of course, there were the women I encountered.

"So I neglected what others call art, literature, work, professional vocation, and instead cultivated the art of living, the vocation most important to me. Since that time, my life has gone by so quickly . . . I have scarcely had time to realize that I was thirty, fifty, eighty years old. And yet I can still remember the boy I was at twenty, a boy whose innocence was then so overwhelming that I am almost ashamed. . . . Sometimes such shame is a good thing. . . . But I have delayed too long in getting to the point, in telling you what means most to me.

"So you must imagine me now, having just finished my studies, a young diplomat setting out for Hungary, and I shall invite you to take with me the first of my train journeys. It is 1913 . . ."

MARIA

Budapest, 1913

First among the women who have made me into what I am today was Maria. Maria von Pallberg. The Baroness von Pallberg . . . I want to talk about her first. I met her at ten o'clock on a Tuesday evening, and I saw her for the last time on the following Friday, at dawn, and yet I owe her more than sixty years of happiness. Another reason for speaking about her first, however, is that she was perhaps the most beautiful of all. From time to time, someone asks: what is the book, the picture, that means the most to you in the entire world— or who is the most beautiful woman you ever met? I would have to answer the stupid people who are fond of asking such stupid questions by saying: Maria.

Maria von Pallberg . . . She was—but I was about to tell you her age, and that was something no one knew. Perhaps Val-Bergot, her oldest acquaintance, but Val-Bergot was far too tactful to have revealed the secret, even had he known. No, Maria was ageless. It was enough that she was beautiful. Tall and beautiful, dark and beautiful, thin and beautiful . . . that was all there was to it. Her lips were a deep red, her nose slightly *retroussé* beneath that half veil she always wore like a kind of mask—a veil that drew attention to the captivating smile below it—her nostrils were finely sculpted, and her face revealed her elegant bone structure, with high cheekbones, a face that ignored age, time, just as Maria herself blithely ignored or sailed calmly through borders, people, Europe, carelessly, casually. Maria von Pallberg was descended from the old Magyar nobility; she was the widow of a Prussian officer whose family had been in Budapest for three generations. Of all those who frequented European high society, from Vienna to Paris, from Berlin to the old Princess Bertolucci's salon in Naples, she was the best at smiling seductively. And it was she who could become serious at nightfall, when the vodka, the champagne, the *raki* had lit up the faces of those around her, and recount her fortunes and mishaps, turning them into stories, bringing tears to all eyes. I say "all," as though I had been a part of such evenings, such balls and dinners, but in fact I was in her company only for the length of a journey from Paris to Budapest, three days in the autumn of 1913.

It was ten o'clock in the evening. In the courtyard before the Gare de l'Est, almost deserted at that hour, there was a sudden activity, an influx of those wealthy migratory creatures who seemed to turn up three times each week on the platform, platform number one. The old Orient Express to Strasbourg, Stuttgart, Munich, Vienna stood ready to depart, to take the more adventurous on to Varna and Constantinople without their having to leave their sleeping compartments, the bar car, those sumptuous accommodations lined with red silk and precious wood that the Compagnie Internationale des Wagons-Lits furnished so that they could cross Europe in the comfort and luxury of an era that was already, in those days, beginning to fade away. Of course, you don't know those rail-bound luxury liners, like great ships of mahogany and Lalique crystal, with their velvet curtains, the lace: as I recount my stories of these women, perhaps you will be able to imagine that you feel beneath you the soft velvet of those surroundings.

But I am wasting time with superfluous detail when I should be getting to the point. As a young embassy secretary, a vice-consul on his way to take up his first post, I was in the station courtyard, and I noticed the long limousine with the glittering chrome and red-leather roof marked with the crest of some foreign embassy—or did I really pay attention at the time? I was in too much of a hurry to find my own coach, to sink into the luxury that was to become my daily lot for over fifty years of life as a professional diplomat and inveterate traveler to notice my surroundings too carefully. Yet I should have paid more attention to the people and things around me. For from that limousine

Maria von Pallberg emerged. I imagine the rapid conversation that ensued:

"You're sure you have all you need?"

"My dear Ambassador, I am—unfortunately—a grown woman."

"Maria, I wouldn't want you to . . ."

"Please, Ambassador, do not concern yourself . . ."

And that tall, erect figure with the lowered veil, that woman anxious to cut short the advice, the fussing, of M. de K., a worldly ambassador with a neat beard—so elegant that every housemaid in his embassy on the Avenue du Bois was secretly in love with him—was Maria von Pallberg. Around her hovered two porters in their blue uniforms, taking her bags; another young diplomat whom I had encountered in certain houses I myself did not frequent too assiduously, Philip Mertens, stood a few feet away, nervously twiddling a cane.

"I'm worried, Maria. . . ."

Maria von Pallberg gave a slight smile, a smile with a touch of sadness, tension.

"It is all on your own behalf, Ambassador."

Her voice held an implicit reproach.

"I know, Maria, I know. But it isn't that simple!"

Again the same slight smile, but the tension had increased; it became almost ironic.

"You needn't tell me that."

Philip Mertens approached the car and murmured a few words to the ambassador, who shook his head.

"Ah, I almost forgot. . . ."

Followed by the porters, Maria von Pallberg was about to leave when the old man with the seductive goatee called her back.

"Maria—the man I told you about, Captain Kruger; he is here."

By now, Maria's smile was openly ironic; she glanced at the man with the pointed mustaches who had joined them. He was well built, forty years of age, and his body seemed to be bound in an iron corset.

"I know Captain Kruger."

Her voice was so full of contempt that the man known as Kruger blushed.

"The baroness knows me when it suits her purposes. I am flattered that she does me that honor this evening."

He bowed stiffly.

Walter Kruger, a captain in the Hungarian army stationed in Paris, had a face marked with two livid scars, old saber cuts; Heidelberg was not the only place where duels were still fought in those frivolous days. In passing, I might remark that it is a pity the second scar on Kruger's face, the scar that descended almost to his throat, had not gone two inches further. Had he been dead, Captain Kruger would not have been able to play his role as Maria's nemesis during this trip.

Yes, I know. . . . Captain Kruger, the ambassador, the youthful Philip Mertens, myself—we are like characters in a play meeting together there on that train platform. I realize that I may be looking back on that scene through the distorted mirror of memory; I may be embroidering on it, dramatizing it. What does it matter? What *does* matter, the only thing that matters, is that on a Tuesday in November of 1913, in Paris, an elderly gentleman, a plainclothes policeman and an officer in civilian clothes had joined to bid farewell to one of the most beautiful women in Europe as she boarded the train to make her final journey. And chance saw to it that I was on the same train, and because of that, I was to meet another woman, the woman who was to become mine. All the rest, all the details—they are fiction, details I am putting in to enliven my story. After all, I am attempting to entertain you, and you will have to forgive me. And, of course, somewhere inside of me there is still a writer, trying to escape. . . .

I had had only a glimpse of the limousine outside the station; it was on the platform that I noticed Maria for the first time. Preceded by the porters with her luggage and followed by Philip Mertens—I forgot to mention that he was a foppish little man, like a rabbit, self-important with a power that he totally lacked—she walked majestically, like a reigning queen of society, like an empress, which she was in her restricted circle of friends. Nearsighted, with the haughty gaze nearsighted people have, she also had the smile of those who smile at everyone for fear they will snub their closest friend by mistake—and so, as she came toward me on the station platform, she smiled at me. I returned her greeting, raising my hat, not able to place her, and our paths crossed. And I seemed to detect something very like sorrow beneath that smile. . . .

Mertens murmured into her ear: "Do you know that young man?"

He meant me—I was almost two years older. But Maria von Pallberg's mind was elsewhere. I spoke of sadness, of sorrow: she was already thinking of the trip she was about to take—and of what awaited her at her destination.

"No, I didn't pay attention. . . ."

Philip Mertens gave a short laugh. "But you still smile at him. That was Paul de Morlay."

In those days, all of us lived in a world in which everyone knew everyone, a group of three hundred, three thousand people constantly moving between Vienna and Paris.

"Isn't he a colleague of yours?"

Mertens' voice was contemptuous: "Barely three years ago, he was still rubbing his behind on the benches in the College of Political Science. . . ."

Maria did not reply; her thoughts were far away. When the foppish young man attempted to accompany her onto the train to her compartment, she turned to him brusquely.

"Thank you, Philip. I detest farewells, handkerchiefs waved from departing trains."

Like Captain Kruger, Philip Mertens bowed . . . stiffly.

"As you wish, Baroness."

From the other end of the coach, Captain Kruger had observed the scene. The foremost objective of his mission was to see to it that Maria von Pallberg was put onto the train for Constantinople. He did not step into the train until he saw her speak for a moment to the conductor, who seemed to be making excuses, explaining something to her; then he mounted the three wooden steps into the carriage. The second objective of his mission was bound up with those excuses and explanations the conductor had been instructed to make.

Another passenger had also caught sight of Maria von Pallberg. André Val-Bergot. Val-Bergot—does anyone read his delicate novels today, those poetic jottings, travel notes with titles like *A Glimpse of Turkey, Our Easterners* or *Our Lady of the Sunflowers*? At the time, however, Val-Bergot was at the height of his fame; every literary magazine in France—including the young *Nouvelle Revue Francaise*—was proud to have his name included in its table of contents . . . and I remember him as a fairly clever writer, at once precious and entertaining. Employing a touch of nostalgia and a touch of worldliness, he was the poet of travel long before the day of writers such as Cendrars, Cassel or Paul Morand. At barely twenty years of age I had read his books, and he had given me a taste for the exotic whose risk did not extend beyond the confines of the train compartments he described so well.

MARIA

When he caught sight of Maria, Val-Bergot smiled. His trip would not be a boring one. Once again—perhaps for the tenth or twelfth time—Maria von Pallberg would make things lively with her melancholy presence. He scribbled a few words on the back of his calling card, beckoned to one of the attendants and slipped a coin into his hand.

"Take this note to the Baroness von Pallberg. She is in the next car."

I entered my compartment. I had already been to Vienna on one occasion and to Prague, prior to this trip, but in those days I had been in my teens, and my attention had not been drawn to the carriage, to the scent of cologne mingled with coal dust, to the shaded lamps and the cut-glass bottles above the washbasin. All I had thought of was leaving Paris, of being able to practice my meager German or to use the few words of Hungarian I could pick up. The taste of adventure—with no more risk than was represented by that polished mahogany compartment—the scent of departure were vivid that evening when, after my six-month apprenticeship at the Quai d'Orsay, I set out for Budapest and my modest but promising first post as vice-consul, a post that after all represented the goal of years of study and examinations, and disappointed hopes, too. It all seemed new to me, exotic, unexpected. I'm not ashamed of that. In those days, I was still something of a child.

Three compartments from my own, the Baroness von Pallberg looked around her. Not because she too was entranced with the countless amenities the train company provided in those days, as I had been, but because her compartment contained a crystal vase full of roses, magazines in both German and Hungarian and a huge box of chocolates, and she was fully aware that all these luxuries were on behalf of the dangerous and formidable men who were awaiting her in Budapest—men whose plans she knew full well.

"They're beneath contempt," she murmured.

She tore the roses from the vase angrily and threw them to the floor. A thorn caught her finger.

"Contemptible," she repeated.

A drop of blood swelled up at the end of her right index finger. Suddenly the beautiful and self-contained woman seemed desperate. A small photograph in a leather frame stood on the mahogany table: it was a picture of a pale, twelve-year-old boy, who smiled at her.

"Contemptible . . ."

She had regained her composure; once again she was the controlled woman known to all of Europe. Someone knocked at the door. As she examined the tiny square of stiff paper with André Val-Bergot's name and his note—his title had always amused her, since she alone knew how ironic it was, "Man of Letters and Traveler"—she smiled again. As had Val-Bergot, she decided that her trip, unpleasant as its outcome might be, could after all be a pleasant one. Val-Bergot knew how to amuse her. . . .

"Tell M. Val-Bergot I shall be happy to join him in the dining car in ten minutes."

Standing at her mirror, Maria began to repair her makeup, to prepare the face she wished others to see; then she drew her veil down over her eyes.

"Dear André! A journey into the depths of Europe would not be the same if you were not along!"

Maria had recovered her air of elegance, and her voice had regained its enchanting tone. For a moment, Val-Bergot held her hand in his.

"How many times have we made this journey together, Maria?"

She gave him a dazzling smile. "Eight, ten times? Who can tell?"

"Fourteen, Maria. It has been fourteen times since that first departure for Vienna in . . ."

She looked at him flirtatiously, somberly.

"Please, André, not the date. No dates, no years! That is my firm rule; it's the only way I can still think of myself as only twenty."

Val-Bergot was gallant, but he was also something of an historian; he knew how to count. "Come, Maria—twenty!—one has only to see how men still look at you . . ."

And it was true: in the dining car, with all its carefully planned details—the Limoges porcelain with its unique, sumptuous design, the pale and dark colors conceived by some decorator in Brussels—the diners, the waiters, the maître d'hôtel, all were unable to keep themselves from staring at Maria von Pallberg, as all of us look at women who attract us when they chance to cross our paths: with admiration, with feigned disinterest, with nostalgic regret. Val-Bergot, however, was seated facing her across a table laden with caviar, vodka and hot toast.

"As you can observe, I am a practiced traveler, and I can survive journeys only by indulging myself. On this train, my meals are planned like a piece of music: from west to east, I have caviar and vodka; in the other direction, Chambertin and *foie gras* . . . with a bit of smoked salmon if I go on to Ostend. Of course, as a literary man—so-called—I admit to *nouveau riche* tastes."

Maria smiled; she was amused, and Val-Bergot knew that his witty facade amused her and made her smile. For all the years he had been traveling in her company, running into her, the only way in which he had come close to possessing her had been to amuse her, to make her smile.

Yet beneath her smiles and amusement, all at once he sensed something like an immense sorrow: her way of biting her lip from time to time, the way her smile would for an instant become fixed.

"But you're not eating. . . . I hope you are happy, at least?"

Her white teeth gleamed when she smiled. "Happy, unhappy, gay or sad, how is one to tell?"

Val-Bergot was as practiced at deciphering women as other men are at reading poetry or a score by Mozart.

"You seem fairly melancholy to me."

Melancholy was the word, indeed. Not happy or unhappy, not truly gay or truly sad. Why should she try to hide it from Val-Bergot? Was he not, after all, one of her oldest friends? Val-Bergot, reading her face, understood.

"It's the thought of returning to Budapest. Am I right?"

"You can imagine how little I like going back. There are too many things there for which I have never been forgiven. . . ."

Baron von Pallberg—her husband, stiff, somber, severe—and his suicide: he had been discovered in the woods a few miles outside the city, with a single bullet fired from the pistol still in his hand. One bullet through the mouth. And in those woods where the spring buds were green on the trees, no traces of any footprints but his own had been found. Although as far as the world was concerned, Wilhelm von Pallberg had been killed in a duel, his family was fully aware that he had ended his life with his own hand. Because of Maria's way of life, her love affairs, her travels—or because of money difficulties, political troubles? People had preferred to say that Wilhelm von Pallberg had been driven to suicide by Maria's misconduct.

"People are pitiless. . . ." Maria's sadness was now clearly evident.

"Aren't you afraid that . . ."

She emptied her vodka glass at a gulp. To the shrieking of steel rails, the train had just sped through a station over the crossing points; the car shook. An attentive waiter sprang forward to catch a bottle that had been about to fall.

"Afraid? You're joking! You know, in the first place, that I am afraid of nothing . . . and you are here to defend me, aren't you?"

I can imagine the feeble protection Val-Bergot would have been against any of Maria's possible attackers. Val-Bergot, with his pen, his desk, his pads of elegant paper which were, he maintained, the only tools with which he could write. Val-Bergot, with his literary preoccupations that were no more serious than passing migraines, like ripples on the surface of a pond.

"I am a writer, ergo a coward!"

He knew how to turn it into a joke. And his trip to Constantinople, the trip he was making because he had heard at the Princess X's that his friends, the V's, had bought a summer house on the Bosporus, and he was off to enjoy their hospitality and to produce another slim volume of souvenirs of the minarets, Santa Sophia and the bazaar—his trip was also a kind of flight from something. Yes, he was a writer, and probably a coward, too. I cannot imagine Val-Bergot being able to protect Maria, but I can readily imagine that his presence on the train on this, her final trip, must have been a comfort to her—for although she did not know what was to happen, she knew enough to expect the worst.

And at the other end of the dining car, his nose buried in a German newspaper, keeping her constantly within sight, sat Captain Kruger, like a wild beast tracking his prey. . . .

"Paul, my dear! It's not possible!"

Interrupting his ironic remarks on the courage of writers and the idleness of the literary man, Val-Bergot noticed a young man who was searching for a table at the other end of the car—a young man who was myself. After a couple of false entrances, I am at last onstage.

"Join us! You are just the person we were waiting for!"

Across his empty plate of caviar, he beckoned to me, and I approached the table. And that is how, at last, formally, I was introduced to Maria von Pallberg. It was Tuesday, the fourteenth of November 1913, at eleven o'clock in the evening, and the one and only Orient Express had just passed through Châlons-sur-Marne.

"You know Paul, of course."

Maria lifted her veil to look at me. I have never seen a more beautiful woman.

She repeated my name. "Paul de Morlay?" Her eyes at that moment seemed to fill with flecks of gold. "No, we've never met. At least, not formally."

Her voice was very low. My taste, my desires, my admiration have always been for very young women. I have told you that Maria was ageless—she was beautiful, and that was enough. Yet in that moment, her beauty seemed so acute that I felt wounded. It was one of those feelings that pierce you at a glance, that leave you changed from what you were before.

"Our paths have crossed from time to time. . . ."

I sat down at the place indicated by Val-Bergot, facing Maria; I ate the caviar he ordered for me, I drank a glass, two glasses, of vodka. And although a moment before, Maria had seemed sad, a deep color now mounted into her cheeks, and her eyes seemed even more brilliantly flecked with gold. She was truly the most beautiful woman.

"So you are going out to your first post."

She returned the slice of lemon she had been squeezing over her caviar to the edge of her plate. I nodded and gave a banal reply: the foreign office, foreign countries, the boredom of embassy life.

"And your first post happens to be Budapest. . . ."

She fell silent for a moment and looked at me: in the depths of her dark eyes, the golden flecks became diamonds. She murmured slowly: "Once, long ago . . ."

And suddenly I remembered. Out of the caverns of my memory rose the face of Maria von Pallberg, whom I thought I had seen for the first time less than two hours earlier on the station platform.

"Once, long ago, I made this same journey with a young man very like yourself, a young man on his way to take up his first post in Budapest, just as you are."

The young man had been my father. What had happened between him and that girl who had not yet become a baroness, who had not yet borne the harsh, cruel von Pallberg name? For a long time, I know, my father had cherished this woman's memory; I know that my mother cried sometimes when she dared mention her. But my mother had already turned into that wonderful, somewhat unhappy woman living in the shadow of my father's career, receiving ambassadors' wives for tea, organizing charity bazaars. And on the beach at Cabourg where I passed my childhood vacations, through circumstances that were far from innocent, the somewhat melancholy young woman who had strolled the beach or the promenade like a figure in a Boudin painting beneath the gray sky of the Normandy strand, that young woman had been Maria von Pallberg.

I stared at Maria.

"The lady with the blue parasol . . ."

She smiled. "So you do remember?"

There was nothing more to say. In those days, in Cabourg, Maria had sought protection under a blue parasol from the mild sun that shone through the low skies. I remembered its shape, its pale color. There was nothing more to say, and yet, in a voice altered by her emotion, Maria spoke about my father then as no woman had ever done before. She recalled his smile, the deep sorrow in him, the tenderness I had never sensed for either my sister or myself. Yes, my mother had suffered. But I realized, I suddenly saw, what his feelings must have been, that serious, lofty diplomat who spent days on end shut up in his office with his files, but who had sometimes led me by the hand on long, silent promenades through the Tuileries or the Luxembourg Gardens; that man had loved. My childhood afternoons had been haunted by the lady with the blue parasol, like the vaporous, impalpable figure of some exquisite, unattainable princess in a fairy tale, standing in a shaft of sunlight after the rain. Val-Bergot emitted a discreet cough.

"And to think that at the time I was rambling around Egypt and pretending to be a monk on Mount Athos in the company of a group of lascivious, bearded papists."

Maria, whose thoughts were far away from the train, from Budapest —and even from Mount Athos, where I could easily have imagined her disguising herself for a dare as a monk, turning the heads of the entire monastery—gave a throaty laugh that seemed to conceal a sob.

"When I think that I am sitting here with two of the most brilliant men in Paris, and my glass is empty! What has become of French gallantry? Did it expire with the last century?"

With a screech of its night whistle, the Orient Express entered the tunnel of Saint-Jean-les-Tourettes. . . . We had just passed the turrets of the Château de Saint-Fargeau—and Captain Kruger had lit an odorous cigar. But he was far away, at the other end of the car.

And the evening went on. . . . All her sorrows laid aside, cast like a mourning veil onto the speeding tracks, Maria was once again the Maria of the legendary days in Paris or Rome. She was practiced at being brilliant, and she shone—down to the tips of her mother-of-pearl fingernails. Val-Bergot too had made a profession of wit, and now he lived up to it. Entranced, I listened as they exchanged quips, glances, allusions that I did not always understand—and when from time to time I sensed that Maria was addressing me directly through the glittering curtain of her laughter, her wit, I was deeply touched. I was not merely a dull and uninteresting young diplomat such as one meets nowadays on every plane between London and Paris, Bonn and Rome—I was a man, a man the Baroness Maria von Pallberg was taking pleasure in amusing.

Around our table, the rest of the dining car had fallen silent; even the wine steward remained frozen in respectful silence, ready to uncork another bottle for us, to remove an empty glass, a group of empty glasses. And Maria talked on. She enchanted us with her conversation, with her laughter that welled up between goblets of champagne, between cigarettes, between the glances full of meaning that we exchanged.

"There are evenings like this when all I want is to be gay, gay. . . ."

Yet why did I feel, at that moment, that deep within her there was a kind of anguished sorrow?

We spoke about the world and its inhabitants in worldly tones: "What is the world, after all?" Val-Bergot remarked. "Ten friends in London, or Vienna, or Venice who dress for the evening in stiff collars and white ties and kiss each other on both cheeks, a little world within a world, all of whom cordially detest one another as soon as they step outside the barriers of that little world."

We spoke about X and Y, of parties given by the Princess de Cardigan and the mad passions of the Marquise de Monteuil, and Maria grew more serious; she, of course, knew why she happened to be on the train. Val-Bergot made another witticism: "In the end, the world doesn't change. Not you, not I, not anyone. Take this train: in all the years—you will indulge me if I am not precise as to their number—I have been making this journey, I have always ordered the same Bordeaux, I have always been served the same overly salty caviar at Sofia. And whatever happens, it will go on like this. Just as before, whether we like it or not. . . ."

Maria set down her glass. "I adore your idleness, my dear André.

But if I did not know you enjoy baiting us, I would call it almost indecent!"

Even had I not sensed her sorrow earlier, I would have felt it at that moment in her words.

Val-Bergot feigned surprise. "Bait *us?* Who is this famous 'us'?"

"All of us, we who know that with each moment that goes by we are coming closer to the end."

Val-Bergot continued to look surprised. "Good Lord, the end of what? Not of smoked salmon in Ostend and salty caviar in Sofia?"

I was no more than a bystander: in all the stories I am going to tell you, I am only a bystander, an onlooker, even if, as in the present case, my own fate will be altered as a result of the journey. But I had read the dispatches at the Quai d'Orsay—and, of course, every morning I read further than the society columns in *Figaro* or the gossip in *Le Gaulois*—enough to know that the Austro-Hungarian Empire was tottering on its foundations, enough to know that throughout Europe men and women and populations that had hitherto been oppressed simply because they formed a minority within the state were beginning to rise up. And Sarajevo was not far in the future. However blind we may have been—even in the College of Political Science and the other hothouses where the brilliant nonentities trained to govern us were bred—some of us still managed to realize, however confusedly, those things Maria had suddenly referred to in this deluxe dining car, surrounded by crystal, Limoges porcelain and engraved silverware provided to the very rich in the name of necessity.

So when Maria replied to Val-Bergot that it was not only the end of caviar, but perhaps the end of a style of insolence on the part of those who ate it so blatantly, and when Val-Bergot mildly called her attention to the fact that she herself appeared to feel little shame at devouring that caviar on this luxury train—"Politics! That is a new line for you, Maria!"—she gave an unhappy laugh. And all at once I think I understood in my confusion that—as she herself had said prior to my arrival—within this woman happiness and unhappiness, gaiety and sorrow, were all intermingled, but that dominating them was something very like fear.

"Oh, as for me, I try not to give too cruel a bite to the hand that feeds me!"

I looked at Maria, Baroness von Pallberg, and for the first time,

she avoided my gaze. If only she had returned my look at that moment
—she who feared nothing—if only she had told me more later on,
I might perhaps have been able to help her. But Kruger was still
sitting at the other end of the car, and I misread female modesty for
what was actually fear. And that fear I should have realized (and
perhaps have shared) faded away with her last words. Once again
Maria von Pallberg was simply Maria, and I found her more beautiful
than ever.

As our meal ended, Paul, the head chef, came to pay his respects.
Maria had known him when he was an assistant chef, and Val-Bergot
when he was a mere scullery boy. Now he stood next to God Himself
—in this particular car, if not on the train as a whole—and like us,
he admired Maria, the fate of every man who crossed her path. With
the attention she always gave to those she liked, Maria thanked him
and then informed us that she was tired.

"The headaches?"

"Yes, the old headaches . . ."

She shared with Val-Bergot an ancient fund of memories that created
something like complicity. "Old headaches . . ." And yet Maria never
spoke of age, or of years, or of the passage of time. She rose, and Val-
Bergot offered to escort her back to her compartment, but she turned
to me.

"Do you know what I would enjoy?"

I understood: we had spoken about my father, and she wanted to
continue that conversation.

"I am going to take some kind of pill, and I think that will relieve
my headache. You may knock on my door in—shall we say ten
minutes?"

She gave one last brief laugh: "Val-Bergot will tell you that I am
not in the habit of seducing little boys. You have nothing to fear."

In a cloud of silks, taffetas, satins and veils, she left us. But nonetheless, she had with the words "little boys" referred to the passage
of time. Val-Bergot watched her as she disappeared down the length
of the dining car, and then he leaned toward me.

"Late in the evenings, Maria sometimes feels the need for something . . . else."

I did not understand him then, or I did not want to understand
his reference to the small silver box I was to glimpse a short while later

on the table in her compartment—a box containing a white powder. But was that really what she intended that evening? Captain Kruger had also risen to his feet, and as he moved ponderously by me, he brushed against my chair.

In German, he swore.

When I arrived at Maria's apartment, the door was ajar. I did not notice Kruger's massive form disappearing out of sight at the end of the corridor. But upon entering the compartment, I saw at once the child's face in the leather-framed photograph, the roses and the small silver box with its strange crest, a unicorn in a monstrous embrace with a serpent. I might have seen next to them that flask with its seal of red wax—but that pertains to tragedy, and so far we are still dealing with a nostalgic, trivial prelude. Maria was seated on the banquette which the conductor had not yet made up.

She rose as I entered and indicated the upper berth, which was still closed. That gesture as she showed me the upper berth was to have more importance in my life than anything that had ever happened to me before.

"This will be my only evening alone here. The conductor is very upset—they forgot to reserve a single compartment for me, and I am going to have company after Stuttgart. A Polish woman, or Hungarian, I'm not sure . . . So I must take advantage of it to entertain until then. . . ."

Motioning me to sit down, she repeated in the same tone of voice she had employed in the dining car: "I was afraid you wouldn't come . . . but it's not my habit to devour little boys."

What did I reply? I probably protested a bit stupidly that I was no longer a child, that I was a grown-up diplomat, and that she . . . But she stopped me.

"We are being silly. Sit here beside me and talk to me. I need someone to talk to this evening."

She shivered, and her beautiful hands twisted a handkerchief of fine lace. She was paler than she had been in the dining car, and her nostrils seemed pinched. She seemed to be breathing more heavily. Perhaps she had had recourse to the contents of the small silver box with its obscene crest. . . .

"I wanted to tell you . . ."

She spoke of my father. She wanted to speak to me of him that evening, to evoke him, to bring back to life a beloved, forgotten ghost. Together, we conjured up the past.

"You resemble him, you know. . . ."

And the ghost took form, became flesh, almost . . . and the memories flowed forth. My father, the man I had found it hard to love . . .

"He wore a mask, you know, and he removed it so rarely. . . ."

The mask of a man of the world, the mask of a diplomat, his tiny mustache carefully trimmed, his official dress, his smile at the end of the day with its trace of fatigue . . . his furtive kiss in the evening before going out, his white scarf and the stiff collar he always wore: all that was his mask.

"But when he laid his mask aside . . ."

And it was at that precise moment that I sensed that the look with which Maria regarded me was not intended for me at all, but for another, for someone I had scarcely known. . . . The conductor knocked at the door, bearing a bottle of champagne, and once again Maria shivered.

"A final glass, to celebrate our meeting again . . ."

I felt strangely happy in her company, a kind of calm and peace— even though I could sense the trembling within her. But I was comfortable, at my ease.

"Let us talk about you," Maria said after a pause.

I shrugged, embarrassed: I was more modest in those days. And I had not yet learned to recount—"expose" would be a better word, I believe—my own feelings as easily as I do today. But Maria knew how to look at me, and for a second her hand had touched mine. I was not the person she sought, of course, but she herself was there, so tender . . .

"Talk about myself . . ."

And I poured out everything: I drank a glass of champagne, the train swayed and I told her of my hopes, my desires for travel, my ambition to write. It all rose easily to my lips because I was saying it to her.

"To write?"

"Yes, to write."

The dozens of novels I had left unfinished, some begun at the age of fifteen on rainy days in the summerhouse, all lying silently in my drawer. My poems full of the fire and naive emotions of adolescence—

what can I say about them, other than at the moment I had thought they meant more to me than anything else in the world?

"And these novels, what were they about?"

Maria had lit a gold-tipped cigarette, Eastern tobacco, whose blue smoke floated in the compartment and surrounded us both with a scented halo.

"About?" I blushed. "About love, of course."

I had been drinking a bit, and I was no longer ashamed to confess everything.

"About love, of course! As one thinks of love at fifteen!"

My novels had indeed been about love, about the woman of my dreams, the woman I still dream about. The pale, blond image of purity and mystery that haunted my adolescent nights. That girl who wanders through the pages of books—do you remember?—Yvonne de Galais, who had just been created; *Le Grand Meaulnes*; those diaphanous, childlike figures in the poems of Laforgue. Suddenly all the naiveté of my fifteenth year came tumbling 'out, inspired by the champagne, and I discerned a smile on Maria's lips.

"But you're laughing at me."

She took my hand. "No, no, I am not laughing at you!"

I wonder now whether beneath my own mask so carelessly cast aside, I had not revealed to her that other man who had brought us together, my father. The masks were different—although as I grew older I began to wear a mustache and stiff collars and white scarves; they became a part of my uniform as well. Perhaps my father too had dreamed of a distant woman . . . but she had not been blond and wrapped in mists, but dark, with golden flecks in the depths of her eyes.

"No, I am not laughing at you. Perhaps all of us cherish the image of a unique love. Only . . ."

"Only?"

Her sentence had been left unfinished.

"Oh, only . . . Things do not always turn out as we may have dreamed them, even if we happen to meet it, that unique love."

She sat silent for a moment longer, her hand still touching mine. Then, softly, she drew away.

"And now I think it best that you go to bed, Paul. . . ."

Was it my name she spoke? I am not sure. There had been the excitement of the evening, the vodka and champagne, the white powder within the small silver box, the memories.

And Kruger, who had visited her compartment prior to my arrival.

So I am no longer certain that it was my name she murmured as her voice sank to a whisper and her face, for one instant, one sigh, drew close to mine.

The compartment door closed upon Maria—one last time I saw her hand, long and slender with scarlet nails, as she slowly shut the door—and I was alone in the corridor, at a loss. I no longer knew. I too had had the experience of memories suddenly dredged up, and I had also seen the face of this woman, so different from the woman to whom I had spoken with such tranquil innocence, and it had overwhelmed me. I returned slowly to the bar car. As I went, the corridor was lit up suddenly by the lights of some small station as we passed through, and the car trembled on the rails as we sped along—then darkness, sound, odors. I was on the express train to Constantinople; I was on my way to my first post, but the excitement of departure had given way to a sensation difficult to define, one in which Maria's profile with its high cheekbones mingled with that other dreamed face that had haunted my youth, that existed nowhere outside my dreams: the girl, blond and misty.

I found Val-Bergot in the bar, and he told me all his friends' opinions as to why Maria was returning to Budapest and to the child whose sorrowful face I had seen on the compartment table, her son. Franz suffered from a blood disease; his case was hopeless; he was finding it hard to die. The family of the Baron von Pallberg, formidable Prussian landowners who had grown more stern in exile than had they remained on their meager native soil, refused to allow Maria to remove the child from Budapest. As the heir to a somewhat well-known name which those who bore it considered illustrious, little Franz was being constrained to live—and to die, as everyone knew—among his own.

"You can understand why she has such sudden flashes of gaiety; it's to conceal her overwhelming sorrow."

We did not remain in the bar long. What Val-Bergot told me about Maria made her even more precious to me—for in a way she had become precious to me, a way I cannot describe. I wanted to be alone now. I was only twenty-three, still of an age when reality can easily overpower even the most cherished image, and in a few short hours Maria had created in my mind a portrait of herself that I was to carry with me all my life.

At exactly 8:25 the following morning, reality finally conquered the dream, the fantasy . . . For at that precise moment, Stephanie entered my life. I recognized her at once: the blond, mysterious girl of my vision. There are coincidences that surpass coincidence, encounters that any so-called realistic novelist would never dare use. Let us say that the vision I had on the platform of the Stuttgart station where the train had come to a ponderous stop was beyond the wildest imaginings of the novelist I would never be. It was she: that was all. I saw nothing of Stuttgart, the Anlagen, the parks and gardens, nothing of the Stiftskirche or the Residenz with its 365 rooms, one for each day in the year—or night? I saw nothing in Stuttgart but a train platform. And her . . .

I had been about to sit down to breakfast with André Val-Bergot, and the waiter had just placed before me two eggs, bacon, hot toast and that Russian tea one finds only on trains going to the East when I happened to look out of the window. There were people moving about on the platform, a few passengers; some soldiers with rifles strolled by. And there was a young girl with a leather suitcase at her side, a very young girl who so resembled my vision of love that I must have grown pale. And I realized in a flash that both solitude and cares had vanished, at least for a time.

"You're not eating?"

Val-Bergot wiped his mustache delicately and set down his cup of Turkish coffee. No, I wasn't eating. His eyes followed mine.

"That girl . . ."

It was she, quite simply. So clearly that, even after she had disappeared from view, I knew I would find her again. Thus, when the train began to move a few seconds later and we entered the suburbs of Stuttgart—gone as soon as one glimpsed them, so sharp was the division between town and countryside in the Europe of those days—I was not at all surprised when Maria entered the dining car arm in arm with her, speaking in a loud voice and coming to our table. It was as it should be, in the nature of things—or of my dreams, I should say—and that was all. Maria, however, was already sitting down at our table, and she motioned to the girl to take the place across from her . . . and across from me.

"You know, sometimes the good Lord gets things right. I wasn't able to have a single compartment, I envisioned God knows what kind of traveling companion for the rest of the journey . . . someone bad-tempered, perhaps with a mustache. And see what heaven—or luck—has provided!"

She indicated the girl, who smiled, not at all embarrassed.

Maria continued: "Allow me to introduce Stephanie Kovaks. She is going on to Budapest, too, like myself."

Val-Bergot rose and bowed; he made one of those harmless, amusing remarks at which he was so talented, but I remained seated, silent, unable to stammer out more than my name as greeting or welcome.

Maria took up the conversation. "Well, Paul? You are very quiet all at once."

Good Lord, what could I have said? I muttered something, because some reply was required. Stephanie Kovaks offered me her hand; her handshake was frank, firm, almost like that of a boy . . . but a boy with the smile, the face, the most delightful figure in the world.

"Doesn't Mademoiselle Kovaks seem to remind you—quite by chance, of course—of the girl about whom we were talking last night?"

"What girl? May I know?"

Stephanie, with the same assurance, looked at me questioningly. But Maria had returned to the tone of voice I had heard the evening before, nostalgic and mysterious.

"That, for the moment, must be a secret between Paul and me."

While our two companions, one new, the other very new, began their breakfasts—and Stephanie devoured eggs, toast and marmalade with a hearty appetite—I quickly came to the realization that this girl had conquered me at one blow. For that is what I was—conquered—and if ever the notion of love at first sight had any basis in reality, it was then, it was happening inside me as I looked at Stephanie. In an instant, everything about her seemed wonderful to me, light, lovely, transparent. She was so much like that image I had cherished in my thoughts for so long. Even today, I have to smile at the naiveté, the suddenness, the spontaneity of that great blow to my heart. It was all so simple, so natural.

Indeed, everything seemed natural. Stephanie Kovaks was the daughter of a Hungarian businessman who had married a Swiss woman; she was one of those girls who in those days were determined to be modern, to learn how to do more than play the piano, speak a foreign language, do embroidery. She had studied political economy in Zurich, she spoke both French and German as well as Russian, English and Italian, and she had suddenly decided to return to her homeland.

"But what about your studies . . ."

Val-Bergot was one of those prematurely aged men with whom I was so familiar, a man who begins to take an interest in young girls when he turns forty; he was fifty-five, and he was listening to Stephanie with an attention that went beyond mere politeness. Stephanie made a gesture as if to toss her hat over her shoulder. Studies?

"There's more to the world than studies, you know."

She was the first girl I had ever met who had studied political economy.

"More? What, for example?"

Maria had leaned toward her. I noticed that this morning, at breakfast, she was still wearing her thin, blue silk gloves.

"What? Well, the world. Living, breathing things."

We were silent, but Stephanie continued: "And suffering people."

Maria's look grew hard. I was not to learn why until later. But Val-Bergot burst out laughing.

"How serious these modern young women can suddenly become! Is that what they are teaching girls in our universities nowadays?"

But Stephanie was not at all put out. She looked at him calmly and turned a sugar cube between her fingers.

"Not at all. That is exactly what they do *not* teach us."

She wore a signet ring on her little finger, a ring with a strange crest. It was a unicorn, like the one on Maria's silver box, but here it was entwined in a bird's embrace. Maria's eyes fell upon the ring and then on Stephanie's face. She relaxed.

"Pretty, isn't it? My father found it in a second-hand shop and bought it for me for my eighteenth birthday."

Stephanie, on that day, was eighteen years, three months and seventeen days old.

Later, we spent hours talking together in the bar car. Why was I afraid—hesitant—to let her know that I was a diplomat, afraid that she would take me for one of those foppish creatures that haunt embassies? Sitting there across from her—that student who had given up her studies—I was suddenly almost ashamed of my overly severe haircut, my austere collar and the silk cravat that along the corridors of the Quai d'Orsay, behind the heavy curtains and padded doors of those silent rooms, was considered the height of taste.

I wanted to show her that I was able to listen, to love, to enjoy the things that I felt she would enjoy hearing, seeing, loving. We spoke about Debussy and the symbolists, about the young Stravinsky, about the Ballets Russes. We spoke of writers, too—Apollinaire, Gide, Claudel, Laforgue—and Stephanie mimicked my tone of voice, my pretension, and ended up bursting into laughter; I did the same, and from that moment on, we were friends. I no longer had to maintain my shameful diplomatic front.

How does one recount such moments as those, when the first words have not yet been spoken? How does one recapture the glances, the laughter, the moments when love has not yet turned into love, but soon will? Or how does one speak of the train as it crossed Bavaria, of the onion-shaped steeples, of the inns with their decorated façades—Mering, Althegnenberg, Maisach—or of Stephanie herself, who was taking pleasure in all I was discovering?

"Ah, when you have taken this journey as often as I have . . ."

She spoke as though she were a seasoned traveler, and I told her that in her company I would be glad to make the trip every month, every week . . . and again she laughed. Is it permissible to hold the hand of a woman one has met for the first time in Stuttgart? I asked that question, and Stephanie laughed once more, and my finger—no more than a finger, a gesture, as if it were a game—rested for an instant on her ring. Yet I did not notice the look Maria gave me at that moment. Her look at us . . .

Nor did I notice the motionless presence of the observant Captain Kruger. Stephanie, equally unaware, talked to me of everything that was important to her.

"There is such injustice in the world. So much oppression, tyranny, poverty . . ."

She told me about the slums she had seen in the German cities through which she had so often passed, of the outskirts of Berlin or Düsseldorf, of the poverty that attached itself like a kind of leprosy to things and to people, slowly devouring them with alcohol, disease, like a disgusting fungus or a rot eating away at the walls of their hovels.

"You cannot imagine . . ."

And she spoke of those who were suffering under the yoke of other police, other states, other legal systems.

"I am Hungarian, and the Hungarians have become worse than the Austrians. Others, anyone who is not one of them, know only one kind of law—the law of the whip, of prison. When it isn't a firing squad at dawn . . ."

Armies of white-uniformed, white-gloved officers with cigarettes in their mouths rode through the villages on haughty white steeds. But for all that, they were sad. Their victims were so beautiful as they danced beneath the whip at saber-point in the small towns that would soon be burned to the ground.

"That surely can't be true, Stephanie. . . ."

"But it is true. . . ."

Maria's eyes watched us, and Kruger watched Maria, as though actors in some tragedy had taken their positions on the stage, each spying upon the other before taking up his cue.

The play was soon to begin in earnest: just after we crossed the Austrian frontier at Seftensee—the old story of a beautiful woman sacrificing herself, paying the highest price anyone can be asked to pay. Before that, however, for example as we sat down to lunch, an enlightened onlooker—and Val-Bergot, I remind you, was such an onlooker—might have seen that Maria von Pallberg's attitude had undergone a profound change. She continued to display great courtesy to Stephanie; she continued to set off the dark fireworks of her golden eyes for the benefit of Val-Bergot and myself, but there were other moments, other glances, when her eyes would suddenly become fixed. Fixed on Stephanie's face and on mine, and on Stephanie's hand. Val-Bergot exerted himself to be witty, but Maria smiled only with her lips; her eyes belied her amusement. Neither Stephanie nor I noticed this, and as for Val-Bergot, he probably attributed such evidences of her sorrow to the wrong sources.

Once, as Stephanie was speaking about someone she had seen who had moved her, with tenderness and animation in her voice, and I was looking at her with the same tenderness, Maria turned to her and murmured: "Why do you have to be so adorable. . . ."

She was moved; Maria was moved by Stephanie, and it was as though she were sorry for it. None of us understood the other. And the train was approaching Seftensee . . . in the next minute, our lives were to be plunged into drama.

It happened very quickly. First, an incredible screeching from every wheel of the train and a sudden stop that sent the passengers in the restaurant car hurtling against one another, shaking bottles, causing pheasant and smoked salmon to slide onto the damask tablecloths.

I can see the steam escaping everywhere, can feel the hot metal; I can imagine the face of the terrified engine-driver as the train ground to a halt a few feet from the end of the tracks—an explosion had torn up the rails for a hundred yards ahead, and they lay twisted on the roadbed.

Then for the first time I noticed Captain Kruger. All the other passengers in the restaurant car were terrified, full of questions, wondering what had happened, but a man dressed in black at the far end of the car was cursing violently in German. He was standing and looking towards us, and my eyes met his. I am not sure he didn't shake his fist.

It was obvious what had happened. Some terrorists had completely destroyed the track between Munich and Vienna a few hundred yards outside the village of Seftensee, on the Austrian side of the frontier.

In an instant, the train was invaded by the atmosphere of fright mixed with curiosity—as futile as it is unhealthy—that always prevails wherever street accidents occur, or when a dog is run over. The passengers poured out onto the tracks to examine the extent of the destruction: the train had stopped just in time; we had come within inches of going off the tracks. Ten yards more, and three or four of the cars would have been hurled from the tracks into an oat field five or six yards below. Twisted metal in the high, autumnal stalks . . . So there were exclamations, shouts of horror and relief on every side. One old lady, a tiny dog clutched under her arm, waxed indignant at the deeds perpetrated by people everyone knew to be terrorists, anarchists, murderers, and a chorus of passengers answered her.

Only Stephanie, who had taken my arm, tried to understand.

"It's not as simple as that, you know. . . ."

In the same tone in which she had talked about working-class poverty in German suburbs and throughout Europe, she spoke to me once again of the struggles of the oppressed ethnic minorities of the Austro-Hungarian Empire—remember, this was towards the end of 1913—an empire that was leaking from every seam like some gigantic ocean liner that had become too unwieldy for its feeble captains and was—very soon—about to sink. As I have already said, Sarajevo was not far distant. And it made little difference whether the bomb had been placed on the tracks by Serbs, Croats or Moldavians.

"You must understand: they're trying to show us that we cannot decide their fate, we cannot sign treaties and form alliances without even asking their opinion!"

I echoed the words of the old lady with the little dog: "But they're murderers!"

She kept hold of my arm.

"This bomb was put there by people who know their job. If they had really wanted to wreck the train, they could have blown up the track a hundred yards further on. On this curve where we are now . . . because of that clump of trees on the left, the engineer would have been unable to see the damage in time, and we would all be in a really bad way."

Her explanation was based on such cold logic that I was shocked. She pressed against my shoulder and burst into laughter.

"Come, come, don't let it upset you too much! I don't know who they are, these people who are trying to draw attention to themselves, but I like them! And if they make our trip last a little longer, they can't be all bad, can they?"

The chief conductor was already assembling the passengers to inform them that during the twenty-four or so hours the train might be forced to remain where it was—time enough to repair the damaged tracks— we would be forced to return to Seftensee, where we would probably be able to put up at one of the inns. As Stephanie and I looked around for our friends, I suddenly caught sight of Maria. She was in deep conversation with the man in black whose presence I had noticed a few minutes earlier on the train . . . a man who—I remind you—had never let us out of his sight.

"This is a real catastrophe!"

Maria started as we came up to her, and Kruger immediately faded into the crowd of passengers standing by the train; the chief conductor was clumsily attempting to herd them back towards the village.

"A real catastrophe," she repeated. She seemed totally overwhelmed. Val-Bergot joined us and took her arm.

"Come, now. Here we are with twenty-four hours to spend in the land of nowhere, in the depths of the country. I find that rather amusing."

Maria seemed preoccupied as he led her away. And I recall the face of the man in black. When I think of it now, I feel he must have been speaking harshly to her as we came up, that he must have been warning her against something.

But Val-Bergot was speaking to her. "What is wrong, Maria? What is happening?"

Again she shivered and quickly recovered herself. She had an explanation ready.

"It's this delay . . . my son is supposed to be having some minor operation, and I would have liked to have been there to . . ."

Had Maria known how fateful her words, spoken only to calm Val-Bergot, were to be . . . She might have gone on to say something else, but her words were lost in the babble of conversation of the passengers who were straggling towards the village—and I might have purposely averted my attention, preoccupied as I was with savoring every additional moment spent with Stephanie. It had been real love at first sight for me, and I had the sudden impression—I was almost certain—that my feelings were shared. Selfish as one is at twenty, I turned my back on Maria, and I helped Stephanie along the tracks.

We arrived at Seftensee to find a village prepared for a celebration, preparing for a celebration, I should say. The little village stretched along the banks of a lake set amid encircling hills. It was being hung with lanterns and garlands; women with long, voluminous skirts embroidered with flowers moved about amid the scents and music of a country fair; a wooden platform had been erected for dancing, and there was a greased pole hung with hams and flagons of Franconian wine for later on. And we passengers from that luxury train that had been halted by a terrorist attack in the depths of Austria—still tainted with the silly, artificial sophistication of those who travel the world but never stop to look at it—we must have looked very strange in that landscape as we came down the cobbled street of the village. Women holding parasols, men in panama hats, people in high heels and city boots crossing open fields spread with sheep manure, we must have looked exactly like what we were: puppets in a puppet world that was on its last legs. We were playing childish games, like Marie Antoinette at Trianon, in our Tyrolean playhouse, while the first rumblings of what was to be the final struggle were already audible faintly in the distance.

The villagers came to the doorways of their houses to watch as we went by, and children followed us as though we were clowns and circus riders—Val-Bergot might have been Harlequin; I a simpleminded Pierrot with my Columbine at my side. And Kruger was the villain in the piece, but I did not know that yet. The village innkeeper, who was busily setting up tables for the evening's celebration, watched us invade his domain as though we were creatures from some other planet.

It took a great deal of argument and discussion before we found places to stay—either in private homes whose inhabitants agreed to provide beds for the night, or in the inn itself. Many rooms in the inn were empty: it was a private party that evening in Seftensee, and no visitors had been expected. Thus began that strange night, and the day that was to follow it, far from the world in the midst of the green countryside . . . while murder, conspiracy, terrorism and war skulked unseen around us.

In relating what happened, I am now forced to abandon once and for all the role I have tried to maintain heretofore: a detached observer recording only what he sees at the moment and ignorant of all in which he is not directly involved. I learned the facts later, after having heard Val-Bergot, Stephanie and Maria herself tell me what they knew—and from now on my narrative will be based on that, a narrative in which I am no more than a secondary character, surprised only to be caught up in the midst of such a conflict of emotions—if that were only all!—a character in a drama between a mature and beautiful woman and a young, very young girl.

However, we were arriving at the inn. As soon as we had obtained rooms, Maria went off in search of a telephone. We had not fully realized how much the state of her son's health concerned her. Val-Bergot was to tell me later that during their walk from the halted train to the inn, she had told him of her premonition that Franz was about to die.

"He has a way of smiling, as though it wasn't at all really serious, that tears me apart!" she had told him.

Later she had admitted: "I sometimes think that those ultra-Prussian von Pallbergs who won't allow him to leave Budapest must be monsters! A bit of sun, the air in Nice or Cannes might help him! In Provence or on the Côte d'Azur, he might get some real color into his cheeks for once in his life—some color not put there by fever!"

It seemed that the twenty-four hours we were fated to spend in the land of nowhere—and free from the presence of Kruger (we shall see the threat represented by that)—had brought all her worries to the surface. As soon as she reached Seftensee, Maria tried to telephone to Franz's nurse in Budapest.

"A telephone?" The stout innkeeper's wife shook her head and laughed. Maria thought for an instant that she had made an impossible request, but the peasant woman beckoned to her. "You couldn't have come at a better time: we have had a telephone for just a month. The first one in the village."

Maria returned almost at once. Having a telephone in Seftensee was one thing; using it was another, and the good-natured girl in the post office to whom she had spoken had promised to call her as soon as she could set up a connection between the isolated Tyrolean village and Budapest.

"And I'm afraid that may take a while. . . ." Maria looked exhausted.

Once again, Val-Bergot took her arm. "I'm here with you, you know."

But she did not reply. Then, with a shrug, she smiled. "But aren't we all here together? And isn't that a good thing?"

All she had to do was hold herself together for a few more hours. Only a few more hours . . .

In her room at the inn, Maria was dressing for the evening, just as she would have done in Paris, Berlin, Vienna. Since she was in none of those cities, however, she had chosen a simple gown, light in color, set off with a lace stole that made her look almost like a peasant girl.

"How pretty you are!" Stephanie exclaimed.

Standing before the mirror on the painted dressing table—there were bright-colored cupids and flowers on a blue background—Maria was combing her hair; she froze.

"Oh, you are such a child! Why do you have to be so adorable?"

She turned back to the mirror, her voice tinged with sorrow, with regret. . . . Stephanie had no luggage other than the leather bag that had stood beside her on the platform in the Stuttgart station.

"What are you going to wear this evening?" Maria asked.

Stephanie did not reply but made a gesture to signify that she had nothing with her save the clothes she was wearing. Maria examined her from head to toe, as if examining a mannequin in a dress shop, a painter's model.

"Just a moment!"

From her own suitcase she drew a gown of some supple material, very like the one she was wearing, and held it out to the girl.

"May I really?"

Stephanie clapped her hands like a child. And when Val-Bergot knocked on the door to their room to see if they would soon be ready, he was greeted with a charming sight: Maria von Pallberg was kneeling before Stephanie Kovaks, in the process of fixing the hem of her dress.

"We look like sisters, do we not?" Stephanie asked when Maria had finished.

And Maria, who had stepped back to gauge the effect of her labors, murmured: "Yes, two sisters . . ."

She moved to the dressing table where she had set her toilet case and removed several objects: a tiny comb in tortoiseshell, a gold clip with a ruby—and the small silver box with its diabolical crest. She was about to slip them into her bag when another object almost fell —it was the flask I mentioned before, a flat bottle made of crystal. Its silver stopper was sealed with wax. Maria closed her eyes; her hand went to her heart. She hastily replaced the bottle, but something had happened to change her mood, and her face hardened suddenly.

"Ready, Maria?"

Val-Bergot was still present in the room. Maria recovered herself as suddenly as she had become upset. She took from her dressing case another bottle, similar to the first, and took off the cap—there was no wax seal on this one.

"Almost, my dear . . . I was deciding what scent to wear. Wild gentian, what do you think—for a village ball? I feel that might suit."

Val-Bergot, who had missed nothing, smiled at her as she dabbed on the perfume with her fingertips.

"I must remember that, should I ever chance to write the story of this forced halt . . . wild gentian. It's just the thing!"

Maria was gazing at her face in the mirror. Val-Bergot went on reassuringly: "In any event, I can promise you that my story will have a happy ending."

Maria did not reply. Too many thoughts were welling up in her mind: the telephone call she was awaiting; the vision of my father my presence had recalled to her; not to mention the bottle with its red wax seal or Captain Kruger who—just one floor beneath her in the same inn—was standing at his window smoking an evil-smelling cigar. So that when Stephanie walked into the middle of the room and twirled around like a fashion model to show off the gown that floated out around her waist, Maria turned to her with a look that contrasted strangely with the kind affection she had shown earlier—a cold, hard look.

I, all unsuspecting, was knotting my cravat before the cracked mirror of the tiny room under the eaves I was sharing with Val-Bergot.

As the first sounds of an accordion drifted up to us, Val-Bergot—who had managed to shake Maria out of her mood—brought the ladies down, and we entered the large dining room of the inn, a room opening out onto the platform for dancing; beyond lay the lake. The ball had already begun, and the first couples were already waltzing.

The contrast between the villagers, all dressed in their Sunday best, the men in lederhosen and embroidered vests, the women in bright skirts over layered petticoats and blouses with puffed sleeves embroidered with gold thread, and we train-wrecked passengers was a strange one. Each of us had made an attempt—for reasons that were quite the opposite of those of the villagers—to dress "simply" for the occasion. Thus, the gentlemen, who were more used to stiff collars for evening wear, were wearing loose ties or casually knotted scarves, while the women had donned their simplest, everyday gowns—although not with Maria's effect.

The passengers occupied a good quarter of the room; we were all sitting on benches at the long tables, upon which foaming earthenware tankards of beer had already been set out. Stout bottles of white wine were also brought out and poured into stemmed goblets of green glass that were oddly elegant. The women were in high spirits, amused at everything around them, and the peasants nudged each other good-humoredly at the sight of us: it seemed natural then that there should be a total lack of contact between the two groups. I realize today that it could hardly have been otherwise. Perhaps only Stephanie was aware of the impassible barrier that separated the villagers of Seftensee and these passengers bound for Vienna or Constantinople who had strayed into their midst. The miracle that had happened to me after the train had stopped at Stuttgart made me oblivious. Stephanie—I can say it without false pride—had eyes for no one else. After all, in addition to the story of Maria, this is the story of the beginning of a love affair that was to last for a long, long time. . . .

The festivities rose to new heights when a huge villager with broad shoulders got up his courage and invited one of the female passengers to dance. The young woman, a girl from Vienna on her way home from Paris, looked at us in a rather startled way, but when we encouraged her she laughed and agreed to waltz. A few moments later, the ice had been completely broken. The accordion and violin broke into a gypsy tune, joined by trombone and fife, the beer began to flow in rivers and huge platters of whole hams, cabbage and potatoes appeared on the wooden tables.

Among the villagers was a young girl, her hair braided on top of her head like the others, dressed as they were in the same skirts and embroidered blouse; she seemed to be no more than sixteen, and she was so lovely that even I caught my breath.

"That creature is ravishing, is she not?"

Val-Bergot raised his glass to me. But I was too much in love, and I turned to Stephanie before replying: "Yes, ravishing . . ."

Val-Bergot turned to Maria, and both of them looked at us, at Stephanie and at me; he shook his head and murmured in the same tone to Maria: "These young people are adorable. . . ."

He was talking about us; Maria did not reply.

Later, Maria spoke brusquely to Stephanie for the first time: everything was going as planned, of course, but Maria was unable to allow herself to show tenderness to Stephanie any longer.

What brought it about? Nothing at all, really. I had once again expressed pleasure at the accident that was enabling us to spend our evening in that village—yet it had been a bomb, after all!—and had spoken casually, to make conversation. Val-Bergot, like the old lady with the little dog from the train, had expressed mild indignation at people who put the lives of innocent passengers in jeopardy just for the sake of some cause about which the passengers were ignorant. As she had done earlier, Stephanie attempted to explain to him, equally mildly, that it was not that simple, that we were thinking only of ourselves.

But Maria interrupted: "Do you realize what you're saying? To kill at random, anywhere, any place?"

Her voice was dry, sarcastic. I had taken Stephanie's hand in mine—
I had by now grown brave enough for that.

"I am only trying to understand," Stephanie replied. "I am only
trying to point out that they may have valid motives. . . ."

Maria had grown very pale, paler than even Val-Bergot had ever
seen her before.

"What motives can ever justify the death of an innocent person?
Or the death of a child . . ."

"Maria . . . Maria . . ."

Val-Bergot had put his hand on his friend's arm, as I had on mine.
"Maria, Stephanie is only eighteen."

Maria looked at her: "I realize her age! But age is no excuse. You
know that as well as I."

The waltz went on, but I knew from that moment on, where Maria
was concerned, everything had changed. When a peasant approached
her with an invitation to dance, she refused with a brusque gesture.

I got up to lead Stephanie away. "Shall we dance?"

It was our first waltz. . . . In order to describe that moment when
for the first time my hands touched the waist of the woman I loved,
you would have to try to imagine the relatively innocent minds young
people still had in those days; you would have to use the simplest,
purest words to describe the trembling feeling, the feeling of sweetness
and tension . . . Some will smile to themselves at my emotion now,
an old man remembering such moments, but I cannot find the words
to describe the magic interval in that village inn when we danced together for the first time. . . .

Maria had remained seated at our table; she ordered another bottle
of the young fruity wine. . . . Val-Bergot attempted to prevent her
from drinking more.

"Are you sure you . . ."

"Of course, I'm sure."

He shook his head. But Maria had already downed a glass, and then
another. Now I know that as she watched us dancing, her inner emotions were turbulent: she saw us—Stephanie, so young, so elegant,
and myself—as we revolved dizzily around the room; she was isolated
and alone—despite Val-Bergot at her side. More beautiful than ever,
yet alone.

"I should so much like to be able to help you. . . ."

For a second, Maria relaxed.

"You're here, André, and that is already a great deal."

But Kruger, seated at a nearby table, was there, too, and that was the overriding factor.

Meanwhile, the waltz continued. What was I saying to Stephanie? "I'd like . . ."

She pressed closer to me. "Don't say anything . . ."

So we danced, through suspended moments, moments I cannot describe.

Then there was an interruption. The innkeeper came to our table and whispered into Maria's ear: her telephone call had gone through to Budapest. She rose, pale, and Kruger also stood up—but Maria moved quickly, making her way through the throng of dancers, and went to the room where the new telephone was hanging on the wall.

I had returned to our table, somewhat out of breath, and Val-Bergot shook his head.

"It's about her son. She is nearly dead from worry."

There were so many undercurrents in that room. Maria, however, was already returning. She, too, was out of breath, and she was paler than before.

"It wasn't for me, after all. It was for a Captain Kruger." She spoke as if she did not know who Kruger was, in a loud voice, so that Kruger, standing close by, could hear her. Then she sat down once more. Val-Bergot put his arm around her shoulders.

"I'm sorry, Maria."

She was trembling, and Val-Bergot poured out a glass of white wine for her.

"There's no need to be sorry, André. For a second, I thought it would be the news I am waiting for, that's all."

Kruger had left the room when he heard her words, and now he returned and came to our table. For the first time, he joined us. He bowed to Maria.

"I thank you, Madame. Allow me to introduce myself. I am Captain Kruger."

His heels clicked smartly. It was, as I said, as though they had never met before. For a second, Stephanie looked at the man in black. She seemed about to ask a question, but Kruger had already moved away. With a shudder, like an automaton being set in motion, Maria rose and spoke to me. "Would you like to dance with me?"

Maria, Baroness von Pallberg, was inviting Paul de Morlay, a young embassy secretary, the new vice-consul in Budapest, to dance.

"I must talk to you, Paul."

Although I had known her for only twenty-four hours, I could tell from the tone of her voice that what she had to tell me was something of gravity. The music, too, seemed to grow stately, grave, and the dancers marked its rhythm with their heels. And all that ensued, the incredible conversation I was about to have with Maria, was like some fantastic dialogue between two lovers who were being forced to become enemies, the one determined to destroy; and the other determined not to pay heed to what was said to him.

"Paul, I do not think it is wise for you to become overly attached to that girl," Maria began, opening the encounter between us.

My reaction was violent. "To what girl? To Stephanie?"

"Yes, Mademoiselle Kovaks. You don't know who she is or where she comes from. Nowadays, you can meet anyone on the Orient Express —not always the sort of people you would know in Paris, Vienna . . . even Budapest. . . ."

Maria's voice was curt, sharp, almost a whisper. I did not understand. "What do you mean?"

Dryer, sharper: "I mean that you know nothing of this girl. She told us her people were . . . bankers of some sort, in business. That's not a reference. How do we know she hasn't invented the whole thing?"

When I heard her speaking those words to me, I felt that a whole solid and secure world upon which I had been ready to base my life had suddenly been pulled from under my feet. I attempted to justify myself, to explain, to remind her that she had been the one who had introduced me to Stephanie in the train.

But Maria spoke to me harshly. "Don't pretend to be naive. You know very well that I had only met her myself a few minutes before! And just because one is forced to share one's compartment with someone from Stuttgart to Budapest, that doesn't mean one is able to vouch for that person's respectability!"

I had to make some reply to her. "Respectability! I respect you, Maria; I respect you enormously. I admire you. But you are taking it upon yourself to speak to me as my mother would never have done."

The waltz went on, accelerating, the rhythm tapped out by hundreds of heels. It was a fantastic dance, insane, sorrowful. I was aware of nothing.

Maria had grown bitter. "I may be speaking to you like a mother. I may even be old enough to be your mother—that is reason enough for me to tell you that to me, Stephanie appears to be a brainless hussy! I know nothing about her, true, but to me she looks like some shopkeeper's daughter seeking adventure, or I'm very much mistaken!"

Maria's voice had become so different from the voice I had known, that voice so full of kindness and tenderness, that I attempted to calm her.

"Maria, please . . ."

But she continued, even more harshly. "Listen to me! You are a diplomat, a French diplomat on his way to his first post. You must be careful with whom you come in contact, my dear Paul! You will be in Budapest for two, perhaps for three years, and now, even before crossing the frontier, you have allowed yourself to be taken in by some girl you have chanced to meet, a girl about whom you know nothing whatsoever! If you feel you owe nothing to your mother—or to me—at least you owe some respect to the career you have chosen. At the moment, you are acting like a high school boy. Try to act like a man, like a responsible man!"

I had nothing to say. The sounds of the orchestra and the dancing feet echoed in my ears. I could have shouted at her; I could have yelled out what I was feeling, but I know that Maria would not have listened. Maria, my friend, the lady with the blue parasol, did not realize what had happened to me. She was betraying me; that was all I felt.

I went back to our table where Stephanie and Val-Bergot were waiting. Perhaps I wanted to show Maria that nothing she had said had made any difference to me; in any event, no sooner had I sat down than I rose once more.

"Would you like to dance?" I spoke to Stephanie the same words Maria had spoken to me a short while before. Stephanie joined me, and that waltz—the last one for the evening—was filled with tenderness, with warmth, with sweetness. Yes, I loved Stephanie, and she loved me; her waist moved under my hand, her bosom pressed against my chest when the movement of the dance brought us together—and her fingers tightly clasped mine. Everything told me that she loved me.

Maria sat at the table opposite Val-Bergot, crying softly. She was no longer drinking.

"I've never wept in front of a man before," she said to Val-Bergot a few minutes later, excusing herself for her show of weakness.

It was when she rose to return to her room to repair her makeup that Kruger motioned to her. Her words to me, my words to Stephanie, had been, "Would you like to dance?" Kruger said to her only: "Would you come with me?"

I am aware of what Captain Kruger must have said as he led the Baroness von Pallberg to the courtyard of the inn, off the area where couples continued to dance. Or rather, I can imagine what he must have said. Like a chief issuing orders, he must have told her that their unexpected overnight halt had not changed their plans in any way.

"But that child . . ."

Maria may have tried to protest, to explain, to talk about Stephanie . . . because, as you have doubtless perceived by now, Stephanie was the subject of their animated discussion.

"She is no longer a child; you know that as well as I." Kruger's voice was the voice of one in authority, but it was the authority of one of those petty chiefs whose job is to arrange for the dirty work of a regime. Despite that, Maria von Pallberg questioned his authority.

"And if I were to refuse, Kruger?"

Captain Kruger's laugh was metallic, sarcastic. "If you were to refuse? But Baroness, you are forgetting your son!"

I can imagine the look Maria must have given him: that same superb look Floria Tosca casts upon her tormentor, the police chief Scarpia, in the Castel Sant'Angelo in the second act of Puccini's opera.

"You are contemptible!"

Because what he had said was true: of course, the formidable von Pallberg family, frozen in their rigid way of life, had refused to allow the child to be taken from Budapest. But above and beyond them were distant, shadowy elements of which Kruger was a part—the tottering Empire's secret police, watching over their master's health. They were indeed contemptible, those policemen in disguise, hiding behind army officers or ambassadors, their victims held in the toils of their vile machinations by blackmail. In their task of maintaining the well-being of the Empire, they would stop at nothing.

"To use a child, Kruger . . . a child!"

Kruger only smiled. Maria von Pallberg, widow of a Prussian aristocrat who had emigrated to Hungary, the victim of plots fomented by the society of decayed nobility that had cast her out, was no more than a plaything in the hands of the Empire's secret police. She had many friends, she traveled freely in the world, she could render service . . . what was more natural? What better qualifications did she need to spy upon the movements, the activities, of a liberated young woman traveling from Zurich to Budapest—a young woman who, it was hoped, would never arrive in Hungary?

"Yet"—and the policeman's laugh became frankly obscene—"this girl's presence disturbs you. Before she showed up, your little affair with de Morlay was coming along very well. . . ."

Maria's reply was to slap his face. She turned and walked swiftly back into the inn and the dancing, the innocent peasant merriment, and Kruger swore under his breath after her retreating figure: "If you think you will get off that easily, Baroness . . ."

Late that night, just before dawn, a bell rang through the inn, now empty of dancers. The portly innkeeper in a nightshirt finally emerged to answer it . . . and then there was a knock on Maria's door.

The baroness slipped on a silk peignoir and went downstairs to the main floor, inhabited only by empty bottles, overturned chairs, extinguished lanterns. Her hands were damp as she took up the receiver.

The conversation lasted only a few seconds; Maria said almost nothing. Then she slowly hung up. There was a click, and silence. With a simple gesture, she brushed aside the concerned innkeeper when he asked her if she had need of anything.

Slowly she climbed the stairs to her room—the room she shared with Stephanie, who was still asleep. We had danced until our feet ached, and when I had left her, she had melted for a moment into my arms. But in those days, young women were still ladies. . . . Maria went to her bed and lay down, staring at the ceiling. For a moment she was motionless. The moon was full, and the room was visible in its cold light: blue and silver, the shadows stood out clearly. On the dressing table lay her toilet case. . . .

She rose again, still slowly. She would have been able to find the dressing table, her case, even with her eyes shut. Her hands moved among the brushes, the crystal bottles.

"It's impossible . . ." She spoke in a whisper. Her fingers had found the bottle with the red seal, and she looked down in horror. Then, quickly, she opened the box with the von Pallberg crest and took two pinches of the white powder.

Her eyes now wide open, Maria von Pallberg returned to her bed.

In the morning, it was like summer: the air was cool, fresh, invigorating, the air of the mountains at first light. The sun had already penetrated into the valley. In the distance, one could see the train, still stopped in the midst of the fields, and workmen on the embankment repairing the tracks.

In front of the inn stretched the lake we had seen when we left the train, one of those Austrian lakes in romantic engravings, surrounded by dark fir trees and lined with steep banks of a strange deep blue. The impression of wild nature was enlivened by the vivid green of fields strewn with yellow-gold flowers, and the scene had all the charm of the Tyrolean or Bavarian countryside. Here and there, tall farm buildings were visible, their sloping roofs weighed down with huge stones.

Val-Bergot had the impression he was the only person in the entire inn who was awake when he arose that morning and gazed at this scene from the window. He had opened the shutters a crack so as not to disturb me and had then gone downstairs to the deserted main floor with its overturned chairs. A deep silence reigned: at seven in the morning following such a celebration, no one wanted anything to drink unless it were a steaming bowl of *café au lait*. . . . Val-Bergot went out and took a few steps in the direction of the lake. There he saw Maria. She had not slept at all.

"Oh, André, if you had not come . . ." She threw herself into his arms. "I mustn't cry . . . I must not cry! Tell me not to cry, tell me . . ."

She pressed her face against the writer's shoulder, but her eyes were dry. Val-Bergot understood immediately.

"Franz?"

"Yes, Franz."

The telephone call in the middle of the night had been quite simple: Franz von Pallberg, the child with the sad, pale eyes, the child held as hostage in the great house in Budapest, had died the evening before as the result of the operation he had undergone. Or had it been that his blood—so pale, so thin—had merely ceased to flow, to nourish his frail body that had already dwindled to a shadow?

Val-Bergot did not speak. There was nothing to be said. He took Maria by the arm and led her along the lake. They walked in silence through the fresh grass. For Maria von Pallberg, a lifetime of tension, of waiting, of worry and concealed hatred came to an end there, on the banks of that unfamiliar lake set in the landscape of legend, in the midst of that rustic tranquillity. If she was unable to cry, it was because at that moment her sorrow was too violent, too brutal for tears.

They walked in silence. Gradually, Val-Bergot began to speak, at first but a few words, a few sentences. He told Maria what she meant to him. Other sentences followed, and then others: the poet, the friend, murmured words to his companion that were not mere words of comfort, random thoughts of sorrow and of life, words spoken simply to be spoken.

"Cry . . . you should cry, Maria. You must not wall yourself up in your sorrow."

The lake and the beautiful baroness in black . . . Her memories were not of waltzes in village inns, but of balls in palaces, in corridors that glittered with gilt and carved wood, with a thousand mirrors reflecting back the image of one woman, the most beautiful of women. But a woman who, upon returning from her ball, had always bent over the narrow bed of a sleeping child to weep.

"Cry, Maria. You will never in your life suffer more than this. . . ."

Although he thought of himself as nothing but a cowardly writer, Val-Bergot had a way with words, the right words.

"Cry, Maria. . . ."

The sleeping child murmured his mother's name, and his mother softly took his tiny hands, his curled fingers, his fingers that were almost blue.

"Cry, Maria. . . ."

The memories flooded back. She remembered a lady with a blue parasol on the beach at Cabourg, the face of the man with a small mustache, wearing my father's mask. Or myself, finally, our meeting on the train, the tying of the threads on this final journey . . . and the young woman who had danced the night away in that room with smoked hams suspended from the beams in the ceiling, that young woman unaware that somewhere in the shadows people were plotting her death.

"Maria, you must cry. . . ."

And at last, softly, Maria did cry. Val-Bergot walked beside her a while longer. They reached a point on the shore of the lake from where they could see a tiny church on an island, surrounded by willow trees. Val-Bergot stopped and pointed to it.

"Look, Maria . . . we seem to have wandered into a mid-nineteenth-century painting. In a moment a bell will toll from that onion-shaped steeple, and we will hear music from some concealed piano . . . Liszt, of course. . . ."

Val-Bergot could not help being a writer; even in moments of deep emotion, he could not avoid literature. But Maria had already ceased crying and pressed his arm, saying simply: "Thank you, André . . . you have taught me how to cry again." In a lower voice, she added: "No one must know. Promise me?"

Val-Bergot promised, and arm in arm, Maria almost smiling now, they returned to the village.

Maria von Pallberg was probably the bravest woman I have ever met.

As the morning progressed, the sun grew almost hot. Work continued on the tracks, and we could hear the sounds of picks and shovels striking the rails, amplified by the echo in the valley.

I had finally arisen, as had Stephanie, and Maria had managed to have a private meeting with Kruger. The chief conductor informed us that we would not be leaving before late afternoon, and we decided to have a picnic. . . . The day went by like a day outside of time, because Stephanie was beside me, and her hand never left my own.

Our picnic? We went off riding in carts with bells furnished us by the innkeeper, and Maria carried a blue parasol. She had changed from her black gown into a white dress, and Val-Bergot sported a magnificent panama hat. Stephanie—she and I shared a cart—wore a pale green riding costume Maria had found for her in the seemingly bottomless depths of her trunk. There must have been other picnickers, too, in other carts, but I did not notice them. I did catch a quick glimpse of Kruger's black figure with two other passengers at the end of the procession.

We climbed the slopes of a hill overlooking the lake. As we climbed, the village seemed to turn into a child's toy set down at the water's edge. Maria was glowing, superbly beautiful, seemingly young and serene; she had recovered the high spirits tinged with nostalgia she had had before our departure from the train. It was as though her cruel words to me the previous evening during our funereal waltz with the peasants had been forgotten.

When we arrived at the picnic spot and descended from our carts, she took me by the arm.

"My dear Paul . . ." She turned to Stephanie before drawing me aside. "I'm only taking him away from you for a moment. I promise to return him quickly."

It was said lightly, almost in jest. . . .

"My dear Paul . . ."

I remember it all: the ground was thick with pine needles, and through the trees bordering the path we could glimpse the lake below.

"I must tell you . . ." She told me to forget her harsh words of the previous evening; perhaps she had had too much to drink. She told me many things. And without truly understanding, I somehow understood. . . .

Later, of course, I realized that that morning she had made a decision, one that was to change everything: her life, my life, but above all, Stephanie's life. She was not as precise as that, naturally. I did not know it until later, through events that were like a blow in the face. She had decided, finally and irrevocably, to give in no longer to her tormentors' blackmail. Since early that morning, Maria von Pallberg had been free, and now she had the serenity of freedom.

"Come, Paul! Go back to Stephanie. You deserve to be happy."

So with Stephanie I walked that path covered with pine needles. We reached a promontory from where the island with its onion-spired church seemed like a child's drawing in a painted landscape. Stephanie's waist moved beneath my hand, and there, for the first time, I kissed her.

Val-Bergot and the lady with the blue parasol were somewhere behind us. Maria had given Stephanie to me; it had been her gift. And Maria, who had found finally both her own youth and her own age, put her hand on her companion's arm.

"Look at those children. . . ."

Her smile at that moment was unlike any of the smiles she had earlier displayed—smiles of surprise, social smiles, smiles of faint amusement worn like costumes, like masks. Thus, when Kruger made his way to her side and attempted to speak to her, she turned to him.

"I have nothing further to say to you, Captain Kruger. It is finished."

She had emphasized the word "Captain" for the benefit of Val-

Bergot, who was standing beside her. The Hungarian grew livid, but she had already turned her back to him. She bent toward Val-Bergot and murmured into his ear: "No questions, my dear André, if you please."

Somehow I think Val-Bergot understood.

At five that afternoon, the tracks had finally been repaired, and we returned to the train. A half hour later, we had again set off on the last stage of our journey, during which everything was to be unraveled.

What was it that Kruger and his cohorts had asked Maria to do? In short: when the train was forced to make an unexpected halt—not this halt at Seftensee!—she was to admit to her compartment two men who would have mounted the train from the far side. What they were then to have done to Stephanie . . .

To "that child," as Maria had called her.

As a student in Zurich, Stephanie had been deeply involved with a group of young Hungarian nationalists who—like so many other groups —were hoping with all their hearts for the Empire's dissolution.

"The role we are forced to play at the instigation of Vienna—the sham independence we have been granted—is ignoble," Stephanie was to tell me a few days later.

Remember: since the compromise of 1867, Hungary had become autonomous; it enjoyed a certain degree of independence from Austria within the monarchy. Those who had come to power in Budapest, however, were even more determined than their friends in Vienna to maintain that power, and they had become formidable oppressors of the minorities they controlled. So there were Stephanie and those like her, all engaged in their struggle, and on the other side were the Empire's secret police forces, in which Kruger was one of the more formidable elements. For such agents, sworn body and soul to uphold a lost cause, it was of prime importance to see to it that Stephanie never reached Budapest. Plans had been made to act during the final phase of the journey to put an end to what, today, we would call her "subversive activities."

However, the unforeseen halt at Seftensee had upset more than one set of plans. But Maria was ready. . . .

Night had fallen when the train arrived at the rendezvous set by the secret police. Kruger had once again made his way to Maria's side and given his orders. "You are prepared to act?"

She had the bottle of chloroform with its red wax seal in her toilet case. But Maria's reply was in the negative.

Stephanie was curious. "What is happening?"

The conversation occurred in the corridor outside their shared compartment.

"Nothing, my dear. The man is importunate, and I was forced to tell him so."

At that moment, as had Val-Bergot during the stroll in the forest, Stephanie must have understood. But Maria had already shut the compartment door behind me—for I had joined them when she had, without any explanation, invited me.

"Paul, my dear, would you be kind enough to keep two somewhat lonely females company?"

My only regret is that Maria did not tell me everything then. Although Val-Bergot had guessed, although Stephanie had realized, I alone that night suspected nothing.

At 7:15, darkness had fallen when the train ground to a halt in the open countryside. Someone had pulled the emergency cord; there were footsteps outside in the corridor, sounds of voices outside on the embankment, and a knock on the door to our compartment.

"Baroness von Pallberg, I order you to open the door."

It was still vital that the men not reveal their plot, owing to my presence and to the other passengers.

Maria shrugged. "It's that bothersome man again. . . ."

At 7:25, the train slowly started up: the chief conductor had been unable to discover who had been responsible for our halt . . . and those responsible, having failed completely, had been forced to give up their plan.

"I don't want to keep you, my dear Paul. Stephanie probably wants to prepare for dinner."

Maria's calm at such a moment was unnatural! But how could I have detected all its implications? So obediently I left their compartment and went to my own to dress for dinner. And later, still calm, Maria came out into the corridor. She was holding her embroidered bag in her hand.

Standing at the far end of the car, Val-Bergot witnessed what happened next. Perhaps he sensed that it would be better were he unnoticed; in any case, he stood in the shadows. He saw it all. . . . Maria

—free, her son dead, her last mission performed—had she intended to kill herself, or had she decided, in cold blood, to kill Kruger instead?

She left her compartment dressed for dinner, clutching her embroidered bag. It contained a revolver—a true woman of the world, Maria von Pallberg was prepared for any eventuality. She stood motionless for a moment in the corridor, as though making up her mind. Then she moved slowly to the rear of the train. At that moment, Kruger appeared. What threats he must have made. . . . His eyes bulged as he swore at her: the train had been stopped according to plan—but Stephanie was still alive on board.

"You must realize what awaits you in Budapest, Baroness!"

His mission had failed. Hers . . . but she answered him through clenched teeth, perfectly in control of herself. "I know. And I also know what awaits you. . . .''

He may have raised his hand to strike her; he may not. He spewed out insults, he swore vulgarly, threatened her. They were standing near the door that opened onto the tracks.

"And what about your son? Have you considered what will now happen to your son?"

Maria brushed his question aside almost indifferently—what state of inner peace had she attained?

"Franz is dead, Kruger, and your hold on me is gone." For a fraction of a second—Val-Bergot was a witness—Kruger seemed to hesitate. Was he surprised? Surprised that she knew? However, he quickly regained his self-control and became even more cynical, more violent.

"As if I didn't know! The little angel has been dead for a week, Baroness! However, on my orders you were not told."

Maria appeared stunned; she stood motionless. Then, all at once, she flung herself at Kruger, striking at him with her fists. She flailed at him desperately, despairingly. Val-Bergot knew enough not to make a move. Suddenly she moved to the door and threw it open.

It all happened so quickly, and when Val-Bergot arrived it was all over. Maria stood alone in the corridor before the door open onto the tracks, onto emptiness. Below, the roadbed sped by with the hypnotic rhythm of a train in a nightmare. Already . . . a hundred, two hundred yards behind . . . Captain Kruger's body was lying crushed against the embankment.

I believe—or so Val-Bergot told me—that Maria had attempted to throw herself out. Perhaps Kruger had been trying to stop her, to hold her back. . . . Did she then push him through that open door? Had it been an accident? Her embroidered bag still concealed a revolver. . . .

"It was an accident, Maria, surely . . . I am a witness, I saw it all. It was an accident." Slowly Val-Bergot pulled Maria back and shut the door. "It was an accident. . . ."

Haggard, Maria did not speak. She allowed Val-Bergot to lead her away. Under her breath, at last she murmured: "Do you think anyone is naive enough to believe it was an accident?"

"Anyone"—those others who had tormented her throughout her life, but of whom she was now free.

After Val-Bergot had led Maria to the bar car, it took her no more than ten minutes to regain her composure. She drank two cups of champagne, one after the other, and to the writer she explained: "You must understand—that girl . . . I couldn't . . ."

Another cup of champagne.

"And there's Paul . . ."

She spoke of me as the son of the man she had loved. She talked, she drank, she talked and drank some more, and within ten minutes, Maria von Pallberg, her son dead, having just killed a man, was once again the elegant passenger on a luxury train, the woman who frequented every aristocratic salon between London and Petersburg.

At dinner she laughed and told stories in a loud voice, stories that were extremely amusing and sometimes even a bit suggestive.

"Of course," she had said to Val-Bergot before joining us, "nothing must be said about this . . . accident."

And, as on our first evening, champagne, vodka and wine flowed freely—it was Bordeaux wine from those enchanted years before phylloxera had done its work—some Château de la Tour, Château Haut-Brion, I no longer remember. Maria played her part, she entranced us, she was in turn sublime, moving, ironic and so tender. As we reached the end of the meal, she proposed a toast.

"My friends, I raise my glass to the most severely tried of all virtues: to youth! Come, drink with me. . . ."

She exchanged looks with Val-Bergot; then Maria lifted her glass again, but this time to me, to Stephanie: "To *your* youth."

She spoke about us. Why did I feel like a fool, suddenly, when she proposed that toast; why was I incapable even of guessing the extent of the gift she had just made me? In the short time of our first dinner together, our brief conversation alone in her compartment, Maria had glimpsed in me the image—more than that, I know now—of her lost lover. What had her dreams been in those moments when violence, death, were stalking her? Then Stephanie had come onto the scene. Maria had hesitated for a few hours, and she had made her decision. Her gift to me was the walk I had taken with Stephanie along that path strewn with pine needles above a postcard lake. That stroll, that first kiss . . . and a whole lifetime . . .

But she had already turned to Val-Bergot.

"You see, André, I have tried to ignore it for too long, the days, the time, dates, years . . . do you remember, André? Do you remember my motto: No dates, no years! Well, this evening I want to forget I ever tried to ignore them. I want to remember everything . . . perhaps so that later I can forget it all more easily! Is that too complicated? Do you know what I mean?"

Maria was drunk; she was marvelously, luxuriously, sublimely drunk. Val-Bergot took her hand. Once again she looked across at us.

"They are the ones who will have the benefit of it. Those children . . . they say one learns with age. Maybe that's it; in forty-eight hours, I have learned everything. And everything has happened. Like that woman who used to get up at night in her palace in Vienna to stop the clocks. I have learned, yes . . . the young Maria, the old Maria . . . the aged baroness . . ."

"Maria, please . . ." Val-Bergot gripped her hand.

"I know, André, I know . . . but I have forgotten nothing." And then, all at once, her sad mood was gone. "I remember everything, André! I remember it all!" She laughed, her head back, more beautiful than she had ever been. "I have forgotton nothing! Paul's father's blond mustache . . ."

Val-Bergot smiled. "Maria, Robert de Morlay had a dark mustache! *I* was the man with the blond mustache."

Maria laughed again. "I told you I had forgotten nothing!"

The next day around noon, we arrived in Budapest. One of my colleagues was waiting to greet me on the station platform. An old woman in a gray cloak had come to meet Stephanie, and two men in black overcoats were waiting for Maria . . . they could have been Kruger's twins. Val-Bergot, who had planned to go on to Constantinople, had gotten off the train with her. She spoke briefly to the two men and then turned to Val-Bergot.

"My friend, it seems that I am obliged to go with these men."

Stephanie came up to her. "Baroness von Pallberg, I look forward to seeing you this evening at Prince Korwathy's ball. All of Budapest will be expecting you."

She spoke in such a way that the two men heard her, as did Val-Bergot and my colleague from the French consulate. In a clear voice, Maria replied, looking straight at Stephanie and then at the two men who had come to arrest her. "I shall be at Prince Korwathy's ball this evening."

Then, followed by a porter and the two policemen, she left the station.

Maria von Pallberg had provided herself with a twelve-hour reprieve.

So my tale ends at this ball—with the final glitter of a world that was waltzing towards the abyss.

"I suppose you know that Prince Korwathy is a notorious liberal."

Standing before the mirror in the room I had been provided at the consulate until I could find a suitable apartment, I was knotting my white tie, and Guy de Chauvins, whose career was to cross mine so frequently over the next forty years, was seated in an armchair puffing on an Oriental cigarette.

"This is the first time for I don't know how many years he has invited all of Budapest society; it's almost a provocation. . . ."

Stephanie had told me before we parted that she too would be at Prince Korwathy's. While being driven from the Orient Express across this city that was to be my home for a year and a few days, I had had the feeling of landing in some operetta kingdom, where no one spoke of anything but balls and military reviews.

"Tomorrow the archduke is to review the honor guard . . . you won't want to miss that!"

And Guy de Chauvins—Or could it have been someone else? All those well-brought-up young men who wrote our diplomatic dispatches looked alike in those days—stroked his mustache with his fingertips just as my father must have done. Just as he would have adopted a slightly bored and ironic tone when speaking of Prince Korwathy:

really, a Hungarian aristocrat with liberal tendencies . . . it just wasn't done!

"You really must attend, if only to catch a glimpse of it."

And so I went.

Prince Korwathy's palace was a vast, neoclassical building whose bulk stared across the Danube towards the Rathaus: above its entrance, the figures of Justice and Faith extended the palms of freedom to the Hungarian nation. There were cars, and even coaches with old-fashioned giltwork and coachmen with high hats—dusty with age and brought out once a year on such occasions—drawn up at the foot of the high steps leading to the entrance, rising like the gradients of some Aztec pyramid.

"All the upper crust!" de Chauvins remarked, tossing back his black cape with a studied gesture and handing it to a white-stockinged valet at the door who stood behind a majordomo wearing a silver chain.

We mounted the staircase to the ballroom, and it too was lined with valets, majordomos. Mingling with the throng of guests were a few odd characters, young people with feverish eyes, tall, eccentric creatures in homespun robes—as though Prince Korwathy, said to be a liberal, had made it a point to gather together beneath his roof every class of the city's society; from students and anarchists to minor grand dukes, Buda and Pest intermingled.

"He mocks at society, and since he is a society man himself, society cannot forgive him," my mentor remarked, with his penchant for convoluted puns.

However, my eyes were drawn to our host, who stood at the end of a gallery hung with immense portraits in the style of Van Dyck—a Magyar Van Dyck who seemed to have painted nothing but women in furs—for at his side stood a young, blond girl who—as of course you have guessed—was none other than Stephanie.

"Ah, yes," she said to me, as we began to waltz together as we had in Seftensee, "I had to come home. My father had asked me to return, and I was trying not to draw too much attention to myself. Well, at least my journey did not go unnoticed!"

We danced. Stephanie's father, Prince Korwathy, had taken my hand with a knowing smile, and the couples revolving around us glanced at Stephanie with curiosity, a curiosity that was very like greed.

"It's two years since I have been back in Hungary. . . ." She had been living in Zurich with young nationalists, all of whom had been trying to change the face of the world in their various ways.

"Sometimes I am so afraid of war! There are so many here who want nothing else but war! It is their dearest wish!"

All those people wanting war, all those people trying to uphold an order that no longer really existed, were well aware that with her Stephanie had brought lists of names, dates, secret meeting places: as a daughter of a Hungarian prince, she was a formidable opponent.

"But I was fully aware of what I was doing. And I also knew that Maria . . ."

She lowered her voice. The gilt, the chandeliers, revolved around us; we were surrounded by the toothless smiles of old people watching from the shadows Stephanie's radiant friends whom her father had invited to his party. The old were living in another world.

"What about bombs?"

"Let's not talk about that . . . let's talk about ourselves."

So we danced on. Then a silence fell as Maria entered the room on Val-Bergot's arm. Stephanie left me to go to Maria's side, and Prince Korwathy offered her his arm: both of them knew what was to happen a few hours later. The prince spoke to Maria in a low voice and kissed her hand. My friend—for she was indeed my friend—was very pale, very beautiful. And it was she who invited me to dance, as she had in the village.

We did not speak. The woman in my arms, dressed in black and gold sequins, was twenty years of age, and the man leading her in this final waltz was a man who resembled me like a father. That was why, when Maria leaned against me from time to time as we danced, abandoning herself to me, she was like a young woman, a happy woman. And my hand on the small of her back was the hand of a man in love guiding the woman he loves on a dance floor; for the space of a single waltz, Maria was my mistress.

The others around us seemed to wear masks: Val-Bergot, Prince Korwathy, even Stephanie were only faces. Friendly glances, inimical glances, flew by as we turned. We danced in the center of the room, I dressed in the evening clothes that were still the fashion as recently as twenty years ago and Maria in her grandest gown: the king and queen of the ball, we allowed ourselves to form the center of attention . . . and I was madly in love with Maria.

Maria was the first to stop dancing when the final violin sounded its final chord. We returned as if from a great distance. She leaned on my arm, but now she was leading me . . . she led me back to Prince Korwathy and his daughter. There, with a slow gesture of her arm like that of a ballerina, she beckoned me forward, at the same time drawing Stephanie to me, giving her to me. We had not exchanged a single word. The Prince, Val-Bergot—both knew what was going on—bowed to Maria, who extended her hand for me to kiss it. I followed her with my eyes. Val-Bergot escorted her to the doorway to the ballroom, with its beveled mirrors, a door that opened onto the vestibule where two men clad in black were waiting. Were they the same men as at the station? They looked very like them. There Maria signaled her friend to leave her.

"We shall meet again?"

"Yes, one day . . ."

A closed car with drawn curtains was waiting at the foot of the palace stairway. Maria entered it, and no one in this world ever laid eyes on her again.

I know I loved her.

Six months later, I married Stephanie. She is now in Paris, and I shall join her there in a few weeks . . . she is resting. Neither of us is twenty years old now, you see. . . .

Paul de Morlay lay down his pen. He had just reread and corrected with meticulous precision the seventy-some typewritten pages that Lise Bergaud had given him the evening before. One by one, he had evoked the ghosts of his youth for the microphone of a tape recorder and which, in a few days, the young woman had managed to bring to life again.

"I was so young . . ."

As though making excuses for himself.

Lise arose and approached the table where he had been working.

"But that is exactly what I find touching."

"My youth?"

The old man had also risen, and Lise Bergaud looked at him. Yes, his youth . . . He was an ambassador to his fingertips in his way of speaking, of behaving, of evoking the years when he had been twenty— and also in the way he stood there before her, tall and forthright, as though he were keeping the years back. Lise Bergaud had explored the corridors, the rooms, the garden of the Villa Manni—there was nothing to make one suspect that it sheltered a man who was almost ninety. Perhaps only the plaid shawl, brought each evening by Barberina and Despinetta when the first cool breeze arose and placed around the ambassador's broad shoulders, hinted at the years that had, nevertheless, flown by.

"Stephanie infused me with her life, you know, with her vivacity. Without her, I am sure I would have been nothing but another diplomat, like all the rest."

Yes, the concern others had for his health was the only tangible sign that this diplomat—unlike any other—was an old man. As for the rest . . .

For the rest, and throughout the week she had now spent in the house, Lise had had the feeling that she was living in the company of a man, a wise man, a gay man, sometimes serious, sometimes melancholy, but a man who was devoid of all sorrow, all regret. It was as though everything pertaining to the past was linked so closely to the present that the two had become one, and that in the heart of the retired ambassador recapturing his past there lived the soul, the mind, of the young man he was remembering.

"Yes, it is your youth that touches me more than everything else," Lise attempted to explain. "It is your way of living in the present as though tomorrow you had only to get into another car, or another train, to rejoin a woman with whom you would fall in love."

Paul de Morlay gave a smile whose meaning Lise Bergaud would understand later. He himself drove his white Porsche between Lausanne and Zion. . . .

"But how do you know that—if not tomorrow, at least in a few weeks, perhaps in a month—I'm *not* going to take that train to meet a woman I love, or with whom I will fall in love?"

In Lise's mind and in the ambassador's, along with the lady with the blue parasol who had disappeared that evening in 1913, there stood another figure, at once more frail and more substantial: that of Stephanie Kovaks, the girl who had become Stephanie de Morlay.

"Your wife . . ."

"Yes, my wife . . ."

Lise Bergaud sensed that each of the ambassador's sentences ended with an ellipsis; it was as though the aged ambassador took a sly pleasure in never finishing his thought. After all, it was her job to draw conclusions. . . .

Barberina and Despinetta now made their appearance, like soubrettes in an old comedy, silky, white as whipped cream. They fluttered around the old man, whispering to him and glancing at Lise Bergaud, and it was as though she, too, were one of the characters in a play who haunted not only the villa's rooms, but also its walls. Each had her role, and—like Stephanie before her—Lise Bergaud guessed that her role was to be that of Columbine.

"Do you know what these young women have in mind?" Paul de Morlay gestured to Lise to come closer. "Do you know the surprise they have in store for you?"

Barberina and Despinetta expostulated; if Lise were told their plan, it would no longer be a surprise. But Paul de Morlay swept aside their protests with a smile.

"When I was six years old, the most wonderful surprise in the world was finding my gifts beneath the tree on Christmas morning. And yet, I had gotten up in the night to find out what was in them!"

Appeased, the maids clapped their hands. "Well then, tell her!"

"These two imps have had an idea of genius: we are going to have a party for you, a party like in the old days, with costumes, masks and fireworks. And we are going to invite all of the handsomest young men in the region. For you. And, of course, for them as well . . ."

And why did Lise throw herself upon the old man's neck at that moment and embrace him with all the tenderness of a little girl opening her surprise Christmas present under the tree on the morning of December 25?

"But that mustn't distract us from the work that still lies before us. Because beginning tomorrow morning, I am going to tell you about someone who meant a great deal . . . and not to me alone. Jenny Fisher. Do you know who she is?

JENNY

Vienna, 1919

The whole world knew Jenny Fisher. She was acclaimed on virtually every stage throughout the world by men of my generation; everyone was entranced by such a voice—with such a face, such a figure, such presence. Whether as the tender, fragile Pamina of *Zauberflöte* or, later, the Marschalin in *Rosenkavalier,* from Mozart to Strauss, all her roles displayed her sovereign beauty. Her voice—thank God, recordings have preserved some of her more moving performances, and, through the mists of time, through the crackling of old wax pressings, those who were not lucky enough to see her in Paris or Vienna, Milan or London, can still manage to sense some inkling of what it was.

However, Jenny Fisher did more than sing Pamina, the Marschalin, Leonora—she was a divided woman, a totally divided woman. I enjoy now my memories of having crossed her path over the years, in Venice, Milan, Paris. . . . She loved, she suffered and she taught me to love.

It is about her that I want to tell you today: Jenny, almost torn apart, yet still needing to believe in happiness. For it is she, more than anyone else, who gave me my taste—still so strong—for certain kinds of music, certain voices, whether it is Elisabeth Schwarzkopf in Schubert or Lotte Lehmann in Mozart, and also, and I'm not ashamed to admit to it, the joyful strains of operetta, *Das Land des Lächelns* or nostalgic songs about that somewhat gray Blue Danube to which Jenny Fisher was to return after five years' absence because she, too, remembered. . . .

I first heard her story from her own lips in fragments, between sobs, as she begged me to intervene—but what could I have done?—to put a stop to that execution, one that would be made to look like a suicide, the next morning at dawn; later, some of the great singer's friends and fans told me the rest. And in the shadows of the whole affair, there were other women, women who loved in silence. One of them, one who had braved every storm, was La Chesnaye's mistress. La Chesnaye is the other hero of this adventure. Another was the nurse who had cared for Jean. Perhaps they—and they alone—were the only ones who knew the real truth. I mean about the deepest, mad motive for La Chesnaye's insane gesture.

When I mentioned La Chesnaye, I used the word "hero"—and why not? To be sure, at a time when every French male of eighteen or more was being cut down in the trenches of Verdun or on the Somme, Georges la Chesnaye had been living a carefree existence—we called it being a dandy in those days—in society or, worse, had haunted gambling rooms and private clubs. What does that matter? This is the story of Georges La Chesnaye almost as much as the story of Jenny Fisher, the story of the most dubious adventurer—and the most generous lover—I ever knew. And if my memories are to be laid like floral tributes at the feet of a group of women, this one is also intended for the memory of Georges La Chesnaye, an unscrupulous gambler, even a murderer, but also the most faithful of friends. . . .

It all began—once again—on a train platform one morning in 1919. The guns were silent at last—supposedly forever—and Europe was binding up its wounds. The treaties—Versailles, Trianon, Saint-Germain and all the others—were being elaborated with codicils and amendments intended to construct that most illusory peace, whereas in Germany itself the last hopes of the Berlin commune were being stifled by assassination, arson, blood and one of the most horrible of crimes against free opinion. For the waters of the Spree had no sooner closed over the mutilated bodies of Rosa Luxemburg and Karl Liebknecht than—with noisy ceremony on either side of the frontier—great acres of death were being inaugurated, sown with their crop of white crosses to the ridiculous flutter of memorial flags. This is by the way, of course, to remind you of what our vision of the world consisted at the time: while determined optimists persisted in repeating to the world (which was only too ready to believe) that we had just lived through the war to end all wars, trainloads of the mutilated, the crippled, the sick and anonymous wounded were being brought back from military hospitals all over Europe and unloaded in the railway stations of Paris . . . when anyone returned at all.

I had fought my war, like everyone else. Yet I had escaped with barely a scratch . . . no more than a touch of gas in the left lung. I was luckier than my brothers—one of whom was now a white cross in the Chemin des Dames cemetery, the other of whom had been lost in an air reconnaissance mission somewhere over Flanders—and on November 18, following the Armistice, I was back in my office in the Quai d'Orsay. It was as though nothing had changed. Outside my window, the roof of the Grand Palais blazed in the setting sun as before, and evening after evening, I would pay calls on the mothers, sisters and daughters of my former comrades who had—like my two brothers and my uncle and my three cousins and my sister Jeanne's husband—paid with their lives for the honor of rotting alive in mud up to their waists. Following a few weeks of frenetic activity—I was engaged in assisting the General Staff in drawing up a list of French troops lost between the Dardanelles and Vladivostok—I was ordered to Vienna. I spoke German, I knew how to waltz and one of my great-aunts had been an Austrian: in those days at the Quai d'Orsay, such things were considered important. . . .

Two months later I was installed in an office overlooking a park with a secretary named Emilie, who kept hidden in her bosom more secrets than were contained in the antique safes of our chancellery, and I was drinking my fill of music, painting, fresh air. As I've said, life was pleasant for those in the Quai d'Orsay in those days. And it was thanks to that life—I had a great deal of free time, since we worked in shifts albeit always ostensibly on duty—that I met Jenny.

So, a morning at the beginning of 1919 . . .

It was chilly in the Gare de Lyon, cold for the time of year, and the interior of the building was filled with opalescent light, a mixture of steam and morning mist. The Geneva Express was standing at platform seven, its windows covered with moisture, awaiting the last passengers. Jenny was there already.

"You're sure you're not making a mistake?"

"Yes, I'm sure."

The young woman, pale, was being given advice by two male friends. The collar of her fur coat was drawn up nearly to her eyes, almost completely concealing her profile and the oddly sensual lips in a face whose other features were thin, almost sharp: her nose was straight, her forehead high, her eyes set deeply in their sockets below incisive, strong eyebrows. And her pale blue eyes swam with something other than the mist. Tears?

"No, I'm not crying!"

She smiled beneath her broad white hood; she laughed. She made an attempt to seem gay, to act as though what was about to happen was normal: after all, she was only going to meet her husband.

"After all this time . . ."

"He's not the only man who was a prisoner!"

Jenny Fisher—for this young woman about to board the train for Geneva, where in a hotel on the lake she was to meet again her husband who had disappeared from sight during the first weeks of the war, was the singer Jenny Fisher, that soprano whose star had risen during the war, making her one of the outstanding young divas of the period—Jenny Fisher shrugged her shoulders. She had to keep up a front, she had to appear to be gay—and, above all, she had to pretend that everything was as it should be. No one must sense so much as a hint of the anxiety that gripped her. Jean . . . Jean. Again she smiled and shrugged.

"I think it's time to board the train."

The last passengers were hurrying down the platform. A tall man smoking a cigar passed them and stared at her—someone else had recognized her. She shivered; it was as though the eyes of men—even in those sad days that people did their best to turn into celebrations—wounded her in some way . . . the eyes of certain men, at least.

"It was so kind of both of you to come to see me off."

Her friends protested . . . they assured her of their friendship. What could be more natural; we weren't going to allow you to go off without a farewell! Jenny collected her baggage, her bouquet of flowers —her trunk and other luggage were already in her compartment—and once again she seemed to tremble. A photographer who had appeared out of nowhere managed to capture that moment, the tiny quiver of her lips, her half-closed eyes, her sorrowful smile. Jenny had tried to keep her departure a secret, just as she had tried to keep a discreet veil drawn over the fact of her husband's reappearance. But someone at the Opéra had disobeyed her orders, and two journalists, one from *L'Illustration* and the other from *Le Gaulois*, had managed to catch up with her at the last minute. With a rapid gesture, Jenny Fisher indicated that she was not prepared to respond to their eager questions— "Why are you going to Geneva, why are you returning to Vienna?"— but the photographer accompanying Yannick Navarre, the reporter from *L'Illustration*, managed to get a picture.

And I have here before me today the yellowed clipping from that long-defunct newspaper, so famous in its day. Beneath the photograph, the caption is uninformative, yet it says it all: "The famous singer Jenny Fisher mysteriously leaves Paris—is she off to Austria and the opera house where she had her first success?" What means most to me, however, is the image of that young, almost terrified young woman in flight . . . departing to meet again the man she loved. . . .

Trying to remain calm, Jenny Fisher clenched with a trembling hand the huge spray of roses her friends had presented to her. The photographer snapped another picture, but it has been lost in the archives of memory . . . and then she stepped onto the midnight-blue sleeping car of the Compagnie Internationale des Wagons-Lits, and the door closed behind her.

Beside the journalists and her friends, another man had been observing this scene—just as Val-Bergot had watched Maria before her disappearance. A man of perhaps thirty-five years of age—at the most, forty—he sported a thin brown mustache, and the somewhat dated elegance of his dress indicated that he was one of those men belonging nowhere, at home everywhere. His traveling cape was from Saville Row, his lizard shoes from Fioretti in Rome—where I myself have spent fortunes in my time—and one sensed that beneath the cape, his jacket, also from a London tailor, had seen hard wear. He was smoking a thin cigarette and leaning against one of the metal posts supporting the iron roof of a magazine kiosk; he seemed to be watching Jenny Fisher's departure with a great interest and at the same time to be keeping an eye on the entrance to the platform. It was almost as though he were waiting for some late arrival who might turn up and leap onto the train at the last minute, unexpectedly, to accompany him on his journey. Not until the stationmaster's whistle had echoed beneath the vast, gray-glass roof of the station and the wheels shuddered, the brakes emitting jets of steam—the chief conductor had just closed the door behind Jenny Fisher amid these clamorous sounds of departure—did the watcher in turn move to the steps of the train. At the very last minute, as the train had begun to tremble in anticipation throughout its steel, iron and polished wood length, he pulled open a door and leapt on board.

"That was close!"

It was the man with the cigar who had seen his hasty entrance into the corridor, but the man in the black cape did not reply. Behind him on the platform, however, from a vantage point behind the newspaper kiosk, a woman in a gray hat raised her veil: the train disappeared from sight in the rain-filled morning. The woman placed her hand on her heart . . . perhaps in relief.

The conductor who approached La Chesnaye—for that was the name of the last-minute passenger—as the train was passing through Melun was in no way surprised to find a traveler on the Geneva Express without either ticket or baggage. In those troubled times there were many like him, men who leapt onto the first train they could find simply because they wanted to seek a different life, at least for the duration of a journey to Bremen, Hamburg, even to Omsk or Vladivostok. Georges La Chesnaye drew from his pocket a well-stuffed wallet, murmured a few words to the conductor and soon found himself installed in a single compartment in the same car where—four compartments further along—Jenny Fisher was unpacking her traveling case.

I will make a guess at what may have been going through the singer's mind as she emptied the capacious leather case a young admirer had given her—a girl named Eva who was to make a sensational debut ten years later at the Theatre Unter den Linden as Eva Manievitz —and took out an elegant crystal toilet set. Jenny Fisher was full of hope. Despite everything, she was full of hope. For Jean had written to her—or, to be more precise, someone had written to her on Jean's behalf. For the first time since receiving the communication from the War Ministry that her husband, believed lost for the past three years, was not dead but rather a prisoner somewhere in a German hospital, she had at last received a real letter asking for a real meeting.

That had been on Thursday evening. She had just walked off the stage of the Opéra-Comique after the first act of *Madama Butterfly* and was resting in her dressing room, bare save for two bouquets of red roses, until the next act. Norbert was also there. I knew him well, Norbert de Saint-Symphorien: he was a junior commissioner on the Conseil d'État, one of those dandies who are too well bred to know when to leave, who spend their entire lives waiting. Norbert de Saint-Symphorien had made up his mind that he was in love with Jenny . . . Jenny knew full well she did not love him. Everyone knew she was a married woman, but everyone looked upon her as a widow. Why had she kept silent about that letter from the ministry informing her of her husband's wound—of Jean Ledoyen's imprisonment in a hospital? Perhaps merely because she was neither sure of herself nor of her talent . . . even though everyone else who had heard her sing was well aware of the value of her golden voice . . . and she had preferred to remain silent. Thus, if she unwittingly encouraged her host of suitors, if she sometimes gave in to their pressure—because she was twenty-five years old, beautiful, alone—she still realized deep in her heart that she would never love anyone in the world but her husband, the man who had disappeared and had now returned, the man hidden away somewhere in a prison hospital and then later in an ordinary hospital because the war had left him so terribly marked and he was not yet prepared to face the world.

"You seem nervous," de Saint-Symphorien had said to her that evening, taking her hand as she came into the dressing room.

She withdrew her hand gently. "I'm tired, that's all. . . ."

Remembering the scene for me later, de Saint-Symphorien told me that he had never found her more beautiful but that at the same time he had never been so cruelly aware that Jenny could never be his. And, of course, as I listened to de Saint-Symphorien's confidences, I knew that although during those years alone Jenny might have been unfaithful to Ledoyen, it had been in the arms of a man quite different from de Saint-Symphorien or any of those refined, elegant aesthetes spared by the war who haunted receptions and theaters as they thanked God for having kept them out of the trenches. No, the men Jenny had desired had not been found in the carpeted corridors of our ministries, in theaters or salons. I imagine them as delivery men, messengers, market porters . . . but that is another tale, the tale of a secret Jenny Fisher, a woman none of us—not de Saint-Symphorien, not Ledoyen, not I—ever saw. Perhaps Georges La Chesnaye had a glimpse of her, because he, too, was a part of that shadowy world. But, of course, he never had a chance to tell of it. And had he known, for that matter, I know he would have kept silent.

So in her dressing room after the first act of *Butterfly,* Jenny Fisher allowed herself to be courted vainly by a man who could never have achieved success. There came a knock at the door.

."A special delivery letter for you, Madame Fisher."

De Saint-Symphorien gave a coin to the messenger, who had remained transfixed in the doorway staring at Jenny—her shoulders were bare, and her Opéra-Comique Japanese kimono had fallen open, revealing her leg to the thigh.

The young woman seemed hypnotized by the handwriting on the envelope—nervous arabesques in violet ink. A woman's hand, obviously, and most likely a foreign woman. She opened the letter, and the words exploded before her eyes: "Madame, your husband has requested that I write to you . . . he is hoping to see you again. . . ." The letter was signed Frieda something; she could not make it out. She trembled, she wept and words tumbled in confusion from her lips: she was ecstatic. She felt an almost senseless joy, the joy of a drunken woman, a joy so profound that it overshadowed every other joy she had ever felt. Distracted, she brushed aside the unfortunate de Saint-Symphorien's attentions with a gesture and ignored the dresser who was refastening Butterfly's kimono. As the stage manager announced the beginning of the second act, she walked toward the stage as if in a dream amid the sound of violins tuning up in the orchestra pit. It *was* a dream, that unbelievable moment filled with happiness. Her husband finally found, her husband asking to see her . . . Butterfly, singing of her hope to the becalmed sea, had never sounded as she did that evening—one fine day, he will return, the man I love! Never had her words been more true, more filled with vibrant serenity, than when Jenny Fisher sang them that evening on the stage of the Salle Favart in Paris. For she was now about to set out to meet the man she had never ceased to love in all the past five years—even in the arms of other men, of strangers—and that evening, in that music, she repeated words that embodied her own joy: *Un bel di vedremo . . . Vedi? E venuto . . .* That was it: he had come back . . . and she was to go to him.

La Chesnaye introduced himself to her at lunch. He had waited in the bar car, had watched her. She was so like the picture of her he cherished in his mind: beautiful, so beautiful, and so fragile. Why are all the heroines of operas such fragile creatures? He sensed something timorous in her that made him suddenly catch his breath, that libertine, that gay dog. He had an urge to go up to her with open arms and embrace her like a tiny, wounded bird, a fragile bird who would find refuge, who would lean upon his shoulder and allow herself—that was it: she would "allow herself"—to find protection. He seemed to divine that, beneath her joy, the joy of finding her husband again (which he did not so much as suspect), she was filled with anxiety. For there was always that question she had not dared ask herself ever since receiving that letter in violet ink written on blue paper (perfumed blue paper . . .) the question that haunted her in the night: what if the Jean who was alive, whom she was about to see again after five years' separation, were in fact a dead man to her? Why had he been silent? Why had he rejected her?

Thus, Georges La Chesnaye watched her drink two martini cocktails in succession—when someone downs two martinis on a train, it must be to gain courage—but he had not made a move. There were other women in the car—one other in particular, wearing a feathered hat—but he had not noticed them. He had eyes for no one but Jenny. Perhaps it was because he had heard her voice; perhaps because he found her more beautiful, more touching than all the other women on the train, more than any of the women whose paths he had crossed throughout the years he had been sailing like a pleasure craft on the seas of beautiful women. Perhaps it was simply because all at once, just like that, he had fallen in love with her.

I asked Jenny later . . . We were sitting on the terrace of a famous café not far from the Théâtre des Champs-Elysées where she had just given a recital, and the Place de l'Alma was blossoming with another springtime. She took my hand.

"What if I were to tell you that I truly believe that no man has ever loved me as La Chesnaye loved me?"

She was then one of the foremost singers of her era, and we had become friends; all at once, I began to love La Chesnaye for having loved her so much.

So, as he approached her table as she was having lunch after her two martinis and a glass of champagne, Georges La Chesnaye was gripped by a violent emotion. He, the cynic, a man who had not quailed when faced by the underworld or by the even more dangerous operators of international high finance, felt his hands grow damp. For a few seconds, as he leaned toward the young woman to ask her permission to join her at her table, he found himself almost speechless. It was not until he had ordered a drink that he finally managed to relax somewhat.

"What do people usually say to a great singer when they chance to meet her on a train and want to strike up an acquaintance with her?"

Jenny Fisher started. She had been miles away from this stranger who had so suddenly approached her, somewhere with the memory of Butterfly and her return to the man she had lost.

But La Chesnaye continued: "Is one supposed to say how much one admires her, that one is passionately in love with her voice . . . or does one talk about her eyes, her smile, her face. . . ."

Jenny stared at La Chesnaye. Could he be making fun of her? She saw his bantering smile; he was obviously making fun of someone, but not of her. He was making fun of himself. For a moment, La Chesnaye thought she might smile—it would have been the first time he had seen her smile—but her face was grave.

"People say what they feel like saying, that's all."

La Chesnaye sensed that her reply was an encouragement for him to continue. He emptied his glass, settled into his chair and began to talk about her.

"So if I were to say that I am somewhat afraid . . . that all at once I feel unsure of myself, that I am trembling like a boy on his first date, would you believe me?"

Now she smiled. He continued his banter as he ordered his meal. Jenny relaxed and began to respond to his mood, and in a short time the ice was completely broken. One should remember that in those days just after the war, those who had survived seemed to share a kind of complicity; relations were somehow easier then. The dessert arrived; Jenny Fisher had ordered the strawberry charlotte that had made the head chef on the Paris-Geneva line, M. Paul, famous in his time. This man who had sat down so casually at her table—and the Mumm Cordon Rouge 1902 champagne La Chesnaye had ordered with his usual *savoir faire*—had put her at her ease; she began to talk about herself. And since La Chesnaye listened to her with an understanding expression, not interrupting her as she spoke, she began to tell him gradually, without realizing she was doing so, about the circumstances that were weighing on her mind: her husband's disappearance and sudden reappearance. One sometimes speaks more readily to strangers encountered on a train than to one's closest friends.

"Can you imagine what it's like to live for a year, two years, without any word from the person you love? Waiting, hoping, and then one day you stop waiting, you stop hoping for anything. One day, everything falls apart!"

She played nervously with her spoon, and La Chesnaye thought to himself as he watched her that it was a miracle a woman like Jenny Fisher should also have Jenny Fisher's voice. No word, no expression she used failed to touch him. It was as though everything around him —and, above all, what he was fleeing from—had suddenly ceased to matter.

"And that is how it is with me," Jenny continued. "First, Jean's letters from the front grew less frequent, less informative, and then suddenly, nothing."

For a moment she fell silent, and La Chesnaye found that even her silence was lovable—it contained great modesty and almost total immodesty—she seemed able to tell him anything and everything all at once.

"When I finally discovered what had happened to him, I began to live again. Because he was alive, and I knew he was alive. . . ."

After the first anonymous message, however, she had had no further word. Silence. The letter she had written to the address given her by the War Ministry—a prison hospital in Bavaria—had been returned to her unopened. All her letters bore the words: "Refused by addressee." With blind obstinacy, Jean Ledoyen had for over two years refused, one after the other, all her written appeals. It was as though his wound, his imprisonment, had erected an impenetrable wall between them.

"Yet I knew he was alive. . . ."

Then, indirectly, word had come. Jean's comrades had gotten in touch with her to tell her that he had been transferred to another hospital, then to another . . . but from Jean himself there had been nothing.

"So when the letter finally arrived . . ."

She drew the sheet of blue paper from her bag . . . the unfamiliar handwriting, the scent emanating from the envelope. After five years of silence, Jean Ledoyen had finally arranged a meeting at a hotel in

Geneva. At that point, she had made a decision: they had met in Vienna in the days when she was beginning her career, still unsure of herself, and now she would return with him to Vienna! She would go back with him. She would recapture all her past in one journey— their youth, their love. She would make the world come to life again. That was what she had written to the hospital in the Valais where he was convalescent, and Frieda with her large and angular handwriting had replied by return mail. Jenny had feared the worst, but Jean had agreed to her plan.

"I used the first performance of a symphony composed by a cousin of mine as an excuse for the trip."

Jenny spoke Rolf's name for the first time—"composed by a cousin of mine"—but La Chesnaye paid little attention. Yet it was to be Rolf who would, with one bullet, bring this story to its final, bloody end. Jenny shook her head; she had been talking too much. Not once had La Chesnaye interrupted her. His emotions were in turmoil. He was familiar with Ledoyen's work, his reputation. Even more: he admired the man.

Perhaps this is the moment to say a few words about Jenny's husband. Jean Ledoyen was one of the foremost architects of his generation; he had conceived some of the plans that we still look on as landmarks, plans that during the years 1910 to 1913 were *avant-garde* visions, rediscovering form, volume, space, from Berlin to Paris. The famous "Villa of Light" in the hills above Nice, for example, bathed in sun on all sides and through the roof was his, the model working-class city near Saint-Étienne, a children's rest home in Chamonix— buildings that revealed not only a fiery and inventive genius, but also a concern for human beings and their problems, a humanitarian vision turned both to work and pleasure. La Chesnaye was naturally somewhat taken aback by the knowledge that the man he so respected was the husband—a husband who was alive, whom she was on her way to see again—of the woman with whom he had fallen so suddenly and so violently in love. He had been prepared to conquer her, to crush anything that might stand in his way, and now he found himself at a loss!

After a moment he offered to escort Jenny back to her compartment, and it was as they stood before her door that she made that mad, unpremeditated gesture that was to bind them together forever.

"Don't leave me," she breathed, taking his arm.

He understood: she needed him; it was as simple as that. He read nothing more into it but that. And so he followed her into her compartment filled with red roses.

For La Chesnaye, the rest of the trip was like its beginning: full of rapture. How far behind him seemed all those anxieties that had haunted him until the very second the train had left Paris. Jenny talked, and La Chesnaye listened to her until their arrival at the Geneva station. When she fell silent, La Chesnaye would revive the conversation with some remark about herself, about one of the roles she had sung, and Jenny would go on without any further urging. He was well aware that she needed the company of another, but he was nevertheless overjoyed that it was he. When she informed him that Ledoyen would not be arriving at the Hôtel Beau-Rivage until the following day, La Chesnaye at once told her that he, too, was getting off the train in Geneva.

"But I didn't know you were going to Switzerland!"

"I'm free to go wherever I please."

It was the first time he had said anything about himself, and his remark could easily have been mistaken for banter. But, in fact, at that moment La Chesnaye had spoken more seriously than ever before . . . and both his fate and his very life had just been decided.

The weather was radiant that evening in Geneva, springlike for that time of year. A light mist rose off the lake, and at the very moment the train pulled to a halt in the Cornavin Station, every bell in every steeple in the old town across the Mont Blanc Bridge began to ring. Other bells answered from the surrounding hills, echoing from the mountains. In the gathering twilight, as Jenny hummed for La Chesnaye the opening measures of *Porgi amor* from *The Marriage of Figaro*—surely the most heartfelt aria of lost love Mozart ever produced—they strolled for a long time together through the streets. Why return to the hotel, why even bother to have dinner, when all either of them wanted was to wander side by side through those streets whose very names—Place du Bourg-de-Four, Rue des Marchands—were redolent of Switzerland, of peaked roofs and cobblestone pavements?

Unlike La Chesnaye, Jenny felt that something very simple had happened to her: for the first time since she had been thrust into the predatory world of men who were ready to stake everything on the chance of possessing her, she had found a man who simply listened to her. A man who seemed to ask for nothing more. Jenny did not question herself further. She could very well have wondered who La

Chesnaye really was, why he appeared to be so free from constraint and obligations, but she was too happy to have found a confidant to think of intruding into his private life. She felt good, it was *good*—that was all. Her anxieties gradually faded, and she began to trust in her forthcoming meeting with Jean, in the trip to Vienna—and that peace she now felt she owed to La Chesnaye. For the first time in her life, beyond the ephemeral pleasure she had sometimes managed to grasp in the rough arms of a passing lover soon to be forgotten, she had found a friend. The transparent mist rose gently from the lake. In the distance was heard the cry of a sea gull, a boat's horn. . . .

And so, after a leisurely dinner—Jenny found herself suddenly ravenously hungry—in a tavern behind the cathedral, they arrived back at the hotel on the Quai du Mont Blanc where they were both staying.

La Chesnaye took her arm in his and asked: "May I come up with you?"

Tenderly shaking her head, she refused. "You are now my friend, Georges," she said.

La Chesnaye, who had known her answer even before he had spoken, smiled and bowed. "You're probably right."

For the first time since their meeting, she smiled truly at him. She had smiled before, but that had been her public smile. Now she smiled from deep within herself. "You know very well I'm right!"

And the revolving door of the Hôtel Beau-Rivage whooshed as she passed through. For a moment, standing in the sudden cold—the low clouds overlying the lake had suddenly thickened, the air was like ice—La Chesnaye stood motionless; he did not want to follow her at once. He did not want to be too near her, give her the impression—or have the feeling—that he was following her. He lit a cigarette and strolled along the *quai*. The mist had thickened into fog, and it surrounded him, but he did not feel the cold at first. Then it began to seep into his bones. After a moment, he halted and then turned abruptly back the way he had come. Did he notice the silhouette of a man wearing a raincoat and a soft felt hat, its brim turned down, standing in the shadows near the hotel?

"He told me he had realized he was being followed, but he did not tell me when he noticed it for the first time," Jenny said during our long conversation over tea Chez Francis, that conversation in which she revealed the entire story.

As he approached, the man must have concealed himself in a nearby doorway. This scene was described to me by the woman who had been watching La Chesnaye at the Gare de l'Est, a woman who was to meet him by prearrangement in Geneva. Worried when he did not return to the hotel, she had gone out to look for him. When La Chesnaye finally came through the revolving door of the Beau-Rivage, Andrea D. remained concealed in a corner of the lobby. She was the only person who knew the risk La Chesnaye was courting by remaining in Geneva, and she also knew that he was flouting the danger to himself because of a woman . . . another woman. Because of Jenny.

But what would any man not have risked for Jenny's love, for her life, her voice—and for the misty blue of her smiling eyes?

The next morning, Jean Ledoyen was surprised to see his wife enter the hotel lobby on another man's arm. The train from Soldanelles, the clinic in the Valais, had arrived behind schedule, and he was late for his meeting with Jenny at the time they had agreed upon, the time he himself had fixed. Once again overcome with anxiety by this further delay, Jenny had been unable to stand the wait, her room. She had gone out and run into La Chesnaye, who was pacing the lobby. He had taken her by the arm, determined to make her forget her troubles if he could.

"Come along! I'm taking you with me."

In the open air and sunshine, La Chesnaye's high spirits had eventually overcome Jenny's concern; thus, she was smiling as she entered the hotel again a half hour later—after all, Jean's delay was probably due to something quite ordinary. Jenny played with fire, but Jean was being consumed.

For he had finally arrived; he had been waiting for her.

I must make clear now what Jean later admitted to Jenny—who had already realized it—as well as to La Chesnaye and later to me when we met in Paris. You have to understand what the war had cost Jean Ledoyen: sights of death, mud and twisted metal had reduced a man with one of the most brilliant minds of his time, one of the finest and most generous characters, into a shadow of his former self. It wasn't only his wound. He had suffered a perforated lung and a crushed leg too, but the most terrible part of his condition was the silent, ever-increasing anxiety. Dead friends—V., the designer, his closest comrade, who had lost his hands; Jacques D., an urban planner and visionary like himself, whose eyes had been burned out; Maurice M., Claude L. D., men he had respected, whose work he had admired, all had been reduced to ruins, to memberless bodies and featureless faces. Jean Ledoyen had expected to be wounded even before it had happened, and he had awaited his wound as irrefutable proof that the world and mankind were standing on the brink of madness that could only be cured by the sacrifice of his own body.

"Think of surviving all of that!" he was to say to me one day, his voice low, staring at his tortured hands, his stiffened leg.

And yet those words were spoken in the days when Jenny's love and La Chesnaye's sacrifice—there is no other word for La Chesnaye's insane deed—had already nearly completed his salvation.

So this ruin of a man, a man exhausted by even the slightest effort, a fragile man who was easy prey to any emotional disturbance, grew pale when he saw his wife enter the Hôtel Beau-Rivage on another man's arm, laughing. And he had waited so long before agreeing to see her again.

"What am I doing here?" he wondered suddenly, opening a newspaper to conceal himself from the new arrivals.

But Jenny had already approached the desk below the vast four-story wooden balcony that rose up in the center of the Beau-Rivage and made it the architectural wonder it was (the same hotel where Elisabeth of Austria had died with a needle-thin dagger in her heart). The concierge pointed to Jean, behind his newspaper.

"Leave me," she murmured to La Chesnaye.

And she went to her husband.

When she told me these details in that café on the Place de l'Alma, the facts that have enabled me to know her version of the Viennese adventure, Jenny said simply: "I no longer remember anything of what happened during those first minutes."

How could she remember? And how can I, a diplomat more familiar with chancellery gossip than with the technique of fiction, invent it for you? The first minutes, the first words, the stammered thoughts, the first chaste kiss, almost shy . . . Frieda, Jean's nurse, who had been watching off to one side as had Andrea X., La Chesnaye's mistress, told me merely: "She took his arm and led him outside."

To live! To breathe! To walk and drink in the suddenly fresh air, to realize that this man on your arm is your husband found again and to rediscover his love, his smile, or perhaps no more than the pressure of his hand on yours!

However, upon their return Jean Ledoyen seemed to be as tense as he had been when Jenny had first entered the hotel. He had not dared question her about La Chesnaye, of course, and the question was still stuck in his throat . . . like a pain in the chest when we awaken after a lonely night filled with anxiety: does she still love me? Jean and Jenny went up to her room, where they were to wait until six o'clock that evening to go on to Lausanne and then transfer to the old Arlberg Orient Express for Innsbruck, Linz and Vienna.

Jean stretched out on the bed completely dressed and watched his wife as she moved around the room. At one point, she slipped out of her dress and stood before him in the light, clad only in her white silk undergarments, her white skin. "Do I desire her . . ." Ledoyen wondered. There was the memory of La Chesnaye's presence at her side in the lobby, and the question still stuck in his throat: "And who is that man?" He knew he should speak, should question her, be reassured, but he could not say a word. He was locked in silence; he was afraid. So, although he should have spoken, he shut his eyes. But at once he saw other images: their first meeting in Vienna at a ball, the scents, the multicolored gowns and the shadow of another man bending over her, that musician, the cousin she had loved and whom they were soon to see again. Rolf. Rolf. Rolf! Ledoyen's skull seemed about to burst.

"And Rolf?"

He spoke the name aloud. Jenny was arranging the flowers she had received from a Swiss-German opera director, a man with a fondness for France and its singers who had learned by chance of her presence in Geneva. She turned and looked at him.

"You know that Rolf is only a pretext. I used his concert in Vienna the day after tomorrow as an excuse to be there with you."

Jean Ledoyen lay motionless, his cane at his side; he said nothing. Rolf. There was not just the man who had entered the Beau-Rivage arm in arm with her—there was also Rolf Freitag, his wife's first lover.

"So," Jenny was to tell me later, "the day passed. I began to think it would never end."

They had gone out to walk by the lake. Since he was still convalescent,

Jean Ledoyen wrapped himself in a brown wool cape with a military air—like those old greatcoats the army used to issue—and Jenny had put on a tiny, pale green pillbox hat, like a piece of mint candy; her hair had been twisted up off the back of her neck, held by two pins.

"I need to breathe," she had exclaimed. "To breathe!"

She guided his steps, and they arrived at the *quai* where the landing stage, on pontoons, stood for the white paddleboats, so reminiscent of those in New Orleans, which plied their way across the lake to the opposite side . . . just as they had done in my grandmother's day: blue water, parasols making soft touches of color in the scene. On the deck of one of those boats, out of the wind, she had leaned against him.

"How lovely it is. . . ."

And for the first time, that stranger who was yet her husband put his arm around her shoulders and drew her close to him, very lightly, with barely a pressure of his fingers.

"Yes, it is lovely. . . ."

All at once an entire, vanished world flooded back into his memory: concerts, songs, laughter. Long evenings before the fire in their apartment in the Rue Daunou—"Just a short walk from the Opéra, so convenient!"—where they had lived for the two years of their married life . . . all at once that world seemed a part of him again. It was as though everything were once again possible: there would be houses to build, houses that would be alive and full of warmth for people now suffering in cold, dead cities. And there would be the love of this woman he had never ceased to desire with his broken body, in his clouded, anguished mind so full of fear and anxiety—away from the forgetfulness, the hospital beds, the silence in which he had attempted to bury himself. At that moment, life revived in a man who had been turned into something like a zombie by the war, by the insanity of generals and by the zeal of those in the rear lines to order further advances. Once again, he increased the pressure of his fingers, his arm, around Jenny's shoulder, and she leaned against him. Then a great gust of wind came, and there in the open air, in the midst of the sea gulls gliding over the white boats on the blue water, her hair tumbled loose and an ash-blond cloud fell over her glowing face, so alive with pleasure. And Jenny also realized—quite clearly, without a shadow of doubt—that everything was once again possible.

She had been waiting five years for that moment—and it lasted the time it took the white boat to cross the lake that lay before the city. Time was in suspension.

And on the café terrace on the Place de l'Alma, as she recalled it, her face suddenly frozen with emotion, I realized that I, too, could have loved her!

The white paddle steamer took an hour and a half to cross the lake. Neither Jean nor Jenny spoke again, but for the first time neither of them felt any need for words; they were not afraid to remain silent. And their silence amid the crystal water and the green shores and the sweeping flight of the sea gulls over the lake could have lasted forever, forever. . . . Jenny may have shivered—from happiness or a sudden chill; and Jean may have felt in his left leg the stabbing of the pain that never left him completely, day or night. But they were together again, and that was all that mattered.

At five o'clock, the boat, like something out of an operetta, returned to the landing stage, and the car Jenny had ordered to take them to Lausanne was waiting. Jean released his wife. When they returned to the lobby of the Beau-Rivage and La Chesnaye appeared at the end of it, bowing courteously to them from a distance, Jean Ledoyen's anxiety flooded back.

"You have to realize that he was still very unwell," Jenny explained to me.

It was as though she were making excuses for him.

Their journey across the lake had been a timeless moment, but now they returned to the real world in which they were suddenly reunited—to the hotel, to the car, to La Chesnaye, about whom Jean knew nothing, about whom he suspected so much. Like a window suddenly closed, the brief moment of hope Jean Ledoyen had experienced came to an end. Mechanically he returned to the room and packed the few articles he had removed from his valise. Still without speaking to Jenny—not a single word, this time—he crossed the hotel lobby ignoring Frieda, his nurse from Soldanelles; yet she was there in the background, watching him, in love with him, like Andrea D. watching La Chesnaye.

All those women, watching those pitiful children that men, whether wounded or not, never completely succeed in growing away from. . . .

Jenny Fisher and Jean Ledoyen, in their double sleeping compartment on the train to Vienna, spoke no more than they had on the journey from Geneva to Lausanne by car, or on the rattling old train that had borne them from Lausanne to Basel. Jenny had caught Jean's anxiety, and now her lips, too, were tight and her hands trembled as she unpacked her bag. Once, holding her long white nightgown over her arm, she turned: across from her on the banquette, Jean was staring at her, and his face was like that of an old man. Her fears grew, and she shut her eyes against the question that sprang up in her mind: what if Jean were lost to her forever?

Two compartments further along in the same car, La Chesnaye was sitting next to Andrea D., who had joined him and was talking to him in a low voice. La Chesnaye listened. A thin smile crossed his lips, but his eyes were serious. When the young woman left him, he opened the elegant leather briefcase that was his only luggage and drew from it a small-caliber revolver; he checked the barrel with an expert movement and slipped it into his pocket. Then, seated on the banquette, he began to lay out a hand of solitaire. His deck of cards was copied from a famous eighteenth-century set designed for another supreme gambler, the Marquise de Pompadour. The first four cards he laid down were all aces. . . . And in the only third-class car, at the tail end of the train, the man in the felt hat with the turned-down brim was reading a cheap newspaper.

How can I be precise about what happened next? At the end of this adventure in Vienna, I will have facts, names: there will be shouts and even deaths when we reach the denouement. But during the Arlberg Express's journey to Vienna, everything that occurred between La Chesnaye, Jenny and Jean consisted of murmurs, brief confessions, avowals and whispers—and underlying it all, a resonant tone of resolve. The resolve La Chesnaye took to do everything in his power —during the short time remaining to him—to bring the couple back together . . . a couple who had never been truly divided, since they had not yet truly been joined. At the outset, Georges La Chesnaye took a step that set up another wall of misunderstanding. Shortly before nine o'clock, he sent his card to Jenny, inviting her and her husband to dine with him, her husband, "to whom I should be happy to be introduced at last," he concluded in his beautiful, almost calligraphic handwriting that was so oddly different in its restraint from what we were later to learn of his character.

Jean Ledoyen came to a decision. "May I ask who this gentleman is?"

His voice was without expression, and the anxiety Jenny sensed in him as he asked the question served to calm her. So that was it—not the only thing, but one of the things that was upsetting him! She almost smiled.

"Oh, La Chesnaye . . ." She explained who he was—one of the last of the *bon vivants* in a time when other people had not yet learned to live again, a passing acquaintance on a train—certainly not a lover. "I met him for the first time yesterday on the express train to Geneva," she concluded.

Jean's look told his wife that she should have spoken earlier to reassure him. He shook his head, already less tense: "Just another passenger . . . nothing more."

But Jean did not voice his deepest thoughts. What did he really think of La Chesnaye? Another idler, a real or sham aristocrat with a tiny mustache who had flitted around in society while others were dying of fear—not to mention a bullet in the skull—in the trenches? Jenny sensed his unspoken reproach.

"There are many men like him. If you only knew . . . and he is probably one of the least.unpleasant." She laughed briefly. "And then, he loves my voice—he says such lovely things about it. . . ."

For the first time, they seemed to understand each other. Jean almost smiled with her.

"Oh, well, if he says lovely things about your voice!" He had not told her, but during his years of captivity and silence, he had saved every newspaper clipping about his wife, every program, every photograph he had managed to lay his hands on. "Oh, if he says lovely things about your voice . . ."

His indifference was only feigned. While La Chesnaye in his compartment continued to lay out his solitaire with a superb insolence, aces and kings falling from his fingers . . .

It was time for dinner. . . . Conversation was difficult at the outset. Ledoyen was stiff, but it was only a protective wall; he was always on the defensive. La Chesnaye, although he was at ease in any surroundings, also felt a certain constraint. He plunged in. What did he talk about? His true thoughts. "You know, I admire you a great deal!" He addressed himself to Ledoyen. Jean looked at him uncomprehendingly, but La Chesnaye continued: "I've only seen a few of your buildings, but I was overwhelmed by them."

In his forthright way, further evidence of his determination not to take himself too seriously, he made it clear to Jean Ledoyen that he knew what he was talking about. He mentioned a complex of artists' studios in Menilmontant, a school in the northern suburbs of Paris, a villa in Nice.

"You are allowed to smile at my enthusiasm, and of course I'm nothing but a neophyte. But when I'm really struck by something as I am by your work . . ."

Jenny was probably the most surprised. During their stop in Geneva, La Chesnaye had told her that he was familiar with her husband's work, but she had considered his words as nothing but small talk, perhaps a bit more—and now to find that La Chesnaye was able to discuss the style of a staircase, that he knew the year in which a school had been constructed . . . she looked at him, fascinated. In turn, conscious of her interest, he may have exaggerated a bit. He was aware of Ledoyen's expression. As he listened to La Chesnaye, the architect recalled his former professional life—a post office in Cambrai, a building in the Rue de l'Est—and deep within his mind, something began to come to life. It was as though something deeply buried were suddenly being brought back to the surface, and he was caught up in a desire to examine it again.

"What I am trying to say," La Chesnaye concluded, "is that I know no work from that period that is equal to yours, neither in scope, nor above all in coping with human concerns."

The very words that were called for.

"You are overlooking Auguste Perret!"

"Perret is different. He has the creative flair, but there's also a kind of art nouveau aestheticism that's very close to mere decoration."

"Perret taught me everything I know."

"But you've forgotten his lessons, thank God!"

Happily, Jenny listened to them talk. These two men, so unlike, appeared to have found a common ground, and, more important, Jean seemed to be revived. Had she been able to perceive the concern underlying La Chesnaye's attention to her husband's words, perhaps she might have guessed the insane plan he was hatching. But Jean Ledoyen was coming further out of his shell.

"I've had an offer . . . a working-class housing development in the north, near Liévin."

Jenny was surprised. "You never said anything to me about it!"

He shrugged. "Oh, I don't think I'll accept . . ."

"I hope you will say yes! You should get back to work as soon as you can. Now. You're needed now!"

La Chesnaye's voice was intense; he brushed aside Jean's hesitation, his unwillingness. And he also recognized his own loneliness in the wounded architect's disordered feelings.

"Too many who might have been able to rebuild the world have been destroyed by the war. You are still alive, and you have no right to refuse!"

"Oh, alive . . ." Jean Ledoyen's laugh was suddenly full of sorrow once more.

"Yes, alive!"

La Chesnaye's voice had been almost sarcastic; his words hung in the air. Jean Ledoyen looked down at his hands. He said nothing. All the while he had been talking, listening, he had been looking around, at the waiters and wine stewards moving to and fro, at the fine wines, the partridges in cabbage, the women with egret feathers in their hair, the pheasant and guinea fowl. . . . At the next table was a dark woman with a South American accent and bare shoulders, delicately lifting small Belon oysters to her mouth and tearing them from their shells with a rapacious tongue. Huge, pear-shaped diamonds hung from her ears; the man across from her in evening dress was pear-shaped as well. He had been glancing at their table even as he spoke to his companion in a low voice. The woman was beautiful; he was ugly, fat, gross—he had paid for her in a bar in Buenos Aires or Santiago. There was another man, a man who was still young, attractive, who kept staring provocatively at Jenny; once again, Jean was afraid. She had been living with this sort of thing for five years! And all that time, in the hospital in Soldanelles, deep in purest Switzerland, there were boys of twenty without arms or legs, and in Berlin communists were being hunted down like dogs. . . . Jean Ledoyen shook his head: one must never allow oneself to forget.

"I think I'll go to lie down. . . ."

Jenny and La Chesnaye also rose; La Chesnaye had noticed Jean's eyes on those around them, the men staring at Jenny. Yet Ledoyen's smile was calm.

"Please . . . you can join me later, Jenny. I feel a bit tired, that's all." He spoke to La Chesnaye, holding his hands for a moment in his own. "Thank you for what you have said, sir. I'll try to remember that I'm not totally forgotten."

He bowed stiffly and left them. Upon reaching the compartment, he stretched out on his back and lay motionless, completely dressed, as he had in the room in the Hôtel Beau-Rivage. The motion of the train was soothing, but he knew he would not sleep.

"Now you know why I refused your offer last night."

Jenny, for a second, took La Chesnaye's hand. "Yes, I believe I can understand. . . ."

They were silent. Jenny's fingers were clenched around the stem of a champagne goblet. Finally she set down the glass and looked at La Chesnaye.

"Do you truly believe the things you said to him? About his plans, his buildings?"

"Yes, I believe them."

"You don't think it's too late?"

"Will you allow me?" La Chesnaye took his time in lighting a small black cigar which he drew from a flat leather case. He blew out a fine cloud of smoke before he replied: "It is up to you. Up to you, principally. If he is to believe in himself, Jean must believe in you."

That look, the look of fear Ledoyen had cast at the men who eyed Jenny. La Chesnaye took another puff on his cigar. He had never been more serious. Speaking to her about Jean, he was laying his own life on the line. For he knew that Jean's life depended upon hers . . . and he was in love with her, too.

"I know it's none of my business. But what are you going to Vienna for? I hear that you intend to remain there. Is that true?"

She paused before answering. "I don't know myself. I want to return there with him, because that is where we . . . But I no longer know."

"You must be very careful, Jenny."

She stared at him suddenly. "Why are you so interested in him? In us?"

"In both of you? Do you really want me to say?"

He did not reply for a moment, and, with a movement of her eyes, a flick of her lashes, Jenny urged him to continue.

"Simply because I admire your voice and your husband's talent, because you are a very handsome couple—and because I could have loved you."

He had said it all in one breath.

"*Could* have?"

"I'm only a passerby. . . . I'll be frank. I'm not really sure where I may be next week, so . . ."

She made a gesture, concerned. She could imagine all manner of things. Suicide . . . "You aren't going to . . ."

"No, no! It hasn't come to that! But this evening, I want to talk about you and Ledoyen. . . ."

Jenny was even less certain of herself when she returned to her compartment. Of course, there was Jean, there was Vienna, but she had not told La Chesnaye everything. Her return to the place where her music, her art, had begun also represented a temptation to see once again— just to see, no more—an entire part of her past, one that she had suddenly begun to realize perhaps she had never completely renounced.

"I'm insane," she thought. "Insane!"

She was mad to play so wantonly with fire. She was mad to have imagined that she could rebuild the past on the old foundations—her childhood memories. And there was the immense shadow of her cousin, Rolf, the passionate, somehow evil music of Rolf Freitag. There were the aesthetic feelings of another era that still clung to her heart, her body. It was of Rolf she had dared not speak; it was Rolf who must now make his brutal entrance into this story that I heard from her lips so much later. His entrance should be heralded by some aggressive, noisy fanfare, a brutal one. Rolf's face is superimposed on that of Jean, his stiff, close-shaven neck, his hard, square hands. Rolf, the Viennese Prussian, Rolf the pitiless, Rolf the possessive, crushing what he possessed. What had she told La Chesnaye—"To give Jean back his self-confidence"? Jenny shivered. She was on her way to Vienna with Jean, but there was also the Vienna of her first love affair. And what else?

In the compartment, Jean was still awake. At the sight of his thin, drawn face with the blue circles beneath his eyes, his taut lips, Jenny was suddenly overcome with a flood of tenderness.

"I no longer knew where I was," she confessed to me later. "I realized suddenly that I was about to see Rolf again, and at the same time I knew that the only thing I wanted, the only truth, was Jean."

She sat down beside him. "You're not asleep."

"I've slept very little these past five years."

His voice was faint. They looked at each other for a few moments. Jenny scrutinized her husband's face with a kind of passionate expectation.

"I so wanted everything to begin again. . . ."

Jean raised his hand to Jenny's cheek. Not touching her—being very careful not to touch her—he outlined her cheekbone, her lips. . . . Waiting, Jenny held her breath.

"I so wanted everything to begin again. . . ."

Which of them repeated that fragmentary sentence? For a moment longer, Jean's hand played over her face; then it slowly descended the length of her neck. His fingertips—only the fingertips—came to rest at the base of her throat.

"Oh, Jean . . ."

She breathed deeply as though at that moment everything might truly have begun again. Jean's touch upon her flesh . . . he should have touched her then, he should have embraced her, have taken her. Oh, Jean . . . She shut her eyes, the train swayed suddenly, and Jean's hand fell away. It was over.

"You had better try to get some sleep," Jean murmured.

After Salzburg and Linz, the Arlberg Orient Express reaches the Danube in the early morning hours. On that day, at the place where the imperial river joins the Enns, the entire valley was like some gigantic funnel catching the night fog which still lay on the sides of the mountains, while high above, touching the sky, the peaks glittered in the cold spring light. In the train as it left the tunnel of night and the last winter mists, one could smell the odor of the mountaintops, exciting, exhilarating, intoxicating: the scent of those snow-covered slopes where, years later in Chamonix, I was carried away in a cloud of crystal powder with a woman I was to love.

"May I?"

They were in the restaurant car. The journey was drawing slowly to an end. Ebelsberg, Traun—both untouched by the war. Another era . . . Seated before his orange juice, ham and eggs and a cup of very black coffee, La Chesnaye looked up. Jean Ledoyen was standing at his table, a silk scarf around his neck, wearing a tweed jacket that seemed too big for him.

"Please, join me."

Ledoyen's movements were at once economical and somewhat clumsy, as though he were afraid of being a bother, as though at any moment he might knock over a glass of water or one of the slim vases of white roses that stood on each table. However, La Chesnaye sensed that he had more energy than on the previous evening. And he was more inclined to talk.

"May I order you some eggs?"

Ledoyen shook his head. "Eggs, in the morning?" He never had more than a cup of tea, a slice of toast. But La Chesnaye had already beckoned to the waiter and had ordered for him.

"Two soft-boiled eggs, tea and toast." He winked at Jean. "You'll see, you'll feel better for it!"

"Somehow I feel better already."

Jean Ledoyen returned his wink, and, a few minutes later, apprehensively but with something very like a real appetite, he cracked into the first of his soft-boiled eggs with the back of a spoon that bore the crest of the Compagnie Internationale des Wagons-Lits.

For the next few hours they talked. It was intimate, male conversation. La Chesnaye told Ledoyen what he had earlier told Jenny: that he must begin to live again, that only Jenny could give him the desire to do so, and that he, for his part, would do everything in his power to help them.

"Because I . . ."

La Chesnaye finally spoke about himself. The train was approaching Tillysburg—home of the great Tilly of the Thirty Years' War, something of an adventurer himself—and for the first time, Georges La Chesnaye admitted his true profession . . . although he did not mention the names of those who were seeking his death; he showed the tiny revolver he had slipped into his pocket.

"It will work for me once, maybe twice. . . . And then . . ."

La Chesnaye's gesture was clear and unambiguous, but he smiled. And I—who have met so many such men, from New York to Yokohama, men for whom death has been in the end no more than the logical conclusion of some final adventure—I believe I can understand today what motivated La Chesnaye, what led him on the humanitarian course he had chosen.

"What might that be?"

"Love, of course! Love . . ."

Jean Ledoyen devoured his eggs with gusto. Alone, at the other end of the car, Andrea D. was not smiling.

At 11:25 A.M. on March 4, 1919, the train from Switzerland via Arlberg and Innsbruck pulled into the Vienna station. Rolf Freitag was waiting on the platform, and he was not alone.

One final moment of hope: at the instant the train was coming to a stop, Jenny put her hand on her husband's shoulder. "You'll see. It will all be all right. . . ."

Jean stared ahead of him. "Perhaps it will all be all right, yes. . . ."

But his illusions were to be shattered at once by the music that blared forth under the great glass roof of the Kaiserin Elisabeth Westbahnhof. It was the clamor of the most grotesque, ridiculous "Ride of the Valkyrie" imaginable, played by ten musicians standing on the platform and conducted by Rolf Freitag, who appeared to be in the grip of some thunderous emotion.

"Impossible . . ." Jenny murmured.

A welcoming committee had turned out in strength to greet her as she descended from the train. There was Rolf Freitag; there was the old Countess Herminie von Bellmer, Jenny's aunt; there were Hans Bebel from the Conservatory; Klaus Martin, the conductor of the Philharmonic; Scheel and Ludwig, the opera directors; and newspapermen, photographers, four or five officers in dress uniform.

"Impossible . . ." Jenny repeated.

The orchestra continued to blast out the incongruous music. The young woman stepped from the train, followed by Jean and La Chesnaye. The officers snapped to attention, and a crowd of curious bystanders attracted by the merrymaking stood around, giving the entire scene a farcical aspect, with Jean's profound unease adding a note of tragedy. Jenny turned to her husband and at once sensed his anxiety. He was overcome by the feeling that his wife was beginning to play a game in which he had no place. She was about to take his arm when Wagner's music came to a sudden stop and Rolf turned to face her.

"Welcome back to Vienna, Jenny Fisher!"

The musicians had spoken in chorus, and the rest joined in: "Welcome back to Vienna!"

Everyone crowded around her, shaking her hand, embracing her, the opera director, the old countess, the musicians, Rolf . . .

"So you have finally returned, my child . . ."

Carried away by the wave of welcome, embraces, congratulations, Jenny was unable to resist. And it was true, she had indeed returned to Vienna. . . .

"All at once, I was overcome. All those people, all those friends I had lost sight of and was now seeing again . . ."

She explained to me her almost childlike pleasure, the joy with which, despite her awareness of Jean's discomfort, she had been filled in those first minutes of her return.

"It was almost like the return of the prodigal. . . ."

There had been music, compliments, emotion before on other occasions, but now there was something in the air, the odor of bitter cold and of hot chocolate, the smoke of beer halls and the ancient dust of concert halls, something unlike anything else.

"I could feel that Jean was unhappy, but . . ."

Of course, I never dared ask Jenny: When you left with him to return to Austria, didn't you realize what might happen? Yet I had every confidence that Jenny Fisher, the great Jenny Fisher, having returned home, almost in Rolf's arms, would then have answered, "No." So the excitement mounted, and, as a little girl in Tyrolean dress recited a greeting, Jean stood in the background. La Chesnaye was at his side.

"That fellow's face is even more unpleasant than I had expected. . . ."

Georges La Chesnaye spoke of Rolf Freitag, Jenny's cousin. The latter had already raked him with his eyes: Who was this intruder? And that same suspicious, wrathful glance was to come to rest upon La Chesnaye more than once during that first day.

The same comedy was performed at the Hotel Sacher where they had made reservations. Rolf had barely shaken Jean's hand in the car.

"Well! It had slipped my mind that you were supposed to come along. . . ."

But he had cast frequent dark looks in La Chesnaye's direction when La Chesnaye had made no move to quit the couple. Drawing Jenny aside, he asked: "Is that a friend of yours?"

Overcome by the emotion of the moment, Jenny had not detected the threat in her cousin's tone. In the hotel lobby, she thanked the proprietor who welcomed her. The old Countess von Bellmer, who had insisted on accompanying them to the hotel, took a long time to say good-bye, telling them in her high-pitched voice of the reception she was giving that evening after the concert, a reception in her niece's honor, her niece whom she had lost and had now found again. She pushed forward a tall fool of a grandson with a short haircut and a pimply, twenty-year-old face, who stammered out a few words on behalf of the youth of Vienna.

"Don't you remember Dietrich?" the old countess asked.

Laughing, feeling like a young girl, Jenny reveled in it all. The opera director, who had caught up with them, added his shouts of pleasure to the general cacophony, like that of a flock of parrots.

It was not until they were alone in the elevator on their way to the suite that had been reserved for them that Jenny took Jean's hand.

"I am so happy to see them all again! You know . . ."

Jean's smile was forced. "With a bit of luck—or misfortune—I could easily have run into your cousin Dietrich at the front."

Jenny brushed his forehead with her lips. "He's nothing but a child."

She, too, seemed suddenly no more than seventeen. As they walked down the vast corridor with its red carpeting and baroque decor, she took a deep breath of memory.

"Can you smell the café au lait? Breakfast with coffee and whipped cream at the Sacher . . . that's Vienna. . . ."

Jean was silent. He seemed to have nothing to say in the face of vases overflowing with red roses that stood everywhere throughout the suite, in the bedroom, the salon, in Jenny's boudoir. Each bouquet bore the same card: Rolf Freitag. And even Jenny herself seemed all at once uncomfortable. She summoned the bell-hop.

"Take the flowers away—the scent bothers me." She took Jean's hands in hers. "Do you realize we're finally home?"

Gently he drew his hands away. "You mean *you* are home."

It was over: all that had been locked up inside him, all that might have been released by Jenny's tenderness during their journey—or perhaps by La Chesnaye's firm certainty—seemed to close suddenly, irrevocably. Jenny would fly forward to the final crisis—and it would be a real crisis, indeed—from this early emotion to the final rediscovery, and Jean would continue to be walled up in his solitude. It would take La

Chesnaye's act—an act I have already described as mad, insane—before that wall would crumble.

The morning's farce went on throughout the day; the porter in his silver chain brought the evening newspapers to my office in the embassy precisely at five o'clock that evening, and the columns spoke of nothing but the return of Jenny Fisher.

"Of course, I should have sensed what Jean was going through. . . ."

How oblivious she had been! First, there had been a mob of journalists, all demanding an exclusive interview. Rolf Freitag had finally suggested that Jenny hold an impromptu press conference, and in a room in the Sacher Hotel she had faced a cross fire of questioning. All the questions had focused on the same subject: had Jenny Fisher returned to Vienna to stay? She tried to deny it, explaining that she had only come for a visit, to attend the first performance of Freitag's new symphony—no one seemed to believe her. The war was over, after all, and what could be more fitting than that one of Austria's foremost singers should return home? And the omnipresent Freitag said nothing to deny it.

"You must be suffering . . ."

Ledoyen was silent. From a corner of the brilliantly lit room, he had listened to the hubbub around him, sunk in despondency. Had he been stronger, more in control of himself, he would have stood up and returned to his room to pack his bag: there was nothing for him in Vienna. But the Jean Ledoyen who, removed and apart, impotently watched the renaissance of Jenny Fisher, Austrian diva, had become more than ever a lost soul.

"You must be suffering . . ."

La Chesnaye had joined him and was watching the scene around them with bitterness.

"I don't understand," Jean murmured.

He did not understand—but Jenny should have made some protest. She should have said something to justify herself, told him that she had returned for his sake, for him, Jean. It was for him that she had returned to the palaces, the Viennese atmosphere, the gardens in which they had first been in love—that had been her promise to him, had it not?—not to take part in this grotesque game of question and answer in which the lies seemed to spring so readily to her lips.

JENNY

La Chesnaye lit one of his small, black cigars.

"You mustn't let it upset you unduly . . . it won't last forever."

But last it did.

That evening there was Rolf's concert. Jenny was seated in the first row of a box, next to Jean . . . although no one took any notice of Jean Ledoyen that evening. The gold and stucco auditorium of the old Kärtnertor Theater was filled with the plumes, diamonds, opera gloves and tight-fitting evening jackets of another era. It seemed as though all the relics that had survived the revolver shot at Sarajevo, that entire, moribund prewar world, had assembled there to pay one final tribute to its lost illusions. And Rolf Freitag's music was a part of that past.

Who remembers Freitag today? Does anyone listen to his music? Among the musicians who were a part of the great post-Romantic Viennese period that followed Mahler and Bruckner—with the exception of Richard Strauss, who is performed today because he was blessed with a kind of genius—does any continue to be heard now? Where are the performances of Korngold and Freitag? Even in those days, when the striking discoveries of Schöenberg, Berg, Webern were already under way, Rolf Freitag's music seemed very rearguard. He was no longer in the running, and he was on the defensive, prepared to wage an all-out battle to ensure the survival of his work. Thus, all those counts and barons, those souvenirs of a vanished empire, had assembled in the Kärtnertor to applaud a music that no longer had any relevance. Yet that music Rolf Freitag, with his shaved head, his heavy-lidded eyes and his solid, square hands, defended against all comers; it was a grand romantic gesture that had long been outmoded.

As Jenny Fisher took her seat, applause broke out. I had gone to the concert out of an almost morbid curiosity, just to take a look at all those people who had been hiding out since the war in their dusty, crepe-hung palaces and who had now emerged in public for the first time. I was a young embassy official, and the Viennese way of life continued to amuse me. It was there that I laid eyes on Jenny for the first time.

"You were very pale, yet your cheeks were flushed, almost feverish," I told her later, recalling that evening.

She blushed then, even more deeply.

"I had no idea . . . I didn't know what I was doing. I was allowing myself to be carried along by the events around me."

It was her first Viennese acclaim after her triumphs in Paris, and she had not even had to open her mouth!

Sitting beside her, Jean Ledoyen was livid. And seated at the back of the stalls, La Chesnaye glanced nervously over his shoulder from time to time, as though fearing his enemies might have already caught up with him.

When Freitag came onto the stage, the applause broke out again. Stiffly, dryly, Freitag bowed; it was as though his body bent in half on a hinge. He motioned toward Jenny, and the applause mounted. Then the lights went down.

I have always taken an almost adolescent pleasure in the atmosphere of a concert hall or an opera house: the moment of silence, absolute silence, before the music swells up. On that evening, I had no idea what to expect, and I was filled with anticipation. I had come to observe, of course, but also to be moved. And whatever the opinion current then about Freitag's music—or about his personality, for rumors had reached my ears—he had still been considered a great conductor for the past three or four years. He was feared for his violence and was not generally liked because he was so harsh to those weaker than himself, but he was respected; he conducted the orchestra like a captain in command of a great vessel engaged in battle with Beethoven or Bruckner. Later, of course, he burned himself out. What had once been vigor became brutality, passion turned into excess. But during those years immediately after the war, he was at the height of his powers, and Beethoven's "Leonora Overture No. 2" with which he prefaced his own symphony that evening was both energetic and inspired.

I was sitting in a stage box, and I was able to observe Jenny Fisher; I stared at her openly—and I was not the only one—through the little mother-of-pearl opera glasses I still take with me every summer to Salzburg and Verona, from festival to festival. I was watching her attentively, and I detected the tears flowing down her cheeks. Did I, I wonder, move my opera glasses a few millimeters to the right to find out what the man sitting next to her—Jean—was like? I doubt it. None of us had eyes for anyone but Jenny, for in those days she was, I believe, the most beautiful singer who had ever appeared on the international stage. Since that time, we have had Maria Callas's beauty, Elisabeth Schwarzkopf's—not to mention the melting loveliness of Meta Seenenmeyer, who was the glory of Dresden in the twenties. But Jenny Fisher, even in tears, seated in the first row of her box, had the face, the body, the hands of all the opera heroines of our dreams.

When the applause that had greeted the final bars of "Leonora No.

2" had subsided, Jenny's face became even more serious and expectant. In that same auditorium, of course, she had met Jean for the first time, in all that oppressive gilt and voluptuous red and garnet-colored velvet; he had just been commissioned to build a sanitorium in the Tyrol, a kind of Magic Mountain on a more human scale. And it was in that same auditorium that she had discovered for the first time, seated in those gilt chairs, Beethoven's D-major concerto played by Eugène Ysaÿe, or the sonatas with the great—the first—Rubinstein at the piano. Then the man at her side had been Rolf, not Jean. Rolf. Her cousin, her mentor in discovery, the man who had revealed to her one by one the pages of the glorious volume of music, the art that was to dictate his way of life . . . and Jenny's.

A chord was sounded, and then another: a long chord, like the music that rises from the depths at the beginning of Wagner's *Ring*, and slowly Jenny abandoned herself to it.

Of course, at the conclusion of the work the audience gave Rolf an ovation. There were bravos and cheers on all sides, punctuated with flowers and tiny bouquets of red roses tossed onto the stage by hordes of his young female admirers—the daughters of the minor nobility that had come out in public again on that evening—all in honor of a man who had become their idol not only because he was handsome and still young, but because his music recalled to them the sounds of a former Vienna, a former Germany. They knew in those ultra-conservative circles that he was one of them, a rabid ultra-nationalist holding aloft the banner of established order—soon that banner would turn into a policeman's cudgel—over all the defeatists, the fomenters of unrest, the Jews, the foreigners.

At the back of the stalls, La Chesnaye realized that around him and in the balconies as well there was a part of the public that was not evincing the same enthusiasm. To them, this symphony with its triumphant horns and trombones, its haughty, classic and predictable chromaticism, led with such fiery élan by a conductor above all desirous of producing an effect, was nothing but an empty, noisy monument to the past that revealed an astonishing lack of inspiration, a bombast that was both boring and syrupy.

"It's shit!" a young man wearing gold-rimmed spectacles murmured into the ear of another young man who was holding a large music notebook under his arm.

"And, if I may use the expression, fucking aggressive shit . . ."

Both young men were mocking the inflated words of praise being voiced on all sides, and La Chesnaye leaned across to them. "Tell me a bit about Freitag's music, please."

He was curious, and the two students—for they were both at the conservatory—were not hesitant about telling him.

In the meantime, the applause went on in an uninterrupted wave, engulfing the hall. Quieting the fervor of his admirers at last with an imperious gesture, Rolf Freitag came to the front of the stage and announced that the work he had just conducted in its first performance was dedicated to his cousin, the celebrated soprano Jenny Fisher. And then, delirium. Smiling faintly at Jean, as though to excuse herself, Jenny rose and bowed, and long after the lights in the Kärtnertor had been extinguished, a group of admirers continued to cheer its two idols, chanting their names over and over in total darkness.

"Oh, Rolf—it was superb!"

Even in her husband's presence, Jenny Fisher no longer made any attempt to hide her joy. We have seen her standing pale and exhausted on the shores of Lake Leman, in the train from Lausanne; now she was bursting with well-being, with joy and pleasure as she stood in the foyer of the theater where a reception had been arranged. Overdressed baronesses and marchallins decorated with ostrich plumes clasped her to their almost-bare bosoms; royal chamberlains, once-imperial generals and effete heirs of an already extinct race bowed low before her, stiffly, to kiss her fingertips.

Haughty and reveling in his glory, Rolf bowed, too; he accepted compliments and steered Jenny from group to group, making certain that she would be closely associated with every moment of his triumph.

"Jenny, my little Jenny . . . it's all going to begin again. . . ."

From a distance I glimpsed the back of Rolf Freitag's head, like the neck of a bull, and I knew that his tanned face would be the face of a wild beast in sight of its prey. . . .

Yet Jenny had insisted on Jean's accompanying her, and like a Pierrot with a broken heart who had lost his beloved, he stood in a corner, oblivious to the noise around him, to the jostling crowd of admirers spouting compliments. He no longer heard or saw anything: he was present only in body. And, once again, La Chesnaye made a move. There was a sudden silence.

What ensued might have been a scene in a play.

"Sir," he said to Freitag, "they say that your symphony is a hodgepodge of all the trite effects with which every conservatory in prewar Europe was littered. Nevertheless, allow me to congratulate you on the success that you have somehow managed to achieve!"

La Chesnaye stood as stiffly as the chamberlains in their old uniforms and the young, effete Viennese fops standing around Freitag. Freitag turned scarlet.

"Sir, I will not permit . . ."

He stuttered with rage. The horde of admirers around him, thunder-struck, seemed to be expecting him to crush the insolent interloper with one blow of his fist—as he could have done, indeed, for he was built like an athlete and strong enough to lift an entire orchestra with one arm. However, La Chesnaye laughed and turned his back on him.

"I see I am preaching to the converted, so I shall withdraw. There are none more deaf than they who will not hear—perhaps it is I who am tone-deaf. However, I wanted to salute you, and I have done so. Sir, until we meet again."

Freitag would have pursued him to demand an apology had not an advance party of that army of young women who had applauded him until their silk gloves were in tatters not surrounded him and buried him beneath noisy enthusiasm. When Rolf managed to free himself, La Chesnaye had disappeared.

There was a dance later at the Countess von Bellmer's. An orchestra played waltzes, and since the old woman's notions were nothing if not advanced, a small jazz combo also performed at the other end of the magnificent expanse of rooms in the Bellmer palace, whose tall colon-nade—destroyed by the bombings in 1945—proudly overlooked a French-style garden laid out with geometric precision, its box hedges clipped to form huge bass clefs.

According to the protocol for this kind of soirée—organized for Rolf, but also for Jenny, since it was obvious that the old Viennese aristocracy had joined in this conspiracy to bring her back into the fold—Rolf had arrived in the old countess's car, and Jenny had followed in the car belonging to the director of the conservatory. Sunk back in the cushions beside her, Jean Ledoyen had said nothing. Jenny was aware of her husband's distress, but on that evening he was locked in his own silence, and she seemed to have been imprisoned in some lofty tower built of golden memories, a tower from which all of Jean's sorrow could not have freed her. She had come to Vienna for his sake, but she had found her youth—and another man.

However, as she began her first waltz with Rolf—all the other guests had stopped dancing to watch them—and he brought up the subject of La Chesnaye, she managed to stand firm.

"He's your lover, isn't he? Ledoyen is nothing but an alibi!"

Rolf held her tightly to him, hissing insults between his teeth; he had suddenly turned into a violent, wrathful lover.

"No, no . . . he's nothing but a friend. And Jean doesn't know him any better than I do."

The waltz went on. Around them, the guests smiled and applauded: Rolf Freitag was stern, threatening, but he kept up his front as a muscular prince charming.

"If I ever come face to face with him again . . ."

Jenny pressed against him. She was trying to stave off the worst.

"I beg you not to do anything. He was a great help to me at a time when I was terribly unhappy, only a few days ago. I must be grateful to him for that. . . ."

She spoke seriously. The waltz still continued. Into Jenny's ear, Rolf murmured all his contempt for Jean, that human ruin she had brought to Vienna with her; Jenny begged him not to go on.

Yet the waltz continued. Rolf fell silent, and Jenny pressed ever closer to him. Finally, it ended, and at last she went to Jean, who had been waiting for her alone near the buffet, waiting for the waltz to end. He told her that he was tired and was returning to the hotel.

Jenny felt a final pang; she attempted a last resistance against the world of memories and emotions to which Rolf had unlocked the door. "Don't leave me! Please don't leave me this evening!"

Jean Ledoyen gave a brief laugh. "Come now, you're hardly alone."

He was the one who was alone, broken. When La Chesnaye met him on the red and white marble staircase that led from the ballroom down to the vast, echoing vestibule—a black and white marble floor and voluptuous, contorted nude statues beneath a ceiling of cupids in golden sunbursts, all of which was reduced to rubble a quarter century later—Jean hardly spoke to him.

"I'm going back to the hotel."

La Chesnaye, curious to see what was to happen, mounted the stairs two at a time, in a hurry as he had always been.

"I think," Jenny told me later, "that what he most enjoyed was playing with fire." She fell silent for a moment, she who had struck matches all her life just to see what would happen, and then she added: "Or Russian roulette . . ."

A single bullet in the barrel, a blackened hole in the forehead . . .

Rolf had led Jenny off to a small reception room hung with French tapestries on the pretext of introducing her to the prefect of Salzburg, who was supposed to be extremely eager to make her acquaintance. There were a few paintings by Boucher and a small Watteau—all of which later disappeared in the war along with the colonnade, the staircase and the other rooms overlooking those sumptuous French gardens. He took her hand, tenderly.

"And the prefect?"

"He can wait . . ."

There was a fire burning in the fireplace. Behind them, through the open double doors leading into the ballroom, couples were waltzing madly, desperately. But it was as though a wall of glass had come down between those ageless, futureless men and women and Rolf and his cousin; no one disturbed them; they were alone.

Rolf held Jenny's hand in his own. "If you knew how I've waited for you . . ."

"Don't say that. . . ."

She continued to protest, and he almost shook her. "Why not say it, since it is the truth. . . ."

Almost under her breath, she spoke Jean's name. Rolf was about to reply, but another couple had entered the room. He led her further, to the open window leading onto the balcony.

"Let's go out. It is quite mild."

The warm night, the gardens of the Bellmer palace, the superb colonnade rising above them: forty years ago, it would have been impossible to believe that Vienna would not always be that beautiful. The great mass of the Schwarzenberg Palace rose before them, and in the distance the Imperial Guard barracks, the Metternich Palace and the Belvedere stood silhouetted against the sky. Nighttime Vienna, a magic stage set built by an architect with a passion for the theater.

But Jenny had said Jean's name. "Jean!"

Rolf Freitag burst into speech: "Jean! He's a nothing, your Jean. A ruin, a wreck! I've made inquiries—how can you go on hoping for anything where he is concerned!"

She pressed her forehead against her cousin's shoulder. "Don't say such things about Jean."

But Rolf continued. He would force her to understand, to decide, to choose. "You haven't come back just on a whim. You know that! You know that you have come back because of me!"

She would have protested, perhaps; she might have tried to explain —but Rolf drew her suddenly to him and kissed her. And Jenny forgot Jean. She was unaware of the eyes looking at her from behind the glass, the lace curtain of the door leading out of the room they had left. Nor did Rolf notice the man who observed them so intently with such a lack of discretion. When he finally relaxed his embrace and Jenny was leading him back toward the ballroom—"We mustn't stay away any longer"—La Chesnaye's appearance on the threshold was too sudden for either of them to manage to replace their masks. And they both realized that La Chesnaye had seen it all.

"Pleasant evening, don't you agree?"

He clicked his heels and bowed, a sardonic smile on his lips. He seemed to be mimicking Rolf. Rolf did not relax his grip on Jenny's arm until they had seen La Chesnaye vanish in the throng of dancers.

"I shall kill that man," he said.

For although Rolf Freitag may have been a second-rate musician, he was an accomplished sportsman, a sharpshooter and an unparalleled swordsman.

Jean had returned to the Sacher. La Chesnaye faded into the blue Viennese night that was soon to enfold him forever; Jenny remained alone with Rolf. What happened next may all be a dream, one of those daydreams, one of those stories it amuses us to invent when we would not dare live it . . . even less write it down.

It was just before Carnival. Groups of revelers hailed each other in the streets, and Rolf had taken Jenny by the hand. He had not said a word, but she knew where he was taking her. So often in the old days, in the days of their youth, they had taken the same route beneath the huge gaslights with their glass globes like thick bunches of grapes in the Viennese night. After the theater or the opera, around eleven in the evening, they would dine with friends from the conservatory, poor students like themselves, in some beer hall . . . or in some fashionable restaurant when Rolf himself or the old Countess von Bellmer's daughter had invited them all. Then Rolf and Jenny would leave their companions.

"Do you think she'll hear us ring?"

"Lotte never locks her door."

Arm in arm, the composer and the singer were on their way to visit Lotte Brenner, aged Lotte, Lotte the sublime, who for forty years had sung at the Vienna Opera all the great roles in the repertory, who had been Jenny's teacher and had taught her all she knew.

Lotte lived on the top floor of a palace that belonged to Herminie von Bellmer behind the Belvedere Gardens, a building that had long been empty. The countess had purchased it from an impoverished *nouveau riche* for her son, the handsome Heinz, but Heinz had perished in a duel before he had been able to move into the vast rooms he had decorated with flashy luxury, a delirious blend of Viennese baroque and French Second Empire. And one day, when Lotte Brenner had found herself homeless, the mourning countess, who now lived for nothing but music, had offered her a room in Herr Vaninal's old palace, an apartment and a few pieces of furniture on the third floor, and the old woman had lived there ever since. She never slept at night. She would leaf through her memories and listen endlessly to the scratchy sounds of old wax recordings or cylinders, to the echoes of voices she had loved, now dead—and as students, Jenny and Rolf had made a habit of ending their evenings at the Vaninal Palace.

"Come," Rolf said on this night again, twelve years later.

He pushed open the door at the monumental entrance with its double flight of baroque stairs: the vestibule was like a vast marble pool, above which hung a huge, draped chandelier. Before them, the main staircase rose in the shadows, at once a piece of sculpture and an architectural form, up to the second story.

"Let's go up," Rolf said, once again.

Jenny's heart was pounding: she had really come back now, and there was a trace of music in the air, like those voices that seem to come from a great distance because they are really inside us. Words, whispers . . . Mozart's countess, the heroine of the *Barber*, suddenly one and the same as they passed through the vast, empty rooms. The curtains were drawn back, and the moonlight cast huge blue and white shadows on the walls and the floors. They were locked in the embrace of Vienna at night.

"Nothing has changed," Jenny murmured.

It was already like a kiss, an embrace. The war had passed, the years had passed, there had been her love for Rolf, her love for Jean . . . and there was still this same outlandish scene of dust-covered furniture, of shrouded mirrors and of gutted candles in dusty candelabra shaped like barebreasted women. They pushed aside hangings, through doorways; they passed through a room where a bed stood ready.

"No, nothing has changed."

It had been their room on so many occasions, and their bed when neither of them had wanted to go on, on those evenings of great music and great joy. Who had made up the bed? The canopy, the curtains with heavy gold tassels, the damask silk sheets . . .

"She's expecting us, I know."

They mounted a final staircase, this one concealed behind a panel in the wall, made a final sharp turn and suddenly Jenny saw, on her right, the lamp: it was the same low lamp with a pink shade, lighting the piano, the scores, the photographs and recordings with which Lotte Brenner surrounded herself: The old woman did not even need to lift her eyes to see them.

"My Jenny, you have come back!"

She had recognized the music of her step—and Jenny was in her arms.

They stayed together for an hour, perhaps two, talking, those two women—teacher and pupil—the woman who had created a voice and the woman who had made it live. Sitting off to one side, Rolf listened to them, but he was there: he had brought Jenny back to her, and Lotte Brenner smiled at him from time to time.

"It's good that Rolf is with you. . . ."

Jenny pressed her old teacher's hand.

"It's good that you have come back."

Jenny lowered her head. And later, when Lotte Brenner went off on a great bout of remembering, Jenny did not respond to her regrets for the days when singers performed in London, Vienna, Paris—but only there—and did not travel around the world seeking ephemeral glory, jumping from one opera to another, from ship to train. What would Lotte have had to say about the singers of today whose lives are based on airline timetables, this morning in Berlin and this evening Milan? Jenny knew that it was Lotte Brenner's dearest wish that she give up her international—Lotte used the word "cosmopolitan"—career and attach herself exclusively to the Vienna Opera, which in forty years of singing had been Lotte's home more than any other.

"One evening in America, ten days later in Peru, and a week later in Africa—I don't call that singing. . . ."

Lotte Brenner's skin was as smooth as a child's, and so taut that it seemed age had passed her by. She had Jenny's pale blue eyes beneath the same broad forehead . . . today, Elisabeth Schwarzkopf has the same look . . . or Marlene. . . .

"In all my forty years of career, the farthest I ever went was to Salzburg from time to time, or a short trip to Berlin . . . beyond that, there was a world I didn't know. For me, there was never anything but Vienna. Always Vienna . . ."

Do you understand, Jenny? Do you understand? The old woman's voice trembled slightly, and there were tears in her eyes, the tears of age; she caressed Jenny's face with her smooth, soft hands.

"You won't leave again, will you?"

She had spoken in a low voice, as though uttering a kind of spell. And when Jenny did not reply, Rolf leaned forward.

"No, Lotte. Jenny won't leave again."

It was he who then asked the old woman to place on the turntable of the ancient phonograph a recording she had made over twenty years before. The voices of Mozart and his Pamina in the *Zauberflöte* rose in the tiny room: the voice sang to the women in the gray and sepia photographs on the wall, to Lili Lehmann, Margarethe Siems, Nellie Melba and to the young woman who had returned after so many years. Lotte Brenner's lips moved silently, gently, speaking from somewhere deep within herself the words she had uttered so long ago in the recording studio:

> *Ach, ich fühl's, es ist verschwunden,*
> *Ewig hin der Liebe Glück!*

Ah, I feel it—all love is vanished, my happiness is gone. . . .

Jenny leaned toward her; Lotte's eyes were open, but she saw images lost in a time far before her pupil's. Lotte Brenner saw Jenny no longer. Rolf took her hand. "Come, let's go. She can't hear us."

Slowly they made their way down the wooden staircase that creaked beneath their feet. From farther and farther away, the music continued to reach them, and it was as though the pink glow of the lamp with its lowered shade still fell upon them, from a great distance, feebly.

When they reached the room that had been theirs seven, twelve years before, Rolf took Jenny in his arms.

It was morning when she returned to the Sacher Hotel. Lying on the bed on his back, Jean heard the door handle begin to turn and shut his eyes. But he had been far from sleep. He heard the rustling sound as her silk garments slid one by one to the floor and the light clink of her jewels and silver chains as she placed them on the dressing table. Then silence: he had not slept during the six hours since his return. He had been waiting.

La Chesnaye had been waiting, too, and he had not slept either. His reasons were equally weighty. As he had listened to Rolf the previous evening, to the court being paid him, as he .had observed Jenny and Jean—and the gulf between them—he had slowly been overwhelmed by a feeling of profound hatred for the composer. It was a violent, burning hatred that devoured his entire being. His only thought was how to bring him down, destroy him, crush him as one crushes a puppet or a toy clown: with ridicule, with silence. He was possessed with hatred. When he returned from the Bellmer palace and opened the door to his room, however, he found a man there waiting for him.

"Surprised to see me, La Chesnaye?"

La Chesnaye was impassive. True—he had another life. There was his flight. And whether it would be Werner or someone else, every man he knew would be hot on his trail, and they were all alike. Andrea D., the woman whom he both loved and had ceased to love, who was also waiting for him somewhere in the hotel, had told him: "You'll see, they will come after you if you don't get away." Yet he had stayed, and now they were here. The man rose. His hands were empty, but La Chesnaye knew full well that somewhere in the pockets of his voluminous cape he had a revolver.

"I'll be brief, La Chesnaye."

The man who was called Werner was short, thin: with his glasses perched on his nose, he looked like a professor of Greek or music in some provincial village in the depths of Carinthia.

La Chesnaye cut him short. "I know what you're after."

They had caught up with him at last. La Chesnaye was fleeing; he should have continued to flee, but he had stopped in Vienna because of a woman, and these men who had for a time been his employers had caught up with him there.

"Yes, the money!"

La Chesnaye breathed deeply. This was what real excitement was, the excitement of gambling. Once again this evening—as on so many other evenings—he was gambling. Double or nothing. This time there was the fake Persian carpet of his luxury hotel room instead of a green baize table, but this time the stakes were his own life. His losses were being called in, and he was unable to pay. Andrea, the woman who loved him, was to tell me later about all those evenings in private clubs and casinos and how, with his own money or that of others, he had gambled on and on, unceasingly. A month earlier, in the back room of a large club in Paris, he had lost—and on that occasion, the money he had lost had not been his.

"You were supposed to bring us the money, La Chesnaye. I'm waiting."

"You know very well I don't have it."

The face of the man with the glasses twitched almost imperceptibly: from now on, the Frenchman standing before him was a dead man. Yet even to a dead man, one shows a certain consideration in his final hours.

"Sorry, La Chesnaye," Werner muttered.

However, La Chesnaye understood the need to gain time. And then there was Jean, Jenny: he had not yet finished what he had to do for them. He cut Werner short. "I haven't the money on me, but I'm expecting it."

"Well . . ."

Gain time. Werner's interest was aroused. He spoke. "So you've come all this way in hopes of getting your hands on the money and then disappearing!"

That was it—the man must be made to think that his halt in Vienna was part of a plan. He gambled . . . again, double or nothing.

"You've figured it out. So much the worse for me."

"And the money?"

He thought for a second. "Tomorrow evening, on the train arriving from Salzburg at five-thirty."

Suddenly the other man joined the game.

"Five-thirty?"

There remained only to set the details of their meeting the next day on the station platform, and then Werner, wrapped in his ridiculous conspiratorial cape, left him alone. But Georges La Chesnaye, a hunted man, now realized full well that he had reached the end of the road. He drew from his pocket his deck of antique playing cards with their strange figures and dealt himself three aces and two red kings in the solitary poker he played against himself in those moments when he realized that life itself was nothing but a gigantic poker game. . . .

He then telephoned Jean Ledoyen in his room—the Sacher Hotel had just installed a fine internal telephone system, with brass mouthpieces and rubber tubing encased in red silk—and told him that Jenny would shortly be on her way home. Ledoyen had not believed him, and neither of the two men had slept.

At ten in the morning, Jenny and Jean were brought two breakfast trays. Lying next to the croissants and brioches and the pot of that steaming black coffee that had reminded her of the odors in the hotel corridors of her childhood, there were three newspapers, each of which, like those of the previous evening, announced Jenny Fisher's return on the first page. And they all quoted Rolf Freitag's statement affirming that the singer had returned to Austria permanently and that she would be creating his new opera, *Cordelia*, at the Vienna Opera in six months.

Jean opened the *Wiener Zeitung* first. As yet, he and Jenny had only exchanged a few brief words. What was there to say? Jean knew, and Jenny knew that he knew. When he had read the article, he dropped the paper and looked at Jenny. She had slipped into a dressing gown of antique Calais lace and was seated at the dressing table combing her hair. Their eyes met in the mirror. Jenny was pale. . . .

"Is it true?"

That she was going to remain in Vienna . . . Jenny did not reply, and the silence hung heavy between them.

Later, because Jenny had no appointments before early afternoon, they hired a car and, as they had planned, took a tour around Vienna— an outing that had been planned, as had the concert the evening before, to be the path of memory along which they would find each other once again. They drove along streets lined with palaces, with gardens in which both plane trees and statues grew; there was a barrel organ beside a church and the little antique shop where Jean had once bought Jenny a silver rose. Neither of them spoke. Jenny wore a white hood like the one that had blown in the wind on Lake Geneva, but now her hair drawn up from her neck was firmly fastened. Jean looked at her: how can a woman one loves suddenly seem so unyielding? Once I knew a woman who told me for months over and over that she had never loved anyone as she loved me. I was flattered. Then, a week later, she left me flat, telling me that I had never loved her properly. I cried for a long time. Her face, her expression when she said, "No . . ." On their outing in that old-fashioned open car through the Prater and along the avenues of the Hofgarten between the Burgtor and the new opera house, Jenny's expression was the same as that woman's.

"If only he had made one move, just one, I know I would have burst into tears. I would have fallen into his arms!"

Telling me later about this scene, she did not make excuses for her own attitude; she tried only to explain. After all, I was the one who had wanted to understand it all. I watched her then, as people walking by us on the Place de l'Alma stared at her—would any of those preoccupied, busy people have understood? For Jean had been away from her, closed up in his private sorrow. Frozen. He had not even been able to try to understand.

The Santos chocolate shop, the art gallery, the Westhof antique shop where together they had found a small baroque painting of Daphne being turned into a tree, a flower, in the hand of an impetuous Apollo: every shop window was a reminder of the past. Had Jean only taken Jenny's hand then . . . But he could not do so. Still in silence, they had lunch at Ross in the Leopoldstadt gardens, and then Jenny had ordered them to be taken back to the hotel.

"I promised my aunt I would be there at four o'clock."

Jean knew that the old countess would have invited a few friends, musicians, journalists, and that Rolf would also be there. He knew he was vanquished. And, in turn, Jenny felt his sorrow flow into her body. As they arrived at the Sacher, as he was getting out of the car, she held him back.

"I'm so terribly sad, you know."

"I know."

There was a brief silence.

"I try to tell myself it's for my career," Jenny murmured.

"That's it. Tell yourself it's for your career."

It was Jean's turn to be harsh, but he was the one who suffered. And when two maids knocked on the door to the suite that afternoon and were admitted, he watched impassively as they packed Jenny's clothes in her trunk . . . the dressing gown of Calais lace, her nightgown with its bluish sheen. . . .

Jenny, as she went quickly up the staircase in the Bellmer Palace, had only one thought: she was waking from a bad dream. At last she would be able to begin to live again.

To live what life?

It was five in the evening. Candles had been lit in the bar of the Sacher Hotel, and two women in revealing evening gowns were seated on high stools drinking the sweet and complicated cocktails that Johnny, the American bartender—born in Budapest—had prepared for them. Jean Ledoyen, his movements still clumsy, embarrassed, had just entered the room, and his eyes had not yet adjusted to the dimness.

"I'm over here."

La Chesnaye signaled to him from the far end of the bar, and the two demimondaines on their high perches looked after Ledoyen with lingering glances. One was clad in black net stockings that were revealed up to her thigh through the slit in her long skirt.

"Am I intruding?"

"Not at all."

Ledoyen sat down at La Chesnaye's table. He had come down to the bar in the hope of finding him, and for a second he had felt a pang of disappointment at not seeing him. Now who could he talk to? Or, more precisely, not talk to . . . but, thank God, he had found him in the murk. Resting his elbows on the table, he said simply: "It's all over."

Bucharest Johnny approached, and La Chesnaye ordered two whiskey sours.

"Alcohol?" Jean Ledoyen seemed almost surprised.

"Why not?" La Chesnaye respected his silence for a moment, and then he repeated Jean's words. "And how do you know it's all over?"

"I know, that's all."

"Well, for my part, I am not convinced." With complete assurance, La Chesnaye then spoke up: Rolf was a contemptible man, and Jenny was well aware of it because she had already left him once before. She had known it then, and she would quickly realize it now. "He's ignoble, don't you see? He is that arrogant kind of man that I find the most loathesome . . . men who see themselves as supermen, who think they are masters. Had he been an officer or a slave master on a galley, or a cop or a prison guard instead of a composer, I wouldn't think much of the chances of the unlucky creatures under his control."

"So?"

"So Jenny will not stay with him."

Ledoyen smiled weakly. "She'll leave with me?"

His words meant: with me, with the wreck of a man I have become? With a weak, exhausted man lacking in courage?

"Yes, she will leave with you."

And La Chesnaye's words meant: with you, the architect who has built buildings and neighborhoods and whole cities, a man who has been offered a commission for a working-class development in Liévin. Jean read the unspoken meaning in the other man's voice, and he gave a short—a very short—laugh.

"But I'm useless."

He knew he could not face the blank paper, his pencils, his drafting board. But La Chesnaye knew better.

"You can, yes, with her you can. You told me so yourself." And he continued. For the first time in his life, La Chesnaye the gambler, the adventurer, the faker, the desperate clown, spoke as the man he had made up his mind to be, a man who spoke the truth from the bottom of his heart.

"I never told you, but I, too, could have loved Jenny. . . ."

Jean, Jenny, they were both mixed together in his mind in one great tenderness. Into what kind of man had he suddenly been transformed, this man who haunted gambling casinos, this hunted man who carried a revolver in his trouser pocket? I can tell you that I have no words to describe what I, too, feel for this man I never knew, my deep affection for him. He was the friend we should always hope to meet one day, that is all. . . .

"In any case, Jenny can never live with anyone but you."

He was convinced, firm. And he would have gone on; he would have spoken for hours had not a harsh, insistent bell suddenly rung out, had the bartender not interrupted him.

"Monsieur La Chesnaye? You are wanted on the telephone."

He pointed toward the booths in the lobby, but La Chesnaye raised his hand. "I'll take the call here."

There was a telephone at the end of the bar. Ledoyen watched him as he went to it, picked up the receiver and listened for a second to what his caller was saying. La Chesnaye then spoke, very calmly. "Listen, old man," he said, his voice curt, "we've still got a half hour, and I have a watch in my left-hand vest pocket. So don't bother me for another half hour, do you mind? I'll be there."

He hung up, but he had spoken loudly enough for Ledoyen, Johnny the bartender and the two prostitutes in evening gowns to hear him. His final act of bravado? He returned to the table.

"Trouble?"

La Chesnaye shrugged. "Nothing out of the ordinary."

The train from Salzburg pulled in to the Kaiserin Elisabeth West-bahnhof at 5:30. Of course, it carried no passenger known to La Chesnaye. Werner, the man with the glasses, was waiting at the entrance to the platform. When he saw La Chesnaye walking toward him with empty hands, he stepped forward.

"You've been pulling the wool over our eyes again, haven't you?"

La Chesnaye shook his head. He had come to a decision, and he led Werner to the station's vast washroom with its magnificent glass roof. "We can't talk here. I've got what you want."

The washroom was empty. There was an odor of cheap soap and disinfectant—that smell of all those anonymous places where final intrigues are unraveled. La Chesnaye opened a door and motioned to Werner to precede him; then he took out his revolver and fired a single shot. He knew that had he asked for another twenty-four-hour delay, Werner would have refused. And La Chesnaye needed those twenty-four hours. The man with the glasses collapsed onto an enamel and faience toilet, made in Manchester. Deliberately, La Chesnaye shut the door behind him and went to wash his hands, taking his time.

He knew what he must do now. A lost man, he had a plan, and he would carry it out to the minute. And as I recreate the itinerary of this man who is lost in shadows as far as I am concerned, who barely emerges from them before he is lost again, I not only like him, I admire him. I admire him just as I respect some public man, some writer or architect—none of my friends, and naturally I include myself, would ever have dared imagine doing what he was about to do. And yet he did.

"No man ever loved me as he loved me," Jenny Fisher was to repeat. "I believe that."

And along with the tenderness and admiration I felt for her, I sensed a kind of rancor in myself: how could Jenny have been so blind?

At seven-fifteen, Georges La Chesnaye entered a small reception room in the Bellmer Palace, the room with the French tapestries overlooking the garden, that same room in which Jenny and Rolf had first embraced the previous evening. Freitag, standing beside the old countess, was holding forth as usual. He was talking about the decadence of German music, of the new school of Vienna, of Schöenberg, Berg, Webern and their ilk, steamrolling over everything that stood in their way, and he was denigrating all their followers.

Inferior men. Foreigners. Jews . . .

How Rolf revealed his true nature in those few words . . .

La Chesnaye paused for a moment in the doorway, listening. Then he stepped forward. Jenny was the first to see him, and she began to rise—as though she had suddenly foreseen the worst and was trying to stop him. However, La Chesnaye smiled. He began to speak. He spoke in a loud, clear voice in impeccable German. He addressed himself to Freitag, and his tone was cutting, cynical, concise. He was insolent as only a man who has arrived at such utter loneliness can be. Freitag's music: it was worthless offal, and everyone knew it. Freitag's talent: the talent of a metronome suffering from *folie de grandeur.* Jenny's return to Vienna: a publicity stunt, nothing more; a trap, a snare. Freitag's future: oblivion. Quick, lightning quick, pure and simple oblivion.

Freitag moved to strike him, but his friends held him back; it was evident that La Chesnaye was prepared to defend himself. Beneath his equivocal and foppish exterior, one could sense the strength of an adventurer. Perhaps you remember the film *Les Enfants du Paradis,* when Lacenaire, played by Marcel Herrand, kills the aristocratic Louis Salou? It was like that. La Chesnaye was also prepared to kill.

Freitag shouted: "Sir, I shall not allow you to . . ."

But he spoke to a blank wall. La Chesnaye bowed—he did it very well!—and feigned courtesy the better to strike: "Whenever and wherever you like!"

"Tomorrow morning!"

Freitag foamed at the mouth with rage. La Chesnaye, however, never stopped smiling. It was all part of his plan, and, now that Werner was dead, he had his twenty-four hours of grace.

"Very well, tomorrow morning. I had planned on it. Since I have few friends here, I shall send a servant from the Sacher to make the necessary arrangements."

Jenny stood motionless, frozen with shock . . . and perhaps with fear. She suddenly realized what was to happen. But La Chesnaye, after bowing one last time, had left the room. La Chesnaye was a true artist; better than anyone else, he knew how to make an exit.

I must imagine Georges La Chesnaye's return to the Hotel Sacher on that night, that final night at the beginning of Carnival. As on the previous evening, the streets were thronged with groups of masqueraders, stopping people, and their false faces were the masks of death: desperate Pierrots, sardonic Harlequins, tattered Punchinellos. There was wild laughter; from time to time a firecracker would explode, and from somewhere, the sound of music rent the night.

"It's cold! You wouldn't leave me alone on a night like this, would you?" The girl who had caught his arm was dressed completely in black, and her mask was decorated with paste teardrops; her mouth was like the mouth of all the women he had ever loved. "Come with me, you can have me. I'll warm you. . . ."

She hung on his arm as she cajoled him, tugging at him, taking possession of him, but La Chesnaye shook her off. "Not tonight, my dear. Tomorrow, all night if you like!" He watched her stagger away, borne on the wind that came up out of the town, through the fine rain that had begun to fall, full of the tastes of Carnival.

"I'll be waiting!"

The next woman was ageless—or rather, she wore her age badly, and the tears in the corners of her eyes were of the same paste as the previous revellers. Her blackened teeth, her glistening lips, covered with sores . . .

"Don't you know me?"

Yes, he had recognized her; she had been the first, twenty years earlier, and this was all that remained. Now her embrace was moist and nauseating. She was rotting where she stood. Even had he torn off her mask to discover she was no more than sixteen, there was still that stench of mud, like the women to come afterwards. He tossed a wad of bills, the old, large, blue-and-green banknotes, behind him, and the women fought over them like dogs tearing at scraps of meat.

He returned to the hotel trembling with fever and briefly explained to the gold-braided porter what he would require of him the following morning; then he went up to his room. The porter counted the bills he had been given. Yes, Jenny was blond and beautiful, but the gaze of her deep-set eyes beneath her smooth brow was the gaze of death.

"When I came into his room, he was lying on the bed fully clothed, and sweat was pouring down his face," she told me.

In that moment, as she spoke, tears were running down her own cheeks: that night and the morning that followed had marked her life more indelibly than had any other night, any other morning.

"I had come to beg him to abandon that duel, to go away. Not to fight."

La Chesnaye had quickly regained his aplomb. He stood up, adjusted his cravat and asked Jenny to pardon him for receiving her in such disarray. Then he replied. No, he would not leave Vienna. Yes, he would go through with his duel with Rolf the next morning.

"But why? It won't do any good."

La Chesnaye helped himself to some cognac from a leather-covered flask that stood open on the night table.

"Yes, it will do good! It will make its effect."

Then he told her everything: about the men who had been pursuing him ever since he left Paris, about his entire life, the money he owed, the murderer he had shot down. About the odor of that station washroom, the perfumes of the women he had encountered in the streets.

"Since I'm done for, in any event, I'd at least like to choose the method of my own death!"

"But this is a duel, Georges, not suicide."

"Do you really think I intend to defend myself? Do you think I would fire a shot at your paragon of Viennese pomposity?"

La Chesnaye's plan was inflexible; he had no intention of changing it so much as an iota. Jenny begged him, pleaded with him, and he heard her out with a smile; but he stood firm. At last, she burst out:

"I will tell Rolf everything! He will listen to me, and he will never agree to meet you under those conditions!"

"You may think so!" La Chesnaye gave a harsh laugh. He was certain Freitag would meet him and that he would shoot to kill—even more readily were he to be told that his adversary did not intend to fire. For that was the underlying factor in La Chesnaye's plan, and everything that was to happen went according to his predictions. He lowered his voice. "You see, Rolf Freitag isn't a man. He's a puppet made of steel, covered with a thin layer of flesh. He's an animal. He is one of those monsters with human faces who bide their time, waiting for the right moment in which they will crush all of us."

He spoke slowly, for he—the gambler prepared to kill to save his own neck—had seen through the Rolf Freitags of this world. He recognized them as killers who murder at random simply because they have power, men who, fifteen years later, were to grasp that power, first in Berlin and then in Vienna, Warsaw, Bucharest, Prague, Budapest, Paris —not to mention Rome and Madrid.

"I will go see him in any case," Jenny muttered. And as she was leaving—she had already opened the door—she said: "Why are you forcing me to do this?"

He looked at her for a long moment, a final moment. "Why have you left Jean?"

In that precise moment—and perhaps only then—Jenny Fisher may finally have understood.

Her breathless conversation with Rolf Freitag, her explanations, her pleas, were fruitless. La Chesnaye had known his man: Freitag was determined to kill. He may even have believed—despite Jenny's denials —that La Chesnaye was his cousin's lover. When Jenny told him, after all her vain arguments, that if anything happened to La Chesnaye she would leave Vienna the next evening, Rolf Freitag had merely stared at her, a hard stare.

"You don't seem to realize that my honor is at stake. You don't seem to realize that that man stands for everything I despise most in the world."

La Chesnaye, in speaking of Freitag, had said, ". . . all I hate the most." It was to be a confrontation between hatred and contempt.

And Freitag had gone on: "I know you'll never leave me because you are in love with me."

JENNY

Jenny left Freitag's apartment in the Maser Palace with the feeling that, at that moment, her life had come to an end. She passed groups of masqueraders in the darkness—Schulerstrasse, Singerstrasse, Stephansplatz—she seemed to be lost in a Schnitzler novella. All the men seemed to be young and handsome, all of them desiring her, but, in the depths of her soul, she hated them all. She had thrown herself upon Freitag, in tears, striking his chest with her fists. "Don't you understand? Don't you understand?"

The masqueraders glanced at her as she passed; they laughed, and they laughed even more loudly when she insulted them.

"Don't you understand?"

Back at the Sacher Hotel, La Chesnaye refused to open his door to her when she tried to see him. Jean had taken a strong sleeping pill, and she was unable to awaken him. Thus, Jenny Fisher's nocturnal wanderings ended in my office at the French Embassy in the early morning hours; I was on duty. She sank into a chair. It was on that night that I spoke to her for the first time; the friendship we have shared throughout our lives goes back to that night. Yet I could do nothing for her, and she knew it. La Chesnaye was French, of course, but there were no regulations or laws that enabled a French ambassador or a member of his staff to intervene to prevent a duel.

The death took place in the Kaiserwasser forest, a few miles south of Vienna. Two musicians in formal attire, as ready with revolvers as they were with their double basses, acted as Rolf Freitag's seconds; La Chesnaye was accompanied by a man in black tie and tails, a mere *maître d'hôtel* from the Sacher in his work clothes. The smile never left La Chesnaye's face as he listened to the instructions of Dr. M., the referee; he refused to acknowledge Freitag's presence and walked the regulation twenty-five paces. For a long moment, he breathed deeply: forest air in the early dawn, the nascent, vivid odor that wiped out the stench of the city; instead of the masqueraders and the Carnival revelry, he heard the song of a bird in the topmost branches of a birch tree. To make his intentions clear, he stood sideways and thus avoided his adversary's first shot. Then he fired his own first bullet into the air and turned to face Freitag's second attempt.

He died instantly.

"Of course, he had it all planned. He had thought of everything," Jenny said.

Even of the letter he had left behind, the letter telling Jean that Jenny would return to him, that all he had to do was to go to her when he awakened, to the old Countess von Bellmer's palace where she would be waiting for him.

"Then," he had written, "you must be strong, you must listen only to your own heart and to no other voice. You must leave Vienna with her on the first train. She won't be able to stay here any longer. But you must not think that then it will all be over—quite the contrary: it will be just the beginning. From then on, you will have to fight against yourself. The war is over, Jean, but life must go on. Jenny, the project near Liévin—it's all up to you now."

"And, of course, Jean came to the Bellmer palace, and I was there, waiting for him."

Jenny's bags were already packed. She refused to see Freitag again, despite the old countess's pleas and the pleas of her entire entourage, all of whom had been told what was about to take place; even pimply young Dietrich had been called upon. When Jean arrived, she simply left with him without a word.

"We talked on the train. He told me what I had wanted him to say: that he was going to begin to live again."

That was all she had waited for. In tears, she had fallen into his arms, and it was he who had, at last, consoled her, like a man. The train bore them away.

In Paris, in London, Milan, New York—even, of course, in Vienna, finally—Jenny Fisher went on to become the great singer we all know. Rolf Freitag had his hour of glory; it lasted for five years and was restricted to Germany and Austria. Then, even his friends abandoned him; his music passé, Freitag turned to politics. His tall, rigid figure in its brown uniform haunted the corridors of the Third Reich until a bullet from a partisan's rifle in Poland brought to an end a career that had long been over in fact. And who still listens to Freitag's music or performs it?

As for Georges La Chesnaye, he was forgotten even before Jenny Fisher and Jean Ledoyen had reached Paris. Only Jean and Jenny remembered him. And Andrea D., who mourned him. And myself, because I would like to have known him.

"May I tell you something?" asked Lise the next evening.

JENNY

Lise Bergaud had just joined Paul de Morlay, who was leaning on the stone balustrade overlooking the garden of the villa where couples were dancing on a wooden floor that had been erected among the white statues. Pierrots and Harlequins, Columbines and Scaramouches were whirling on the lawn.

"I thought I had made it quite clear that you can tell me anything at all. . . ."

"Yes, I know . . . but this is something I've just thought of, and I'm wondering if this is the right time."

Among the statues, the couples danced on.

"If this is really the moment?"

All the young people the ambassador had invited to the party in Lise's honor were young, good-looking. Of course, he had invited the men for her benefit: students from Vicenza and Padua, young men from the noblest families in Venice; and women, too—so young as to seem almost children. Anyone happening upon the scene would have wondered how this old man had managed to bring together around him such a wealth of very young women . . . almost his grandchildren. His pleasure at seeing them dancing in their light, filmy dresses on that summer night, without a hint of any winter to come, was evidence that his guest list had been prepared with the help of a conspiratorial friend well aware of his tastes. That was why Lise felt somewhat hesitant about distracting Paul de Morlay at that moment.

"But it's your party, Lise! And you can do whatever you like. Even talk business!"

And it was almost business she wanted to discuss with him, standing there beside him in a low-cut gown that revealed her breasts, naked, soft and very white.

"I've been thinking about the story of Jenny and Jean. But I've been thinking above all of what you managed to tell me along with their story. Perhaps without even realizing it . . ."

Amused, he protested. True, nothing happened without the ambassador's realizing it. As though excusing herself for her clumsiness, Lise also rested her elbows on the stone balustrade overlooking the garden, and her cheek touched the ambassador's shoulder.

"What I'm trying to say is . . ."

She wanted to tell him that what had surprised her the most in each of his narratives, but particularly in the one he had finished the previous evening in that gallery with its wicker armchairs, was his concern for people, for the world. It was the acute awareness he seemed always to have had of the sufferings of others—and his deep hatred of violence, blindness, war. . . .

"You mean my hatred of people like Rolf Freitag?"

"Among other things, yes . . . And the way you talked about Berlin after the war, about Rosa Luxemburg, about the rise of fascism of all kinds . . ."

Paul de Morlay shook his head. "Ah, my child, if only there really were clearly defined categories in this world, laid down once and for all! The 'good' on the one hand, well-dressed people for whom unhappiness, poverty, the absolute evil of warfare or any kind of tyranny doesn't exist; and then the truly sincere people—people like yourself. So many people, too, believe their hands are cleaner than ours because they happen to be journalists, writers, idealists—or simply because they aren't well dressed. Ah, my child, how quickly you will discover that everything is not that simple!"

Below them on the terrace, a couple was dancing to a rock group. The girl might have been fifteen, and Lise followed the ambassador's eyes, which were fixed on the dancers even as he spoke. Once again, he smiled.

"As if even though one loves women, even though one has grown very old and has become idle—so very idle—one doesn't sometimes also want to cry out."

Paul de Morlay, at the tragedy of Jean Ledoyen, had had the urge to cry out.

Lise looked at him then, her eyes serious. "May I ask you one more question . . . the last?"

"Of course."

"Jenny . . . did you go to bed with her?"

The ambassador's eyes were now serious as well.

"Yes, I went to bed with her, but long after that Viennese adventure . . . and by then we had become friends, old friends, not really lovers."

"And Jean—Jean Ledoyen?"

Lise seemed cold, and the ambassador put his hand on her shoulder. "I remain one of his best friends. And now you're going to please me and let one of the handsomest young men at this party invite you to dance. You know that this party is wholly for your benefit . . . and you must stop asking yourself too many questions." He took his hand from her shoulder. "And I," he continued, "am going up to bed."

Lise moved closer to him. "Would you like me to . . ." The ambassador smiled. "No, no, my child! You must enjoy yourself. Despinetta or Barbarina will measure out my seven or eight drops of sleeping potion I must take in order to fall asleep each evening, and tomorrow I'll be fresher than the freshest of your young men."

Before Lise Bergaud had time to protest, the ambassador had left her.

The couples continued to dance in the garden, on the terrace and in the salons; they danced with serious expressions on their young faces, expressions twenty-year-olds have when pleasure is still a serious matter. Leaning over the balustrade after Paul de Morlay's departure, Lise watched them. They were all handsome, with the perfectly smooth faces of young patricians—all those youths who traveled from Saint Moritz to some dazzlingly white yacht moored in the Aegean, roaming the world without seeing anything of it—but their expressions were masks of indifference. Suddenly Lise Bergaud felt a kind of hatred for them, for all those too handsome young men, those flawless young women. They were so self-enclosed, so grave: they were serious when they laughed; they were serious when, beneath the shadows of the trees, they sought the shadow of pleasure. None of them could have looked back in memory to the death of someone like La Chesnaye or to the murder of an innocent in Berlin, people whose demise was fixed in Paul de Morlay's heart like a wound in his side.

"Aren't you dancing?"

She started. One of those young men had approached her and was standing before her . . . the handsomest of them all, perhaps, with the most perfect tan, the most dazzling smile. Paul de Morlay might have chosen him especially for her. He was wearing a blue silk shirt and faded blue jeans that were molded so tightly to his body that they looked like another skin. He had the air of an athletic gigolo, and the heavy gold bracelet encircling his wrist added to that impression, although the signet ring on his right hand bearing the crest of the noble B. family of Venice identified him as something more.

"Aren't you dancing?" He was already leading her away. . . .

So they danced. Before long, Lise had melted into the crowd gyrating to the disco rhythms being blared out by one of Italy's most famous bands, hired by Paul de Morlay for the occasion. Lise moved with the others, with her entire body, but at the same time she felt she was watching herself, observing at some great distance away from that blond girl who looked so much like herself, that girl gradually caught up in the whirlpool that brought her constantly into contact with the solid arms and body of Vincenzo B. with his glittering teeth.

Dance followed dance. After Vincenzo B., she danced with Patrizio C., Maurizio D.—they were all alike, but Vincenzo was the handsomest among them. It was in his arms that she found herself dancing a slow, melancholy blues when dawn began to appear through the pines and white statuary of the park. And it was he who followed her up to her room under the ironic gaze of Eugenio, the chauffeur with the face of an angelic killer, who had acted as master of ceremonies after the ambassador's departure. Lise Bergaud succumbed to the young Venetian's caresses with a violence she had never before experienced, a violence that was very like hatred, while he, blithely unaware, took her again and again . . . pleased at her moans, her tears, as they made love.

"All men are idiots!" That sentence rang in Lise Bergaud's ears when she finally woke up.

Vincenzo B. was still asleep, sprawled across the bed, his brown, almost golden torso as perfectly smooth as his haughty face. On the floor at the foot of the bed lay Paul de Morlay's manuscript, the story of Jenny Fisher. Suddenly Lise felt ready to cry. Quickly she got up and, completely naked, went to the window with its closed shutters. Vincenzo B. was sleeping too soundly to enjoy the sight of her elegant, pale, superbly modeled body; when Lise pulled open the shutters, he merely groaned in his sleep. The sunlight flooded into the room, and the curtains at the windows swelled softly like sails in the morning breeze. Outside lay the garden, the park, the countryside below the terrace and the gallery. She had a sudden longing to be there, to leave her room, that bed, that young, overly handsome man whom she hated with such sudden ferocity.

Slipping on a filmy dressing gown that did not really hide her nakedness, she went down to the kitchen. On the way she passed Eugenio, but he stared straight ahead; she lowered her eyes. In the kitchen, Barbarina and Despinetta chattered like giddy, amusing magpies when she appeared, still under the influence of the champagne that had flowed so freely the night before. As Lise entered they nudged each other, and the girl blushed deeply.

Despinetta came forward with a broad grin. "You have a right to amuse yourself . . . and he was so handsome."

Lise did not reply, but Barbarina answered for her, with the same words Lise had thought upon awakening: "What difference does it make? Men are idiots!"

She directed Lise to the covered gallery where Paul de Morlay was already enjoying his breakfast of toast, tea, orange juice. Lise burst out laughing: how right Barbarina was! She joined the ambassador, and when Vincenzo B. appeared two hours later, still a bit groggy, somewhat taken aback to find his mistress for the night so deep in conversation —almost conspiratorial—with a man old enough to be her grandfather at whom she was not looking as one looks at one's grandfather, she greeted him casually, with a gesture.

"I'll call you . . ." the young man muttered.

"Yes," Lise said, he should call her, but the young man clearly understood that she would not accept his telephone call. When his white Maserati disappeared from sight, the ambassador leaned toward her.

"Why?" he asked.

He meant, why so indifferent? But Lise had already forgotten Vincenzo B. In reply, she donned her huge, round sunglasses. "Because I'm waiting for what's going to happen next," she said.

ANTONELLA

Venice, 1924

The years passed. The threat La Chesnaye had so clearly discerned lurking behind Rolf Freitag and those like him suddenly began to become visible to everyone: the world—Europe, at least—was heading toward the edge of an abyss.

But did any of us really realize it then? Did any of us understand that the March on Rome, the rise of Italian fascism with its gradual elimination of other political parties, was really only the harbinger of a tempest that was to spare nothing we loved? We politicians, diplomats, men who were so involved in all those stillborn treaties, those futile discussions that resulted only in torn-up scraps of paper—we argued, while the boots of the militia, paramilitary forces and bands of killers were resounding on the cobblestones of our city streets. I had Jewish friends in Berlin, Rome, Warsaw—which of them realized that the short forms they were asked to fill out so innocently were only the first of those thousand and one forms, questionnaires, files that were to bring them yearly closer to the gas chambers?

But we are in 1924, and who could have suspected then? Yet the story of Antonella, which is also the story of all those early warning signals of apocalypse, could have, should have warned us all. Carefree, radiant Antonella, caught up in that tempest—who could have guessed?

ANTONELLA

It started like a comedy, like an American musical comedy, almost, one about a professor being seduced by an attractive student. I envisage Cary Grant in horn-rimmed glasses, an absentminded professor at work on an elixir of youth in his disordered laboratory. And the student would be played by . . .

But I can't pick a name. For the student was played by Antonella; she is the only person right for the part. Antonella: youth, gaiety, the joy of living. Antonella, who devoured every day whole for fear she might miss a single crumb. Antonella, whose laugh was unlike the laughter of anyone else, who loved as people have forgotten it was once possible to love.

"She was twenty years old, with the laugh of a child," George Mac-Larren was to tell me one evening after it was all over.

George MacLarren was my British counterpart in Venice in those days, a man who drank as only a consul of Her Britannic Majesty can drink when he has been set down and forgotten on the edge of some lagoon: whiskey at nine in the morning to recover from his hangover of the previous night and so on through the day with gin-and-tonics, a bottle of wine with every meal. But more of him later.

In his jovial, desperate way—at once rigorous and a bit grotesque, but also generous when he at last came to understand—he was the darkest element in my uneasy conscience throughout my stay in Venice. He, at least, knew, and because he knew, he paid for it. He was the one who welcomed into his small palazzo near the Academmia that odd couple, Peter Charley and Antonella, and it was in that palazzo that one November dawn the sound of fists and boots beating on the door was to shatter lives. Yet Antonella had hoped until the very end.

"There was one moment," MacLarren was to tell me, "when I thought she was going to teach even us to live again."

He referred to himself and to Diana, both of them human wreckage . . . castaways that England had deposited in that damp, frigid building in the heart of the world's most beautiful city. But a city where the storm that was already beating against the walls of those deserted palazzos, like abandoned ships, rose to a tempest . . .

"As a matter of fact, I think that what Diana felt for Antonella was something very like love at first sight."

A flash of lightning? More like a whiplash! Diana MacLarren, George's wife and also one of my oldest friends, was another who drank to excess, but she was still capable of great feats of generosity and revolt—unlike George, she was not yet completely burned out.

"I'm a ruined man!" MacLarren always said when he downed what was supposed to be his last glass. And then he would stagger up to bed, stopping to catch his breath on each step of the huge stone staircase in the Foscarini Palace which housed the offices and residence of the British consul in Venice. One evening, while still lucid, he had added: "That kid with her hazel eyes and curly hair almost managed to shake us out of our stupor!"

Superb, insouciant Antonella, who so profoundly affected the lives of everyone whose paths she chanced to cross—some of them, like Peter Charley, never recovered completely, not to mention those who died because of it.

As for Peter Charley, he is alive today in his apartment near Kew Gardens. We exchange Christmas cards every year. Once, in a note written in his minute, upright hand in violet ink, he mentioned Antonella . . . without regret. Too many years had gone by since that brief, unhappy love affair, that tragedy. . . . And yet it had all started like a musical comedy.

It was at Victoria Station on the first of November 1924.

There was that childish air of expectancy that always seems to prevail at English leave-takings: this time it was the train for Venice, but it might just as well have been for Brighton or Cheltenham. On the platform inside the station, even in the courtyard outside, there was that smell so typical of English railways in those days: a reek of pipe tobacco and cinders, an odor that is now almost nostalgic. In those days, the newspaper vendors looked like grocers; the ticket collectors were like historical figures. The train for Paris was about to depart from platform one—there were still cars that went on to Venice direct.

"Even at the beginning, Peter Charley worried . . . but then, he was the kind of man who always worries. . . ."

George MacLarren had known Peter Charley during their time together at Cambridge, and they had remained friends, linked by their common memories of the past. George MacLarren was a good judge of men, and he was able to describe Peter Charley to me as though he had actually seen him himself, pacing the platform outside of car seven, looking at his watch, dropping his raincoat, impatient, grumbling, furious.

"It's unbelievable! But it's not like her to be this late!"

The girls around him giggled behind their hands. They had come in a body to see him off on his train, their professor of Renaissance art, girls of eighteen or twenty still dressed like schoolgirls, enrolled in his courses at London University.

"Everyone liked Charley, you know . . . he wasn't like other men."

I mentioned Cary Grant, wearing horn-rimmed glasses in some American film: he was an absentminded professor, still handsome, tweed jacket, checkered shirt. He had something of the air of a gentleman farmer in his Sunday best who had wandered into an art gallery, the section devoted to the sumptuous nudes of Veronese or Tiepolo; it was a look that amused and even moved his female students beneath their giggling and winking. Everyone knew that his wife was a dragon. Everyone knew he had children, friends and one great passion—Venetian painting—but nobody had ever seen him in the company of any woman but Mary Charley, the dragon. . . . However, she lived in Putney or Wimbledon and almost never emerged from her suburb to accompany her husband to faculty dinners. Half seriously and half in fun, Peter Charley's students all dreamed about him but without, of course, ever trying to make their girlish dreams a reality. But he had such green eyes, such pepper-and-salt hair, the athletic physique of one of those shy, absentminded men who spend their vacations alone climbing all the rocky peaks or snowy slopes of the Cairngorms in Scotland, as men today might ascend Annapurna. And all his students adored the smell of his pipe.

"It was a sweetish tobacco he used, really awful, but those girls adored it, I know!"

I sensed a kind of envy in MacLarren's voice; at least, Charley had not fallen apart like he had.

Standing on platform one of Victoria Station, London, on that November day, however, Peter Charley seemed on the verge of nervous collapse.

He was a man whose life was based on principles, the foremost of which were punctuality and exactitude. He could not imagine how it had happened that Miss Perry, his longtime assistant, devoted as she was dumpy, was not at the station to greet him. She had both their tickets, and the conductor for car seven—albeit a fine fellow and a native of Bradford like Peter Charley—was stubbornly refusing to allow him to board the train.

"The train will leave in ten minutes," Maggie Parnell-Smith, the student with the reddest hair, announced. And they all burst into giggles, as though they knew something. . . . Which, of course, they did.

Charley swore under his breath. "You think it's funny—six months of planning and study, all for nothing."

He may have been ready to give it up, to return home, who knows? But at that moment, Antonella made her entrance into our tale.

"Are you making fun of me or something?"

By now Peter Charley was nearly speechless with rage. He stammered; all his somewhat grumpy good humor was gone. He looked very funny and—Antonella was probably thinking—charming.

"No, Professor, I've never been more serious."

Standing before the mirror, Antonella Walden was drawing a red line around her lips. Her calm served only to increase Charley's anger.

"You're crazy and scatterbrained."

"Not at all, Professor. I'm only doing you a favor!"

A favor! Peter Charley took his pipe from between his teeth. A favor! A fine favor she was doing him! Now both of them, professor and almost unknown student, were thrown together in one compartment and would be forced to spend the entire trip to Venice in those intimate surroundings. She was doing him a favor because faithful Janet Perry was remaining in London, and he was setting out with an assistant who had dropped into his life out of nowhere to help in the delicate research that only his regular and trusted collaborator could help him to accomplish.

"It's not my fault Miss Perry caught whooping cough! But you'll see, I'm as good a photographer as she is!"

Antonella seemed amused, but Peter Charley didn't find it at all amusing. Yet when the attractive young woman, loaded down with photographic equipment and bursting with good feeling, had appeared on the platform with their tickets in her hand, what could he do but allow her to board the train with him? It was now 12:57, and the train was due to depart at 12:59!

Antonella's explanations, panted out as they handed their tickets to the conductor and tossed their luggage into the compartment, had been succinct: Miss Perry had implored her to go in her stead . . . that was all.

"But couldn't she have telephoned me herself and asked my opinion? Couldn't she have explained to me herself?"

Antonella was too busy to answer. Miss Perry's absence was one thing—but one compartment for them both? When they found themselves in the compact space with its two beds, one above the other, and Peter Charley had given a horrified groan of dismay, Antonella had merely replied that it was the only one available.

"Wé would have had to wait until Friday, otherwise. And you wouldn't want to wait until Friday, would you?"

She was very sure of herself, ready to do battle and in charge; her photographic equipment was already strewn about on the banquettes. Antonella took care of it all, tipped the porter and lowered the window to say farewell to her companions.

"Don't you want to say good-bye to them, too?"

The train was about to leave . . . as though Peter Charley had any inclination to smile and call farewells to those girls who had so obviously known what was going on and who had appeared to be making fun of him as they waved their handkerchiefs.

"Bon voyage! Have a good time, Professor Charley!"

He shrugged and turned his back to the window. A minute later, the train pulled out of the station, and Antonella, standing before the mirror, was repairing her mouth with pink lipstick.

"Are you making fun of me or something?"

But Antonella was not making fun of Peter Charley at all.

Not until they were nearly finished lunch did he stop frowning.

Throughout the meal, which was served immediately after their departure, Peter Charley had continued to rage at her. He called upon the ghosts of his predecessors, the girl's respectable family; he mentioned the gossip at London University and voiced his indignation at Antonella's thoughtlessness in organizing such a trip.

"Have you stopped to think how my colleagues will leer at me when I return?"

He vigorously chewed his way through the second-rate menu that even in those days was prevalent on the British leg of that journey, and Antonella, with lowered head, waited for the storm to blow over and counted the limp french fries piled on her plate. And when Charley finally grew tired of talking to himself over his charred steak and suspiciously green peas, she looked up and gave him one of the smiles that only she knew how to smile.

"Had I known my company would be so unbearable, I assure you I . . ."

She stopped, blushed and feigned innocent confusion. Peter Charley looked at her over his glasses. Antonella was able to simulate tears with very little effort. He was apologetic at once.

"That's not what I meant. . . ."

He stammered again, but this time out of discomfiture at the sight of a young girl on the verge of crying.

"You hate me, don't you? And if you only knew how I want to go on this trip with you! All of us did, for that matter; we almost came to blows trying to decide who would come along when we found out that Miss Perry was ill. But I won!"

Suddenly she looked so sweet, so upset, that at last he smiled at her. "No, of course I don't hate you!"

Thus, when the train arrived at Folkestone and the cars were being shunted onto the Dunkerque ferry, Peter Charley had finally managed to convince himself that he had not made such a bad bargain after all in trading the ample, somber Miss Perry for this pretty twenty-year-old girl who had begun to smile again.

The remainder of the first day of their journey was for him an enchantment—it was more: it was a revelation. Listening to Antonella talk, watching her as she leaned at the rail of the ferry or drank a glass of red wine with him in the ship's bar, purchasing tobacco from the purser: it was like a journey into another world, a world he had been unaware existed.

"When I think of what I had been missing for forty-five years without knowing it!" he told George MacLarren during one of the long evenings they spent together in the Palazzo Foscarini.

And, indeed, the twenty-four hours of that journey from London to Venice via Dunkerque and the Simplon Pass were a veritable awakening for Peter Charley. Antonella, of course, had managed it all. She had only to laugh, and it was like a celebration, that superb display of her lovely teeth, like those of some small, wild creature, and her tender, amused expression that belied that hint of cruelty the somewhat thin line of her lips might otherwise have suggested. She had only to talk, and it was like a flood of surprise, of funny or suddenly serious and pertinent comments that, as the hours flew by, gave Peter Charley a feeling he had never experienced before, a kind of stunned rapture:

that this girl, so young, so beautiful, should suddenly be there close to him surpassed any of his dreams.

"You aren't still angry?"

He jumped: across from him in car seven on the opposite seat of their compartment—the train had been reattached after Dunkerque—Antonella was smiling.

"Of course not; I'm not angry any longer. I was never truly angry, for that matter. I was surprised, more than anything."

She lowered her eyes.

"I know I'm impossible, but if you really want something, you have to take chances, you know. And I love to take chances. . . ."

What he read at that moment in her eyes moved him as he had never been moved before.

"One has to take real chances," she repeated.

At that moment, Antonella Walden was not pretending. As for Peter Charley, he listened and learned: one had to determine to take chances.

Their dinner, this time served by the Compagnie Internationale des Wagons-Lits, lived up to legend: lobster *mousse* and duckling with currant sauce, *noisette* of lamb on a bed of spinach and a pineapple *soufflé*. By now, M. Paul had become an unparalleled chef. Antonella, her cheeks aglow with pleasure, devoured everything that was set before her . . . and more. She wiped her plate so assiduously that Peter Charley finally offered her what he had left on his own, and, without interrupting her nonstop conversation, she drank glass after glass of champagne. She chattered on about whatever came into her head: stories of student life, childhood memories of her youth in Venice—it is not without importance that she had lived in Venice—along with comments on paintings they both admired, and Peter Charley fell ever more deeply under her spell. It was as though he had been asleep for years among his books and pictures, with long, suburban Sunday afternoons and his dull Putney spouse, and he was now suddenly discovering a unique new quality: gaiety.

Antonella was gay as Peter Charley had never imagined anyone could be gay.

"You know, Peter—I may call you Peter, may I not?—all the girls at the university are crazy about you."

She peered at him through the bubbles in her glass of champagne; it was amazing how different Peter suddenly seemed, seen through champagne bubbles. His heart was young, even if his face was not, and now he had all the attractiveness of one of those forty-year-old men who so often haunt the dreams of schoolgirls at night, alone on their narrow cots. Such girls have the knack of coaxing smiles from such so-called older men.

"Yes, crazy about you . . . First, it's because of the way you talk to them about art . . . eroticism in Veronese or Tiepolo. Not many professors talk that way! But that's not all. There's something else, too."

"Something else?" Peter Charley had drunk more than usual himself; he was prepared to believe anything.

"Yes . . . There's something sad about you."

He laughed. "Sad? Me?"

"Yes . . . So they all want to comfort you."

I think it was Giraudoux who wrote somewhere that in order to seduce a man, a woman must tell him how handsome he is, but that she can make a man weep by telling him she wants to comfort him. Antonella took his hand. Was it the champagne? She thought suddenly how soft and solid a man's hand was. She was more sincere than she had ever been. There was a small, hard, discolored area of skin near the end of Peter's middle finger, the writer's bump where his pen rested. Suddenly sensitive, Peter Charley allowed her to examine it, and then he withdrew his hand.

"I have tired old hands, you know. . . ." He couldn't think of anything else to say.

When they returned to their compartment, it was to find that the conductor had had the two berths made up—one above the other, with two pillows, two bolsters. A nightgown was laid out on the lower berth . . . not transparent, but filmy, nonetheless.

Peter Charley hesitated, suddenly sober again. Even though in those days young women had already become fairly daring . . .

"Are you certain there isn't another compartment free somewhere on the train?"

"I'm sure. I asked the conductor."

She was lying—she had not asked anyone—but she happened to be telling the truth, for there were no free compartments. I am not really certain whether she had actually planned the whole thing, what was to happen. She was just completely gay, a bit giddy, daringly insouciant. For reasons that will become clear later, she had to go to Venice; she was now en route, and suddenly her companion seemed very charming, with all the charm men of his age who have not forgotten that it is possible to be a boy in the body of a middle-aged adult. What process had Antonella set in motion by her frivolity? For what was to occur was something Peter Charley never forgot.

Peter offered to undress in the washroom. As she watched him leave, Antonella seemed to be wondering why. With his pajamas in his hand, a dressing gown he had taken from his bag, he looked somewhat confused.

"Well, I'll be off. . . ."

When he returned to the compartment, Antonella was lying on the lower berth. She had turned off the light in the ceiling, and only the feeble glow of the blue night-light lit the compartment. Peter Charley hesitated. He felt silly, standing there with his clothes over his arm, the suspenders of his trousers dangling down.

Antonella beckoned to him. "Come sit here, if you like. . . ."

She edged closer to the wall of the compartment to make room for him, and he sat down gingerly on the edge of her berth.

"I think I must be a bit drunk."

She gave a tiny hiccup . . . and then she giggled. She smiled and stared at him. Drunk? Well, perhaps she was a bit, but, above all, she was suddenly touched by this adolescent and grown-up man whose open pajama top revealed the graying hairs on his chest. She put out her hand. "I've probably had too much to drink," she said again.

That was no excuse, but it was the best one she could invent. Gently, Peter Charley bent over her.

Later, Peter Charley talked as the train sped through the night. It was his turn to tell her everything: Cambridge and London, his youth, his wife, the other women he had met—and the paintings he had loved instead of loving those women. The train clattered over crossing points and through stations whose harsh lights sometimes threw clear white bars of brightness across the ceiling and walls of the compartment. He talked on. Antonella lay beside him, cradled in his arm, her head on his chest. He felt an immense, limitless, unreasoning pleasure at that moment as Antonella turned upon her back, still close to him, and he gazed down on the lovely landscape of a woman's body. The body of a very young woman, the swaying of the train, their caresses filled him with a desire to take her again, to begin over.

"Never before, you know . . . never . . ."

Little London girls grow suddenly melancholy and tired after making love . . . afternoon tea, and that taste that lingers in the mouth after one has left them.

"You see, with you . . ."

Peter was delirious; he felt like breaking into song, like shouting his joy, his marvelous astonishment at finding that twenty-year-old girl with her twenty-year-old body laughing in his arms. She did not speak. He took her in his arms. "You're very quiet."

She murmured: "I'm fine." Later, she said: "You won't hold it against me, will you? What's happened? You won't hold it against me?"

She seemed to be asking a favor, but Peter Charley was not really listening. He was savoring his happiness. Yet her words should have been a warning to him. "I was already so afraid of hurting her!" he was to tell George MacLarren. Afterwards . . .

There was a shock awaiting them at the Italian frontier. They were brought back down to earth with a start. They had entered enemy territory. The day before, there had been an abortive attempt on Mussolini's life and all the newspapers were full of it; some unbalanced Englishwoman had indulged in marksmanship practice with *Il Duce* as target, using a small-caliber revolver. No one had been injured, but reprisals had followed—banning of political parties, a stricter control of public gatherings and, of course, close surveillance of foreigners. Especially the English.

It is at such times, remembering the moments of pleasure passed on a train, that we are brought to a realization of how close we are to the edge of the abyss. I mentioned Antonella's innocence—but we should rather speak of Peter Charley's innocence and the innocence of all those like him, living isolated in art and books while half of Europe had already begun to tremble!

The Italian policeman who violently threw open the door to their compartment might have sold *lasagna* in some Roman shop: in that case, we would have described him as adorable, picturesque fellow in an enormous cook's hat, who whistled tunes from Verdi in his kitchen. But the voice of the man in the police uniform had all the brutality that such a uniform can give to the uneducated of this world.

"English?"

The officer and his henchmen systematically emptied all their bags.

"English!"

They had orders to search all British citizens thoroughly and to confiscate any weapons they might discover. Unable to find any, they only searched the harder.

Peter Charley had slipped on his dressing gown. Antonella remained in the berth with the sheet and blanket pulled up to her chin. Charley made an attempt to protest.

"I'm a professor of art history. I'm here at the invitation of the Italian government. . . ."

The officer merely shrugged. A professor? That was even more suspicious. He picked up a notebook filled with Peter Charley's notes and reference materials, holding it by a corner, and shook it like some filthy object too impure to be opened and examined in any normal fashion. He bent down and picked up the photographs that had fallen out, and when he saw that they were without any strategic or political interest, he tossed them to the floor again—Veronese nudes! Through clenched teeth, he repeated: "English!" When he examined Antonella's passport, his tone changed. He turned to her suddenly: "Italian? With an English passport?"

The girl explained calmly. "English, but born in Venice of an Italian mother and English father. I've been brought up in England; I've only spent vacations in Italy."

The *lasagna* cook turned brutish policeman looked at Antonella with a kind of hatred mingled with contempt. She was not only English, she was a turncoat. He ordered his men to search everything, down to her toilet articles, and did not even grin when one of his men, with a suggestive snicker, held up a collection of pink and blue panties.

"I'm sorry about that," Antonella murmured when they had gone.

They had left behind them piles of disordered filmy lingerie, men's underwear and art history books. Antonella's high spirits had disappeared; they had indeed arrived in Italy, and, in 1924, Italy was already a land of fear and violence. By saying, "I'm sorry," Antonella was suddenly remembering that she was half Italian and feeling almost ashamed of it.

The train went along the shores of Lago Maggiori, through a post-card landscape that stretched on either side as far as the eye could see, and Peter Charley attempted to restore the mood he had experienced as he had held her in his arms a few hours before. Antonella, so gay, so light, so young, had grown serious, and when he tried to embrace her, she gently disengaged herself.

"Forgive me, Peter, but I don't feel well."

Did he have any inkling? In any event, for the first time, he became afraid of losing her. What if the entire affair, that moment of perfect happiness that night, were ended forever? As they drew nearer to Venice—Verona, Vicenza, Padua—the smell of the city already in the air, Antonella recovered some of her smile. And when the train drew into the Mestre station fifteen minutes behind schedule—Mussolini had not yet seen to it that all trains in Italy arrived on time—she leaned toward him.

"Forgive me . . ." Her lips brushed his. "You must forgive me. I was nervous."

"Are you feeling better?" He needed her reassurance.

"Better, yes . . ."

With a screech of metal that was answered by the shrieking of Adriatic sea gulls, the train came to a stop.

I've always had it in the back of my mind that someday I would write a book about Venice. I lived there for three years; I've visited it thirty times since then, and each time I took notes, made sketches, wrote fragments, but the more I came to know the city—from the deserted Zattere on a December morning to the crowded Merceria in the June heat, or the empty rooms of museums like the Querini-Stampalia Palazzo and the far corners of the Napoleonic wing of the Procuratio—the more I had the feeling that Venice escaped me. Are those things Venice? But what about the Ghetto Nuovo? Or the children running barelegged, revolving like tops in little squares . . . What about the noble contours of the Arsenale? The island of Saint-Francis-of-the-Desert? How to write about a place when so much has already been said?

So I have kept silent on the subject of Venice, as well as everything else. And just as I have told you about other people rather than about myself, I shall tell you only of the Venice Peter Charley and Antonella knew . . . you arrived there on the same train as they; I'll be describing things that you have seen. The first wonderment . . . that smell of the autumn sea that takes your breath away, the sharp wind, the movement on the canals that you notice as soon as you come out onto the *quai* in front of the Santa Lucia Station. And then that crowd, so unlike any other, men in double-breasted jackets waiting patiently for a

ANTONELLA

vaporetto; girls hurrying along the Rio Terra, revealing a glimpse of white calves as they cross some humpbacked bridge; children playing at the very edge of the dark water on the mossy steps of some palazzo.

"I feel it is like a miracle just being here, every time." Standing before the Santa Lucia Station, his luggage around him, Peter Charley took a deep breath. "And each time, I tell myself that it may perhaps be the last time I'll see it."

He looked around him at the crowd he loved, but Antonella had become worried once again. A few yards away, two blackshirted teenagers were strolling by: the joy of her return faded. Yes, Venice in 1924 was that, too: a black shirt, the arrogance of the powerful. Peter did not yet understand it, and once again he tried to regain the lyric enthusiasm he had felt during their journey.

"One of the rarest of Tiepolo's frescoes used to be in the Scaldi Chapel next to the station. An Austrian bomb destroyed it all during the Great War. Now there are only a few fragments left, in the Academmia. But the gesture of that old man embracing a child who looks like a woman . . ."

Antonella was not listening: the men in black seemed to rivet her . . . with a fascinated horror . . . the way everyone moved out of their path to give them room . . .

"Yes, that's Venice," she said to herself.

Peter Charley had begun to fret: where was his friend the consul who was supposed to be meeting him at the station? Where was the consular gondola that was to take them to the Palazzo Foscarini? On the *quai* before them stood a row of *vaporetti* and passengers leaving the station . . . and that was all.

Antonella took charge. "We can just as easily take a vaporetto."

Followed by two porters, they made their way to the dock for line number one. The gray-blue wooden boat rocked gently on the water.

Peter Charley never stopped talking throughout their trip along the Grand Canal, still oblivious to the change that had taken place in the girl. He spoke with the same enthusiasm, the same jubilation: "Every time I return to Venice, I recite the names of the palazzos along the Grand Canal like a kind of secular litany. Ca d'Oro, Barbaro . . ."

The Ca d'Oro, where today the greatest of Titian's nudes have found asylum; the Palazzo Barbaro—how could Peter Charley have known that Antonella's mother, an anarchist journalist in the days just after the war, had sought refuge in six gilded rooms on the top floor of the Barbaro, among the vestiges of Tiepolo and Bernardo Strozzi?

"Every time I return to Venice . . ."

The Franchetti, the Loredan, the Vendramin—but Peter Charley's memories are shared by all who love Venice. Wagner, the poet Browning on the *entresol* of the Ca Rezzonico, Henri de Regnier at the Palazzo Dario—not to mention Henry James, whose ghost haunts so many deserted houses, or Ruskin, or even Proust—and, above all, Paul Morand, of whom I think this evening because he, too, is a part of the book you are going to write for me, since I shall never write one. All those people who, word by word and book by book, have made Venice what it has become in our eyes . . . Antonella, lulled by the sound of the motor, closed her eyes. Venice—yes, she, too, had returned. Slowly she was beginning to realize what lay in store for her here.

"When Peter and Antonella arrived at the Foscarini, I had gone up to lie down," George MacLarren told me, making excuses.

He was being euphemistic. The previous evening had been a bad one; the gin had been worse, bitter and of poor quality. He had had a restless night, plagued by the heat of the bedclothes and the late mosquitoes, bred in the pollution of the lagoons, that filled the closed courtyards of the Zattere even in November. At dawn, he had finally lost consciousness, and Diana had risen alone. The house was empty: Fernando, the head butler, had disappeared as he did every night— "The shit!" Diana had murmured, knowing that he left every evening to report to the police (or some other more questionable and dangerous organization) all that occurred at the consulate—and Camilla, the maid, was snoring in her den at the level of the canal in the arms of some gondolier she had lured in by showing herself half naked at her window.

"I'm terribly sorry—George is still in bed. He's very tired these days."

She attempted to put up a front for Peter and Antonella, who had arrived on foot through the little gateway that opened onto the Rio Terro Antonio Foscarini. Later she would let her mask fall. Diana MacLarren, in a dressing gown, her hair in disarray, went through the house, calling out, and eventually managed to rouse Fernando, who condescended to carry the new arrivals' luggage up to their rooms. Peter, who was still reveling in his happiness, noticed nothing, and Antonella was lost in her own thoughts.

"You'll have to forgive the mess. Help isn't what it used to be in Venice."

Bottles and empty glasses stood about on tables . . . and beneath Diana MacLarren's eyes there were gray-violet circles. Peter Charley, who had been in love with her for a few months during their young days in Cambridge, did not notice them either. The explanations he felt compelled to give concerning Antonella's presence were like the excuses a child makes before he has been accused of any wrongdoing.

"Miss Walden is one of my students, and she's an excellent photographer."

"Oh, yes?" Diana MacLarren glanced back over her shoulder. "I've put her in the room next to yours. I hope that will be convenient."

Then she went off toward the kitchen to see to dinner . . . or so she said.

George MacLarren did not put in an appearance until seven that evening. As the years of his residence in Venice had gone by, he had grown more somber, more bitter, more prone to a heavy irony that he directed to everything around him. It was as though he felt called upon to protect himself from any sensitivity or openness he might feel with regard to other people. I knew George MacLarren well. At twenty he had published two novels that the critics had praised with just enough reservations to give him the urge to write a third. Yet he had not done so. Shunted from Ankara to Berlin—where he had witnessed the horrors of 1919–1920—Spain, which he had loathed, and Peru or Ecuador, with their shoddiness that had taught him to be indifferent— the Indians, the poor, were dying like flies there in those days—he had gradually withdrawn into himself. As for Diana, ten years younger than he, she too had gradually abandoned what had for a long time been her reason for living: those huge, brutal canvases filled with nightmarish figures she had painted from Berlin to Ecuador. She had stopped painting at the same time George had given up writing and, like her husband, had sought refuge in the restorative virtues of gin and whiskey, consolation for her lost youth, her beauty. She was gossiped about in Venice for her short, unhappy flings with various young men about town, affairs about which George feigned indifference. They lived apart, destroying each other, in the dark, echoing rooms of the Foscarini Palace, in a torpor from which only the duties of George's consular post—soirées, meetings, cocktail parties—which he

managed to fulfil despite everything roused them and saved them from
utter collapse.

"That's why I say that Antonella woke us up, in a way," George
MacLarren had said once, when he had given up drink for a month
or two before he went under completely.

He had been instantly attracted by Antonella's youth, but he had
also discerned beneath her gaiety that deep, inner seriousness she became increasingly less able to conceal.

At dinner, which was meager and badly served, George MacLarren
and his wife led the conversation, making ironic comments about the
hard times they were experiencing. Peter Charley, preoccupied by his
dreams of happiness, seemed oblivious to the sharp tones in which his
two friends addressed each other. Only Antonella realized the extent
to which the MacLarrens, who had once been in love but who existed
now in a state of total indifference and lost illusions, had drifted apart.
Whether discussing the food before them, about which MacLarren
made several disobliging remarks, or life in Venice, which they both
criticized contemptuously, each seemed eager to outdo the other in
bitterness and acid comment.

"You must forgive us, my dear," MacLarren finally said to Antonella, "but you are seeing two rare specimens, pure products of the
British Empire on its last legs. After it, the deluge—and after us,
nothing!"

Diana's gaze froze for an instant: yes, she had been beautiful once;
she had once been twenty. I can remember that Diana MacLarren—
Diana Brush in those days—galloping headlong on a white horse
through the countryside around Abergavenny in South Wales. That
Diana still remembered George's poems, his novels: "After us, nothing!"

At that moment, despite the passionate attention he was devoting to
his new assistant, Peter Charley should have taken Diana's hand. But
then, we never know, do we? Or not until too late . . .

When Diana had accompanied Antonella to her room and had herself retired for the night, MacLarren and Charley remained alone in
the vast salon with its painted, tattered furniture, too real to be the
film set it so resembled.

"I'm afraid we haven't given that child a very savory foretaste of
middle age," MacLarren muttered.

He got up to pour another drink, and Peter, on the broken-down sofa, agreed for once to a second whiskey.

"I think she has all the virtues of youth and that whatever gloom or sorrow there may be will pass her by without touching her."

She had managed to deceive him, too, to appear to him as an innocent child. Had that really been her intention?

"You mean things touch her without really corrupting her?"

"Perhaps . . ."

George MacLarren gave what sounded like a nasty laugh, his famous bitter laugh that resounds throughout this adventure. "Of course, I don't know her, but I don't think she's that innocent. . . ."

"Oh yes, she is innocent. . . ." Leaning back against the couch, his eyes half closed, Peter Charley watched the flames crackling in the fireplace. "Oh yes, she is innocent. . . ." And in a voice that the unaccustomed alcohol made almost toneless, he tried to explain all that Antonella meant to him, what she had taught him about the virtues of innocence, about spontaneity, about her freshness and her determination to get her own way that left him breathless.

"With her, you see, I suddenly feel both like an old man—I'm so much older than she!—and like a boy her own age: the youth fermenting in her is so strong, so healthy, that she communicates it to me; it's as though she had inoculated me with a vaccine against bitterness, fatigue, lassitude. . . ."

He stared into space and talked, and everything, all his confused feelings since his first anger towards Antonella in the restaurant car had suddenly abated and he had become aware of her, assumed a coherent, logical form in his mind. He was in love with Antonella, that was clear! His wife, all the women he had ever known, had been nothing but shadows. Only Antonella had given him this zest for living, seeing, grasping with both hands for beauty. Just as Antonella greedily ate her breakfast!

"So you're in love. . . ." George MacLarren summed it all up.

Peter Charley rose and went over to the fireplace. "Yes, I'm in love. You're right. I'm in love. . . ."

George MacLarren shook his head. "I envy you, you know."

And when Peter Charley had gone up to his room, the consul stayed in his chair by the fire for a long time. A bottle of whiskey was within reach, the only mistress who would never deceive him.

Peter had tiptoed into Antonella's room and listened to the girl's breathing; she was asleep. For a second he had been about to go toward the bed, to wake her up, embrace her—but, held back by the puritanism so deeply instilled in him by twenty years of London academic life, he turned and gently closed the door behind him. At the end of the corridor, a watchful shadow waited until Charley had entered his own room, and then it faded away. How could Charley have known that Antonella would never again be the laughing, open girl who had given herself to him so generously in the train from London to Venice, blinded as he was by the innocence of first love? Without his knowing it, and without her awareness of it yet, she had undergone an irreversible change—Venice suffered under the fascist boot—a change that had totally destroyed her marvelous innocence. The city had turned her into someone else.

The next morning, however, was one of those November days that occur in Venice only in rare and happy years. The sky was blue, the water in the canals was blue and the Giudecca across the water was like a white, luminous frieze of abstract motifs—palazzos, churches, that seemed to be placed there solely to give relief to the horizon. There were the cries of sea gulls, the hooting of barges anchored at the entrance to the San Marco basin; the sun was like the sun of early springtime. Peter Charley awakened with his heart full of the same euphoria he had felt the previous evening. In a few minutes he was dressed and ready to go out, eager to set to work.

In the kitchen, Diana MacLarren was preparing a pot of very black coffee. "Do you want some?"

He forgot that he had drunk nothing but tea in the morning for more than thirty years.

"I've warmed you a brioche."

Diana, her acerbity and bitterness of the evening before having evaporated overnight, seemed almost young again. "She was truly beautiful once," Peter thought as he spread honey on the slice of brioche she handed him; a moment later, he corrected himself: "She *is* beautiful." She had pale blue eyes, a tanned complexion, black hair touched with gray falling in a wavy mass around her face. This morning, Diana MacLarren was making a real effort with her appearance, and at the same time she had regained something of her youth.

"It's good to see you again," she said, sitting down next to him on a white wooden chair. "It's nice, being here like this, the two of us."

Peter, who was looking at her with the old tenderness that went back to their days in Cambridge, replied that he, too, found it pleasant to be with her in the city he had always loved. Diana's face grew dark. To her—like Antonella—Venice, once so bound up with all her feelings and affections, had gradually turned into a perfumed trap, a diabolic snare that still reflected back the delicate arabesques of moving water, but where anxiety seemed now to ooze from every leprous facade of its abandoned palazzos.

"Yes, Venice . . ."

Caught up in his good spirits, Peter Charley did not pay any real attention to Diana's words. He was isolated in a world in which politics was art and Veronese and Tiepolo the only masters. Diana was trying to tell him that Venice had become a city living on borrowed time in which hatred and violence lurked on every street corner, at the edge of every canal, only waiting for a propitious moment to erupt.

"You mustn't think George is unaware of everything that's going on. It's just that he doesn't want to talk about it."

George had felt fear mounting, as had she—the police gradually being shorn of their power by the blackshirts, suspects being tracked down, lists drawn up, communists and liberals brought in for questioning.

"So you can understand how the beauty of a Palladian facade or the purity of some Bellini virgin . . ."

Peter's surprise grew as he listened to her. Though so removed from everything foreign to his beloved painting, all at once he began to understand that Diana MacLarren, whom he had always thought preoccupied with herself, was now experiencing a whole world of emotions that were completely strange. When she told him of a frightful scene she had witnessed in front of the church of San Trovaso—an old man had been attacked by a group of teenagers and kicked senseless under the indifferent eyes of the police—he was unwilling to believe her.

"Aren't you exaggerating a bit?" In Venice, the home of Carpaccio, Titian, Tintoretto . . .

But Diana's voice became even more serious: "You can't imagine the kind of things that are now going on. You've no idea . . ." She sat facing him, her cup of black coffee grown cold between her hands. "And we're too cowardly to do anything about it. Or even to try to tell the truth! You've said it yourself: is it really possible in the shadow of Titians or Tintorettos!"

He would have questioned her further in an attempt to understand, but Antonella entered the room. She looked tired; she told them she had slept badly.

"You see," Diana MacLarren said to Peter, "the air of Venice isn't what it used to be!"

Shortly afterwards, he set out for the Palazzo Labia.

A specialist in Venetian painting, an art historian trained in the school of Tietze and Hestler, to work from originals, Peter Charley had undertaken to draw up an inventory of the Tiepolo frescoes that still existed in the sites where they had been painted—the story of Iphigenia or of Rinaldo and Armida at the Valmarana; the apotheosis of the Pisani family at Stra; and, on this occasion, the sumptuous groupings in the Palazzo Labia, the meeting of Cleopatra and Antony in the presence of slaves, goddesses, lackeys. In those distant days when photographic documentation was available only to specialists in museums, he had come to Venice for the purpose of preparing an exhaustive catalog, accompanied by critical notes, which a London company wished to publish in an inexpensive edition. In his way, Peter Charley was in the vanguard of the distribution of works of art in reproduction, in its infancy in those days.

On this first morning, when he found himself inside the vast, dilapidated salons of the Palazzo Labia with Antonella, he was embarking on the preliminary stages of his research.

"What I'm after is a group of photographs that will be as inclusive as possible, omitting none of the details in the frescoes. Afterwards I can choose . . ."

At his side, Antonella was giving instructions to the Italian photographer who had been assigned to assist them: here the close-up of a face, there a hand, and that marble inlay over the festive table.

"I want to be able to play on the feelings that inspired Tiepolo as you would on a keyboard. A blue eye, blue-black hair, can have the same erotic intensity as a naked breast or limb, an undraped thigh: you have to be able to bring out that eroticism and separate it from the cloud of mere decoration that sometimes obscures it."

From a distance a man was watching them. He wore a black suit and a long raincoat, belted at the waist. Peter Charley indicated him to Antonella with a jerk of his chin. "Our guardian angel?"

The man was a police inspector placed at their disposal by the Italian tourist bureau to facilitate their access to the various monuments and palazzos in which they were to work, to assist them, as someone at the bureau had told them, should unforeseen problems arise.

"He's watching us!"

Antonella looked worried. But Peter Charley seemed to attach little importance to this unasked-for "assistant"—as though the perpetual presence of a policeman were no more than a formality. Peter Charley's world was distant from reality . . . Antonella, however, made her feelings clear: "He looks like a killer!"

Peter laughed—so long as he didn't disturb their work. The girl had set down the small camera she was operating herself.

"That's the only thing you care about, isn't it—your work?"

He nodded: yes, it was the only thing that mattered, but there was also his joy at working in her company.

"It's as though the evocative power of these Tiepolo nudes were suddenly speaking to me in their own language, and I can suddenly understand every word!"

Without replying, Antonella took up her camera.

Peter Charley's first day's work must have been intoxicating, alone with the most sumptuous frescoes left us by eighteenth-century Venice, in the company of a girl such as he had never known before. He went from room to room of the vast Palazzo Labia, giving instructions— "Here you can feel Veronese's influence on Tiepolo. Just look at that grouping of figures . . ."—and at one point he drew Antonella aside. "If you knew how happy I am, being here with you!"

His happiness: he had come to believe in it so strongly that on the second day of his visit he informed George MacLarren that he intended to get a divorce. "After what I have experienced with this girl, I can't go back . . . do you understand? I can't go on living as I did before."

He barely listened to his friend's advice that he wait a bit, that he not be hasty, that he give things time. . . . "Wait? Why, when I've found a girl like Antonella?"

But on that second night, as on the first, Antonella had gone up to bed early, and she was already asleep when Charley went to her room a second time. As he had on the previous evening, he returned to his own room alone—and the shadow that spied on him from an alcove in the long corridor was the shadow of Fernando, the butler, the informer.

It was scarcely surprising that Antonella should be tired. When she and Peter packed up their bags at the end of their day's work, she asked him to excuse her, and, on the pretext of visiting an old childhood girlfriend, she started out on her long quest through the streets of Venice that was to make Peter so anxious that he gradually became a man at the end of his tether. Antonella had come to Venice in search of something, and she was looking for it.

First she went to the old library in the modern street that runs alongside the church of San Moise. There she waited for a bookseller who had been a friend of her mother's—the anarchist who had lived amidst the dilapidation of the Palazzo Barbaro—and with him she had a long conversation. Don Gasparo, however, a specialist in books about old Venice, apparently had not been able to tell her what she wanted to know, for she left him and set out for the Campo Santa Maddalena.

In that ideal Venice where I used to imagine I would eventually live one day, the tiny church of Santa Maddalena, with its Masonic symbols, has a special place. Situated on a canal bordered by a covered passageway, at the corner of a square with a well in its center that serves as a playground for hordes of children who scatter like a flock of sparrows at the arrival of a stranger, Santa Maddalena has always seemed to me like a temple for some forbidden cult of little girls and affable prostitutes, who combine in fleecing tourists or in loosening the purse strings of any half-way sympathetic passerby. It was there that Antonella knocked on the closed shutters of a shop until a shrewish woman dressed in tatters finally opened the door to her. . . .

Later, the man in the raincoat, the man assigned to assist Peter Charley in the Palazzo Labia, was to see Antonella leave the sordid shop on the Campo Santa Maddalena and walk to the Merceria. In the maze of streets, full of pedestrians at eight in the evening, at once a meeting place and an endless labyrinth, she managed to get away from him, and the raincoated policeman had had to trail home.

As for Antonella, she did not return to the Foscarini Palace until nine-thirty, and she was exhausted.

"Sometimes it's difficult to be in love with kids like that, when we aren't twenty years old ourselves!" Sunk into an armchair, George Mac-

Larren was trying to pour himself a glass of whiskey with a trembling hand. "But it's even more difficult to stop loving them!"

With a somewhat embarrassed laugh, Peter Charley had told him what had happened the night before—and the night before that—about Antonella's deep slumber. The consul had tried to find an explanation for the girl's behavior, an explanation his friend was unwilling to accept.

"It's not that! She's just tired, that's all."

Insidiously, however, his doubts began to grow. When MacLarren told him about a party he was planning in his honor, Peter Charley barely listened. What was Antonella doing prowling the streets of Venice alone that morning, the previous evening? Later, back at the Palazzo Labia, he had told her what he wanted her to do for him, and it was clear that she was not even listening to his instructions.

"But Antonella, it's not all that difficult! All you have to do is focus on the little blackamoor with the lace collar!"

The little angel-blackamoor with his girlish features was indeed adorable. Antonella had started: "I beg your pardon! I was thinking about something else!"

"That was obvious!"

And even though Peter Charley wanted terribly to know what was on his assistant's mind, he had not dared ask her, and another day had gone by without his having been able to recapture the emotion of their journey. At five-thirty Antonella had left him, as she had the evening before.

The policeman following her found himself led to a cinema, to a youth club and to the house of a priest who lived next to Santa Maria Formosa.

Finally, on the third evening, Peter attempted to talk to her. George MacLarren was staring dully at a newspaper he was holding upside down, and Diana had gone to the kitchen to wash up the dishes that the maid had left undone.

Antonella seemed very unhappy. She was beginning to sense what Peter was feeling, and I know that she regretted it.

"But what do you want me to say? Of course, nothing has changed!" she exclaimed.

They were sitting in a loggia overlooking the entrance hall and the time-worn white stone staircase—on which their adventure was to have its tragic denouement a few days later. At the moment, seated on an ebony chair inlaid with mother-of-pearl, Antonella was nervously puffing on a cigarette.

"And you know very well it's not the same," he was saying. "The other evening in the train . . ."

Antonella took his hand. "Please, Peter . . . I'm very tired right now. It's Venice, the atmosphere . . ."

And, Peter Charley was tempted to add, all those walks you take alone through the streets the minute we finish our work . . . but he kept silent.

"Please be nice, don't press me," the girl concluded.

On that evening, as on the others, Peter Charley did not press her.

Three days later, as they were once again at work in the Palazzo Labia, a message arrived for Antonella. Its bearer, a twelve-year-old boy, had been told to say that one of her girl cousins wanted to meet her and would be waiting in an alleyway off the Rialto. For a moment Antonella hesitated: a few yards away the plainclothes policeman in the raincoat lit a cigarette, tossing the match on the floor—not quite the behavior of an inspector employed by the Office for the Preservation of Historical Monuments. Charley, who had not noticed her hesitation, urged her to go.

"Go ahead! The light has begun to fade anyway, and I think I'll knock off, too." The knowledge that she was going to meet a female cousin had somehow reassured him.

Antonella's eyes met those of the man in the raincoat, who was feigning total indifference.

"I'll meet you back at the consulate." And she left, followed a few seconds later by the plainclothesman, hot on her trail.

They walked for a time, one after the other, along the Rio Terra San Leonardo and the Strada Nuova, and then Antonella turned left towards Santi Apostoli. The policeman was following only a few yards behind her, making no attempt to conceal himself.

"I'm sure she was unaware of him," MacLarren was to tell me. "When Antonella had last been in Italy, three years earlier, the situation was completely different, and all that she had heard since from friends in England was only 'hearsay.' She had to see things for herself in order to realize finally . . ."

And, she was to realize, finally, indeed!

After having passed the church in which Tiepolo's sublime Saint

Lucia lies surrounded by candles like some profane Madonna, she turned into the narrow street leading to the cul-de-sac where she had been told to go. She had just entered the alleyway when out of nowhere a hand was put over her mouth.

"Say nothing!" The voice was that of a youngish man with a Venetian accent. She tried to struggle, but his arm around her waist drew her back violently. "Don't move!"

She tried to cry out, to free herself. But the man who had drawn her back into a doorway held her fast. A few steps away she saw the policeman in the raincoat hurry by in the street, obviously concerned at having lost sight of her.

"Don't move!" The man whispered into her ear, and his hold on her relaxed imperceptibly. "Follow me. . . ."

She turned. The man facing her was in his thirties, with a thick black mustache and curly hair. He wore a gray suit, and his shirt, which had once been white, was open at the throat. He was not wearing a necktie.

"I'm a friend of Mario's. . . ."

That was all she needed to hear; she had reached her destination. Peter, of course, was still in the dark, but he had begun to think that Titian, Veronese and Tiepolo were not sufficient for a man's happiness. And all over Venice, men in black were lurking. . . .

A few minutes later, Antonella and her guide reached the top floor of a narrow house overlooking the Calle Zenordeni and a canal. From the window they saw the policeman in the raincoat retracing his steps; he noted down the number of the house at the end of the cul-de-sac before striding away, probably in search of reinforcements. Only then did Beppo—that was the name of Antonella's abductor—signal for her to follow him.

They were now in a boat moving slowly across the lagoon. Despite its huge, noisy motor, it was one of those old, flat-bottomed barges that are used to move heavy cargo on the inner canals of the city. A little old man with a cigar between his teeth, dressed as a sailor, was at the rudder.

"That's Antonio. You can trust him," Beppo said to her.

The barge entered a narrow canal between two bare, low islands. Antonella and her guide were lying on the floor of the barge; Beppo was not really hiding, but it was just as well to stay out of sight of any patrolling police boat or the customs. He lit a cigarette and finally felt able to speak.

"With all your searching and running all over Venice, you might have ruined everything for us!"

He seemed amused at the girl's surprised look. Yet he knew that both of them risked serious danger and that other, even more real dangers, threatened them.

"But what about Mario? He told me to write to him as soon as I could, but I didn't know where to find him."

"You should have waited! You should have waited for a signal!"

And as the boat moved towards the tiny island of Saint-Francis-of-the-Desert, on which a community of Franciscans had lived since time immemorial, Beppo explained to Antonella what had happened. Three days later she passed these explanations on to Diana, who told me, along with Antonella's version, what happened next.

Half-Italian, Antonella had remained in touch with a group of friends who formed part of a small network of determined opponents of the Mussolini regime, which was then being set in place. Through students living abroad, school friends or mere tourists, they were thus able to exchange a certain amount of information—if not calls for help —between London and Paris, Rome and Venice. In those early years of fascism, Italy was a paradoxical place, a place where on the surface everything seemed completely normal. Tourists were able to move about freely, and Italians who so desired could leave the country un-hindered. Behind the facade of liberalism, however—one that even a cursory examination of the controlled press or the tone of official speeches would even then have sufficed to raze—things were far more somber. Anyone suspected for any reason of not being in total agree-ment with the new ideas was put under close surveillance; their actions were spied upon, their movements watched, their correspondence opened and read. The police were circumvented by an immense net-work of parallel, but official, organizations. Without having returned to Venice, Antonella in London had been an essential element in that movement of ideas and people. In addition, at one time she had been engaged to a certain Mario Ruspoli, a Communist student who was wanted by the police and of whom she had had no news for several weeks . . . thus the motive behind her trip to Italy.

"First of all, you shouldn't have dashed here to see Mario; you shouldn't have left without telling anyone. And since your arrival, you've been behaving like a child."

Antonella, who had taken umbrage at his tone, shrugged. "Then why did you send that boy to me a while ago?"

It was her companion's turn to shrug. "You'd already caused enough trouble, hadn't you? Going around to see all our friends . . ."

She tried to protest. "I had no way of knowing I was being followed."

"You only had to turn around and look behind you! Now Mario has had an accident, and things have changed. Now we need you . . . we really need you!"

At that point, and not before, Antonella grew pale.

When the boat finally docked at the small island of Saint-Francis-of-the-Desert, they were met by a monk with a serious expression.

"Quick! It's no use attracting attention!"

The garden of the monastery was still in bloom; chickens and ducks wandered about it, pecking at the ground. It breathed peace and tranquillity, a strange background for the conspiratorial air of the brother who guided them.

"The police came this morning. They claimed there was an influenza epidemic, and they tried to force one of their doctors on us. The abbot managed to get rid of them, but they will be back. . . ."

They traversed echoing corridors. A panel hung on the wall, a sign in black and white: "No women beyond this point," but neither Father Bruno—for that was his name—nor Beppo paid any attention to it.

"Your friend is in a cell on the second floor."

A moment later, Antonella was in Mario's arms.

His story—and that of Beppo—was simple: a group of Blackshirts had burst into their meeting place near the Rialto, where Mario Ruspoli and his friends published a newspaper—not even a clandestine newspaper—a newsletter for a student organization. It contained no hint of politics . . . at least on the surface. For those who knew how to read between the lines, it was a mine of information: meeting places, announcements were distributed throughout the region in its columns —and not only for students. Who had betrayed them? Who had denounced them?

"It was that bastard Scarpio, I know it!" Beppo muttered.

However, Scarpio had disappeared, and—most important—one of the attackers, a leader of the Blackshirts, had been killed in the fighting that had preceded the destruction of the printing press. The man's companions had recognized his attacker despite the confusion in that ground-floor workshop: it had been Mario who, wounded himself, had managed to escape just before the police arrived.

"You can see why I haven't had time to write to you since then!"

He had first hidden out on the *entresol* of a palazzo on the Grand Canal, and then his friends had brought him to the monastery, where he had been concealed for three weeks.

"But you cannot stay here any longer, Mario," Don Bruno said. "The father superior has told me to warn you. Our relations with the authorities are too shaky as it is: I wouldn't want to make them worse."

Father Bruno had grown even more serious, but he had nonetheless brought bread, wine and cheese. Antonella, ravenous as ever, fell to.

"Since I'm the one who brought you here, I now have to ask you to help me out of this mess!"

Mario had taken Antonella's hand. He was pale, his cheekbones prominent, and the knife wound in his thigh had not yet healed; he seemed to be shaking with fever. He saw that Antonella had noticed his condition.

"In addition, I think I'm coming down with an attack of malaria!" He attempted to smile but failed. The pain in his thigh made him grimace.

Antonella leaned over him. "'You've got to get out of here!"

A wave of bygone tenderness, of memories and images of the childhood they had spent side by side in those stately mansions along the Brenta, flowed into her mind.

"I'll get you out, you'll see . . ."

The three men looked at each other. Of course, with a British passport, living in the consul's house, Antonella might be able to help them. But how?

Antonella returned to the Palazzo Foscarini to find her friends concerned about her. It was almost ten o'clock at night, and—probably on the urging of the plainclothesman—an inspector from the prefecture of police had called with a request that the two English visitors present themselves the following morning at a commissariat located on the far side of town, in order to "regularize" their situation. Peter

ANTONELLA

Charley had begun to protest, but George MacLarren stopped him.

"They're only doing it to help, you have to understand. They're making it easy for you to get into all the places you want to visit, so it's only normal that they know your intentions every two or three days."

"But it's a police summons!"

"So? It's only a formality, old boy. A mere formality!"

Diana motioned to Peter not to insist; George was having one of his bad days. Indeed, before long he would withdraw to his room, after having passed through the kitchen to collect a bottle of cheap whiskey . . . all the alcohol left in the house.

"Times are hard, old chap! Not even any scotch! This whiskey was probably made in Ethiopia!" He gave a deep laugh, but his eyes were unsmiling. And Fernando, the butler, watched him as he climbed the vast staircase.

"That one," Diana exclaimed, referring to Fernando. "We'll have to get together the courage to kick him out on his ass."

She was fully aware, however, that neither she nor George would ever work up that much courage. She then shut herself in the salon with Peter.

"Don't worry . . . we'll hear your girlfriend if she knocks on the door."

Peter joined her in another cup of very black coffee. Then with a nervous gesture he pushed back a lock of hair that had fallen over his forehead.

"I know, old man; it's difficult!" Diana murmured. She understood Peter's devouring concern. "I've been through the same thing myself! He was twenty-five. . . ."

She might have continued, but Peter stood up and went over to her. He looked down at her: yes, this woman, his friend, had been twenty once herself. She had been beautiful, very beautiful, and for a time he had believed he was in love with her. The long rides together on horseback in Wales . . .

"Oh, Peter!"

She had risen, too, and she threw herself into his arms, weeping. I can see them so clearly, those two middle-aged people trying to convince each other that it was all over for them; I can even see myself in them. Yet in those days, I was barely thirty-five!

When Antonella finally knocked at the outer door, she crossed the vestibule rapidly, muttering that she was tired and wanted to go straight to bed. The expression on the face of Professor Charley of London University at that moment was very like that on my own at the same moment, a few houses further along the Zattere, just because some little Venetian prostitute was about to leave me! She was seventeen, with firm breasts and a tiny mole, and she had hips that moved beneath your hands like a small wild animal always ready to escape.

"I don't understand anything," Peter Charley muttered as he returned to sink down beside Diana in an armchair.

"There comes a time," Diana told him, "when one begins to understand things only too well."

I can imagine what Peter Charley was feeling. Above all, I can imagine the dismay the girl's sudden change in attitude had caused this man who until then had thought of nothing but his work, his research, and then suddenly discovered a world of tenderness in which everything was new. Even though his ecstasy had lasted for only a few hours, was it possible for him to return to earth? Above all, after such passionate playfulness, such playful passion, how could a young woman so suddenly—and so matter-of-factly—become totally indifferent?

For that was what Peter Charley now sensed in Antonella: indifference.

"Come," Diana murmured, "let's go up to bed. It's late."

On the wall of the corridor leading to their rooms, a bad copy of a pastel by Rosalba Carriera smiled ironically down at them. . . .

Diana herself told me the next part of the story.

It was seven in the morning, and she had already come downstairs to the kitchen to prepare the strong coffee so characteristic of that household, as was her habit.

"Some Venetian music was playing on the radio, Cavalli, I think . . ."

The pale, flat light had already begun to seep through the narrow windows that overlooked the Rio Terra Antonio Foscarini. She was pouring boiling water over the coffee when Antonella entered.

"Am I disturbing you?" She had recovered her smile, and she seemed to be a young girl again, alert and gay, as she bustled around the kitchen. "Can I help?"

As she prepared toast and squeezed orange juice, Antonella chatted to Diana about her life. She spoke—as she had never done before—

about her anarchist mother, who had been the daughter of one of the city's oldest families, and the years she had spent in hiding.

"The Palazzo Barbaro—when I think I used to play hide-and-seek there, while in the next room my mother listened every second for fear the police would come . . ."

From palazzo to palazzo, their conversation inevitably led them to the Palazzo Foscarini in which they found themselves that morning, and which Antonella suddenly expressed an urgent desire to explore.

"I'm sure there are lots of pictures, marvelous things."

"I'll give you the complete tour," Diana said.

She took down a huge skeleton key that hung on the inside of a cupboard door and led the girl through the house.

How can I describe to you the world of staircases, corridors, shut-up, unused rooms, hidden alcoves in the "small" Palazzo Foscarini? It had been built at the end of the fifteenth century as a place for Senator Antonio Foscarini to hide when he had been unjustly accused of having passed on the secrets of the Venetian Republic to some foreigners in the service of the Duchess of Arundel. There the Doge's police had found him, and he had been sentenced to die on the scaffold following his summary trial: a few weeks later, those who had borne witness against him had also been caught out, and they had suffered the same fate. At the "great" Palazzo Foscarini adjoining, a delegation had arrived in great pomp to begin his official rehabilitation. During the work undertaken to fill in the canal flowing alongside the palazzo, the street that was to be the Rio Terra Antonio Foscarini, a section of the "great" palazzo had been razed, and the "small" palazzo was all that was left to remind anyone of the unfortunate senator and his fate. But there were still Pietro Muttoni's frescoes in the vast dining room, the miniatures of Palma Vecchio that had once hung in the main gallery and were now in the Academmia to testify to its past grandeur . . . as well as its vast maze of corridors, stairways and alcoves.

Antonella followed Diana from cellar to attic with unusual attention.

"I must admit, I began to wonder about it right from the start," Diana told me when I questioned her later.

Antonella's entire attitude, her exclamations, her sudden curiosity— "And where does that little stairway lead?"—were enough to arouse anyone's suspicions. Yet Diana MacLarren methodically showed her everything . . . to such an extent that when Peter Charley appeared two hours later, he found them sitting down together to a second break-fast.

Diana whispered to Peter, with a conspiratorial smile: "Your girl-friend seems to have regained her good spirits, as you can see."

Two hours later, Peter and Antonella were once again at work in the Palazzo Labia. However, their usual photographer had been re-placed by a young man who explained that his predecessor had been taken ill. The plainclothes policeman in his raincoat noted the name and address of Peter Charley's new assistant in his small, black-leather notebook, and Antonella, who seemed worried, paid scant attention to the instructions Peter gave her concerning their morning's work.

"That woman's face has all the glory of a woman who knows she is deceiving a man and that her victory will be absolute, ephemeral, and brutal. . . ."

Peter Charley went on describing the frescoes, as though the girl's recovery of her good mood at breakfast had filled him with renewed hope.

"And yet, such tenderness in her smile . . ."

Finally Antonella set to work. But when they stopped to rest, a time during which they usually went to have coffee together at a bar on the San Geremia piazza, Antonella complained she had a headache and disappeared. Alone in the palazzo, Charley ordered a coffee to be sent in, and he was wandering through the deserted upper stories when he heard the sound of voices whispering. All at once his fears flooded back: what if Antonella . . . He opened a door, pushed aside a hanging and saw Antonella and the photographer talking softly to-gether in a window recess. The young man had hold of Antonella's arm, and she was standing very close to him, nearly in his arms.

Frozen, Peter Charley returned to the *piano nobile*. There, standing before "Cleopatra's Triumph," that "absolute, total, ephemeral female triumph," was the policeman in his raincoat, looking at his watch.

"It was on that same evening that I gave the small party I had planned for Peter, the one I had told him about."

We were on the terrace of the Hotel Monaco and Grand Canal. Before us, the continual movement of the *motoscafi* and gondolas was interrupted from time to time by a larger *vaporetto*. At the table next to ours, two youngsters in black shirts were arguing loudly, laughing. In a rattan chair, his hand trembling as usual as he lifted his glass of whiskey to his lips, George MacLarren that day seemed to me like a very old man. And the same old man was the boy who had once written verses filled with hope, an ironic, clever novel about a boy's sentimental education at Eton. . . .

"I'd invited a few people from the English colony to meet him, a few professors and art historians, painters, artists: none of the provincial civil or military authorities. I was still taking pains not to compromise my own position."

However, Peter Charley had been late in arriving at the small cocktail party in the large salon and the gallery on the ground floor, beneath the copies of Palma Vecchio. He had come straight from the Palazzo Labia, he said, but once again he had lost Antonella along the way.

"If you only knew the state I'm in . . ."

His friend took him by the arm: he had to put up a front, at least for the duration of the party. Peter barely heard him.

"I'm going up to change."

The guests had already begun to arrive downstairs. It was the usual fauna—and flora?—to be found at such gatherings: elderly ladies who now lived for nothing but just such cocktail parties, like crested pheasants leading gigolos in their wake, a countess flanked by her balding husband on one side and her bejeweled lover on the other. There were a few professors, to, among them Dino Grossi of the University of Padua, who had written a few second-rate pages on Venice but who was being turned into a master of art philosophy by the present regime.

"Professor Charley will be down in a minute."

George and Diana greeted their guests; both of them were good at their jobs, like a couple falling apart and only able to function normally when performing professional duties. George MacLarren had put on an almost-new suit, while Diana was wearing a long gown with folds that clung to her suddenly rejuvenated form.

When Antonella arrived, both the consul and his wife were able to breathe more freely: Peter Charley might now, at last, condescend to join them. And indeed, a few minutes later Antonella—who had obviously been running and was out of breath when she arrived back at the palazzo—came back downstairs, after having gone up to repair her makeup, with Peter Charley on her arm.

"But where have you been?" Charley barely had time to whisper to her before the girl led him down to the main floor.

"Nowhere . . . I went to see a girlfriend."

How could Peter believe her a second time? But he tried to put a good face on it. And then Antonella had taken his arm.

"Please. Trust me."

They entered the crowded room.

"Tell me, Professor, that grace you see in all those women who were painted by Veronese or Tiepolo . . don't you think that perhaps it might have really been . . . grease?"

Pleased at her pun, the wife of the Venice correspondent for some obscure Scottish academic institution clapped her hands.

"Don't you think that perhaps an illustrated volume such as the one you are preparing might not perhaps be a bit . . . frivolous?"

They were very aggressive, those birds in their fine feathers invited by the British consul! However, Peter replied to their questions with indifference, all the time trying to keep his eyes on Antonella; she seemed as far removed from it all as he. Several times he noticed her consulting her watch, and his heart pounded.

Professor Grossi had cornered him and was explaining, with much gesticulation and many signs of affection, that the friendship between England and Italy extended back to the Venetian seventeenth century and that the authorities in Rome—*Il Duce* in person—would be happy to provide him with a sabbatical year in order that he could pursue his work in Venice with fitting independence.

"The government values too highly you foreign specialists who come here to study our culture not to encourage you insofar as it is able, and I've been entrusted to offer you this invitation on the highest levels."

Peter Charley suddenly realized that Antonella was no longer in the room, and he stopped listening to what Professor Grossi was saying. "If you'll excuse me . . ."

He was about to leave, to his companion's consternation, when two women who were even fatter and more grotesque than the others—and equally bedecked with fake jewelry—took him in tow.

"We are dying to ask you, my dear Professor . . ."

George MacLarren was afraid his friend would do something really rude, but Diana stepped in smoothly.

"Professor Charley will answer all your questions once he has had a drink. He has been very tired these past few days. I'm going to take him away from you for two minutes."

She led him to the buffet, holding tightly to his arm to prevent his escape. "For heaven's sake, Peter, try to respond."

"But Antonella . . ."

"Please, Peter. Later!"

Her hand gripped his arm so tightly that it was almost painful—but he went with her.

"Diana has a grip of iron when she makes up her mind," George MacLarren remarked to me later on the terrace of the Monaco and Grand Canal. For the first time since the beginning of our talk, he smiled.

As I have said, Diana had suspected something from the beginning. After she turned Peter over to one of her friends at the buffet, asking her to keep him there, she hastily left the room, only to stop, hesitating, in the vestibule.

Near the small door that gave onto the canal at water level, a gondola had just pulled up. It contained three men: Beppo, the gondolier and, of course, Mario.

"Let's hope she's on time."

Beppo looked around him. It was already dark, and there was no light on the boat. Nor were there any lights showing in the windows of the tall facades lining the Rio. At any moment, however, they might hear the roar of a police boat or, perhaps, merely the sound of the barge of some upright Venetian who would be only too happy to ingratiate himself with the authorities by giving them a piece of information that had cost him nothing.

"We were beginning to live through the darkest days of our lives . . . and that was only the beginning!"

Mario, too, was growing impatient. The wound in his leg was beginning to throb again. However, none of them moved—all they could hear was the sound of the water slapping against the decaying wall. Then the door opened at last.

"I've done all I can. . . ." Antonella was out of breath. She was holding a flashlight in her hand. "Quickly . . ."

She reached out her hand to Mario, who took it and, with a heavy movement of his body, heaved himself across the water and onto the step, rotten from the water and sticky green moss, that led up to the house. Beppo made as if to follow him, but Antonella stopped him.

"Better not. I can't get you back downstairs, and the house is full of people."

The man spoke angrily: "And was this any time to . . ."

But he was dealing with Antonella now, and she had recovered all her self-assurance once she had made up her mind to act.

"Exactly. *This* is the best time."

She emphasized the word "this." Beppo was about to protest, but he thought better of it. A second later, the gondola had slipped away down the narrow canal toward another side canal that led out to the Giudecca.

Once on the narrow staircase leading up to the main floor, Antonella became aware that she would not be capable of getting Mario up to the attic room she had discovered beneath the roof on the tour through the house with Diana. The young man was shivering all over, and he leaned on Antonella's shoulder with increasing weight. Yet she tried.

"Hold me around the waist . . . there, like that. . . ."

They began to climb again. One step, then another, then a third. Mario was about to slip away from her. She glanced back behind them: they were in total darkness, but below was the dizzying drop of the slippery stairway, and at the bottom was the open doorway leading straight to the canal. She almost shut her eyes, but then she took a tighter hold on her burden and grasped him more securely. He gave a soft moan.

"Don't be afraid, I'm here. . . ."

But she was the one who was afraid. She climbed up two more steps and came to the door to the alcove off the servants' pantry on the ground floor: she had locked it behind her, and now she had to get the skeleton key from her pocket and insert it into the keyhole. Mario had fainted and hung on her, a dead weight. At that moment the door opened.

"Quick!"

Diana stood in the doorway, holding out her hand. Between them, they managed to drag Mario up to the hideaway Antonella had prepared for him.

No one in the salon had noticed Diana's absence. The moment she had seen Mario safely installed, she sent Antonella back down to rejoin Peter, so as not to alarm him further. And she advised Antonella to avoid Fernando on the way; his feigned indifference suddenly seemed threatening to her.

"Above all, see that George doesn't suspect anything."

Thus, as if by magic, Antonella reappeared at Peter's side; she led him back to Professor Grossi who enthusiastically finished extending the invitation with which he had been entrusted.

"But I'm certain Professor Charley will accept. For that matter, I, too . . ."

She made an effort to be cordial, and as she pushed back her hair, Peter Charley looked at her in astonishment. How could anyone change so drastically, so quickly? Had the story I am now telling you not ended in tragedy, I might be giving this tale of Peter Charley's apprenticeship an almost ironic title—something like "Bringing up Peter."

"Every time I have to watch those grotesque creatures milling around and uttering the same stupid remarks they have been repeating since they were old enough to eat ravioli, I wonder why I don't chuck the whole thing and become a bum on the Zattere!"

George MacLarren had collapsed into an armchair on his guests' departure, a bottle of gin within reach to compensate for the twenty-four hours of abstinence he had forced on himself in order to play his role as a working consul with complete sobriety. Diana, facing him, knew that what he said was true: although he seemed to revive only on those occasions when he was playing his role, he hated the play . . . and, even more, the fact that he went along with it.

"Do you know what I'd do? I'd tell all those dusky penguins and cockatoos that their perfume smells to high heaven and that the skin of their asses is worn raw from kowtowing to people who despise them!"

Of course, he meant "the skin of their knees . . ." Peter smiled. After the cocktail party, Antonella had remained in the salon, and Fernando, assisted by two underlings, was placing dirty glasses on a tray one by one in total silence. It had begun to rain, and the wind was rising: already it was hitting against the windows and sounding like a storm.

"It will be *acqua alta* soon," Diana said, "high water time." The time of the November floods, when the Piazzo San Marco was often under nearly two feet of water . . .

Antonella clapped her hands: "I'd like to see that."

Diana looked at her: she could not help but admire the girl's self-control. She was to tell her so later, when they were once again alone at Mario's side.

"Oh, you know . . . It's never hard to play a part!" Her voice was bitter. And a second later she added: "What is really hard, after all, is to be serious."

She was thinking of the look Peter Charley had given her: what would happen when he found out?

. The evening dragged on until late: it was as though none of those four English people—for Antonella was at the moment behaving like a young English girl of good family on vacation—had the courage to go to bed. Who knew what anxieties lay in ambush for them there? Nevertheless, Antonella and Diana were waiting. It was not until nearly midnight that they went off to their separate rooms, and the women were finally able to return to the upper story.

Diana told me only portions of the long conversation they had then, but I know that that night the wife of my friend the consul came to know all Antonella's strength of character, her nobility. All she had done—her journey to Venice, her search for Mario—Antonella had done not so much out of love, although she had loved Mario once and must certainly have loved him still—but out of a sense of duty. Her help had been needed and she had come, just as, a few weeks later, she would leave. But she realized the pain she had caused Peter, and it made her suffer.

"If I could make him understand . . ."

That she had used him? She attempted to explain. "It's not really that. Of course, when I persuaded his assistant to let me come in her place, I did lie a bit; I couldn't do otherwise . . . but later, what happened on the train . . . No, that wasn't part of the plan!"

Before she had found Mario again, she had never foreseen a situation like the one in which she was now enmeshed. With Peter Charley, she had started by acting the part of a giddy girl; with the help of the champagne—and with a certain tenderness as well, for Peter Charley in his way could be very touching—she had played her role too well. Until the end.

"It was when I found myself back in Venice—this atmosphere, all these anxieties, that I realized how foolish I had been!"

But then it had been too late, and Peter Charley had become the wounded creature he now was, not understanding why he had been thrown over so quickly—two seconds of hope, a glance at a Tiepolo, and it had all been over—by a girl who had seemed to love him.

"George, too—he mustn't suspect anything."

Diana was thinking: do they have any idea of the things we are capable of, our men, those grown-up children when hurt! Since Mario was beginning to mutter in his delirium, she told Antonella to stay with him and went back down to her room. Alone, Antonella finally gave way. Lying close, pressed against the body of the boy she had once loved, she cried for a long time, shaken with sobs, her hair in disarray, her makeup running down her face in long black and violet streaks and onto the white pillowcase. She did not sleep until dawn.

Peter did not sleep at all. At two in the morning, he had gone into the girl's room and found it empty.

The next day was a morose one. Their usual photographer had returned, but Antonella's tired face, her swollen eyes, betrayed her almost sleepless night, and Peter Charley was in little better shape. Up until now, she had been acting on the spur of the moment, out of need—to get to Venice, to find Mario, to take him to the Foscarini Palazzo, to hide him there—but now she had time to think. And she did not know what to do, either about Peter, to whom she would eventually have to say something, or about Mario, who could not remain in his new hiding place for long. She had to come to some decision.

Peter Charley brooded over his own disappointment: he felt exhausted, breathless, cornered. This man with fixed ambitions, up to a certain point concerned solely with his art, his work, had been turned into what Peter Charley now was all because of a simple love affair—all because of a woman!—a weak, empty man wandering through the echoing rooms of the Palazzo Labia, staring vacantly and weakly at the loveliest frescoes in Venice.

It was Diana—and she alone—who gained new strength from this adventure. Helping Antonella, saving Mario meant learning to begin to live again. I asked her why she had thrown herself so wholeheartedly into that desperate affair, and she had replied, smiling, with the truth Peter had already made me realize: "But don't you see that, in their way, those youngsters saved me?"

She meant Antonella and Mario. During the two days Mario Ruspoli was to stay in the Foscarini Palazzo, Diana had spent long hours beside his bed. She had talked to him; she had listened to him talk.

His youth, perhaps his beauty, but also the struggle in which he was engaged all moved Diana deeply, and with a maternal tenderness— ever so slightly incestuous—she had embraced both Mario and Antonella.

"Before, I was an old, dead thing. I no longer believed in anything. Suddenly they gave me back a taste for living." And she added: "In a way, it's also thanks to them that George, too, learned how to live again."

She was thinking of his terrible rage on the evening of the *acqua alta*, George MacLarren and the bloody face on the black and white tiles, the age-worn floor of the Foscarini Palazzo.

It was Diana, in any event, who had the idea that would, she thought, save Mario. Diana, washed out with exhaustion, that poor, fallen goddess, would be their *deus ex machina*. . . . It all seemed quite simple. She needed only to steal from George's safe a blank passport and make it out to a certain Mark Bedlam. They would then wait until Mario had recovered and smuggle him out of Venice in a group of British students that a friend of theirs was guiding through northern Italy and the Veneto.

"And until then?"

"Until then we'll have to keep our wits!"

Antonella took Diana's hand. It was one of the gestures only she knew how to make. "You're wonderful, you know that!"

Diana, who was uncomfortable with compliments—especially when deserved—merely shrugged. "Sure, sure . . . I'm wonderful!"

For two days, Diana was indeed wonderful. She dashed from cellar to attic, she kept the doors locked between people who must not meet and at the same time she managed to reassure Peter, explaining to him that Antonella was still very young, that no one could expect her to . . . But Peter remained as gloomy as on the evening of the party. And each night Antonella's room remained empty.

When Mario regained consciousness, they talked for hours. He told Antonella what Italy had become—or, more precisely, what it was going to become—and Antonella realized that her studies, her comfortable exile in England were a dream, just as the few services she had been able to render for friends she had left behind in Rome or Venice were no more than an alibi. Above the splendors of Veronese that she had been studying in books, far from the elegant parties she had attended in Mayfair or Belgravia, a threat was gathering day by day—a threat not only to Italy but to all of Europe as well, and no one who might be affected by it could afford to ignore it.

"We've gone around with our eyes closed for too long," she exclaimed to Diana. "There are some things we have no right to put up with any longer."

They were in the attic beside Mario, who was asleep. Diana put her hand on the girl's arm. "You love him, don't you?"

"I think so . . . but that isn't the reason. That's not the question."

For her as well as for Diana, Mario's presence in the palazzo, his entry into their lives and the disturbances he had brought with him—all these had been a revelation. He was asleep, his head turned to one side on the white pillow.

"Nothing can ever be the same again now."

And, indeed, nothing ever was to be the same.

The evening Diana had chosen to prepare Mario's false passport marked the arrival of *acqua alta*, when the waters began to rise. It had rained throughout the day, and boards had been laid on sawhorses across the Piazzetta and the Piazzo San Marco, the city's main arteries. The sky was laden with thick clouds, and it looked as though a storm was about to break; there was a strange glow on the horizon beyond the Giudecca. All through the day, Peter had tried to talk to Antonella, but, apparently absorbed in her work, she had been careful never to be left alone with him for a moment. Diana had even come to fetch them at the Palazzo Labia to avoid that very thing. It was a conspiracy, and Diana had quickly become one of the key figures.

Dinner had been a somber affair to match the weather. The authorities had taken certain steps with regard to British residents, and a number of adopted Venetians had already decided to return to London or Edinburgh. All of this meant added work for George MacLarren, additional worries for which he was little prepared. Diana was beginning to wonder whether the butler who so obsequiously handed round the plates—the meals at the Foscarini Palazzo were still just as scanty—had begun to notice the strange comings and goings in the house; she was counting the days that remained before the group of students, the pretender Mark Bedlam among them, would return to England. As for Peter, he had made up his mind to have it out with Antonella that evening, come what may. Once having reached that decision, however, he did not know how to proceed, and he was afraid of alienating her completely.

After dinner, George MacLarren turned to the *Times* crossword, and Peter, seeing that Diana and Antonella were chatting together in low voices by the fire, went up to his room. Everything in Venice seemed to be coming apart around him; he was no longer filled with joy; he no longer had any taste for his work. He brooded over the papers, plates and photographs he had spread out on the table he was using as a desk. Perhaps he had been mistaken. Perhaps when in a little while he sought out Antonella, she would tell him that everything that had happened during the past few days had been no more than a bad dream, and they would go off together. It would be as before, better than before . . . he felt all the distress and hope of a person in love. . . . He heard the hour strike from the tower of the Gesuati church. Opposite, on the Giudecca, the church of Santa Eufemia, then the Redentore, replied. From time to time, a rapid footstep echoed from the street below. At one point, a couple stopped, two lovers talking together in the darkness, and their murmured voices were painful to him. To a lover who has given up hope, the happiness of others is almost offensive.

"It's not true," he said to himself; "it hasn't affected me that much."

He was now watching the progress of his sickness with a kind of surprise. It was as though he had come down with some unknown virus that he never believed could really affect him, until it had begun to turn fatal. He had reached that point, and the anxiety that now gripped him—an anxious fear that completely paralyzed him, that blocked the workings of his brain—finally made him throw himself onto his bed, unable to catch his breath. He heard Diana come upstairs, and he knew that if he really intended to speak to Antonella, he must get up and go to her.

Of course, the girl's room was empty. It could not have been otherwise, and yet he had continued to hope up until the last minute. Now her turned-down bed and the light burning on the night table beside it destroyed the last of his illusions. He told himself that Antonella could not have gone out—all the doors were bolted at night—and he set out to search for her somewhere in the house. It was the most horrible night Peter Charley, Professor of Art History at London University, was ever to spend—and it was about to begin.

First he moved at random along the corridors, opening doors, exploring closets on his own floor. He opened each door with a kind of cold rage, almost not caring about noise or that the other inhabitants of the house might be aroused. Finally, convinced that Antonella was not on the *piano nobile*, he explored the ground floor, the cellar, in the same wild way. From time to time, some bell would ring out through the almost total silence, or there would be the cry of a cat, a child, far off in the night, sounds that the utterly motionless city contrived to echo as though coming from nearby. The storm had subsided; it had stopped raining.

"She's with her lover! She can only be with some lover!" He was muttering under his breath; without realizing it, he had guessed correctly, even though her lover—still seriously wounded—was incapable of anything more than a pressure of his hand on Antonella's.

Above in the attics, the anxiety was also increasing. It was as though the storm that had been pounding the city had left behind it an even more awful silence.

"You won't leave me. . . ." Mario said softly. He, too, had guessed. "I'm afraid all at once. You mustn't leave me. . . ."

He begged her insistently. To reassure him, Antonella lit the lamp they usually extinguished at night out of precaution.

Peter Charley was coming closer. He had surprised Camilla, the maid, in her basement, busily engaged in making love, and he had heard George snoring in his private study on the third floor in a separate wing of the palazzo. Now he had begun to climb the narrow stairway leading to the attics.

Diana, who was to rejoin Antonella in the early morning hours with the passport prepared, had left open the only door she should have been careful to close behind her.

"Slut, whore," Peter was muttering under his breath as he advanced down the corridor that led to the narrow arm of the building that formed a connection between the old Foscarini Palazzo and the present "small" palazzo of Mario's hideout. Slut, whore . . . he said the words, but Peter did not believe them. He would go to the end of this corridor; he would make certain no one was hiding anywhere there, and then he would return to his room. After all, perhaps Antonella was already back. Peter Charley had already given up. It was then that he spied the ray of light underneath the door.

His heart stopped beating.

He took a few steps further along the corridor and reached the door: he pushed it open.

Antonella looked at Peter, her eyes filled with sudden, nameless terror. In the space of that second, she realized that this timid professor was in the grip of a madness he could no longer control and that he might do anything.

"Peter!" She screamed his name. "Peter!"

But Peter had left without a word, the door wide open behind him. As he was to tell George MacLarren, "I felt as though I had been struck down."

Mario raised himself on one elbow and held Antonella's hand. "Don't leave me! I beg you, don't leave me!"

Antonella pulled away from him. She had to catch up with Peter . . . and, as though adding an appropriate sound track to the scenes of horror that were to follow, the storm broke out again with even greater fury, and once again the rain beat against the windowpanes.

The rest of the night was like a bad B picture in which events occur with no concern for logic, but only to lead to the final catastrophe on the last page of the script.

First, Peter regained his room, locked himself in and refused to open the door to Antonella.

"I think he cried. . . ." George MacLarren told me, trying to explain.

And it was probably true that Peter Charley, obsessed as he was with what he had seen in that room under the roof—the woman he loved in the arms of another man—did cry like a child. When he finally stopped, Antonella was gone. He heard a door open, furtive whispers, steps creaking along the floor of the corridor, and then silence once more. Outside, in the night, the storm was raging. He went to the washbasin in his bathroom and looked at himself in the mirror above it: yes, that was he, that fifty-year-old man. Wrinkles, gray hair. He felt sick. He was ugly, old and tired. Had someone loved him? What a joke . . . For a moment he stood there, motionless. Then, without any motive other than a sudden desire to breathe again, perhaps to talk to George or to Diana, he went out into the corridor. All the lights had been extinguished. In the dark he descended the great stone staircase, almost running into the Gothic armchair on the landing off the *loggia*. He swore in a low voice, a sign that perhaps he was beginning to feel better.

"Yes, I was feeling better," he explained to George MacLarren later. "I only wanted to go out for a walk in the street."

To breathe deeply of night air in the storm. But when he reached the vestibule outside George's office, he stopped. And suddenly, standing there before the closed door, he seemed to understand. He threw it open.

"I knew it!"

Leaning over George MacLarren's desk in the middle of the room, caught red-handed, Diana and Antonella looked at him, speechless.

Diana quickly recovered her composure and moved toward him. "Don't move. I beg you! And say nothing."

Say nothing? When he was bursting with rage? Say nothing? When everything that had been collecting in the pit of his stomach for six days had suddenly risen into his throat, with that desire to vomit that clutched his body? Say nothing? And for the first time in his life, peaceful Peter Charley, the timid, lovesick, absentminded professor, Cary Grant in horn-rimmed glasses, completely lost control.

He screamed.

He shouted, raved, threatened, wept. Drunk with pain, Peter Charley threw his agony back into the faces of those who he thought had injured him. "You, too, Diana!"

That was it: both of them, both those women, had betrayed him . . . all women.

Well-behaved, cautious, timid Peter Charley mouthed foul imprecations. The Peter Charley who had been so calm, so sure of himself, had suddenly become a puppet convulsed with jealousy and anger.

Just as he had begun to run out of breath, George MacLarren joined in. His Majesty's consul had entered the room only a second before and had taken in what was going on, but his attention was centered on one fact alone: his wife Diana had opened his office safe. And from that safe she had taken a blank passport and was in the process of forging it. He would have been able to accept anything but that. It was while he told me about it, repentant, of course, but still somehow indignant, that I began to understand the deep secrets that can lie beneath even a failed diplomat's career. This man, half destroyed by alcohol, his hopes disappointed, betrayed by his wife, abandoned by his foreign office which ignored him completely, had nothing other than that very position to hold him up. Literature, poetry, love, he was dead to all of them. He had only duty . . . or a certain notion of duty.

That was what he told Diana in short, cutting sentences that surprised even her. She who knew, nevertheless . . .

"That, I shall never forgive you for that. . . ."

He fell silent. Each man had had his say; one had spoken out of thwarted love—or love destroyed—and the other had spoken on behalf of the shred of honor remaining to him. And then each had fallen silent. Facing them, the women were silent, too. Outside the house, the storm also seemed suddenly to abate: at that moment, a noise of violent knocking resounded from the street door.

"Don't disturb yourselves. I'll see to it."

Fernando, the butler, appeared in the half-open office door.

"Fernando, I order you not to open the door!" George MacLarren spoke with force; he issued his order. But the butler who—as he was later to explain, "had called for help because he had heard shouting"— had already opened the huge door.

A group of ruffians was standing on the threshold, a paramilitary group in black shirts, boys of twenty who had spent the night in an office they used as a barracks. They were drunk and looking for blood. The one who seemed to be their leader stepped forward.

"There's a Communist in this house. We are aware of it and have come to arrest him."

George MacLarren advanced toward him three paces. "Sir, you are in the consulate of Great Britain in Venice. This building is under diplomatic immunity, and I must order you to leave."

It was the same voice with which he had spoken to Diana when he had seen the passport she had stolen. Duty . . .

"Consulate, my ass!" one of the boys replied. They began to enter the house.

"Gentlemen, I cannot allow this!"

The boy who had spoken acted at once. With a heavy blow meant to cause the maximum pain, he struck George MacLarren in the face with his fist; George fell to the ground.

"This way, gentlemen . . ." Fernando indicated the stone staircase and, beyond it, the other hidden stairway leading to Mario's attic.

"Fernando, you bastard!" George MacLarren managed to shout before he lost consciousness under the kicks of the Blackshirts as they passed him.

"Bastard!" Antonella shouted.

But she knew there was nothing to be done. Diana held her back: drunk as lords—on blood as well as alcohol—the Fascists would have turned on her.

Peter hesitated. He was suddenly aware of what was going on, and now he realized the awful machinery he might have set in motion with his fury, his shouting. He suggested they call the police, the true police, but Diana signaled him to do nothing; the police were neither able nor willing to intervene. For a few minutes, the three of them—George was still lying unconscious—waited. Above, then on the staircase, they heard shouts, calls for help, dull, thudding sounds, but none of them dared move.

The sounds grew nearer, and the shouting could be clearly distinguished as cries of pure hatred. Then came a clearer sound, a sound of something falling, something falling several times as though being struck down.

"Mario . . ." Antonella murmured. She moved forward to the vestibule. And what she then saw . . .

"Horror. Utter horror," Peter Charley would later recall.

Four of the Fascists were dragging Mario's dead body down the stairs like a sack. His head, now no more than a shapeless red mass, was striking each step, and the blood flowed from his body and over the stairway through his tattered shirt. Fernando watched them pass, standing at attention. Behind them, the heavy black armchair fell down into the vestibule. There was nothing to say, nothing to be done; the heavy door of the consulate closed behind the monstrous, gesticulating, laughing mob. . . .

The following day, the Municipal Council of Venice sent a note to Consul George MacLarren. It made no reference to the events of the previous evening, nor did it make any criticism of the consul's ambiguous attitude. It merely informed him that he was harboring under his roof two British subjects—the word "British" was underlined—whose presence had become unwelcome in Venice. It referred to Professor Charley and his assistant, Miss Walden, and it stated that Peter and Antonella could remain in the city—only until that evening's train.

Diana accompanied them to the station. Shut up in his room and probably dead drunk, George had refused to bid farewell to his friends. Of course, later . . .

On the platform of the Santa Lucia station, Diana held first Peter and then Antonella in her arms. She said nothing to Peter, but she felt for him a great swelling of tenderness, made up of all their common memories and mixed with that conspiratorial emotion shared by those who have been defeated and have had to make do their entire lives. Perhaps there was still a bit of light visible for them, at the end. To Antonella, however, Diana had tried to say in a few words how she had changed their lives.

"You have awakened us. . . ." She meant George and herself.

Then the train pulled out. This time Peter and Antonella occupied separate compartments, and they did not meet again until supper time. At first they were silent. Each knew that he was partly responsible for what had happened.

Then Antonella spoke: "You must know, Peter, that I was never pretending. Of course, I wanted to get to Venice. But in the train that first night, I wasn't lying to you. . . ."

Peter Charley heard her out in silence. In simple words she told him what she had felt, of the trouble she had brought him.

"I was overwhelmed by you. And happy, lighthearted, and then . . ." Her voice faltered. "And then we arrived in Venice."

That was all. There had been Venice, the dark, terrible shadow hanging over it, the threat, Mario . . . and there was no more to be said.

Peter took her hand and said very simply, "I am the one who should ask your pardon. If I hadn't shouted as I did, like an insane man, maybe your friend . . ."

She cut him short. "The butler had already denounced him from the first day."

Around midnight they left the restaurant car, and Peter accompanied Antonella back to her compartment.

"You've given me so much, you know."

She gave a rueful laugh: "Your book isn't even finished."

Peter Charley shrugged. He was filled with an immense sorrow, but he, too, had been awakened. . . . "I guess there are things more important than my book!"

Charley was right. Antonella *had* given him a great deal. And even though with the years he was to revert to what he had been before, a professor for whom only his studies, his research, his books and his paintings counted, for a few months, a few weeks, he had, thanks to Antonella, glimpsed something else.

As for Antonella, no sooner had she arrived back in London than she took the first train leaving for the south of France. From there she crossed clandestinely into Italy. One of her closest comrades in arms noted the day and hour of her death. Antonella Walden was shot down by a firing squad of German soldiers at dawn on February 5, 1942, in the courtyard of a prison in Turin. It had been snowing gently, and Antonella, who had been kept in solitary confinement and tortured for several weeks, had weighed no more than eighty pounds.

"But she was younger and more beautiful than ever," Beppo was to say.

"How horrible!" Lise Bergaud murmured as she lay aside the ambassador's manuscript.

"Yes, horrible . . . And even more vivid suddenly, because . . ." Paul de Morlay stopped, as though not daring to go on.

The girl, still overcome by what she had just read, urged him to finish his sentence. "Because . . . ?"

"Well—but you have understood already . . . it's because Antonella looked like you."

It was true: there had been something about the heroine of that journey to Venice, her zest, spontaneity, tenderness, concern for others, her last words to Peter—"And your book isn't even finished!"—that Paul de Morlay seemed to see duplicated in Lise, almost with sorrow. Even her features reminded him of those of Antonella, now dimmed by time.

"And there is more. Antonella, as you must have guessed, was someone I could have loved. . . ."

They had met only at a dull, consular cocktail party in some shabby palazzo. Later MacLarren had showed him the yellowed photographs Charley had kept: a girl dressed in the fashion of the day, her hair cut short, standing smiling on the Rialto bridge or in front of the facade of the Palazzo Labia.

"I wish I had seen those photographs," Lise murmured.

"One day, when we have returned to Paris, I shall show them to you."

It was late afternoon. Suddenly neither of them had any desire to work further, and the ambassador summoned Eugenio, the chauffeur with the face of a fallen angel.

"Shall we go for a drive? All at once, I need to see something supremely beautiful."

A few minutes later, the white Bentley was on the way to Castelfranco. The ambassador had shut the window between them and the driver, and he sat silent. As though it were the most natural thing in the world, almost automatically Lise took the old man's hand.

"Some things, you know, I shall never forget. And that's also why I wanted to tell you about her," he murmured.

Flat fields stretched on either side of the road, edged with trees, and here and there they saw familiar factory smokestacks, ugly high-tension lines.

"Every time I feel tired or unhappy, I take a trip to Castelfranco."

Away from the world, the town in which the man who was perhaps the greatest painter of the Venetian sixteenth century was born is still only a large village, surrounded by red walls like those walled Chinese villages Paul de Morlay had dreamed, as a young embassy secretary, of describing . . . and which he had never seen. Outside the moat, there were modern streets, the crudely colored neon signs of the new town, but Castelfranco itself, with its right-angled alleyways, its neoclassical theater, its dome and its deserted museum, was a village suspended in time and gray dust.

"And, of course, there's the *pala*."

The *pala* of Castelfranco is Giorgione's "Madonna," one of the fifteen or twenty pictures that can be attributed with any certainty to the master's hand. The others—copies, copies of copies, works by Bellini, Titian—who knows? But the "Madonna" of Castelfranco . . .

"Her lowered gaze, so serious, so tender . . ."

Lise and the ambassador stood before the famous panel. In the background there was the cloudy landscape that had inspired an entire century of painting: two saints, *orantes*, interceded before the valleys, the hills and houses, the distant, everyday life, but the only thing that mattered was the Virgin's face.

"All the tenderness and resignation in the world, as though she could foresee the fate of the child in her arms . . ."

Above all, all the gentleness in the world . . .

"I imagine that at the last moment, when she realized it was all over, Antonella, too, was resigned and accepting, just as she is. Revolt—the kind of hatred that inspired Stephanie—lies deep inside the heart. Why direct it against your killers?"

The old ambassador and the girl left the white cathedral and walked for a while through the streets. Evening was falling, but the street lamps with their forged-iron lanterns had not yet been lit; it was calm and very silent. A dog could be heard barking in the distance, a child crying, that was all.

"Well, come," Paul de Morlay said brusquely, "we must snap out of it. Since you have arrived, I've become very sentimental, terribly so."

Lise smiled. "Not terribly, but yes, sentimental—and why not?"

And he repeated, nearly word for word, one of the first things he had ever told her, the afternoon of their first day together. "It is because my entire life has consisted solely of the faces of women."

Lise, who had understood him from that first day, tightened her hold on his arm. "That's what all of them must have loved in you."

He stopped short where they stood. "In me? But we mustn't talk about me. We must talk about them. . . ."

The ambassador did not speak as they returned to the villa, sunk deep in the emotion aroused by his memories and the visit they had just made—and the few words he had spoken to Lise. It was not until they were passing through the lions at the gates to the villa that he murmured in a low voice: "Sometimes I'm afraid of running on, of boring you. There are so many young people in Venice or Padua with whom you could be spending your evenings."

Lise thought of the handsome Vincenzo B. and shuddered. "You know I prefer being with you!" She had almost shouted.

Neither of them noticed the imperceptible smile on the face of Eugenio, the handsome chauffeur with the killer's eyes.

"I promise you that tomorrow we will have a real detective story," the ambassador said finally. "And I promise you it will be more amusing."

But Lise was not asking Paul de Morlay to be more amusing. . . .

HELENA

Bucharest, 1933

To begin with, of course, I won't be amusing at all. . . . For I must tell you something about that period, the early thirties, when at least some of us suddenly began to realize the evil that Antonella had foreseen—the leprosy she had been so quick to diagnose beneath the gold and woodwork of those Venetian palazzos and which was to strike her down among the first. It began to spread throughout Europe. Violence? Do you know what violence is? It is Fascists in black shirts dragging a body of a man already dead down a stone staircase, yes, but it is also shouted orders, screams of hatred, harangues, processions of quite another kind. . . .

The thirties had already begun, and the Reichstag in Berlin had been burned down; they accused the Communists. Vast crowds of people were already going to Nuremberg to raise their arms in salute, while in quiet streets in quiet little German towns shops were being pillaged every night, just for fun—just because the shopkeeper was called Isaac or Jacob. In a very short time, they would be burning books. And although nobody was really concerned about the first camps already said to exist in the depths of East Prussia or Siberia, it was because the prisoners sent to them were only Communists!

And, of course, all of these sparks that were so soon to become

torches were reflected in that isolated world of diplomacy where I—
along with so many others—was engaged in the usual futile game.
People talked about the occupation of the Ruhr, about reparations;
Ethiopia and the war in Spain soon appeared on the agenda of meetings, and the parade of sinister puppets and murders went on. At the
time of which I am going to speak, however, the great question was
rearmament. It was 1933, and the arms limitations conference was in
constant session . . . but with no result other than to record the new
monthly infractions of the laws it had itself established in one useless
amendment after another. Germany, since it was determined to rearm—
Hitler was already in power—was threatening to withdraw from the
conference and to leave the League of Nations as well: in brief, it was
a period in which our last hopes began to fade.

I was then living in Geneva. When the serious *Revue des Deux
Mondes* asked me to write about those days a few years ago, I obliged.
I described the Palais des Nations that had been built at the edge of
the lake, the gardens planted with trees from every country. There
gentlemen in frock coats would stroll in the chill air voicing their disappointed hopes, while in the hall, with its ceiling and walls decorated
with frescoes by Maurice Denis and other official hacks with a passion
for depicting the trappings of patriotism, the empty, pompous speeches,
made by men who continued to uphold a belief that everything could
be solved through treaties, pacts and olive branches, echoed resound-
ingly.

Stresemann, the German who had wanted peace, was dead; so was
Briand, and Kellogg, the American who had dreamed of outlawing war,
was almost forgotten. You encountered their successors in the hallways
of diplomatic missions, or holding forth in private homes and great
hotels like the Grand Hotel des Bergues, always surrounded by journalists, up-and-coming politicians and diplomats, all more dashing than
in real life, men chosen by the Quai d'Orsay to retrieve whatever peace
they could. It was like using a small piece of paper to cover a pot that
is boiling over—but you can be sure that no one ever got his fingers
burnt!

I was first secretary to the French delegation to the arms limitation
conference and had already grown fairly cynical because of my comrades' conduct. I've told you that I believed in the League of Nations
for six months, but I had now been in Geneva for two years. The Old
City was picturesque, of course, and the dinners given by the society

women of Geneva who deigned to receive foreigners were charming—
if not of very high quality—but I was beginning to feel awfully bored.

So I tried to interest myself in other things. Of course, there were
women to distract a diplomat in his leisure time. Stephanie was then
living in Paris. We were still just as much in love, but we spent only
two weekends a month together. There are nothing like international
railways to cement happy marriages! Don't misunderstand me: the
bonds that united—and still unite—me with my wife are the bonds of
the greatest tenderness; but Stephanie had her life and I had mine. Both
of us had been lucky to meet the other, and perhaps our only unhappiness was our lack of children—but that is another story. Living alone
in Geneva, therefore, I had a few female friends, one liaison, many
"relations." In those days, we still called them "acquaintanceships. . . ."

My relations were drawn from a vast pool of a thousand and one
clever secretaries, translators, stenographers who all bustled around the
League of Nations, the conference and the minor committees. They
spoke every language, and there was one for every taste: Norwegian
girls pleased the Italians; and the unfortunate republicans of unhappy
Spain took advantage of the little time they had left in our company
to taste the delights of Finnish girls or red-haired Irish lassies. For my
part, I indulged in every race and political coloring without discrimination. I can recall a fine Soviet girl who had escaped the steppes and was
serving as a secretary, but who also could play the piano. . . . What
were almost pleasure trains rolled between Geneva and Paris, Geneva
and Berlin, Geneva and Brussels, Geneva and Budapest, all filled with
beautiful foreign women. It was like a Congress of Vienna on wheels
and wearing petticoats—all managing to enjoy themselves despite everything, always en route.

I won't say anything about my woman friends, for they are my
deepest secrets. They told me too many things about themselves—and
they have all been gone for a long time, for that matter—for me to
indulge in the indelicacy of revealing any of their confidences. So I
shall tell you only about my official liaison—official for us both, but—
thank God—unknown to anyone else. Her name was Helena Petresco.

Do you remember Maria? It was perhaps the memory of Maria von
Pallberg that attracted me to Helena. As you are well aware by now,
I have always had a great weakness for very young women, and those I
have referred to as "acquaintances" or "relations" were always drawn
from those ranks. Helena was no longer a girl. Not that she was old:

she was just thirty-two, the precise age at which so many women enter their greatest period of beauty. Ripe, blooming, she burned with an inner fire that gave her her great appeal; the eye was drawn to her lovely features and her almost diaphanous pallor contrasted with deep red lips. Above all, as I well knew, she had an iron will.

What was she doing in Geneva? She lived there. She lived there, halfway between France, her true homeland, and Rumania, where she had been born. And she lived there very well, I must admit. Indeed, Helena had a considerable income at her disposal; like Maria, she was said to be a widow, and people who knew her had mentioned lovers, but that made no difference to me. I'm not saying I was in love with her: what I felt for her was more like profound respect; and I think that in my way I amused her. But that form of tenderness can rapidly turn into love. Because she was Rumanian and had lived in Bucharest, and because she was now acting more or less as the Swiss representative of a Bulgarian import-export firm, I had to separate work from pleasure and take care never to reveal in our intimate conversations—particularly in the society in which we moved together—the little information I possessed with regard to the great feats we diplomats were not accomplishing. But that was the law in our particular jungle for the exiles in Geneva, and had it been otherwise, we would all have been spying on each other, and had we begun to look for secret agents, we would have found them. All that is by the way, just to let you know that, although I was happy, I was not a true believer. . . .

One morning in September of 1933, the Yugoslavian representative at the arms limitation conference called together his partners in what was then known as the Petite Entente—the group of three countries that had elected to stand firm against the power being exerted by the nascent Berlin-Rome axis: France, Rumania and Yugoslavia. Lukas, for that was the Yugoslavian's name, had told us he had something highly important to communicate to us. His revelation was important indeed . . . but we have already arrived at the nub of my story.

"My friends," Lukas began, standing in his vast office with its oval windows overlooking the lake, "I think I can inform you that I have at last come into possession of the evidence we need."

Enesco, the Rumanian, and I were well aware of what he meant: for the past several weeks, Lukas had been moving mountains in an attempt to come up with irrefutable proof for the special committee that Germany—in secret and contrary to all its public assurances—had been receiving large shipments of military equipment from third countries. Everyone who had agreed to come forward and testify before the committee to attempt to prove such arms traffic and name those involved had excused themselves, one after the other. Of course, Moelher, the head of the German delegation to the aforesaid committee, could be fiendishly persuasive. . . .

"However, I am today in a position to inform you," Lukas continued, "that tomorrow morning an emissary will arrive from Karavalov, here in Geneva. He has carte blanche from his employer to tell us all we want to know."

Karavalov's name went off like a bomb in our midst. Later, in the course of my story, you will discover who Karavalov was, piece by piece—or who he is, for I am certain that in his shady way, and despite everything that was revealed later, the Karavalovs live on. For the moment all you need to know is that he was an adventurer, a shady financier, a ladies' man and—above all—a dealer in armaments. His name was known and respected from the Rhine to the Vistula, from the Baltic to the shores of the Caspian. He was one of the greatest of the magnates controlling machine guns and bombs, men who, with a total lack of discrimination and with evenhanded largesse, supplied both sides in every conflict anywhere in the world. He was also respected because he was known for honoring his contracts and because he had at his disposal a team of henchmen who saw to it that the other side honored theirs, if need be. I might add—and this is an important point —that no one had ever managed to set eyes on him. I've said he was a ladies' man; there were a thousand stories about him; but what woman he had possessed would have admitted in broad daylight that she had spent the night in his arms? Or even that she would be able to recognize him were she to see him in the street? It was said that Karavalov could be extremely persuasive when convincing others, women included, to respect his anonymity. Karavalov was a man without a face. He had become a myth from the Caspian to the Vistula. . . . Now—from what motives?—he was to send us an emissary who was prepared to reveal all, to tell us everything about those depots and factories across the Rhine that were officially described to overly curious tourists as innocent garages or factories for agricultural implements. Fine threshing machines they made—the harvest to be blood!

Enesco, the Rumanian, was the first to speak: "I won't ask your sources, but I'd like to know how far we can trust them."

I, too, made a few cautious remarks, inspired by Lukas's utter certainty, but the Yugoslavian reassured us: "We have a firm commitment from Karavalov through very tortuous sources. Karavalov is finished; it's all over for him. He wants to go out with a bang, to burn all his boats behind him, in hopes of ending up with a Swiss passport and a nice numbered account in the most distinguished bank in this lovely city. He has played too many interests against each other, and now the time has come for him to call it a day. I'm already in touch with Lucien Maurice of Swiss security, who has given me carte blanche. Even though it is neutral, you know how the Swiss government likes everything clear-cut, even when they're involved up to their eyes."

I knew Maurice and I knew the Swiss, but I knew Lukas, too . . . and, above all, I knew Karavalov's reputation.

"Let's wait and see," I said simply.

What else was there to do?

And how could we have known that Moelher, the chief of the German delegation to our conference, was waiting, too? Like Lukas's and mine, his office also overlooked Lake Geneva, but Moelher was a sentimental man with a penchant for *Lohengrin,* and, since he was also a punctual Prussian, it was his habit to feed the swans on the lake each morning at precisely ten o'clock. Wtih infinite tenderness, he would toss crumbs of buttered brioche onto the water. . . .

At precisely ten-thirty, the man we were to know, for only a few minutes, as Dimitri arrived at the Cornavin Station in Geneva. He was short and thin and carried one suitcase, lightweight and cheap-looking. He paced for a moment in the station courtyard; then he hailed a taxi and asked the driver to take him to an address in the Old City.

On the way, he apparently changed his mind and asked to be let out on the Quai du Mont Blanc at the edge of the lake. Twice, as the old Mercedes with its Italian driver went down the Rue Chantepoulet, he turned, as though fearful he was being followed.

At the Quai, he paid his fare with a large bill, and the driver took a few minutes to give change. Then, in the sunny morning under the bright blue sky, the man called Dimitri walked along the edge of the lake. He breathed in the crisp, dry air of the lovely autumn morning; it was warm, and he opened his tweed coat. At that moment as he took his deep breaths, was he thinking that life could indeed be beautiful?

A man coming toward him bumped into him and apologized politely.

In Bulgarian. For an instant, the short man in the open overcoat did not realize that someone had spoken to him in Bulgarian in Geneva. When it dawned on him, he had already walked on for several steps—and he had already felt a twinge of pain on his left side, just where the courteous gentleman had bumped into him. He stopped, put his hand to his side and fell.

Like Sissi—the Empress Elisabeth of Austria—Dimitri had been stabbed through the heart with one thrust of a narrow blade. And, as with Sissi, the murder had occurred in Geneva on the Quai du Mont Blanc; similarly, the weapon had been almost invisible, the wound extremely small. Only one small patch of blood seeped through the tweed.

"Bravo," was Moelher's only comment to the man who brought him the news.

"Shit!" Lukas swore, two offices further away.

I was close to saying the same thing. That evening, however, Helena was being particularly tender to me, and we went to the opera to hear a very pleasant *Barber of Seville*. Rossini's enchanting minx, laughing at men in general: it should have been a forewarning. On our way back to my apartment, Helena told me that she would soon be returning to Bucharest—and that journey, too, is important to our tale. . . .

"I like you a great deal," Helena told me after she had informed me of her impending journey.

My friends and I—the countries of the Petite Entente—as well as Europe and perhaps even the cause of world peace had all just received a body blow, but Helena was so beautiful that I spent a part of the night listening to her talk about herself. Anyway, I had few illusions about the efficacy of our committee's work. . . . She told me of gypsies and wild Bucharest nights, about deserted palaces still haunted by Moldavian princes who would wrap the gifts they sent their mistresses in ropes of pearls. She told me about men who, flat broke, were professional parasites—the word for them was *mossafiri*—and when I kissed her, it was with passion, for she knew better than any woman how to bring the spirit of an entire city alive in the arms of a lover.

"Bucharest and Paris—apart from them, nothing means anything to me!"

And yet she meant everything . . . for another week. . . .

Morning brought reality flooding back: Lukas's plan had failed, and, since all of the contacts he had recently managed to establish with

Karavalov had been made through Dimitri, Lukas now had no way of getting in touch with the adventurer, at least for the moment. The special session of the committee before which the Karavalov dossier was to have been presented was scheduled for the following Monday; it was now Tuesday. In other words, we had less than a week in which to find Karavalov, reassure him—the murder of his sole envoy had probably upset him—and persuade him to testify before our colleagues.

"Otherwise, Moelher will come out on top again."

Lukas was further irritated because the leader of the German contingent to the conference was such a dilettante, such an aesthete—the swans and Lohengrin!—and because he assumed such an expression of outrage when anyone chanced to cast doubt on the purity of his intentions whenever and for whatever outlandish reason he demanded a suspension of the meeting. Indeed, had it not been for Lucien Maurice, the head of Swiss security, who had been greatly upset by what had occurred on the tranquil shores of the least tranquil of Geneva's lakes and who was prepared to give us his total support, we would have been at a complete loss.

"He's the one who put us onto this Dimitri, for that matter," Lukas told us.

Lucien Maurice, fat, blue-eyed, typically Swiss, lowered his eyes modestly. Lucas—no sooner said than done—had invited him into the office where we were meeting.

"I've already explained my idea to your colleagues," he said to me, indicating Lukas and Enesco, who had been waiting for me in the anteroom of the Yugoslavian delegation's suite. "But I'd like your opinion."

Lucien Maurice spoke to each of us individually in order to convert us all to his way of thinking. He led me into the park that sloped gently down towards the water.

The proposal he laid before me was completely incredible, and it was probably for that reason he had wanted to make separate explanations. Had we been together, we would have been confounded by his plan of gendarmes searching out thieves in some foreign city. However, it was the only feasible approach.

"Perhaps it will surprise you," he began, "but your own people helped us contact the unfortunate Dimitri. You French diplomatists at the Quai still enjoy such prestige in certain areas of the world that

Karavalov has so far agreed to deal with us only through the agents of your foreign ministry."

I was only faintly surprised to learn that certain diplomats at the Quai had been mixed up in these transactions, although the British specialized more in acting as double or triple agents as a rule. I allowed him to continue.

"I have an address in Bucharest that Dimitri passed on to me. The Hracin mansion in the center of town, on the Chaussée Kisselhoff. It is there that Karavalov receives important visitors when he wants to single them out for special attention. He's never there himself, but I'm told that some of his people are always in residence."

I didn't see where he was leading, but he gave me a friendly thump on the shoulder—one of those demonstrations of Swiss affection that can throw a normal man a good ten yards. "You still don't understand, right?"

He gave a sly smile, his eyes bluer than ever.

"Well, if Karavalov won't come to the mountain—in this case, Mont Blanc, which you can see over there above the lake—then the mountain will have to go to him. . . ."

He burst out laughing, pleased at his Genevois humor, but still I didn't see what he was driving at.

"Do you mean that you are going off to Bucharest?"

He looked at me with his straightforward gaze. "Oh, because you think I'm the mountain . . ."

He laughed harder, and I, too, began to laugh at the picture of Lucien Maurice disguised as Mont Blanc.

"No," he said, "I've told you that devil Karavalov will only trust an agent from the Quai."

My laughter subsided at once. I looked at him incredulously. True, I was an odd sort of diplomat, but I would have made a highly unlikely spy. Thank God, Lucien Maurice quickly put my mind at rest.

"Don't get upset, de Morlay"—he emphasized the *de* in the way the Swiss sometimes do, relishing the few relics of aristocracy that France still retains—"you're too useful here where you can keep Moelher busy in case there's an unexpected delay. No . . . your Quai d'Orsay can find some youngster for us, can't they? One of those young men of good family who are dreaming of adventure in the chancellery hallways . . ."

He spoke a language with which I was so familiar that I had no doubt he was right. Thus it was that the next morning I made the acquaintance of Georges Damiens, the "youngster" from the Quai d'Orsay.

When I first laid eyes on Damiens, he was so like myself at his age that I was almost shocked. Yes, that young embassy attaché with his somewhat pompous air, his mixture of shyness and sudden bravado, his avid desire to see everything, know everything, experience everything, his innocence and breathtaking naiveté, typical of the lowest secretary in any embassy who is just coming to grips with life outside the hermetic world of the office—he was just like me. But as I had been twenty years before, for twenty years had passed since Paul de Morlay had met the gaze of Maria von Pallberg on the platform of the Gare de l'Est one evening in 1913.

I felt an instinctive sympathy for him when I set out to explain to Georges Damiens what it was we expected of him. I had a lot of free time in which to do so since Helena, as she had informed me, had gone back to Bucharest, and the young Danish stenographer, with whom I had been planning to end my afternoon at the Perle du Lac restaurant overlooking the lake and the sailboats gliding across it, had gone off the previous evening with a Russian, a member of the OGPU—how much would he learn from that little blond siren? Therefore, I invited Georges Damiens instead to the Perle du Lac for the hot chocolate with whipped cream and the *petits fours* I had ordered for someone else. I told him what we expected of him. As I could have foreseen, he was terrified. He had not been polished at the Ecole Libre des Sciences Politiques and waxed and buffed to a high glow at the Paris Law School merely to play the spy on a train from Geneva to Bucharest! For that matter, his overlords in Paris—our beloved directors in their plush offices—had told him that he was going to Geneva, period. However, since I was twenty years his senior, he was forced to succumb to my persuasion.

"Can you imagine me asking pedestrians in the streets of Bucharest if they know where I can find your Karavalov?"

The boy had a quick sense of humor, with his hair somewhat too severely combed back in the fashion of those days, his loose flannel jacket and matching gray trousers of the same material, his Sulka scarf tied elegantly around his neck. Added to all that, his round glasses—

a bit like Harold Lloyd's—gave him a somewhat bewildered air, which was only on the surface and quickly dispelled by the ironic fold at the corner of his mouth. Indeed, Georges Damiens, beneath his disguise of awestruck juvenile, was really not at all naive—luckily for him, as it turned out!

"I'm a bit . . ." he said.

I reassured him, at least partially. Our friend Lukas, who thought of everything, was putting one of his men at our disposal in Bucharest, a man named Kangalovich, with whom Damiens was to make contact.

"Kangalovich has a very bad reputation in his branch of the service; Lukas finds that a perfect recommendation. He'll act as your assistant, your bodyguard, your marksman if need be. It would be incredible if with all that you didn't come back with at least a piece of Karavalov!"

I was joking, of course, but Georges Damiens—the young man so neatly combed, so elegantly dressed—jumped involuntarily as I mentioned a bodyguard.

"Because . . . it might be dangerous?"

I didn't know myself, but since I imagined the operation might well entail certain risks, I assured him of the contrary and told him that Kangalovich's presence was only a precaution, no more.

"And then he can help you get around in Bucharest . . . if only to find the address in question and speak to the concierge."

So Georges Damiens agreed. We lingered for a time, watching the sailboats skimming over the lake—a light breeze had sprung up—and then I accompanied him back to the Hotel Beau-Rivage where he was staying. At ten that evening he took the train for Bucharest at Lausanne.

The train arrived at the Bucharest station on the appointed day at eight-ten in the morning. To say that Georges Damiens had had a restful journey would be untrue: he was too excited at the prospect before him—and too curious to find out how he would succeed—to have been able to sleep. So he had read. He was a young man of taste and quality and he adored Stendhal: for nearly forty-eight hours and almost without interruption he had reread Stendhal's *Journal*, his *Rome, Naples and Florence* and part of the *Promenades dans Rome*. Stendhal tells us things not to be found in any *Baedeker* or *Guide Bleu*—and it was as good a way as any to cross central Europe.

Thus, when he arrived in Bucharest, he was very tired, but he was also quite ready to confront whatever Moldavian hazards his mission might entail: has Stendhal not taught us that whatever happens, it will always be the worst?

"Monsieur Damiens?"

He was startled, and yet he had supposed someone would be on hand to meet him. The person who had spoken his name, a man with long hair pulled back and an abundant mustache, had a suspicious air, but he was none other than the chauffeur for M. de Lupières, French ambassador to Rumania.

"The ambassador regrets, but he was unable to come to meet you himself."

The driver had a heavy accent with rolled r's that were almost a caricature. On the platform, peasant women in shawls and multiple petticoats mingled with men and women wearing the latest fashions from Paris or Vienna. Debonair policemen strolled by. . . . I am too familiar with such crowds to find them unusual, but Damiens looked wide-eyed at the scene.

"The ambassador should really not have thought of bothering."

Damiens protested, but he was secretly flattered at the importance his visit seemed to merit. He was also flattered when the chauffeur, after putting his one suitcase into the trunk of the huge Panhard-Levassor that stood waiting in the station courtyard, informed him that a large reception was to be held at the embassy that very evening and that the ambassador was looking forward to seeing him there. There had been a moment when he had been afraid that his role as a secret agent might oblige him to remain holed up in his hotel room, awaiting instructions.

At the Athenée-Palace Hotel on the Calea Victoriei, he was greeted by a uniformed doorman who seemed to know in advance that he was dealing with a young, brilliant diplomat; Damiens was led up to his room with so much courtesy and consideration that he told himself that his mission was getting off to a most auspicious start: finding Karavalov would probably be no more than a formality.

At the very moment that Georges Damiens was entering his hotel room—not the least of whose glories was a magnificent chamber pot in light blue faience—Moelher was requesting to speak at the nth meeting of the special committee—with all the oratorical talent at his disposal, which his opponents were the first to recognize. And he had almost managed to persuade the chairman of the meeting, a Norwegian who was completely neutral, to postpone for two weeks the examination of a case submitted against the Turkish government and to skip to the next item on the agenda. The next item just happened to be the Yugoslavian request that had been scheduled for the following Monday, the one for which we were awaiting Damiens' return from Bucharest —an item that was based entirely on Karavalov's forthcoming testimony. . . .

Lukas and I exchanged a dumbfounded glance: the Yugoslavian had himself requested that his item be given urgent attention, counting on the information to be provided by the real—or false—Dimitri.

Siegmens, the Norwegian chairman, looked around the table, not without an innocent aside to Lukas: "I'm sure the request will please the Yugoslavian representative."

Moelher's tiny eyes glittered maliciously. He thought he had just played a good joke on us . . . and we, for our part, were convinced that he knew all about Damiens' journey to Bucharest; he was trying to embarrass us, and he was about to succeed.

"Any objections?"

Silence: there was no plausible reason to oppose the consideration of any so-called urgent question. I think Siegmens was about to pronounce the fateful phrase, "Request adopted," when a voice was raised in protest.

It was the Turkish representative, who was insisting that the item with which his country was concerned remain on the agenda as decided, somewhat to the surprise of the remainder of the committee since the matter in question was, to say the least, embarrassing to the government in Ankara.

The Turk's lisping voice was insistent: "My government has given me precise instructions, my case is ready and I don't see why it should be put off, now that the committee will certainly absolve my country of all the insulting insinuations that have been made against it. . . ."

The item dealt with an unsavory matter of Armenians exterminated with automatic weapons whose origin was in question: any possible exporter had refused to confess to manufacturing them, and the officials in Ankara had finally found a shady Montenegrin who was willing to serve as a scapegoat. Once again Moelher's eyes glittered, but this time with fury. He had quite forgotten to tell his Turkish

colleague about his maneuver in advance. Of course, Mehmet Adjel
would have agreed to remain silent, but he couldn't do that if he knew
nothing about it!

The chairman therefore let fall his gavel: "Request rejected."

Georges Damiens now had six days to return with the evidence we
needed.

Standing before the mirror in the huge Second Empire wardrobe
in his neo-Victorian hotel room, Damiens took a good hour making
himself ready for the evening. At this, his first ball as a diplomat
abroad, he wanted to flaunt the banner of the younger generation at
the Quai and the typically Parisian elegance characteristic of it. He
may also have had some obscure notion that on that evening he would
meet someone who would completely change his life—and mine. I can
see Georges Damiens as he adjusted his white cravat and checked the
four ruby studs in his dress shirt. With brilliantine in one hand and
his boar's bristle brush in the other—made in England, of course—
he must have brushed vigorously at the rebellious cowlick that he had
never really been able to tame completely. Finally, at ten o'clock, he
was ready, and he rang for the bellboy. Ten minutes later a car arrived
to take him to the embassy and waited at the hotel entrance.

In the lobby, next to the American bar with its deep leather armchairs, a burly man with a short, thick mustache, cold eyes and an
aquiline nose—perhaps a bit heavy, but the weight was mostly muscle
—watched Damiens leave. He took a small notebook out of his pocket
and jotted two words on the only empty page, after having licked the
tip of his pencil with the tip of his tongue. An attentive observer
would have noticed a suspicious bulge under his jacket at the level of
his left armpit.

"Monsieur Georges Damiens, secretary to the embassy!" the majordomo standing at the entrance to the heavily gilded salon announced;
the room, with wood paneling, opened onto the suite used for embassy
receptions.

Standing on a Savonnerie carpet found nowadays only in the foreign
residences of our most senior heads of mission, M. de Lupières was
receiving his guests. He was an ambassador in the old style, related to
Norpois and Marcay and Paul Cambon. He wore a silky white mustache;

his hands were narrow and elegant; his body was short and elegant; his nose was narrow and elegant. Everything about him was elegant, almost translucent, and yet, in the way he looked at people and the world around him, one could detect a questioning glance—amused without being complacent—a glance that contained a high degree of irony.

"Ah, our young paragon!" he exclaimed as Damiens was announced. He shook Damiens' hand with a vigor that belied his apparent fragility and introduced him to the ambassadress. "This is the young man who is to replace Desormières. I've spoken to you about him."

Like her husband, elegant and refined, Mme. de Lupières extended her hand for Damiens to kiss, managed one or two smiles and assured him that he would not find his post boring; life in Rumania could be highly amusing. Bucharest was Paris in miniature.

"You are a bachelor, are you not?"

She gave him a brief, understanding smile, and Georges Damiens comprehended that so far as anyone knew—including the ambassadress —he was there under false pretenses and that everyone thought he was to take up a post at the chancellery that had been vacated. M. de Lupières took his arm: "I'll see you again soon—when my guests have arrived and I can permit myself a free moment for a little chat. For the nonce, however, duty calls!"

He spoke completely naturally, but Georges Damiens knew that the ambassador had instructions to pass on to him. In the meantime, he launched himself into the salons and towards adventure.

You must realize that a first post, a first mission, means a great deal to a young diplomat. Suddenly everything seems possible to him—a diplomatic passport is intoxicating—and at the same time so many things are forbidden him. So he observes, he blushes. With time he will cease to blush, and he will become so used to observing that he will forget to look when he should. All those well-meaning, neutral, formal mannequins after their breaking-in period—all of them are alike. Georges Damiens, however, was still filled with all the fortunate weaknesses of his youth; he was still able to blush, and he still knew how to observe. . . .

And observe he did . . .

It all happened very quickly! The ambasador's ball was well attended. Countesses, marquises, princesses, actresses, worldly women and demimondaines. All of them spoke French in every accent of Europe, all had come from some fashionable *salon de thé*—Capsa or some other one—and all had spent several hours in some dilapidated palace, gathering together what riches remained to them, powdering their noses. There were many wives, a few unmarried girls—and a beautiful stranger, the Unknown Woman, the Foreigner, who, as soon as she made her appearance, drew all his attention. From that moment on, he had eyes for her alone.

She was tall, pale, with scarlet lips and hair arranged in tiny, dark curls that formed a kind of halo around her face. Her chin was firm, her nose straight; she had a high forehead and prominent cheekbones. Her low-cut dress revealed a bosom as pale as her face but hinting at voluptuousness; she smiled, as if to herself, standing alone in a corner of a large gallery by a window, and her smile itself was an invitation. . . .

"You seem to be as lost as I am," the woman in black murmured to Georges Damiens—for she was wearing black, with plumes.

Georges Damiens blushed; he smiled; he raised the glass of champagne that had just been handed him by a footman in knee breeches. "Shall we drink to being alone? My name is Georges Damiens."

The woman in black smiled again. She raised her glass, touched the champagne to her lips and gave Damiens a smile that might have broken the hearts of an entire class of junior diplomats. "And my name is Helena Petresco."

For, of course, as you have already guessed, the woman in black was none other than my mistress, who had left me the evening before on an urgent trip to Rumania.

"I've just arrived in Bucharest," Damiens felt impelled to explain.

"And I have just returned . . ."

Helena and Damiens got along famously at once, but I did not know at the time that I had just lost forever a very beautiful woman whom I might have loved. And at the same time there began an amazing scene of worldly banter, one that was to end in the flash fire of a sudden passion such as can only be experienced by young diplomats when they suddenly come face to face with the most beautiful foreign woman they can imagine.

"You can't imagine," Damiens told me upon his return—as though he knew anything with precision himself!—"you can't imagine that young woman's beauty. She was all gravity and tenderness and assurance, at the same time with a profound confusion . . . and . . ."

I knew I had lost Helena so I encouraged Damiens to continue. "And?"

"And she looked so like that image of a foreign woman a man like myself always dreams of meeting on his first posting. . . ."

He had said it all. Helena, the Foreigner: I can easily imagine her being more foreign than ever, rolling her r's and strolling through M. de Lupières's magnificent salons with their paneling hung with Gobelin tapestries.

"I, too, have just returned to Bucharest," she repeated.

And from that moment on, Damiens and Helena were fated to be together, at least for that evening. They began to talk. . . .

"I don't even know why I was invited here this evening," Helena admitted after a moment.

They had drawn aside from the crush and were standing in a small corner room beneath a fairly good copy of a Boucher. They were playing together the comedy of first seduction; both of them, perhaps for different reasons, were eager to please. It was one of those tender moments in which each person, already attracted to the other, knows that he will be able to play the game, so each starts out towards the destination, taking care only to carry the other along with him.

"If it's chance, let's say chance has been clever. . . ."

Helena's forehead became thoughtful: she explained to him that her father had served in the French army during the Great War, something of which I was unaware myself, and that had perhaps been the explanation for her invitation from the embassy. Damiens spoke of the other guests, who passed at a respectful distance from the sofa on which they were sitting as though it was understood they wished to be alone.

"Everyone here is so . . ."

A bit like Jenny, seemingly surprised at seeing in Vienna the waxwork figures of another era emerge from their boxes still smelling of mothballs, Damiens, too, found that M. de Lupières's guests were reminiscent of an earlier day.

"But my dear friend, it's the crowd that always shows up at this kind of reception, and you'll have to get used to it! For the next forty years, throughout your career, this is what you will be meeting, and almost every evening!"

Georges Damiens gave a short laugh to express his mock horror at the prospect. "You make me shiver; let's talk about something else, shall we?"

From Cairo to Tehran and Khartoum, from Lisbon to Santiago— he was even to serve as consul general in Hong Kong—this was indeed what awaited him. However, after glancing into the vestibule where the ambassador was still receiving his last guests, he rose and bowed to Helena, just a shade too formally: "Shall we dance?"

They danced. . . . A few weeks ago, I told you that I was describing the first dance between a man and a woman who were already in love but had not yet said it. The first waltz between a man and a woman who know they will make each other happy, who are on the brink of love, is also unique: it is that one wispy moment when everything hangs in the balance. Helena and Damiens' waltz surpassed such moments. Ought I to say that I began to be jealous at that moment and that I still am? No, I don't think so. Too often I had managed to win a woman I wanted to hold it against someone else for doing the same thing, still less for succeeding in supplanting me. And, of course, Helena had never really been in love with me; we had been good together. I was forty-five. That evening, in Damiens' arms—he was barely more than twenty—she was quite simply sublime, even though I don't believe she loved Damiens any more than she had loved me.

Helena Petresco, that strange foreign woman, was more like a tenderly incestuous sister. Perhaps she was transient, but she left a wake behind her. Georges Damiens was smitten, and then there was the dance that drew them together in its concentric circles with all the magic of a hundred violins and a hint of gypsy magic. As for Helena, she knew, like a true magician, the secret of words and how to use them: how could Damiens not have been fascinated by the luminous, glowing snares she employed?

"All the same, it's amazing," she murmured into his ear. "And marvelous. We don't know each other, we meet like this one evening—and after two glasses of champagne, one waltz, a few words exchanged on a sofa, we are about to tell each other the story of our lives."

The orchestra played Strauss, Strauss, more Strauss, and Helena's waist, so lithe and slender beneath its spiderweb of black lace, bent under Damiens' fingers.

He attempted to come back down to earth. "Perhaps it's being away from home, the exotic surroundings."

Helena twirled faster; she laughed with greater abandon. Damiens' ardor, his enthusiasm, must have moved her. Had she been able to be more than just an episode in his life, she would have loved him. She was *right* with him. More than that . . . but that was already a great deal.

"Exotic! You must be joking! Every reception, every embassy party in the world is alike, from Ostend to Istanbul."

Damiens drew Helena to him. "Perhaps it's that the unknown women one meets in such surroundings are not like you."

Helena was to admit to me one day—and it was not an excuse, not even an explanation: "You must remember that he was barely twenty. . . ."

When she came to tell me that, twenty years had passed—and another war. . . . And she had blushed when she added: "You have known such evenings, such nights, from Bucharest to Vladivostok, and you ought to understand."

As I said, I didn't need explanations, for I had already understood.

When the waltz ended, Damiens returned with his partner to what had become "their" sofa, which no one had preempted. A footman passed bearing a tray with tall crystal goblets of multicolored sherbets, and they sipped the iced liquid—pink and orange—through straws.

Damiens had already told Helena many things, and he tried to make excuses. "It's because you make me want to talk. . . . Your mysterious charm, dark, different, like central Europe and the Balkans—perhaps it's your accent . . . your smile. . . ."

She smiled even more. "Alas, you'll soon discover my innermost secret! I'll have to use an awful word, but I am just an awful business-woman. I cannot stay in one place; I live here, there, all at once . . . anywhere I have to. I travel, I make money, I meet people, and time goes by."

Damiens felt like shutting his eyes; he felt suspended outside of time. What difference did it make if he were forced to lie to her, to pretend to her that he would be staying in Bucharest for several months? Deep inside, he felt that he had been created to find her and that he would find her again.

"Yes, time goes by. . . ."

He was already dreaming, and at that moment Georges Damiens had only one thought, one desire: to stretch out his hand to hers, in its silken glove, and take it in his own. That was all he wished.

"Most of the time, I live in Geneva," Helena murmured.

Damiens sat up. "Geneva? But how strange—I've just come from there!"

It didn't matter to her, for, as she had said, she lived here and there.

But Georges Damiens drew closer to her and looked at her seriously. "You look so solemn all at once." His hand approached hers slowly.

"I'll give you a simple answer, with reference to what you said a few minutes ago: it's you who are making me solemn. I don't know why. . . ."

She gave a slight laugh, almost embarrassed. Georges's hand had almost reached hers, and at that moment M. de Lupières coughed discreetly. He was standing before them, and thus this first scene of tenderness and recognition came to an end.

"Dear Madame," the ambassador said to Helena, "will you forgive me if I take my young colleague away from you for a while? I must get acquainted with him."

Damiens rose with that almost too-perfect alacrity, that total ease also characteristic of cavalry officers in society, of majordomos in great houses, and he, too, bowed to Helena. "May I hope to find you here again when I return?"

Helena's smile was intended as assent. Damiens smiled back at her and followed the ambassador.

"My young friend," Ambassador Lupières began, lighting a gold-tipped cigarette, "it will hardly surprise you to hear that your presence here is embarrassing to me. However, you know as well as I do that instructions from the Quai are orders to be obeyed. A telegram . . . I have been told to extend to you all my assistance, and I can assure you of my entire sympathy. As for the rest, I can promise you nothing. . . ."

The ambassador's study was lined with books: a few months away from retirement, M. de Lupières was finishing a biography of the Prince de Ligne, from whom he was descended through a slightly adulterous great-great-aunt, and at the same time he was beginning to assemble his memoirs to add them to the thousands of memoirs that fill the shelves of a thousand and one ambassadors in almost as many studies. He was thought of as literate, he was known to be elegant, but these were not adequate conditions to make what he would write interesting to others, even though he believed in it firmly himself. Despite his "embarrassment," I suspect that he was highly pleased at the notion of being involved in the Karavalov affair, which would not fail to make a charming chapter in his forthcoming book.

"All I can tell you," M. de Lupières went on, "is that I don't know Karavalov any more than you do and that no one of my circle has ever claimed to have spoken to him personally. Of course, we have an address, that of the Hracin mansion, which you know as well, but as for the rest . . ."

Georges Damiens listened to the ambassador's words with all due attention, but he had realized at once that the older man had nothing to tell him. Thus, while he listened intently, his imagination was elsewhere. On the one hand, he was wondering whether he, too, would look like this old man when he got to be his age, and if youngsters starting out on their careers would then look at him with the same complete indifference tinged with irony with which he himself regarded the elderly gentleman. On the other hand, he was thinking of Helena, and any dreaming in that direction was totally permissible, since at thirty-two Helena was the incarnation of a certain kind of ambiguous beauty created to cast mystery.

"I shall nevertheless emphasize once again"—and the ambassador's voice took on a confidential tone—"that we must respect this Karavalov. In his way he is a remarkable man, even, it is said, a cultivated man . . . but he is nonetheless an adventurer. And although I would not presume to criticize the confidence the Quai is putting in him in any way, I should like to warn you: the mission entrusted to you is a dangerous one; there can be no doubt about that."

At the word "dangerous," Damiens had pricked up his ears; yes, something was to be dangerous . . . he had almost forgotten it. Helena, danger, Karavalov and his own secret mission: he was being offered such a fabulous taste of life! But he had only one wish: to return to Helena. As for danger, he would wait and see. Fortunately, the ambassador, who had remained behind his Empire desk while speaking, was already coming around the table, empty of any document save for a first edition—1843!—of the letters of the Marquise de Custine about Russia. He advanced to the center of the room.

"It remains only for me to tell you that in this affair the greatest discretion is necessary; it would be highly improper were the embassy to be mixed up in it in any way. According to everyone here, you have been sent to take over the post of young Desormières—one that those rogues in Paris, let it be said in passing, have no intention of filling—and I shall explain to my colleagues that I am giving you a few days' leave to familiarize yourself with the city."

M. de Lupières opened the door to his study; waltz music flooded into the room.

"I nearly forgot!" the ambassador exclaimed before leading his guest back to the salons. "I've been asked to tell you that the Serbian who has been assigned to you will meet you this evening at your hotel. Good luck! My sources tell me that he's a killer!"

He might have been a killer, but, despite his bulk, he cut a good figure. Kangalovich was now pacing between the American bar in the Athenée-Palace hotel and the entrance lobby, where the first revelers returning from their clubs and private parties were lingering at the bookstand which was still open, examining the reviews from Paris in order to avoid spending a few cents. Here, too, the sounds of a waltz could be heard, but here the comeliest of the maids on duty at that late hour were all over sixty, and the only prostitute still waiting in the bar had lurid, violet lips that attracted Kangalovich only very mildly.

He glanced at his watch and grumbled: "They last late, the frolics of these diplomatic gentlemen!" The bulge under his left armpit was generous; the weapon was a powerful one.

In the meantime, Georges Damiens had returned to Helena, who had not moved from the sofa. She flashed him one of her generous, warm smiles which I knew so well. "Well, have you remade the world?"

Damiens sat down beside her. "You don't know how true that is!"

But Helena had now risen, and she, too, glanced down at her watch. "Unfortunately, all good things have to end, even wild evenings at the French embassy! I must be up very early tomorrow morning. I have a car . . . may I drop you?"

Wild or not, Georges Damiens' evening was far from over. First there was his return to his hotel in the huge Rolls with the crest of a Rumanian count. A chauffeur dressed in a voluminous white overcoat

and a cap bearing the same crest—black and gold, gold on black—
opened the door for Helena with an almost obsequious bow. Then
through the dark night of a city that had suddenly reverted to what
it really was—a small provincial capital with neither skyscrapers nor
factories, but only its history, heavy with legend—the car had rolled
along.

Although the weather was damp and mild, Helena was enveloped
in a huge fur which stood out around her like a flower, leaving only
her eyes, her nose, her scarlet mouth to emerge from the darkness.
Neither of them spoke, but once again Damiens felt himself gripped
by an emotion that was more than real—their travels, the night, the
silence, the woman—I can imagine that with his round glasses and
flushed cheeks, he must have looked slightly ridiculous. Later he would
be a diplomat playing at being a secret agent, an emissary, a courier;
now he looked like a man in love at the end of his tether.

"This evening has been almost like a dream," he finally murmured.
"Bucharest, the ambassador . . . above all, you. It's as though all
at once I had been plunged into one of those novels I'm so fond of:
the young romantic diplomat and the beautiful foreigner . . . Even
our conversation was like some sophisticated dialogue, even when we
were being serious."

His voice seemed to come from a great distance, from somewhere
deep inside him, from his feelings.

Helena put her hand on his. "Dialogue? Sophisticated? Do you
really find it so?"

He laughed slightly but with a serious note. "You can tell that now
I have no desire to be either sophisticated or to make dialogue. . . ."

Helena's voice was full of the same feeling . . . and I know that
never more than at that moment—except when she had spoken to me
in the same tone—had she been more sincere. "You are very charming, Georges."

"And you, Helena . . ."

She stopped him; there was another touch of his hand, and it was
over. Suddenly they were so near to each other that they needed only
signs to understand.

"No, don't say anything . . . somewhere else, some other way,
some other time, perhaps . . . Not now. I must go home."

The car turned heavily and silently from the Carol Boulevard into
the Calea Victoriei; further along on the right the Athenée-Palace

was still brightly lit up, and the porter in his braid was already approaching the Rolls as it glided to a stop at the curb.

Georges Damiens got out and turned to take the hand Helena extended to him. He bent over it for a long moment. "I will see you again, won't I?"

She flashed him the smile that had been capable of persuading me to agree to anything, even the most intimate betrayal. "You are staying in Bucharest, are you not? So we shall meet again. I am sure of it."

"But when?"

Damiens was about to insist; he knew that the length of his stay in Rumania would be short.

But Helena gently withdrew her hand. "Let's wait and see, shall we not? Europe suddenly seems so small."

She gave the chauffeur an imperceptible signal. Damiens remained standing at the curb for a moment watching the car draw away; then he turned and briskly mounted the four steps of the entrance.

The door of the Athenée-Palace hotel was a revolving one, and as it turned he was projected into what he had temporarily forgotten: adventure.

"Monsieur Damiens?"

He started. It was true, yes; he had forgotten.

"Monsieur Damiens?"

It was the corpulent, solid man with his somewhat sly, grumpy smile, but a smile that was still debonair beneath his mustache, even with the large revolver under his left armpit.

"I'm Mikhail."

For a second Damiens was not sure he had understood. The other man looked amused.

"Kangalovich, if you prefer. It could be Braun or Schmidt, but at the moment it's Mikhail Kangalovich. Don't you think that has a nice ring to it? I believe Lukas and good old Lucien Maurice in Geneva have told you about me. And since we're going to be spending some time together, maybe we could have a little chat? What do you think?"

Georges Damiens had returned to earth by now; his mind was nimble, and he was able to adapt to almost any situation. Still, this man with the smell of adventure and the barely concealed weapon under his jacket shook him.

"Can I come up to your room?" Mikhail Kangalovich was going on. "I'm not staying here . . . cops and diplomats don't mix very well, but nothing's to prevent me from coming to your room. Just to get acquainted . . ."

Without waiting for Damiens to reply, Mikhail led him toward the lift. "All aboard! It's late, and if I don't get my six hours of sleep, I end up with the reflexes of a Polish cop."

That was probably an obscure reference to some misfortune suffered by the Polish police, but Damiens did not understand it. He laughed, nevertheless; in his bluff, rough way, Mikhail at once had inspired him with a kind of instinctive sympathy.

For that matter, it must have been reciprocal, for when they entered Georges's room and Mikhail had rung to order a bottle of champagne—"May I?" he had already rung the bell—and lit up a huge pipe—"I hope you don't mind a bit of smoke?"—the Yugoslavian gave him a friendly clap on the back. "It's the first time I've been teamed with a Frenchman . . . it calls for a drink."

He then turned to more serious matters. He had no doubt that Karavalov had deliberately planned it so that nearly everyone in Europe would know the address of the Hracin mansion. It was obviously more than just a letter drop, and it should be the starting point for any search. However, Mikhail had no doubt that Karavalov was wary, that the murder of the man named Dimitri—whom Mikhail had known— had not made their task any easier and that, above all, they would have to act with circumspection and at the same time inspire Karavalov with confidence.

"Karavalov may be a myth, even a legend, but that didn't stop a man being murdered three days ago because of him, and that probably wasn't the end of it!"

Mikhail's voice was as calm as an announcer predicting the probable outcome of a tennis match.

"So," the Serbian continued, "we have one thing in our favor: your status as a French diplomat. People like Karavalov are funny—they like labels! Yours he likes, and I'm sure that he will finally stick his nose out . . and when I say 'nose' . . ."

Mikhail had ordered up a second bottle of champagne; the smoke from his pipe filled the room with a heavy, floating blue cloud, and Damiens felt himself sinking into an amused torpor.

"It's almost funny," he remarked during one of Mikhail's rare pauses. "I leave Paris and my office lined with green and gray files, with sound-deadening carpets and a nearly ninety-year-old secretary who is avid to know everything about my personal life, and I end up here in eastern Europe playing at being a spy."

Mikhail gave vent to a roar of laughter that ended in a coughing fit. "Spy! Cop, more like it. And who said anything about playing?" He suddenly grew serious: "It could end up in thousands, maybe millions dead, give or take a few."

But he soon recovered his high spirits. "Come on, now, you mustn't let it upset you. Everything will come right in the end, you'll see. You have charm, intelligence, know-how—and as for me, I can bring down a man at a hundred yards or open a safe for you in two and a half minutes; we're made for each other. And as for Karavalov . . ."

For another hour, possibly even two, Mikhail talked about Karavalov, about the legends that were current, about his women, his murders, his sudden bursts of generosity—an honorable bandit, perhaps, intoxicated by money, a *mafioso* who had a finger in every pie, but a man who had at last come to a decision.

"You see," Mikhail finally concluded before he stood up heavily, still in control of his movements despite the vast amount of alcohol he had drunk, "what pleases me the most about this whole affair is getting a chance to see him. To find out what he looks like."

As I said, Karavalov was known as the faceless one. . . .

Exhausted, Georges Damiens fell asleep as the bells of the Metropolitan Church rang out in response to those of the Stavropolos Church, sounding an hour he preferred at that moment not to know.

Damiens awoke with a heavy head and a coated tongue, but the next morning in the hotel lobby Mikhail was as fresh as a daisy . . . a 220-pound daisy. . . .

"Greetings to my favorite diplomat!"

He was heavily ironic, but Damiens could detect in his voice a warmth that already spelled friendship. Mikhail had been right; they were going to make a good team.

In my office in Geneva, surrounded by the books I was reading to pass the time between prolonged adjournments of my committee, I harbored few illusions. The chairman, the Norwegian Siegmans, still had to put up with Moelher's assaults, delivered with one hand on the heart and the other on a briefcase full of documents, all in the German's attempt to jump ahead in the agenda agreed to for our forthcoming work.

"It should all turn out well," Lukas assured me, nonetheless. "You've said that Damiens seems all right, and I have every confidence in Kangalovich."

And I, of course, had every confidence in Helena.

The Hracin mansion stood on the corner of the Chausée Kisseloff and an alley that led to a dead end abutting the garden of an old monastery. It was like all those gigantic structures erected in the 1980s by rich merchants who had not presumed to call them palaces. Its first owner had been a Czech émigré, who had loaded it with every sort of decorative element: a monumental entryway, neo-Baroque sculptures of caryatids on the facade and a profusion of cornices; inside, in the center of the house, there was a vast stairwell large enough to contain some half dozen of the poor gypsy dwellings standing in the no-man's-land outside the city, Bucharest's *mahalla*.

"*Mazette!*" Mikhail breathed—the Serbian equivalent of "Wow!"—as they approached the huge mansion of gray stone. "He doesn't go to any pains to conceal himself, this Karavalov!"

The mansion had indeed been designed to create an effect: everything signified fame and costly luxury; yet the entire building seemed to be strangely empty.

They knocked several times on the heavy street door at the main entrance. After receiving no reply, Mikhail shoved against the tall, carved wooden panel of the door, which swung back on its hinges. The first vestibule led into another, which opened onto the stairwell. Other doors on each side led to endless suites of rooms, all the furniture draped in dustcovers.

"Shall we go up?" Damiens suggested.

Mikhail's right hand had moved instinctively to his left side.

As they climbed the staircase, their footsteps echoed eerily, noisily, almost musically; their slightest whisper seemed amplified to the resonance of a Russian choir. They reached the next floor.

"It doesn't look as if anyone's at home," Damiens remarked.

Mikhail walked down the enfilade of rooms with their polished floors and rolled-up carpets, all filled with dustcovered furniture and dismantled chandeliers. The entire house seemed to have been closed up, if not abandoned.

"Hello! Anyone there?" His voice rang out like some prize Boris Goudonov in some stage Kremlin; the only response was another echo —then silence.

"What do you think?"

The men looked at each other. They had to find something, some-one, some indication or clue. Without that, this would be the end of their search and of their journey, too.

"It looks almost as though things had been packed up after a funeral. . . ."

Karavalov, faceless or not, dead or alive, had thought of every-thing. . . .

They mounted another story to the third floor, the fourth, still through the same dust-filled silence.

"The rats have evidently left the ship."

They had now reached the topmost floor, and Damiens, almost un-thinkingly, had opened one last door; they heard a woman's voice, and all at once everything happened very quickly. The woman had shouted something in Rumanian after a man, who now came running down a sort of service stairway that must have led up to the attic. Before Mikhail and Damiens could say a word, the man brushed them aside and ran down the main staircase, taking four steps at a time.

The fugitive was slight, short, with generous red sideburns. The woman—an old woman wearing an apron and leaning down over the brass railing of the banister—continued to shout down abuse at him as he went.

"What's she saying?" Damiens asked.

Mikhail shrugged. "I don't know—wait!"

Suddenly the old woman turned on them and began to shriek a torrent of what seemed to be imprecations. Unhesitatingly, Mikhail grabbed her by the shoulders, and they exchanged a few brief, almost laconic words, interspersed with more shouts and even two or three squeals. Damiens was able to understand the old woman's last words; the word for death is comprehensible in almost every language. Mikhail released his hold on the old woman, who, with one final curse, slammed the door to the service stairs behind her.

"What was she saying?" Damiens asked, although he thought he already knew.

Mikhail's face had grown somber. "She said Karavalov is dead, Dimitri is dead, too, everybody is dead—and then to top it all off she said that all hearts were empty . . . obviously a bit of Rumanian folk poetry."

Damiens glanced down the stairwell, which gaped empty below him like the hearts in the old woman's rhetoric. "But that's impossible. . . ."

"She says it was an accident. Karavalov is supposed to have been run down by a car yesterday morning. The house is closed."

"You don't think that . . ."

Mikhail made a gesture of discouragement. "We'll get nothing more out of her."

The entire house was silent again, and in silence Mikhail and Damiens started down the huge stairway. Now the sound of their footsteps seemed muffled by the dust, the coverings, the emptiness.

As they reached the bottom step, they heard a voice: "Gentlemen! Psst! Gentlemen!"

Someone was calling to them from the top floor. High above them, the face of an old man peered down at them; he had spoken in French. Mikhail and Damiens dashed back up the stairs.

"Gentlemen! Gentlemen!"

The two men arrived breathless back at the top. A tiny old man was standing there against the light; he had a huge, bald, wrinkled head, and he grinned broadly, revealing toothless gums.

Damiens spoke first: "Is it true that Karavalov is dead? What happened?"

The old man's face closed up like a trap shutting. His smile vanished. "I know nothing of that. I know nothing about it. I don't mix into things that are none of my affair."

Mikhail, as forceful as he had been with the woman, grabbed the man by the shoulders. "So why did you call us back?"

The old man seemed to be trembling in every limb. "I don't know . . . I have a message for you, that's all. Aren't you the two men who are to leave on tomorrow's train?"

Damiens quickly grasped that the old man had just given them a piece of essential information: they were to leave Bucharest the following day. Mikhail maintained his grip on the old man who continued in the same tone: "I don't want to know anything about it. I was just told to tell you to be at the Café Central after midnight. You're supposed to ask for Ghizka, say that Radu sent you."

"Who is Ghizka . . and are you Radu?" Damiens asked.

Mikhail released the informer, who disappeared through the stairway to the attic; they could hear his departing voice as he continued to mutter through his empty gums: "I don't know anything, I don't want to know; the old woman was right . . . I was wrong to try to help. . . ." His voice faded away into the uppermost reaches of the house.

"So, that's not a bad start," Mikhail said.

He stopped short. He drew in his breath and signaled Damiens to do likewise. Once again there was utter silence, and then suddenly, as if to confirm Mikhail's premonition, a new sound was heard on the staircase. This time, it was the sound of a woman's high-heeled shoes, descending the stairs below them almost gaily.

"Quick!" Mikhail shouted. "It's a woman!"

They dashed down the stairs. Two floors below, they could still hear the echoing sound of heels.

"She'll get to the bottom before we can."

Despite his two hundred twenty pounds, Mikhail was agile, but not agile enough; before he reached the second floor, the entrance door closed behind the unknown woman with a dull thud.

"We've missed her. . . ." Damiens muttered.

The closing mechanism of the street door appeared to be stuck, and Mikhail lost several seconds opening it. When they finally emerged onto the street, they saw a woman—a young woman in a black veil—getting into a long limousine parked further down the street. At once it pulled away silently, leaving the two men standing baffled on the steps of the Hracin mansion.

"What was all that about?" Damiens wondered as they caught their breath.

"It seems to have been very well planned. . . ."

They walked side by side down the Chaussée Kisselhoff; on either side of the street behind rows of still leafy trees there were mansions, interspersed with restaurants shaped like pink pergolas. The street was filled with an incredible mixture of ox-drawn carts and luxury cars.

There was a scent of the country, of fresh manure, earth and urine . . . the odor of the plains.

"Planned?"

"Of course, it was planned! The whole thing is a plan! That empty house, the old woman with her dialect—she wasn't even really speaking Rumanian!—the redheaded man who ran into us, the other man who called from the top of the stairs, the woman's footsteps in the deserted house . . . doesn't that all seem a little too well set up to you?"

They had reached a crossing: on the tree-filled islands in the center of the avenue, children were playing, shrieking and laughing as though life were flooding back after their hallucinatory experiences in the Hracin mansion.

"What do you think?"

Mikhail shrugged; his entire body seemed to rise up and then fall back into place as he did so. "I don't think anything. They've put us on the track. The hotel, the Hracin mansion, now the Café Central . . . so we'll just have to follow it to the end. You'll see."

"But what about Karavalov? Do you think he's still alive?"

Mikhail's shoulders rose and fell once more. "How can anyone know? Let's wait until this evening. I'm a cop, not a seer."

A red ball thrown by a little boy rolled against their legs. Mikhail bent down, picked up the ball and pretended to play with it for a moment as the children waited expectantly. Then he threw it back to them.

"Catch!" He laughed, and his mustache quivered with little, jerky movements, making him look like a clown gripped with an irrepressible urge to sneeze.

Later that evening, when Mikhail entered Damiens' hotel room, he emitted a similar laugh when he saw the latter standing before the mirror adjusting his cravat.

"See here, old man, we're not going to a wedding!"

Taken aback—he had not yet applied the hair oil, and his cowlick was standing rampant—Damiens stared at him through his round glasses.

"Of course, if we're to believe the good news we were told today, maybe it will be a funeral!"

Every hair of Mikhail's mustache seemed to tremble, and even when they reached the street, the huge Serbian was still chuckling over his latest witticism. In a short while, through the fine mist that had arrived with nightfall, they began to hear the sounds of music coming from a *brasserie*: they had arrived at the Café Central.

"Here we are," Mikhail announced, pushing open the door.

At once they were overwhelmed by the smell of smoke and tepid beer, heat, sweat and other less distinguishable odors. There was a mixture of grilled sausage, meat, mustard, fried onions—heavy, cheap smells.

The Café Central consisted of a series of rooms grouped around a large central hall with a low beamed ceiling. Drinkers were seated all about before steins of beer or glasses of a colorless liqueur set on bare wooden tables; waiters hurried among them, holding six, ten steins of foaming beer in one hand. On a wooden platform in one of the rooms an orchestra was beating out a heavy waltz rhythm; the drinkers marked time with their feet. There was an accordion player, a pianist, a couple of violinists and a zither player, but the fantastic, almost dreamlike atmosphere of the *brasserie* was due most of all to the mingling of all those smells, colors, heat, to the crowd of drinkers, the blue-green clouds of smoke hanging heavily in the air and the almost deafening music. . . .

"Typical local color," Mikhail remarked as they entered; he would have made a good tour guide.

He threaded his way among the tables and managed to stop a one-eyed waiter who seemed to be the patron. "Have you ever heard of anyone named Ghizka?"

He had to shout above the noise; the waiter jerked his head towards the platform.

"Ghizka, he's the one playing the zither." He had already turned away to dress down a young waiter who was not clearing the tables with sufficient alacrity.

Damiens joined Mikhail, and together they approached the platform.

"It's up to you," Mikhail said. "I'll leave it to you. After all, you're supposed to be the diplomatic one."

Any chance of speaking to Ghizka was doomed to failure for the moment; the music was growing louder, more piercing, deafening. There was a pause when Damiens felt—in that dreamlike atmosphere among all those indistinguishable faces—that the music had slowed down a bit. He took a step toward the zither player, but a tall, thin man with a pale, heavily pockmarked face pushed forward.

"Play, Ghizka!" he shouted. "Play! Music makes me forget my sorrows!"

The music again swelled in intensity while the man with the scarred face rocked from side to side. "Play, Ghizka, play, little father . . . only you can comfort me!"

As he spoke, the man turned to face Damiens, as though—Mikhail was to remark later—he wanted to make sure he had been noticed.

Damiens once again moved toward the zither player. "Are you Ghizka? Do you speak French?"

The musician, apparently rapt in his art, nodded.

"Are you Ghizka?" Damiens repeated. "Radu sent me. I'm looking for Karavalov."

All expression washed from Ghizka's face at the mention of the arms dealer's name: it was like a curtain coming down. The musician straightened suddenly, stared blankly into the hall and went on playing his instrument.

Damiens persisted: "I said we're friends of Radu's. We have to know if Karavalov is alive."

Caught up in the music, Ghizka pretended not to hear. Since Karavalov's name appeared to create such an effect in Bucharest, Mikhail began to repeat it over and over at the top of his voice until Ghizka became frightened enough to talk.

"My friend said we're looking for Karavalov! Karavalov! Do you understand—Karavalov!"

No longer able to feign indifference—Mikhail had a Bulgarian bass voice that was both deep and powerful—the zither player bent toward them.

"In a little while—but keep quiet, for the love of God!"

The tall, pockmarked man looked at them, but he was too drunk to matter. Ghizka turned to him also and appealed to him out of the side of his mouth: "And as for you, Dimitriu, will you leave me alone, for God's sake? Go drink somewhere else."

The accordion player, who seemed to double as leader, had been casting increasingly furious looks at his zither player. Ghizka's fingers now began to dance frantically over the strings of his instrument, launching into a tune that made the reflections shimmer in the mother-of-pearl inlay like pale beams of moonlight in the ruddy glow of the smoke-filled tavern.

The waiter whom Mikhail had questioned when they entered now returned bearing two glasses of a strong, sweet, burning white alcohol containing cloves; without asking, Mikhail and Damiens sat down at a table alongside the other drinkers.

"Rumania is oriental, don't forget," Mikhail murmured, downing his glass with a gulp. "Time means nothing. Anyone who shows up for a meeting less than an hour late is early and also ill-bred. Let's have another glass of this *tsuika*, shall we?"

Damiens, who had attempted to drain his glass in imitation of Mikhail, felt an intense burning pain at the back of his throat that extended down to his stomach, as though all the fire in all the sidewalk braziers on the Bucharest street corners in wintertime had descended his gullet along with that single swallow of raw plum *tsuika*.

"Great, isn't it? The local drink!"

Damiens imagined that Mikhail's mustache was trembling more than ever with amusement.

Not until an hour had gone by and the orchestra had made way for an odd-looking man in a tight suit with a waxy black mustache did Ghizka signal for Damiens and his shadow to follow him.

"We're being summoned backstage, old chap!" Mikhail said as he rose—a bit more heavily than when he had sat down.

Onstage, a gypsy began to sing one of the characteristic laments of his race, a *doinu* that sounded very like a dirge, and conversation came to a halt throughout the hall.

"Some of these singers are nationally known stars," Mikhail explained. "People come here from all over the city to hear them."

Two elderly men were weeping copiously as they listened to Mitica Dona intone his vagabond nostalgia, his song of endless, homeless journeying. Next to them, drunker than ever, the man whom Ghizka had called Dimitriu was completely dry-eyed, watchful. . . .

"Sir," Ghizka began, "you must be crazy! You must know that there are some names that mustn't be spoken here in a loud voice . . . particularly since what happened a few days ago. What do you want to know?"

He, too, was a true gypsy with swarthy skin; his eyes had a strange metallic gleam, a pearly luster almost like the lights that reflected from his zither in the smoke-filled room.

"I'm looking for Karavalov," Damiens replied, undaunted. "We've been informed he is dead. That's not true, is it?"

A group of girls in multicolored dresses, skinny young gypsies with half-naked breasts beneath their low-cut blouses, came down the hallway where they were standing behind the stage against the peeling wall. They were singers who were to accompany Mitica Dona in the famous *doinu* the audience was noisily demanding with much applause. One of them threw Damiens a bold glance as she passed, but it was not the time to indulge in such frivolity. Ghizka was speaking, his eyes glittering more than ever.

"You know very well Karavalov's not dead: other people may die, but not he!"

His voice expressed pride, as though in some way he and the adventurer were joined in a shady conspiracy that outweighed any fear.

"We have to talk to Karavalov. Where is he?"

Ghizka shrugged. "Radu must be mad to have sent you here. . . ."

Mikhail seized the gypsy by the shoulders and began to shake him.

"Listen, comrade Ghizka. Friends who can be discreet are a great asset, but friends who can no longer talk are worth nothing. You're a friend of Karavalov's, and we're two people he has to see. So be useful to us, or you'll soon be good for nothing!"

Ghizka understood. He lowered his voice and whispered: "Go to Roberte's this evening."

Damiens raised his voice. "Roberte?"

"Roberte, the Frenchwoman. You'll find her at the end of Calea Dudesti, number eighty-three, Pavlica's house. But you're sure no one followed you here? It's a matter of Karavalov's life. . . ."

In the room the applause burst forth, and Ghizka glanced toward the small, curtained doorway to the stage. "I must go. I've told you all I know. Karavalov is hiding, you know that as well as I do."

As they left the tavern, Damiens turned and noticed that the Café Central bore another sign. "Three Eyes in One Bed," it read on a painted wood panel, and there was a vulgar caricature of the patron—the one-eyed man—who had welcomed them lying in bed with his wife: two eyes plus one. The counterpane was painted a bright red.

"Just local color, diplomat! Local color!" was Mikhail's only comment.

HELENA

* * *

The policeman and the diplomat set out together on their strange nocturnal errand across that city on the edge of the East, a city so unlike any other. There must have been something incongruous in that journey made by the young man and the portly policeman, the Frenchman who had been highly polished in the best schools and the jovial Serbian who could cheerfully down a bottle of *tsuika* laced with vodka or rum in half an evening without his eyes showing the slightest effect.

"Calea Dudesti, on the other side of town. It's almost in the suburbs!"

They hailed a horse-drawn cab, and the next leg of their journey took them to a distant address: Pavlica's house, a brothel. Above the doorstep to which the driver pulled up, a red lantern was lit according to the laws of hospitality; the driver cursed when his horse slipped on the damp cobblestones. A fine rain had begun to fall, and suddenly Damiens thought of Helena.

The girls in that house, girls who crossed themselves as they passed the icons on the walls, probably could have given hours of pleasure had one lain in their arms . . . but Helena's arms were so pale, so long. . . .

"Wake up, old man. Here we are!"

They were forced to comply with the preliminary ceremonies that often prevail at such places. Pavlica's house was "private," but it seemed particularly so that evening, for Mikhail was forced to engage in a fairly lengthy discussion with the heavily made-up woman who opened the peephole in the door to check them out before they were admitted.

"I'm French," Damiens said, for in those happier days being French opened many doors.

Mikhail was frank. "I've come to see Roberte."

"There's no one here by that name!"

The woman's voice was firm, but Mikhail could be equally firm: "Ghizka sent us . . . from the 'Three Eyes'. . . ."

The woman's face relaxed, and she opened the door just wide enough for them to slip inside.

In those days, the brothels and taverns of Bucharest were an important element in an illicit night life that was too unusual for us to pass over without any notice at all. My friend Paul Morand once told me that he had seen in that city a house of pleasure called Castelful Spermuli. Allow me to translate: the Castle of Sperm! Without the noble pretensions of Castelful Spermuli, of course, Pavlica's house was nonetheless admirable in its way. It had a large central room heated by a vast green porcelain stove; wooden galleries led to the upper stories, forming a long rectangle of parquet flooring that echoed beneath the footsteps of the girls and their customers, almost as noisy as the mattresses on their beds with the broken-down springs.

The prostitute who had opened the door led them straight to another woman dressed in black whose face was painted chalk white, powdered like that of some languid Louis XV marquise, although she was wearing what appeared to be a Viennese cadet's uniform.

"Roberte is busy, sir," this under-madam replied with a thin smile, "but we can offer you an entire regiment of equally charming girls who, I can assure you, have every element of their profession at their fingertips, not to mention the tips of their tongues."

I can imagine Damiens' expression, dreaming as he was such tender dreams about Helena! Mikhail replied for him. Once again, one more time, he spoke Karavalov's name. The effect on the Austrian sergeant major was instantaneous: although she did not show fear, she almost snapped to attention!

"Follow me," she said. She preceded them up the wooden staircase with its treads of huge planks—solid enough to withstand regiments of hussars in heat—that led up to the galleries. On the way, a pale blond giant with albino eyes and a coat with a fur collar stood aside to make way for them.

"*Vive la France!*" he said to Damiens with a pregnant look.

Damiens had the impression that the albino—like Dimitriu in the Café Central and the redheaded man in the Hracin mansion—was making it a point to draw attention to himself. The woman in black paid no attention.

"It's room thirteen. Roberte likes to tempt fate!"

She knocked on the door bearing the number thirteen; it had been nailed on with the numbers turned backwards to thwart evil, just as boats used to go backwards down the Danube. A head with a mop of tousled red hair emerged . . . along with a pink breast from a gaping nightgown. The women exchanged a few words; then the door closed again.

"Wait," the under-madam told Mikhail.

A minute later, Roberte reappeared, but not the breast. Her makeup was now almost too perfect, as though it had been undisturbed for hours, but her voice was hoarse and she smelled of plum brandy.

"I don't know whether the man you're looking for is a friend of yours or not, but he's no longer one of mine," she began.

She was on the defensive, but Damiens, who had recovered himself —he was not forgetting Helena, but he was curious to see where the tracks would take them—adopted Mikhail's technique. He seized her shoulders . . . they were soft and thin and covered with freckles.

"Listen to me. I'm not leaving here until you've told me where I can find Karavalov. It's a question of his life. If indeed he is still alive!"

The prostitute burst out laughing, the laugh of a woman who is not really all that drunk. "As though Karavalov could die! You're as bad as the albino, Ionica! But then, there can't be two people in Bucharest who can manage to believe in the impossible!"

She was about to continue, but the whole scene suddenly seemed to accelerate, as in some "advanced" film, in which a couple of quick fades, a dissolve and a final cut lead directly into a denouement that is really nothing at all. First a voice was heard from inside the room calling out in German: "Roberte? *Was ist das?*" Then, as the girl turned back to reply, the pounding of fists was heard from the front door; one of the women who were standing so scantily clad around the porcelain stove cried out: "Police! Police!"

Mikhail moved to the door of room thirteen, but Roberte, now completely sober, barred his way. "Not this way—out the back." And before either of the two men had time to ask her any further questions, she hissed: "Return to your hotel at once. You'll find what you're looking for there."

Like the Café Central, Pavlica's house, along with Roberte and the Viennese sergeant-madam, seemed to dissolve into the night. A fine rain was still falling on Bucharest, and the morning ox carts, heavy with provisions for the city, were plodding towards the Calea Victoriei and Carol Boulevard.

At the Athenée-Palace, the atmosphere seemed completely normal. The night porter handed Damiens a narrow envelope with a red seal. It contained two tickets for the next morning's train to Lausanne and reservation slips for two compartments: numbers five and seven, in car number four.

"Just by chance," Mikhail remarked, "five and seven . . . with six between them. Of course, that's just by chance, too."

"Do you believe Karavalov will be in number six?"

The Serbian shrugged. He seemed suddenly tired. "He who does not believe can hope for nothing. And I am still hoping."

The lobby of the hotel was empty. The last prostitute, tired of waiting for one more client who would never come, had abandoned her post. A jaded gigolo with tired, romantic eyes, such as one finds only in Bucharest, did not look up at the two men; like so many of his compatriots, he was strictly specialized and probably famous among ex-countesses from Russia or aged Viennese princesses—all over sixty.

For the rest of the night, in his room with the blue chamber pot, Damiens dreamed. He dreamed that when he awoke in the morning, the door of his room was locked, and that in order to join Helena, who was waiting for him on the Orient Express with the impassive Karavalov (whose face was a clock without any hands), he had to climb over the guard rail in the window, across a balcony and down the fake baroque facade of the Athenée-Palace. And then, when he arrived at the station, the train was already disappearing in the distance with Helena Petresco on board, locked into her compartment as he had been in his hotel room, crying.

"Well, we were about to leave without you!" Mikhail said when Damiens arrived breathless at the Filaret Station just before the train was about to leave.

The platform was alive with the usual animated scene: a soldier smiled, his weapon on his shoulder, and another was questioning in Rumanian a tall, bearded character who looked like a defrocked orthodox priest. Mikhail, a bottle of beer in hand, had a worried expression on his face, but he welcomed Damiens with a laugh.

"Just a minute to spare!"

As the porter took the Frenchman's bag to his compartment, Mikhail leaned over confidentially: "Our client is already here. In number six, as we predicted. . . ."

"Have you seen him?" Damiens was brought up short, incredulous: was the man without a face going to agree to show himself in public?

But Mikhail shoved him in. "What do you think! He was already shut up in his compartment when I got here, and he's given strict orders not to be disturbed."

In the corridor, while Damiens was settling into his compartment and his reservation was being checked, the conductor had the same knowing expression as Mikhail: "Your friend doesn't seem overfond of company. . . ."

He was referring to the passenger in compartment number six, which was situated—the layout is important, as you will see—in car number four, between compartment seven, occupied by Mikhail, and number five, where Damiens was opening his toilet case. When he had arranged his things and emerged into the corridor—the train was about to start—he nevertheless felt impelled to make certain.

"Are you sure it's he?"

"Who else could it be? Now that we've started to play this cat-and-mouse game with him, we've got to respect his rules until the end, that's all. Karavalov wants to remain a man without a face, and Dimitri's death has just strengthened his desire for discretion. He knows we're here: why should he show himself, even to us?"

On the platform, the stationmaster was waving his red flag, and the whistles blew.

"Well, in that case," Damiens said, "I suggest that we stand guard in turn outside his compartment."

Mikhail's mustache twitched with amusement, but he he seemed to be preoccupied.

"Our diplomat is beginning to learn the trade! Go have a drink. You can relieve me in a little while."

Alone in the corridor, Mikhail first checked to see that the door to compartment six and the communicating doors in five and seven were locked. Reassured, he filled his pipe, took his time lighting it and then leaned at the window: with a huge blast of steam, the Simplon-Orient Express, en route for Lausanne via Subotica, Zagreb and Venice, pulled out of the station.

It started like any other train journey. Alone in the bar car, the young diplomat ordered a very strong coffee; after all, he had just spent a short, restless night. Then he sank into a deep Pullman chair and leafed through a week-old number of *Le Temps* he had bought the previous evening in the lobby of the Athenée-Palace. But his eyelids grew heavy, and gradually he fell asleep.

When he opened his eyes, he received his first shock. The train had left the outskirts of Bucharest and was now traveling along the muddy waters of the Danbovita. The car swayed gently in three-quarter time over the rails, and three people—only three people—were moving about. "Moving about"—the term is exact. In slow motion, the three passengers changed places with each other, from the bar to the arm-chairs, from the armchairs to the windows and from the windows to the low table piled with reviews and magazines as though performing some strange, unreal ballet around Damiens, a ballet of which he was the sole spectator. The scene would not have been quite so remarkable had not the first of the three men moving about so restlessly in the bar car been the very man who had run into Mikhail and Damiens on the staircase of the Hracin mansion; had not the second man been the drunk named Dimitriu to whom Ghizka had spoken; and had not the third been the debonair albino Ionica they had encountered in Roberte's brothel. The more they moved to and fro in the car, which was now going faster as the train picked up speed along a stretch of straight track, the more they seemed to be taking particular pains to behave as though they did not know each other, to ignore each other's presence.

Damiens took a few moments to become fully aware of what was going on around him. Then, once over his first astonishment, he began to grow suspicious. There was only one explanation for the presence of these three men on board: Karavalov. He pulled himself together and got up. He would have to warn Mikhail. He hurried breathlessly back to car number four; he had suddenly begun to fear the worst.

However, Mikhail was still leaning at the window in front of com-partment seven, and even before Damiens could tell him what he had just seen, the Serbian lowered his eyes with a worried expression.

"I know. They passed me. Of course, I recognized them! Indeed, they made sure of it. . . ."

Damiens was about to reply, but Mikhail stopped him with a gesture.

"And that's not all!" He looked as though he were joking, but his voice was serious. "Look down there."

At the other end of the car, a figure of a veiled woman in black was disappearing from view, and this time Damiens could not help but recognize her.

"Yes, indeed," Mikhail murmured, "the beautiful lady who brought you back to the Athenée-Palace the other night."

"You saw her?" But Damiens was no longer in a condition to be surprised at anything.

"That's my job, isn't it? Come, our guest is well guarded."

All Damiens' aplomb had faded at the vertiginous amateur spy adventure into which he had been plunged. His eyes grew as round as his glasses, and he had a horrified expression. "But you can't think that she is also . . ."

Mikhail's sarcasm was biting. "Did I say that? All these ladies and gentlemen are just plain tourists, like you and me! Haven't you understood? You may not believe me, but this Orient Express is only a pleasure train."

Damiens clenched his fists. The memory of Helena was a tender one. Her image was too beautiful. Of course, she was the foreign woman encountered perhaps but once in a lifetime.

"I'm going to talk to her," he said.

And he set out for the bar car towards which Helena Petresco had disappeared with such an obviously conspiratorial air, Helena Petresco, whom even I had been a million miles away from imagining would ever have indulged in such a pastime. . . .

At the threshold of the Pullman car, Damiens stopped short; what he saw was truly fantastic. Standing at the bar, Helena Petresco seemed to be deep in conversation with the three men Damiens had observed there ten minutes earlier. And when he entered, the ballet recommenced. One after the other—as though casually going through a series of quite natural movements—the three men drew away from Helena, who was already smiling at Damiens as he approached.

"Yes, it's me."

Her smile deepened, but Damiens was wary. "Am I intruding?"

"Not at all! I was trying to get a light from these gentlemen, but none of them seems able to provide one. Could you by any chance help me?"

She extended her cigarette—the same gold-tipped cigarettes!—and Damiens was disarmed at once. Yes, he had found her again, the same as before, relaxed, smiling. So calm . . . And yet she had pretended not to know the three men with whom she seemed so clearly to be linked. . . .

A few minutes later they were sitting side by side in the deep Pullman chairs with their lace antimacassars, and Helena was sipping a glass of tea, Russian style.

"I told you Europe was a small place. . . ."

Appearances had to be kept up; everything had to seem natural, but Damiens protested: "This time I don't believe in chance!"

"You're mistaken. Chance is the only lover who has never deceived me. He has always faithfully come up with the unexpected!"

Nothing about her had changed: not her smile, not her spirited repartee.

"However, you have to admit that your presence here on this train . . ."

Helena's smile did not change, but she made an imperceptible gesture, not an ill-humored gesture, not an impatient one, but a signal that indicated she wished to end this boring conversation and turn to more pleasant subjects.

"So, Georges, and what about yourself? What about your presence on this train? Isn't that rather extraordinary, too? You interrogate me just because I happen to be on the express to Lausanne, whereas you yourself—if I'm to believe what you told me the other evening—should be sitting at your desk in Bucharest! So allow me to ask you the same question in the same way: what are you doing on this train, Georges?"

Damiens looked troubled. For a moment he hesitated, and then he stammered: "I'm . . . traveling. . . ."

Helena laughed. "Perfect! You're traveling. I'm traveling. We're traveling. You have your reasons, and I have mine: let's travel together then, without arguing, shall we? The Slav-Latin foreign woman and the romantic young diplomat, remember? It didn't start off too badly, so why not continue?"

She extended her hand to Damiens, who suddenly relaxed.

"Why not?" He took Helena's hand and held it. "As you said the other evening: someplace else, another way . . ."

"Who knows . . ." Helena laughed, a laugh unlike any other . . . perhaps Maria's . . . and the flirtation between her and Damiens might have entered its second phase at that moment had not the train been suddenly shaken by a distant explosion, followed by a piercing sound of screeching metal and tortured rails—the sound of braking.

Helena was almost thrown into the young man's arms. "What was that?"

But Damiens understood. "Don't move!"

He dashed towards car number four.

* * *

In the corridors of the train which finally ground to a stop, there was the usual excitement created by such incidents. Shouts, calls for help, advice.

"Has there been an accident?"

A conductor was running along the embankment outside.

"No one is to leave the train!"

Damiens took some time in reaching his car: at the entrance to compartment six, Mikhail and an agent of the railway company were vainly trying to force open the door.

"It's blocked from the inside. . . ." growled the agent.

Mikhail shrugged his shoulders in response to Damiens' questioning look. "A bomb! A time bomb must have been put inside."

There was no sound of life from inside the compartment; Karavalov had to be dead.

"I'm going to break down the door!" Mikhail shouted finally.

He exerted all his strength, and the partition gave way: the compartment, the seats torn apart by the bomb that had obviously been placed beneath them, was empty. Tattered bits of fabric and baggage were strewn about everywhere.

It took the actors in this scene a few seconds to recover from their shock. The conductor stammered that his colleagues at the station in Bucharest had assured him that . . . Mikhail seemed equally taken aback. As for Damiens, he had barely recovered enough to notice that Helena was standing in the corridor behind him, silent.

"We were watching an empty compartment," was all he could mutter.

Mikhail was the first to react. Suddenly he turned to Helena, who was now smiling ironically.

"My dear lady, I think it's high time the three of us had a little chat!"

Helena's smile broadened. "Do you really think so?"

She followed them into compartment number seven.

As Damiens explained to me later, Mikhail had at once taken the initiative and attacked, realizing as he did that Helena's presence on the train was not fortuitous. In self-defense, Helena had immediately counterattacked.

"I know you're going to say that you find it strange that you encounter me wherever you go. For, of course, as you have guessed, I was the woman you saw on the stairs in the Hracin mansion."

Helena spoke aggressively, firmly. Mikhail, however, was in no mood for pleasantry: "Shall we stop beating around the bush?"

Damiens joined in. "My friend is right, Helena. You have to tell us what you are doing on this train."

Helena Petresco smiled and replied with her usual superb nonchalance: "Haven't you understood? But, of course, I'm the wife of the man you know as Karavalov! And I, too, like yourselves, want nothing more than for him to arrive in Geneva alive. So I am here to look after him. . . ."

Under the surface Helena was, I think, laughing. Passing herself off as Karavalov's wife was a stroke of genius to explain her journey between Bucharest and Switzerland with no apparent motive. Of course, she might actually have been telling the truth, in which case I—more than anyone else—had been taken in by her when I had held her in my arms by the shores of Lake Geneva. But Damiens had no way of knowing this, and her words left him speechless.

Mikhail did not give up so easily. He pursued his interrogation: "Why the empty compartment?"

But Helena had an answer for everything. "Just an extra precaution, my friend! You ask me who I am, but can you tell me who you are? And even if you do, what proof have I that you are telling me the truth?"

There was no suitable reply to that, but Mikhail attempted one: "You will have to trust us now and tell us where your husband is."

Helena flashed a smile that would have disarmed the most stolid of policemen anywhere along the Danube. "No, no, my friend . . . you know very well that I shall not tell you that. That is the supreme precaution, that no one know who Karavalov is. I shall not tell you. Why insist?"

Mikhail seemed inclined to pursue the matter further, but at that moment the conductor knocked on the door to inform us that the train was about to start and that, since Damiens' compartment had been damaged almost as much as the spectral Karavalov's, he would henceforth have to share Mikhail's accommodations.

"After all," Helena remarked ironically, "this finally brings us all three closer together, am I not right, sir?"

She had spoken to Mikhail who was obviously in a bad temper; for the next several hours, the Serbian's face wore a scowling, grumpy expression. Even though Damiens was fully aware of his friend's unhappiness at the situation and that he continued to regard Helena with a good deal of suspicion, he himself was highly gratified by the intimacy she had mentioned and of which he intended to take every advantage. The fact that Helena was married or not married did not unduly concern him: above all, she impressed him as being a liberated woman. Perhaps her marriage to Karavalov had been nothing but a business arrangement. And then there was that evening they had shared in Bucharest. . . . So as the train carried them ever further along the path toward the impossible, he devoured her with his eyes, he drew her out and made her talk simply because he liked listening to her. But no matter how he attempted to employ all the meager diplomatic resources at his disposal—after all, he was new at the job—he was unable to get her to reveal which of the passengers on that train that was now rolling across miles of low-lying marshy yellow plains was Karavalov.

"But we're here to protect him!"

She continued to shake her head in silence, or she diverted the subject. At last, when one of the three unknown men from Bucharest passed them in the Pullman car, Damiens made a final effort to get her to tell him at least whether one of them was Karavalov—but she cut him short.

"I thought you were more quick-witted, my dear Georges. Karavalov's life is at stake, and the murder of our friend Dimitri was a warning to all of us. You have been given abundant proof that your presence on this train has not stopped our adversaries. The fewer of us who know who Karavalov is, the better for him. Believe me, he has always lived like this—why do you want to change things now, when he is a hairbreadth away from abandoning this kind of life for good?"

Damiens was somewhat abashed by her speech and did not know what to reply, but she had already risen.

"Now I'm tired. I shall return to my compartment." Yet she leaned toward him. "Don't be angry with me, Georges, I beg you. We shall meet again very soon." Her hand caressed the young diplomat's neck. . . .

After she had disappeared, Mikhail arose and came to sit next to Damiens. "Well, what do you think of the whole thing?" He was still asking questions, concerned, gloomy.

"I believe her, of course."

"I can't share your certainty, but that's not the question."

Damiens knew very well that that was not the question; the question was Karavalov. They had set out together on a train journey across nearly the whole of Europe with the purpose of accompanying and protecting a man, not knowing who that man was! There was something so preposterous about their present situation that Damiens suddenly felt inclined to laugh, but his companion's somber mien stopped him.

Mikhail continued: "I think there can be no doubt that one of those three fellows is Karavalov, and that the other two are along to throw us off the track. But which one . . ."

Like a schoolboy eager to respond to a question from the teacher, Damiens raised his hand. "Unless Karavalov is someone else, someone we've not seen but who is traveling under our very noses."

Mikhail shrugged, annoyed. "Or perhaps even on another train. Maybe he's really dead, maybe he doesn't exist, maybe we've dreamed the whole thing! Anything is possible, but just to be safe . . ."

He glanced down to the far end of the bar car: now making no attempt to ignore each other, the three unknown men were sitting together at the same table, drinking silently.

"Just to be safe, I'm going to keep an eye on my three tourists. You're not to let Madame Karavalov—if she is Madame Karavalov—out of your sight. I hope that doesn't upset you too much?"

Georges Damiens nodded in agreement: as far as he was concerned, it was a perfect division of labor.

Mikhail had no great problem in striking up an acquaintance with the three men. Night was beginning to fall, and he approached their table; they had begun to play poker, and it seemed quite natural that he ask if he might join them.

"Two of a kind beats a straight?"

The words acted like a charm: with a deliberate movement, the gypsy from the Café Central motioned to Dimitriu to pull up a chair for Mikhail, and the four of them were soon involved in the game. Each of the three Rumanians knew that Mikhail was watching them; Mikhail knew that they each knew. Now all he had to do was pick up his cards and win. Damiens, who had returned to the Pullman car after dinner, felt renewed admiration for his companion: Mikhail really knew how to deal with all situations! Following the latter's advice, Damiens was fully occupied with Helena.

Thus began the first of the two evenings they were to spend on the Bucharest-Lausanne express, evenings Georges Damiens would remember for the rest of his life, evenings about which he would later speak with a tender, somewhat intoxicated, somewhat mournful nostalgia. He would look back to what he referred to as his "nights on the Orient Express"—the Orient Spy Express, he would always add—and for the remainder of his model diplomatic career that would see him appointed to head two or three of our largest embassies, he would feel a delicious thrill whenever he remembered.

The first evening was fairly banal. Sitting beside Helena, who had retained her amused smile but who was slowly beginning to share some of her companion's emotions, he talked. He talked to her about himself, about herself. A few yards away from them in the bar car, now transformed into a gambling den and smoker, thick, dark clouds from the players' cigars and pipes floated in the air as Mikhail and his companions won or lost considerable sums of money which Damiens saw his colleague handle with sovereign assurance.

"So much for me," Mikhail would exclaim at regular intervals, losing to the man who seemed to be winning from all of them—Dimitriu, the tall, pockmarked drunk from the Café Central—and pulling huge wads of banknotes from every pocket.

Dimitriu and his friends downed glass after glass of *tsuika* with vodka chasers, but their faces remained impassive.

"It's nice, at any rate, to have abandoned our masks," Helena remarked, sitting down in an armchair beside Damiens.

Damiens, who had completely forgotten her alleged married status, agreed: "I've finally begun to recapture the feeling that I've found my beautiful foreigner from the embassy . . . truly found her. . . ."

She drew closer to him; the warm air, the smoke, the plum brandy began to affect them. "I told you then, remember: another time, another place . . ."

For a moment Damiens seemed to recall that somewhere on the train there was still an unknown man named Karavalov . . . but Helena made a gesture that seemed to mean: "Can't you forget him for a while?"

She smiled wistfully. "Let's talk about ourselves, shall we? I'd like you to tell me something, anything . . . a love story."

We must remember the ambience: the alcohol fumes, the cigar smoke, the slow swaying of the train—and perhaps even the feeling of some obscure but imminent danger symbolized by the four men at the other end of the car. Helena, like Damiens, was prepared to forget many things that evening. Or to bring new things to life . . .

"A love story? Which one? Perhaps the foreign woman and the diplomat! There are only three basic plots, after all, and we are only characters, perhaps, clichés, stylized. . . ."

Damiens tried to mask his feelings under a bantering surface, but for once Helena did not seem to be smiling.

"No, Georges, it's not a novel now. . . ."

Damiens suddenly relaxed: no, he had no desire to pretend either. "You're right. The only story that matters now is the story of a man and a woman meeting on a train. The woman is very beautiful, the man is attractive enough and they are about to spend forty-eight hours together. . . ."

She held out her hand. "A great many things can happen in forty-eight hours!"

With the heavy blue smoke, the alcohol, the darkness and the motion of the train, the evening went by quickly. Damiens and Helena spoke the words one speaks at such moments, words no one would care to repeat in other circumstances. She told him of Geneva—I think she even mentioned me, referring to me as "a friend." He told her about Paris, his life, his hopes. He was so like me, Georges Damiens—like the Paul de Morlay you met on the first train to Budapest—that he must have told her about novels he had written as a young man; perhaps he described his image of his ideal woman.

"She would be very pale, with high cheekbones and very red lips. . . ."

She must have gazed deep into his eyes, as she knew how to do so divinely with that art that was hers alone, so that neither of them were able to look away.

"I am happy I've met you, too, Georges. . . ."

Meanwhile, hand succeeded hand at the poker table.

"Dimitriu has the luck of the devil!" Mikhail growled; he was losing heavily.

And Helena and Damiens gazed at each other as though meeting for the first time. The evening, I repeat, passed quickly. When Mikhail finally rose from the table, the game ended, he was staggering slightly, but the winner, Dimitriu, his pockets stuffed full of winnings, had to support himself on the walls of the carriage on the way back to his compartment. Helena and Damiens watched them leave uncaring; for the space of that night, he and she were in a world that contained no spies, no policemen or thieves, a world in which they had been brought together by fate. . . .

At around two in the morning, Damiens escorted Helena to her compartment. He hesitated in the doorway for a few seconds, but she brushed his lips in a rapid kiss.

"I'm exhausted this evening. . . ."

In those happier times, a woman's fatigue was sufficient reason for a true gentleman not to press further. Georges Damiens, therefore, confined himself to hinting that he would have liked to have followed her in. . . .

Back in the compartment he was now sharing with Mikhail, the Serbian, drunk as a Pole, was already snoring noisily, but a happy smile played across his face. In his sleep, Damiens' companion seemed to have regained his good humor. And as for Damiens, his heart was so light that Karavalov was more than ever forgotten.

In the morning, however, his tongue coated and his head heavy, he was assailed by the darkest premonitions. He had slept badly; Mikhail's snoring had disturbed him throughout the night, and plum brandy leaves formidable headaches in its wake. In short, Karavalov and the mystery surrounding him had moved back into the center of his thoughts.

Damiens took a few hesitant steps in the compartment. Mikhail's bunk was empty, but he was glad of that; he would have been totally incapable of carrying on any kind of coherent conversation before he had downed a cup of boiling hot tea or a glass of orange juice. He stood for a long moment before the mirror and scratched his head thoroughly. Then he swallowed a glass of water that stood next to the crystal carafe on the washstand; it tasted bitter. The mixture of *tsuika* and vodka had definitely not agreed with him! He made a cautious toilet and dressed with slow, careful movements.

Two of the Rumanians with whom Mikhail had been playing poker the previous evening were already in the restaurant car drinking hot tea. Only tall, skinny Dimitriu was missing; Mikhail was sitting a few yards from them, puffing on his pipe.

"Well, no one would accuse you of looking in top form this morning!" His mustache had recovered its usual twitch, as though the previous night had affected him quite unlike the way it had affected Damiens.

"I got to bed a bit late last night. . . ."

"That's not being serious, my dear diplomat . . . not serious at all."

Nevertheless, despite his habitual flow of talk, Mikhail's expression indicated that he was preoccupied. When the Frenchman asked, "Anything new on Karavalov?" his companion only shrugged.

"Still nothing. Total darkness. Either the fellow is fiendishly clever or . . ."

"Or?"

Mikhail never finished his sentence. Something was happening at the far end of the car that attracted his attention: a conductor had approached the two Rumanians and was whispering something to them. At once they jumped up, agitated, as though the news had been of the utmost importance.

"Come along!" Mikhail said.

He pulled Damiens after him. At that point, as though from nowhere, Helena stepped between them.

"It's beginning!"

Helena's voice was even more ironic than it had been the evening before . . . but she was right. *It* was indeed beginning. Lying on his back in his compartment at the end of the train, Dimitriu wore the same white shirt he had worn the previous night, but now a large red stain covered the area above his heart. The banknotes he had won were strewn about the compartment, as though his murderer were expressing contempt for any sordid question of mere money. . . .

Horrified, the two surviving Rumanians stood looking down at the body. Helena, behind them, remained impassive. Yes, *it* had begun, and they still had almost twenty-four hours of travel before the train was to arrive at the station in Lausanne. The pleasure train had suddenly become a train full of phantoms. . . .

There were formalities, and there was a long delay when they stopped in a small rural station where the body was removed. There a typically Croatian police inspector questioned all the passengers who had had any contact with the unfortunate Dimitriu, while the rest exchanged guarded looks. After all, there was a murderer on the train; it was like an Agatha Christie novel.

Before the train started again, Damiens, who was feeling increasingly exhausted—he had a headache, sudden fits of dizziness—took a short stroll with Mikhail on the station platform. They had killed a second time, and there was no reason to think it would be the last.

"And what if Dimitriu was Karavalov?" Damiens asked.

Mikhail swept his hypothesis aside with a gesture. "If he was Karavalov, as you say, you can be sure that your lady friend would have behaved quite differently. No, the poor guy was nothing but an underling, some kind of lieutenant. A bodyguard not even able to guard himself!"

"So now what do we do? Wait?"

Mikhail continued to pace back and forth. "Wait! Wait for what? Until they wipe out every passenger on the train, one by one? What a clever idea! No, it's up to us to make some move. And first we've got to make that woman talk. We can't just stand around any longer."

He would have gone on, but Damiens stopped him. "You'll have to forgive me. . . ."

He leaned against the wall of the station; the train and the passengers on the platform swam before his eyes.

"Don't you feel well, old man? You don't look too good to me."

Damiens shrugged. "It's nothing . . . I'm better."

He did feel better, but the sweat was still pouring down his forehead.

"Shall we get back on board?"

They returned to compartment number seven. Mikhail handed Damiens a glass of water. "Drink that. It'll do you good."

Damiens stood motionless for a second, the glass in his hand, as though thinking. "And what if it's better the way it is? Aren't we protecting Karavalov even more effectively, not knowing who he is?"

Mikhail did not answer. He looked at Damiens with concern as he stood there, holding the glass of water.

"But I suppose you're right," Damiens went on. "I'll talk to Helena in a little while, but first I want to lie down for a bit."

And he drank the glass of water he was holding at one gulp.

A large part of the day had gone by before the train finally pulled out. A telegram had been sent ahead to Ljubljana where two Yugoslavian police inspectors were to come on board to pursue an investigation, and no passenger had been allowed to leave the train. Having slept for two full hours, Damiens awakened even more tired than he had been in the morning. He searched the train for Helena, only to find that she had locked herself in her compartment with the expressed wish not to be disturbed. Despairingly, the young diplomat returned to his own compartment and again lay down, but the two aspirins he swallowed one after the other, with an additional two glasses of water, left him feeling seedy still. Mikhail had gone back to playing poker with the two surviving Rumanians, but the three men were watching each other more warily than ever.

When Damiens arrived at the Pullman car shortly before dinner, the scene that confronted him seemed hallucinatory: it was as though nothing had happened. Only a few hours before a man had been found murdered, and now, on this second evening, everyone seemed unconcerned. Some stood at the bar, some were reading magazines, some were playing cards. Helena, in the armchair that had begun to seem her personal property, sat in the middle of the car smoking a gold-tipped cigarette; the unreal, disjointed atmosphere of the entire scene was enhanced by the fact that all the passengers had dressed for dinner—in long dresses, evening clothes, white ties. Damiens felt as though he had entered a wax museum in which every character that had haunted his nightmares had been assembled, frozen in familiar attitudes like stiff dummies in a Madame Tussaud's.

His arrival would have gone unnoticed had not a sudden movement of the car thrown him against the bar.

"Come, sit here!"

Helena had risen and came toward him; neither Mikhail nor his two poker-playing companions moved. The tall albino from Pavlica's brothel was winning . . . Ionica, the madam had called him.

"Georges, you're very pale. What is the matter? You don't look well." Helena seemed concerned.

And, indeed, Damiens felt nauseated. He made an effort to reach the armchair next to hers and sank into it. Around him he could hear vague murmurs, voices: Mikhail swearing over his losses, another man speaking Russian and Helena's voice as she leaned over him, still concerned.

"You should lie down."

He made a gesture of refusal; the idea of being alone in his compartment was suddenly frightening. Then, slowly, as the car and its occupants began to spin faster and faster around him, the feeling rose that something was about to happen, something he should be fighting against.

Helena put her hand to his forehead: "You don't feel feverish."

He caught hold of it. "Don't leave me. . . ."

Without realizing it, he had spoken in a very loud voice. The bartender, a tall Englishman with a red mustache, was moving among the Pullman chairs. Most of the passengers—those stiff mannequins—had gone to the dining car, and no one, absolutely no one, seemed to be paying any attention to him.

He suddenly stiffened: "I don't want to!"

Mikhail looked at him, motionless, expressionless. . . .

"What don't you want?" Helena asked, her voice like an echo.

He was not aware that once again he called out. He held the woman's hand in his, ever more tightly, but it seemed to him that for a few seconds—the thick smoke, the smell of the car, alcohol—he lost consciousness. When he reopened his eyes, Mikhail was standing before him holding two glasses of vodka.

"Drink this. It will pick you up."

The jovial Serbian's expression was cold, and the two Rumanians, who had stopped their game, had the same steely look in their eyes, as if all of them were in collusion against him.

"Mikhail is probably right. Drink . . ." Helena urged.

All of them were in collusion against him and against Karavalov. Even Helena. He pushed her hand away, and once again his eyes closed: the whirlpool of crystal vases and fringed curtains, the bar car, the entire train, became a mass of blue and white clouds that parted to let him through.

"Take him away," Helena murmured.

When Damiens awoke again in his compartment—he was lying on his bunk—it was to complete darkness. Despite the torpor that had overcome him a few hours before—had it really been so short a time?—he felt himself again. He sat up and flicked the switch of the night lamp at the head of his bed. A small rectangular card, Helena's visiting card, was lying beside him, a few words scrawled on it in violet ink: "Sleep. I'll have news in the morning." Someone had hung his jacket on a hanger, but otherwise he was completely dressed.

He sat up fully and looked at his watch: it was three in the morning, and he was suddenly terribly thirsty. Then he listened: from the accelerated motion of the train, he realized it had picked up speed, probably to make up for its long halt in the tiny Yugoslavian station. Now completely awake, he got up for a drink. It was then that he noticed that Mikhail's bunk had not been slept in.

As he reached out for the crystal water carafe, he seemed to hear from a great distance the sound of a scream, almost lost in the noise of the train. His hand remained suspended for a second over the carafe; then, hearing no further sound, he poured himself a glass and lifted it to his lips. There was the same bitter taste as the evening before. He was about to drain the glass anyway—he was very thirsty—when a violent knock pounded at the door.

"Open up! Open up!" a man's voice called. "Helena!"

He leaped to the door and opened it. The tall albino from Pavlica's house stood in the corridor; his hair was tousled, his shirt collar was open and he was panting.

"Come quick! It's Helena. There's a man in her compartment."

With another bound, Damiens was in the corridor. Half a minute later, the two men arrived at the door to Helena's compartment.

"It's quiet now," the Rumanian whispered. "But a minute ago she screamed." He put his hand on the handle of the door, but it did not move.

Damiens had recovered his presence of mind. "Go find the conductor. Quickly!"

Indeed, it was the climax. The conductor arrived and handed his passkey to Damiens, who entered the adjoining compartment, terrifying an old lady who was already frightened at the sound she had heard a short while before.

"Take this," the Rumanian said, handing Damiens a revolver he took from his pocket.

The conductor, who understood what was going on, told him they would be reaching a tunnel in a few minutes. "You can take advantage of the noise it will make."

While he waited those few minutes for the train to enter the tunnel before breaking into Helena's compartment, Georges Damiens, gun in hand—he told me this himself—counted the ties as the train rolled over them.

"I was sure I was going to find Helena dead," he said.

The train entered the tunnel at the 117th tie. At that precise instant, Damiens turned the conductor's passkey in the keyhole of the connecting door between compartments three and four of car number seven.

Helena was in the compartment, but she was still alive. She was crouched huddled up at the foot of her bunk. Standing before her was the massive figure of a man. Damiens did not fire immediately—shooting a man in the back is not the habit at the Quai!—and his pause was almost fatal.

"Drop your gun, diplomat!"

The man had turned; he, too, was armed, and he was prepared to kill. The man was Mikhail.

Damiens let his gun slide to the floor; from the expression on Mikhail's face he knew that the Serbian was going to fire. He shut his eyes, and the explosion burst deafeningly in the room at the very moment the train emerged from the tunnel.

"It's over," a voice said.

He opened his eyes. No, he was not dead. It was Mikhail who had slid to the floor, just as had his own revolver—silently. Helena was kneeling on her bunk gripping a tiny revolver she had taken from beneath her pillow.

"Sorry, Mikhail. . . ." Damiens murmured.

Only after she had drunk two glasses of vodka did Helena explain to Damiens what had happened. At the next table, the tall albino from Pavlica's and the short man from the Hracin mansion were now innocently playing dominoes.

"I suspected one of you from the start . . . Mikhail or you."

She spoke like a leader, a person in command, coldly. But beneath her irony, there was the same tenderness. . . .

"It was just hearsay, rumor . . . I knew that one of Karavalov's bodyguards was not to be trusted. So I asked three of my friends to keep an eye on Mikhail, and I decided to look after you."

There was a short pause; it was almost as though she were excusing herself.

"I had no way of knowing, did I? And then Mikhail decided he would take care of me."

Georges, who had been drinking a cup of very strong coffee, looked at her through his glasses; one of the lens was broken . . . when had that happened? It made him look even more naive and foolish. He was slowly recovering from whatever it was that the Serbian had slipped him—what powder had been mixed into the carafe's contents?

He said what was on his mind: "But Karavalov; you can't be Karavalov!"

Anything was possible, and it would have been rather piquant to find that the man I had sent someone to bring back from the other side of Europe was really the woman who had spent almost all her evenings in my bed!

Helena burst out laughing. "No, Georges! No, Karavalov is dead, well and truly dead. But not yesterday or the day before, and not from an accident with a car, not from a machine gun. No, he has been dead for three years, and of a simple heart attack. But myths are hard to kill, and so my friends—his friends and mine—found it more practical to keep him alive. The man without a face . . . it wasn't very difficult."

Georges Damiens needed another cup of coffee before he began to understand. Yet the rest was quite simple: Helena, who had never been married to Karavalov—she was one of his woman friends, if not *the* woman friend—had taken over his business; she had succeeded him, so to speak. And now, because she sensed that the truth was about to come out, she had decided to forestall it and to testify before the Geneva committee whose work she knew fairly well. It was in Geneva—and sometimes in the very corridors in which world peace was being debated at such length—that she sold her weapons to all customers.

"You see, everything is simple in the end; it's only important to try to live. So a bank account and a Swiss passport were the best way I knew to get out of the game. And then, Europe's getting to be too small. I have an idea that somewhere between Rio and Santiago, things must be being done on a bigger scale. . . ."

She smiled. Her lips were as scarlet as a cherry, and her skin had never been more luminous. "You're not angry with me?"

How could Damiens have been angry with her? Like myself, he had been taken in. But aren't we all, in one way or another, taken in by women? By Maria, Antonella, even Jean Ledoyen by Jenny.

"You're not angry?"

He took her hand, and this time he did not let go of it. "You know very well I'm not!"

It was Helena who proposed to him: "May I spend the rest of the night in your compartment? I don't much relish the idea of sharing mine with your friend's corpse!"

Georges Damiens awoke at around seven-thirty. He had slept only a few short moments, but he felt well and healthy, calm and light. Lying beside him was Helena: Helena's legs, her face, her breasts. I cannot dislike poor Damiens; he had earned it.

In turn, Helena, too, awoke. She stretched for a few seconds, tender, open, caressing. Then suddenly she sat bolt upright! "Seven forty-two! Good Lord! We'll be there in ten minutes!"

Helena was right—she was always to be right—for the train had made up its delay, and the engine-driver had made it a point of honor to arrive on time; they pulled into Lausanne ten minutes later. Helena was out of bed in an instant. In two she was dressed. In three she had made up her face. Georges Damiens was no longer quite sure where he was or with whom he had spent the night: widow, Mata Hari, arms dealer or ardent lover. However, he made a laudable attempt.

"I asked you this question on our first evening: will we see each other again?"

Helena perfected the already perfect outline of her mouth with a brush stroke. "Of course. . . ."

"That's what you said the first time. But if you are leaving for South America right after you testify . . ."

She turned to him; with her veil drawn over her eyes, she was once again the woman in black in the Hracin mansion. "I told you, it's a small world! Do you want proof of how small it is? There are already two men, Hitler and Mussolini, who think they can hold it in the palm of one hand!"

Damiens tried to laugh. "Helena, you frighten me."

Helena did not laugh. "I'm frightened, Georges. And not only of my clients or my arms-dealing comrades with whom I've done so much business. I'm afraid of a great deal more than that. That is why I'm getting away."

It was seven-fifty, and the train was in the station. On the platform, Lucien Maurice of Swiss security and Lukas, the Yugoslavian, were waiting for Damiens. He approached them and spoke to them in a low voice. I knew that Karavalov was supposed to arrive on that train, but Helena had not informed me of her return, and so I was not there to greet her.

Moelher, the head of the German delegation, was shaving when he received the news of his agent's death. The real Mikhail Kangalovich, or a man calling himself that, was no better off; he was lying beneath the water of the Vistula! Moelher's ill-humored reaction caused him to cut his chin—he was not the type to survive the night of the long knives.

A car was waiting in front of the Lausanne station.

"I think it would be best if we parted here," Helena murmured.

Damiens was holding her arm, and he said in a low voice, "Who knows? Perhaps one day, some other way . . ." With his broken eyeglasses, he looked very like a schoolboy who had been expelled.

"Until we meet again, Georges . . ."

Helena had already gone. Two hours later, she herself told me all that had happened: how could I be angry with her for having pretended to be Karavalov—even in the arms of a colleague twenty years younger than I—since the following day she presented his evidence before our committee.

Three days later, while Helena's boat was leaving Marseilles for Buenos Aires—Swiss bank accounts are easily transferable all over the world—Moelher and his entire German delegation pulled out of the League of Nations and the arms limitation conference.

We were entering a new era, but, although the credulous continued to hold sway, there were at least some of us who knew it.

"It's true," the ambassador murmured, "that from that time on everything changed."

Suddenly Lise Bergaud felt like laughing. The way in which Paul de Morlay had described his own role in this adventure—misadventure, rather—amused her. De Morlay as a cuckold made a droll picture.

"You never take yourself seriously, do you?"

The ambassador, who had seemed deep in more profound thoughts, shrugged and smiled. "No, never! Sometimes, when they deserve it, I can take others seriously, but that's tiring enough!" Leaning toward her, he added: "You, for example. I take you seriously. Terribly seriously. Perhaps because I know nothing about you. . . ."

Once again Despinetta or Barberina appeared in the open gallery overlooking the garden, bearing tea, hot chocolate—"My chocolate is delicious!"—and Lise realized that the ambassador was speaking the truth. She had never—or only in passing—spoken to him about herself. Completely engrossed in listening to the ambassador talk, she had forgotten for the past five weeks that she, too, sometimes liked to talk about herself. to share her feelings and the things that had happened to her.

Paul de Morlay grumbled: "It's true, I've become too much of an old egotist to know how to listen."

Lise protested; everything the ambassador had told her testified to the opposite—so much the opposite. "I think that I'm the one who has forgotten everything these past five weeks."

"Anything I might have told you would have seemed very colorless!"

She meant: dull, too plain next to the vivid stories you've told me, next to all those names, those cities, the violent deaths and the unknown women in silk veils wandering along the corridors of the world's trains. . . . After a Helena, an Antonella, how could one bring up the name of a Michel or a Daniel or, least of all, a Vincenzo?

"But I would like you to tell me . . ."

For Paul de Morlay had not lost his consuming desire to listen, his need to understand, his thirst to give. Thus, and for the first time, Lise Bergaud leaned back in her wicker armchair and talked about herself. She spoke in a low voice, a murmur, like music hummed or a fountain playing softly. Around them in the fresh morning the garden was still covered in an almost opalescent mist that made the contours of the trees seem fluid; all was quiet. The gardener moved to and fro, trimming the last roses. He was an old man in a blue apron whose age-lined face was the twin—but more wrinkled—of Paul de Morlay's. Later Despinetta would return on tiptoe to remove the tray of thick chocolate. She would never forget the scents of the garden, of the last roses, of the smoke of burning leaves that rose in the distance. Leaning forward, Paul de Morlay listened.

"My father . . ." Lise began.

She told him of her life, and it was so like that of Stephanie, of Antonella. She had the same ardor, the same daring, the same youth. . . .

In the cool shade inside the villa, behind a thin curtain, Eugenio, the angelic young chauffeur, stood listening. When Lise stopped speaking, the ambassador sat silently for a long moment. Beneath Lise's habitual mask of gaiety and gentleness, behind her vivid desire to do, to create, to live, was the face of a little girl—vulnerable yet temperamental; fragile yet stubborn. She was still a child who throughout her life had sought a kind of repose, a refuge, a port where she might linger for a while and lay her head on someone's shoulder, or simply shut her eyes.

"I would never have believed that any autumn could be as beautiful or last as long as this one," she said finally.

Over the past weeks, or even in those that remained for her in Paul de Morlay's villa in that Veneto in its suspended autumn, had she found that port, that harbor?

"You know that you can stay here as long as you want," the ambassador said at last.

She did not reply at once. When he stood up and looked down at her, the girl's eyes were filled with tears. "I'm happy here," she said simply.

Eugenio went away on tiptoe. He had already guessed, and that same afternoon he drove them into Venice.

"I wanted to wait for a while before bringing you here," the ambassador said when he and Lise found themselves sitting alone together in one of the small inner rooms of the Café Florian.

On the painted glass walls, goddesses of the previous century spread garlands of flowers at the feet of other goddesses with beatific smiles.

"I wanted to wait because I came here for the first time with Stephanie, just after the war—the first war!—and since then Florian's has been special to me."

Across from them, seemingly isolated in their indifference, one couple appeared to be arguing in low voices and another to be making love.

"However, I came to Florian's on another occasion, after my stay in Venice when I met Antonella. That was in 1938, and on that occasion everything was in place for the drama to begin."

Paul de Morlay closed his eyes. It had been at a table in this same café in March 1938, before the deluge—he had come to Venice between two futile conferences—that he had drunk iced coffee and read newspapers full of the glory of approaching slaughter.

The previous August 26, Santander had fallen to the Fascist rebels; the following September, Mussolini had been welcomed to Berlin with wild enthusiasm. The pawns were being advanced. On November 5, Hitler had announced his firm intention of bringing all German minorities back into the Reich, and two days earlier Shanghai had fallen to Japanese troops. People had still kept their eyes shut. In

December, in order to ensure itself a free hand, Italy had left the League of Nations in its turn, and on February 12, 1938, Hitler had summoned Schuschnigg, the chancellor of Austria, to his Eagle's Nest in Berchtesgaden. In the face of that threat, the unfortunate Dollfuss's successor had been forced to appoint the Nazi Seyss-Inquart to the post of interior minister, despite the promise Germany had given that Vienna's independence would be respected.

"Mussolini had given his total support to the Austrian Nazis in order that the Anschluss might proceed without any problems, and on that day in 1938 there were crowds on the Piazza San Marco shouting Il Duce's name," the ambassador murmured.

Spain, Manchuria, Ethiopia, soon Czechoslovakia and at that moment, Austria; with virtuous resignation, on every occasion the democracies had bowed to the worst.

"Soon Daladier was greeted with acclaim on his return from Munich, and as he came down the steps of his airplane, the French statesman regarded the men who were waiting to receive him as the idiots they were for believing that he and his colleague Chamberlain had achieved peace."

At that memory, Paul de Morlay shivered. "While on the Piazza San Marco . . ."

On that March day in 1938, in the most beautiful public square in the world, the good people of Venice had paraded with banners flying from the Piazza to the Piazzetta, firmly convinced that God and right were on their side.

"I was alone in my booth in Florian's, and I was afraid. The more the crowd cheered, the more the excited soldiers cheered that flag which, alongside that of the Reich, was soon to bring bloodshed to all of Europe, the more angry I became. All at once this square and all the memories attached to it—even the Café Florian—became repugnant to me. So I got up, forced my way through the unseeing mob and returned to my hotel. I hated Venice as I had never before in my life hated another city. As one hates a woman who has betrayed you, perhaps."

It was at that very moment, as the German troops were crossing the Austrian frontier, that Jane Belloc, the heroine of the next story Lise was to hear, stood watching the trucks packed tight with soldiers armed to the teeth, wearing gray-green helmets, pass by. She watched them with complete indifference.

"I'm going to tell you about Jane Belloc, all the same," the ambassador murmured.

Suddenly a thousand pigeons swooped down on the Piazza like a shower of dead leaves.

JANE

1938

As counterpoint to the blood and tears unleashed in Europe, the story my old friend Robert Miles told me of Jane Belloc's passion, while also a story of tears, even of blood, perhaps, has a bittersweet, even smiling glow. The story is fairly banal: no murders this time, hardly any police or criminals . . . but it moved me more deeply than many another bloodier melodrama. Jane Belloc, its heroine, was the archetype of those appealing people who for fear of being hurt go through life almost furtively but who are no less damaged because of that.

"She was approaching forty, the typical girl destined to be an old maid like hundreds born every year between Edgeware and Putney, Harrow and Streatham or Croydon," Robert Miles began by telling me, not at all sure I would be interested in what he had to say.

But first a word about Robert Miles himself, for he, too, was almost a stereotype of a certain kind of Englishman prevalent in his day and age. He was a little like Peter Charley, a "typical" professor. But whereas Charley was the absentminded type, with round eyeglasses—like those of Georges Damiens'—and his head in the clouds, Robert Miles's feet were firmly planted on the ground.

I met him on a trip to London. We ran into each other in an old bookstore in Great Russell Street near the British Museum as we were both reaching for the same copy of that entertaining volume, *The Feasts and Courtesans of Greece*, a work whose title is a tiny bit racier than its sober contents, but whose fourth volume contains a delicious Venus. I may show it to you one day. . . . Since both Miles and I wanted the book, we nearly came to blows—all very courteously, of course. The whole thing ended in a pint of bitters in a nearby pub, and we came out of it great friends. Since then, for that matter, we have continued to trade addresses of bookstores in complete harmony, and Robert Miles is now a specialist in Greek and Hellenic priapic cults, whereas I was appointed ambassador to Athens two years later. We were fated to meet, therefore, and we have run into each other at regular intervals every two or three years for more than forty years now. With his pipe and his heavy, vested tweed suits, Robert Miles has scarcely changed at all. I think he is a doctor *honoris causa* at ten or twelve universities, but he was then, and he has remained, a bachelor.

"However, Jane Belloc could almost have made me change my mind. . . ."

But Jane Belloc and Robert Miles, who met on a train and traveled a distance together, were not meant to meet again; they were the kind of people who are meant to pass like ships in the night.

"And yet Jane Belloc . . ."

At the time she passed through our lives, she was thirty-seven years old—Miles's life, I mean; I knew her only for a moment. Thirty-seven, with a head of pale blond hair which she wore parted in the middle and drawn soberly back. A college classmate had once told her she looked like Charlotte Brontë; since then she had cultivated the resemblance, and because she had always looked older than her years, when she began to age luckily she remained unchanged in appearance. For twenty years, in the eyes of those who happened to cross her path, she would retain that look of those who hover somewhere around forty. She wore no makeup, but she did apply some powder sparingly to her face. Who does not recall that scent of rice powder, so typical of willowy or stout women, women who once haunted lecture halls and who now show up at exhibitions and vacation clubs?

Jane Belloc was one of those women. Her mother had been a French instructor in a girls' school, and she had married a village vicar with a living somewhere between Lewes and Brighton, in Sussex. She had taught her daughter a love for Stendhal and Henri de Regnier; like her mother, Jane Belloc detested de Maupassant and Zola, whom she found vulgar. And of course she sang: all French music, from Duparc and Fauré to Satie—whom she naturally took far too seriously! But she also loved bouquets of wild flowers and English composers: Elgar, Holst, Vaughn-Williams. In short, at twenty-one, still a pure-hearted virgin, Jane Belloc was also a young lady of quality. I can imagine that she, too, might have married a vicar, a parson, a teacher in a boys' school near the girls' school in which she in turn had begun to teach young things with stiff braids that Molière and Racine were, after Shakespeare, the greatest playwrights in the world. But an accident, a terrible accident, occurred, and everything changed.

With priestly elegance the Reverend Belloc drove a pretty little English cart to which a dappled gray horse was harnessed as he went through the green lanes of Sussex. It was a charming contraption of polished beechwood that looked like mahogany, and it had real leather seats: it was the cynosure for every villager in Acton Green, Sussex, particularly when Mrs. Belloc was also seated in it, all fluttering umbrellas or parasols. Alas, one fine May morning the dappled gray mare bolted at a level crossing. Jane's mother was killed on the spot beneath the wheels of a meandering little rural train which sliced her to bits; the Reverend Belloc, his spinal cord broken, survived in a wheelchair to bemoan his wife and curse himself continually for having caused her death.

As for Jane, her life consisted of pushing the wheelchair, drying her father's tears, caring for him, feeding him, bathing him like a child. Since she was a model daughter, she left her school and the town where she might have made a career and met boys her own age to walk out with between cricket matches and devoted her entire attention to her father. Since the Bellocs were able to keep an elderly housemaid to look after him a few hours each day, Jane took a post as a part-time teacher at the parish school in Acton Green, and that was the end. Fifteen years went by without young Jane—tall, thin, but with a dazzling fresh smile—noticing that she had turned into Jane Belloc, the knock-kneed, somewhat clumsy schoolteacher in whose heart still bloomed whole fields of violets and forget-me-nots. She grew fond of romantic novels, she wept at the cinema over the love affairs of Clark Gable, Spencer Tracy or Conrad Veidt and—without ever daring to say so—she came to feel that she vaguely resembled Katharine Hepburn, whose hairstyle she imitated for a time.

Then the Reverend Belloc died; one morning he did not wake up, and Jane was unable to feel any real pain. She must have reproached herself later for what she considered her lack of emotion. Not until several days after the funeral did she realize that henceforth she was alone, completely alone. There were still teas with elderly ladies, the annual school fete and the annual church charity bazaar given by the young rector, whose hands, it was whispered, occasionally lingered for too long on young boys, but that was all. There were the pharmacist and the doctor in the neighboring village—both of whom were nearly seventy—and a few groups of somewhat wild young men who bicycled around the countryside shouting and laughing, but they frightened her, and, like the other inhabitants of Acton Green, Jane Belloc considered them rowdies. When she chanced to run into them outside the King's Head, the green and brown pub on the Market Square, she would hasten her steps, but hurry as she might, some of those twenty-year-old boys she passed so quickly emitted an odor of sweat, of dusty roads, that made her tremble. And the emotion she felt then . . .

When Jane Belloc made up her mind to travel, the prospect of departure changed her life. At first it had been no more than an idle thought, a notion she had gotten into her head when she heard that Kathleen Farrar, one of her pupils, was going out to join her parents in Egypt where her father had been appointed aide-de-camp to a general with a red mustache.

"Egypt . . ." she had said to herself.

The following Sunday, at tea with the Misses Pinchley, she had spoken it aloud with greater assurance: "Egypt!"

The old maids had exclaimed: What? Was Jane not aware that the Orient was rife with indecency and depravity? That in those countries ten or twelve women were required just to satisfy one man and that the men, it was said, had odd habits . . .

"Of course, you'll come back forty pounds overweight from gorging on Turkish delight because you will have been afraid to leave your hotel room!"

Jane Belloc had let the matter drop, but the notion had persisted. Egypt, Turkey, the Riviera: paradises of turpitude that seemed to exist in a luminous glow in her mind. Ah, to shut one's eyes in some casino in Nice or Monte Carlo, while beside her the fingers of a handsome, young gambler . . .

Or to glide in a boat down the Nile or on the Bosporus, leaning on the rail and sensing at her side the presence of a foreign man with fire in his eyes who would not say a word but whose sighs would be more eloquent than any speech, while the scarlet sun glittered as it sank beneath the golden waters . . . Jane had a penchant for clichés and even made up her own.

At the same time, she remained clearheaded; as the notion of departure began to take more solid form in her mind, she buttressed it with a group of alibis in order to make it seem—to herself as well— completely normal. She would travel in search of culture, and Greece and Turkey—not Italy; Greece and Turkey had the advantage of being even further away—would provide limitless ruins and limitless scope for the ideas she cherished. Any encounter with a handsome foreigner, if that should chance to occur, would be fortuitous, that much more unreal and marvelous. She did dream of the handsome foreigner—he would be young, of course, and so gentle and tender . . . perhaps with a mustache, obviously with black hair and he would have a trace of a Mediterranean accent to lend poetry to "*Je t'aime*" and "*Ti voglio bene*" which the meager "I love you" of the carefully tended fields of Sussex could not equal. "*Te quiero*" was exotic; it sounded like adventure, and even the thought of it made Jane Belloc tremble as she trembled in the vicinity of the King's Head. But the Don Juans of the Greek islands and the Athens taverns seemed to her quite different from the slick-haired rowdies in the Market Square.

Thus, one March morning in 1938, Jane Belloc set out for London and from there to Dover and Ostend, her traveling case in her hand and her two bags behind her in the baggage car. Did I mention that, after her fashion, she was beautiful? She was determined to arrive in Istanbul by sea, and she was to travel on the old Bucharest-Varna line. . . .

Robert Miles saw her for the first time on the platform at Ostend. It was in the mists of early dawn, after a sleepless night spent on the ferryboat that had tossed about during the crossing on a rough sea. Contrary to all her background and upbringing, Jane Belloc had proved to be a good sailor, and perhaps alone among all the passengers—with the exception of Robert Miles—she had not been sick during the trip. As the green-faced, tired-eyed passengers disembarked to board the Orient Express for Bucharest and Varna, with connections for Istanbul or Athens by the most indirect route, only Jane Belloc had fresh cheeks and a healthy color. In addition, the prospect of her impending journey filled her with such anticipation—and such hopes—that she glowed with a pleasure she made no attempt to conceal.

Robert Miles was already installed in his compartment in car number two, leaning from the window and smoking his pipe, when he saw her come onto the platform. He felt a throb in his heart at once. He was forty-five years old, and his liaisons were restricted to two mistresses whom he loved in tandem but whom he had also thrown over, one after the other, when he had begun to detect in them a growing fondness. They had both begun to want more than those few evenings each month or the pleasant weekends on the Suffolk coast passed in eating lobster and oysters and strolling arm in arm along the deserted beach. He was completely unattached out of choice, and the appearance of this woman who was still young—and glowing—touched him all at once. He must have told himself that he could look forward to spending several hours, several days, traveling in her company, and that must have been a pleasant prospect.

He was watching her pass the car with a combination of tenderness and curiosity when he noticed another passenger talking to a conductor in the uniform of the Compagnie Internationale des Wagons-Lits, a short, portly, mustachioed man with a black hat perched atop his head, who seemed to be engaged in an animated and obviously unpleasant discussion.

For a moment Jane Belloc seemed hesitant to interrupt them, standing indecisively with her ticket in her hand; then she stepped forward.

"Excuse me, sir. . . ."

The porter following with her two bags stood behind her, waiting. The short, fat man with the mustache turned on her furiously: "Can't you see that I'm talking to this man?"

Alas, he was French, and the worst of the breed—the kind who cannot endure in silence anyone stepping on his toes in a crowded subway car. The interruption of his conversation with an underling— it was a dressing down, actually—was a crime of lese majesty. Thunderstruck, Jane Belloc stood there hesitantly, ticket in hand. Then, after a rueful smile from the conductor who looked as discomfited as she, she decided to find her compartment by herself and walked past Robert Miles, who gave her a welcoming nod. Not knowing what to do and not daring to say anything, feeling very tense and uncomfortable, Jane merely acknowledged his greeting with a slight change of expression and hurried by.

The interior of her compartment enraptured her. It was situated in the middle of the car, newspapers in every language had been laid out on the seat and—the utmost in forethought on the part of the train company—six red roses had been arranged in a slender crystal vase. With a gesture that revealed how moved she was, Jane Belloc lifted a rose to her nostrils while the porter arranged her luggage in the rack and departed, highly gratified at the enormous tip the young woman— yes, "young" is the word I used—had handed him, unaware of what a proper amount might be.

"Only princes or peasants hand you silver five-franc pieces," the porter remarked to one of his colleagues, who had whistled enviously at the sight of it.

A peasant turned into a princess, Jane Belloc was making herself comfortable, completely happy. She drew a few books from her traveling case—Byron, Shelley, a *Baedeker Guide*—and she could feel the combined intoxications of Don Juan and Childe Harold rising up inside her. Ah, the great Byron—even if it had all ended for him on that deserted beach where, finally vanquished by fever, the hero-poet had been cremated, before then there had been Missolonghi, the frieze of the Parthenon and the Oracle of Delphi (for whom Jane had already prepared several questions). Her happiness was complete; it had been darkened only for a few seconds by the unpleasant behavior of odious M. Lenoir, which was the name of the short gentleman on the platform, but more of him later.

How marvelous she felt. Jane looked in the mirror and found herself pretty. "I feel young. . . ." she said to herself.

From her seemingly bottomless case she drew out a filmy, transparent nightgown she had gone all the way to London to purchase for fear of causing talk among the good people of Lewes or Acton, not to mention Brighton. She took out a long cigarette of oriental tobacco and a tiny gold lighter her father had given her when she had left university, because young girls had not only begun to bob their hair, they had even begun to smoke.

She murmured aloud: "It's marvelous."

The smoke floated in the air.

Miss Belloc's cigarette smoke, sweet and acrid as it was, did not float undisturbed for long. Alas, the odious M. Lenoir suddenly burst into her compartment, observed by Robert Miles, who was missing none of the scene.

"My compartment!" he shouted, his voice hoarse with rage. "Who has permitted this woman to install herself in my compartment and toss her things on my berth? Who has given her permission to read my newspapers?"

M. Lenoir spoke with a Belgian accent; he was a Frenchman from Brussels. Even before poor Jane Belloc had time to understand or to explain—even to make herself heard—the potbellied little man, followed by two porters, had summoned the conductor he had been insulting on the platform outside and begun to protest.

"If you did your job as you should, no one would have intruded on my privacy!"

The unfortunate conductor flashed Jane Belloc the same rueful smile he had given her earlier on the platform. It was only then that the young woman understood that she had misread her ticket and that she was not in compartment number eleven, but in compartment number one.

"My compartment, in the middle of the car!" M. Lenoir continued to grumble, complaining at the same time about the smell of blond tobacco while he himself was chewing on a smelly cigar.

Jane Belloc's spirits were too high to be unduly affected by this outburst. She understood that M. Lenoir was a boor, and philosophically, under the apologetic gaze of the conductor who felt responsible for the entire incident, she repacked her things.

"If Madame will allow me . . ."

He preceded her down the corridor, and Robert Miles stepped aside for them; this time, a real smile passed between them, and Jane Belloc accompanied hers with a tiny, ironic shrug of her shoulders. What did it matter, after all? The main thing was that she was on the train, and three days later it would reach Varna. The rest was nothing but a tantrum by a spoiled child; between her aged father and the students of the parish school of Acton Green, Jane Belloc was used to that.

Now in compartment number one—which was directly over the wheels—she drew from her blouse the red rose she had managed to steal from the irascible little fat man, put it in a water glass and once again looked at herself in the mirror. How beautiful life was!

In his compartment, Robert Miles was also finding life beautiful—more than that, he found Jane Belloc charming.

They did not meet until later. At lunchtime, Robert Miles had taken care to choose a table for two and to sit facing forward so as not to miss seeing Jane Belloc when she entered the restaurant car. In addition, he had opened *The Times* of the previous day and had spread it out over most of the table in order to prevent anyone else from taking the seat opposite. He was prepared to fold it up as quickly as possible as soon as the young woman appeared so that he could invite her, with a smile, to share his table. Unfortunately for our professor, his strategy was doomed to failure. Jane Belloc was charmingly myopic, and, since she had decided not to wear her glasses unless it became absolutely impera-tive—to examine an antique stele, perhaps, or a marble Apollo—she passed Robert Miles's table without seeing him, seating herself beside an elderly woman wearing a pair of old-fashioned spectacles.

"May I . . ."

The elderly woman smiled and invited Jane to join her. On the other side of the central aisle, another woman, much younger and with her face half-covered by a short black veil, was tending to two children to whom she was speaking French with a slight, charming but guttural accent that could have been either Czech or Hungarian. She, too, was a part of that other world I knew so well, a woman for whom a journey on an express train between Paris and Sofia was as natural as hailing a cab at the corner of the Rue des Saints Pères in Paris. All at once, Jane felt intimidated. She lowered her eyes and unfolded the huge damask napkin the Compagnie Internationale des Wagons-Lits provided for its customers in those days. . . .

"Welcome aboard, Madame," the elderly woman said with a charm-ing smile that included both Jane Belloc and the woman in the veil, as well as most of the other passengers in the car.

Jane blushed without replying.

"From the look of you, I can imagine that this is the first time you've made this journey. Allow me to introduce myself: Madame Dujardin. Widow and traveler."

She was obviously enjoying herself, and all at once Jane Belloc recovered the pretended aplomb she had lost for the second time in one morning.

"Jane Belloc," she said. "I'm English."

Once again, Mme. Dujardin smiled—at the information the young woman had felt impelled to add—and she launched into a dissertation that was to last for the entire meal, barely allowing Jane to interject a comment from time to time.

."I've been making this journey for fifty-one years," the old lady began. "And I am seventy-four. . . ."

Her memories, tender, amusing, poured out. She recalled the "great people" who had traveled on the Orient Express, Mata Hari, whom she had seen, or a nabob who had met the woman of his dreams in a sleeping car and had waited twenty years until she had become a widow and he could finally marry her, while in the meantime they had become inveterate travelers, always on night trains. . . .

"Ah, the Orient Express is not what it once was! I can remember the days when Prince Rostov used to light his cigars with ten-pound notes . . . just like that, to make an impression!"

Jane Belloc stared in amazement at the old lady.

"Ten pounds!"

She had lived in her Sussex village with her father and the elderly maid for one entire month on one ten-pound note. She didn't know whether Mme. Dujardin was serious, joking or merely trying to impress her, but nevertheless a new, incredible world was opening before her. Even better, she seemed to have entered into one of those magazine stories that were the favorite reading matter of shop girls back in Acton Green, girls who commuted daily to London to work.

Mme. Dujardin continued: "And old Durand-Siegmund! There was a famous rake!" All the suitors in morning coats of my father's era and their black-veiled women with gray gloves and powdered white faces, all those compartments with drawn curtains, passed before her eyes. "Ah, anything in skirts . . ."

The elderly lady sighed nostalgically, and Robert Miles, seated three tables away, never took his eyes from Jane Belloc's face; how charming she was, that girl on the verge of forty. . . . But Jane had eyes only for her companion, who was deriving such evident pleasure from providing this glimpse into such a fabulous world of which the old lady herself did not now remember clearly what had been dream, what merely fact. These charming outpourings by an adorable old narrator probably had a lot to do with Jane's state of mind and with what happened next.

"Well, I'm one of the last women to have known such things," Mme. Dujardin was going on. And then she talked about herself—about her son, who had been killed in 1914, about her husband, who had died three years later, about her vast fortune, inherited from a score of deceased relatives. Now she had only herself to please, so she traveled.

"You see, here I am on the way to Austria at this very moment." She owned a property near a tiny village called Blächen, left to her by some Austrian member of the family; there was a house by a lake, mountainous pastureland, peasants in flowered skirts . . . she went there each year.

"And the company"—she meant the train company—"are so kind. They stop the train for three minutes at the Blächen station just for me, just so I can get off near my home."

A luxury train stopping in an out-of-the-way spot solely to enable an elderly lady, eccentric but rich, to be met by her twenty-horsepower motorcar and be driven to her home—yes, Jane Belloc felt she had entered a legendary land! It is not surprising that the stare of some honorable but undoubtedly quite ordinary and very British professor from London University—Robert Miles, who never took his eyes from her—would not have attracted her attention. She was too busy staring at Mme. Dujardin.

"Well, well," the old lady murmured, "things have changed quite a lot!"

Then, one by one, she told Jane about the passengers in the car. As the porter at the Ostend station had said, the days of princes had given way to the days of peasants. For example, that man in the tweed jacket over there was only a suspended salesman, the other man an out-of-pocket newspaperman; the woman with the tasteless hat wasn't even a demimondaine, only the wife of an obscure decoding clerk in some German embassy on her way to rejoin her husband . . . probably she had never even been unfaithful to him.

"Ah, things are not what they were!"

As for that common M. Lenoir, he was some administrator for the Compagnie Internationale des Wagons-Lits . . . whence his arrogance.

"Whereas, in the last analysis, he's nothing but a tradesman, isn't he?"

Only Robert Miles found favor in the old lady's eyes, for she knew of his work on ancient Greece, and of course he was wearing a worn tweed jacket with elbows reinforced with leather patches; that was always a good sign.

"And then that lady over there . . ."

That was all: she herself, Miles and Mme. Nagy "over there," also a widow who traveled all over the world with her two children, both very well brought up, and who could carry on polite conversation in six different languages.

"As for the rest . . ." Mme. Dujardin concluded eloquently.

She made a gesture that brooked no appeal, but Jane Belloc was hypnotized: her table companion's summary biographies had been a marvelous introduction to the marvelous life that was to be her own for four weeks. She closed her eyes with pleasure.

It was at that very moment—they had reached the dessert course, and Jane Belloc had duly appreciated each of the dishes M. Paul, the veteran head chef on the line, had prepared, apparently for her personal delectation—that Mme. Dujardin's flow of conversation suddenly came to a stop. All at once, as though awakening from a dream, Jane returned to the real world.

"What can be happening?"

The young woman had noticed nothing, but Mme. Dujardin's ears were always alert. For several seconds—since the frogs' legs, to be precise—the train had not been traveling at its accustomed speed, even though the countryside through which they were moving was completely flat.

"This isn't normal!"

Mme. Nagy was also looking out of the window, but it was Mme. Dujardin who finally summoned the chief conductor as he passed through the dining car, looking worried and holding a piece of paper in his hand.

"My dear sir, what is happening? It seems to me we have slowed down considerably."

Mme. Dujardin, a familiar figure on the line, known both for her volubility and her kindness, enchanted all who came into contact with her; the chief conductor, therefore, took time to give her all the necessary information. Yes, something was wrong with the train. The axle on one of the cars was overheating dangerously. They had thought they might make it as far as Cologne, but now there was every possibility that they might not be able to change cars there.

"Does that mean a delay?"

"Alas, yes, so I fear."

However, Mme. Dujardin smiled, and that was it. After all, she had once spent three days and three nights snowed in, immobilized by drifts on a stretch of track near Dubrovnik, and on another occasion she had been stopped by the unexpected closing of the Serbian border for forty-eight hours in a godforsaken village where there had been a plague epidemic—she was not the sort to be intimidated by something as minor as an overheated axle.

"Well, we shall arrive sooner or later," she philosophized.

And she ordered peaches flamed in Armagnac; Jane Belloc greedily followed her example.

My friend Miles was not able to speak to Jane Belloc until that afternoon. I'm surprised it took him so long, for in those days, when travel was a way of life, nothing was easier than to strike up a conversation with an unknown woman on a train.

In the event, circumstances worked in Robert Miles's favor. Jane Belloc had settled in the Pullman car and had spread out on the table before her a pile of guidebooks, maps, street plans, all clearly indicating that her destination was Greece. Lulled by the rocking of the train which was still traveling at a reduced speed, she had ordered one of those drinks that were then fashionable, a gin fizz or Marie Brizard cocktail, which added to her feeling that she was tasting forbidden fruit.

"Is this chair taken?"

She looked up at Miles, who, pipe in hand, was indicating the armchair by the table with the maps and guides. Since the remainder of the car was almost deserted, she blushed slightly. . . .

"Of course . . . please . . ."

Robert Miles sat down across from her, and, after a few minutes of silence, he took the plunge: "If my eyes do not deceive me, you are going to Greece."

Jane Belloc laughed. Miles was the kind of man who could entertain her, amuse her—or, if need be, help her were she in need of help—but he was in no way a handsome foreigner with voluptuously rolled r's to make him the exotic man she dreamed of meeting. In addition, from the outset she treated him with a mixture of polite irony, almost camaraderie, and brusqueness typical of young women like herself who know that dreams are not often realized in real life but who remain nonetheless firmly attached to them, rejecting the more available reality.

"Do I understand you are going to Greece?" Miles said again.

Her response was quick, immediate: "You're very perspicacious!"

Robert Miles should have been amused by her quickness, but instead he seemed taken aback. "Please forgive me. Perhaps I'm intruding into what does not concern me. . . ."

Happy to have found someone to talk to, and a man at that—Jane was also one of those independent women who take pride in being so but who soon find solitude boring—Jane Belloc grew more receptive. Even cordial.

"Not at all, not at all . . ."

So they began to talk.

"My name is Jane Belloc," she began by way of introduction.

Miles looked at her for a moment.

"Any relation to Hilaire Belloc, the writer?"

The young woman was flattered to be associated with such a well-known name. She smiled without answering, and Robert Miles introduced himself in turn.

After that, their conversation turned to Greece. Jane was going to Greece, and Robert Miles knew the art and history of that region better than those of Sussex or the City of London.

"If I can be of any assistance to you . . ."

Bending over the maps, they explored various routes across Ithaca and the Peloponnese, from Delphi to Corinth, from forbidden Mount Athos to the bottommost tip of Lesbos, retracing step by step the same itinerary made by Pausanias when he had traveled the region some 2,500 years before, writing the first *Baedeker*.

Robert Miles was brilliant and amusing. He trotted out a thousand and one anecdotes, which is what Hellenic mythology is: stories that, taken together, form the basis of all our tragedies and our culture. And, of course, he wanted to attract her . . . for Jane Belloc had attracted him.

He was both pleasant and pensive. "In fact, we all harbor the dream of some lost paradise. For me it's Crete. Since I was fifteen, I have been obsessed by the tale of Theseus and the Minotaur. I've even written a lengthy book on the subject. The Ariadne myth . . ."

Jane Belloc was familiar with it, having taught it to her pupils in her provincial school. "Ariadne's thread? Ariadne on Naxos, alone and abandoned . . ." She, too, grew pensive.

Miles went on in the same vein: "*Ariadne, Ma Soeur,* yes, that's it.
. . . Do you know that they have finally decided that the Minotaur
was actually only the head of the Cretan army? And that Minos, the
king, simply had him assassinated by some foreigner named Theseus . . ."

Jane's thoughts were crowded with images; yes, this was adventure,
too. However, she stopped him. "Please don't destroy all my illusions!
In a minute you'll be telling me that Achilles' heel was no more than
a sprained ankle!"

I'm fond of Miles, but he was a professor above everything else.
"Historical research can be pitiless where heroes are concerned!"

Jane Belloc had lived much among professors. "Then it should be
left to specialists. Mankind needs its heroes."

Jane and Robert could have been friends but never more than that.
All too human, Jane Belloc needed a hero.

"Mankind also needs truth," Robert Miles said.

When, a moment later, he twice expressed his regret that he would
be unable to stop over with her in Greece and retrace in her company
the itinerary he had sketched out on her map, Jane was almost curt.

"I'm very independent, you know."

Miles smiled, looking uncomfortable. "I beg your pardon!"

To change the subject, he raised his voice slightly to remark that
the train seemed to be slowing down again, and, as night began to fall,
their conversation continued. Later they had dinner together at the same
table, beneath Mme. Dujardin's indulgent eye, but the spell of travel
that Miles had somewhat optimistically hoped would work on Jane
remained ineffective. He talked, he talked a great deal, but Jane Belloc
was all the while reminding herself that the next day she would be
closer to the sun, warmth, those Greek marbles of which she dreamed.
As the evening went on, Robert Miles began to seem more and more
like colleagues of his whom Jane had had occasion to meet. People
don't take the Orient Express to have dinner with colleagues, even university professors. Thus, when he grew more confidential and began
to talk about himself, his life . . .

"I have a not unattractive house off Great Russell Street, near the
British Museum."

She cut that topic short. "Really? I've always wanted to live in
Venice, or Naples. . . ."

And when Miles began to probe for information about her, her touch of brusqueness only served to make her more attractive.

"And you, where do you live?"

Her dry response was almost irritated. "In Sussex. I told you I was a teacher, do you remember?"

Robert Miles did not pursue the matter. He had understood, finally. After that, Jane rose, explaining that she was very tired . . . which was, after all, quite true. Or rather, she was anticipating the next day, and the day after that, and all the days to come, and above all she wanted to get as much out of her journey as she could. So ten hours of sleep seemed as appealing to her as did a languid, protracted evening in the company of a man she could have met on any street in London without having the slightest desire to turn to look at him again. Jane Belloc could be cruel, quite unintentionally, and this only served to make her more touching, since her opinion of herself was so mediocre.

She left the Pullman car with a smile that was charming but distant; Miles, left alone, reached out for a newspaper a German passenger had left behind on the table. Across five columns was spread the announcement of the imminent Anschluss and Germany's final ultimatum to Austria.

In dwelling on Jane's still youthful face, her gauche behavior—that of a young woman on the verge of discovering the joys of living—I have wandered far from what is nevertheless the point of all my stories: history, and the growing threats that were soon to turn all Europe into a battlefield.

I have mentioned what was then happening in Austria; the countries that did not back Berlin trembled. They trembled, but they were also very careful not to interfere. I suppose that each of us must have thought that outside his own borders, the events that were occurring on the other side of the Rhine and beyond were just differences of opinion, more tempests in teapots among German principalities that had erupted throughout history. Like Herr Hitler himself, we may have told ourselves—good Frenchmen that we were, or good Englishmen who were not about to get involved in another war when they could be protected by Mr. Chamberlain's umbrella—that if people speak the same language, they might as well live together in the same country. The handful of journalists and diplomats—and the thousands of Communists and Socialists who were already being imprisoned or hunted down inside Germany—who sensed that what was about to take place would spread over the entire globe found themselves opposed by people who preferred to reassure themselves by saying that that nice Mr. Hitler and that dear Mr. Mussolini had at least built excellent superhighways and gotten the trains to run on time. Wasn't that something in their favor?

However, Robert Miles was one of those who knew. His hatred for the new regimes that were coming to power was almost visceral, for he was an Englishman and a liberal. He was for freedom and all that that implied; tolerance and all that that implied; freedom of speech and all that that implied, the good along with the bad! He wasn't at all a revolutionary, not even a Socialist. It was simply that he could not abide the hordes that stood at attention in Nuremberg, noisily hailing a few simplistic ideas; he could not abide books being burned or barbed-wire fences being erected to contain men and women. The German newspaper he had found in the deserted Pullman car, victoriously announcing the imminent conquest of an unarmed country by a country armed to the teeth, rekindled his feelings of indignation and horror that only since Jane Belloc's arrival on the train at Ostend he had allowed himself to forget.

While the Orient Express rolled on towards Cologne more slowly than ever owing to the accursed axle on car number two which was still heating up—Ostend-Cologne in ten hours was some kind of record! —Robert Miles returned to his compartment. History was winning out, and his hopes for a chaste adventure with the Englishwoman—not overly young but still attractive—faded away.

In her compartment, standing at the mirror above the washstand, Jane Belloc was brushing her teeth. Her mouth was full of toothpaste and her hair had been tucked into a hair net; she stopped short to look at herself. She was not happy with her appearance. Then, like a child, she made a face at herself in the mirror, upon which she looked so truly unattractive that she had to laugh.

In the transparent nightgown trimmed with handmade lace that she had bought in London, her body was far more attractive shaded by the flattering light of the compartment than it was in the gray suit she wore in public. In short, it would not have taken much to awaken Jane Belloc, thirty-seven-year-old orphan. A mere nothing: a gesture, a spark, a glance . . .

That gesture, that spark, that glance occurred at seven-thirty the following morning in the Frankfurt station.

JANE

The train had pulled slowly into the platform. It was March 13, 1938, and armed soldiers were everywhere. Gray uniforms, green uniforms, black uniforms. All the soldiers had the same impassive expressions, and the rifles that were slung across their shoulders were all held with the same obedient grasp. The few passengers waiting to board the train had to pass through a double file of police, who were checking the papers handed them with implacable thoroughness. Among the passengers boarding the train, Miles noticed a young man, short and slender, dressed in black and with a small black mustache who was pacing nervously back and forth.

Coming along the platform were two employees of the station buffet who seemed totally unaware of the police or of the somber atmosphere of the station. The men were in their thirties, at most, and were joking together as they pushed along a cart loaded with bottles and sandwiches. As a newspaper vendor passed them, bearing a bundle of the latest edition announcing that a referendum to approve the Anschluss of Austria to the Reich had won a crushing majority, their faces grew serious. As soon as the vendor had passed, however, they smiled again, good-humoredly ringing the bell that signaled their arrival. Robert Miles had been leaning from the door—he had wanted to see some of Germany, after all—and by the time they reached the level of his car, he had been watching them for some time. One of the two was wearing a white waiter's jacket; the other, perhaps a bit older, was dressed in a dark serge suit and carried a satchel on his shoulder.

At the very instant the train began to pull out—it was precisely 7:28 —the man in the serge suit jumped aboard. His companion had been standing at the door to the next car, arguing with an English passenger who did not understand why only light beer was available, when with one jump the man—whom I shall henceforth refer to as Gaetano— leaped onto the steps of car number two and into the corridor.

Robert Miles had witnessed this maneuver. The white-jacketed man had turned away, ringing his bell, and the train was pulling out; by one of those miracles that occur only for the most daring, the man, obviously some kind of fugitive, had managed to board the Orient Express under the very noses of the German police. He was young— around thirty, as I mentioned—and handsome. Jane Belloc's watch read seven-thirty, and it was now time for her to awaken . . . for her to fall in love. . . .

* * *

"That was close!"

Completely at ease—there was barely a trace of sweat on his fore-head—the young man who had just leaped on board the Orient Express at the very last minute smiled broadly, revealing glittering white teeth, and addressed the young woman who was standing beside him in the corridor. With an even broader smile, he bowed and, in perfect Italian, said, "May I introduce myself: Gaetano de Montefeltre."

When the young woman did not immediately reply, he repeated his words in French, in German and finally in English, still with the same smiling formality. Overwhelmed by such charm and exquisite gallantry and by centuries of culture—all of which she sensed in her new companion—the young woman blushed violently.

"Jane Belloc," she managed to say.

For, of course, the young woman who had suddenly met the handsome stranger of whom she had dreamed all her life was none other than our English passenger. What was to happen is perhaps the most moving love story I have ever been told, moving because it involved Jane Belloc, because of its intensity and because the handsome Gaetano's fate was to be a strange one, caught as he was in a mortal trap. . . .

In a way, the remainder of this tale and this journey will be nothing but one long conversation between a man and a woman who should never have met. You know about Jane Belloc, but you have not yet really come to know Gaetano.

"Your name is Montefeltre? *De* Montefeltre?" Jane Belloc asked when she had composed herself somewhat. "Like *the* de Montefeltres?"

For the name de Montefeltre evoked many images for Jane, many historical memories: the ancient de Montefeltre family of Urbino, whose small princely court had been one of the outstanding centers of Italian culture during the Renaissance, an unlikely mixture of great lords and poets, of beautiful women and philosophers, all traced out for us by the painters of the time on the walls of their palaces. In Italy in those days there were the de Montefeltres and the Malatestas . . . and now all of a sudden she found herself faced with a real de Montefeltre!

Gaetano smiled with a becoming modesty. "Oh, there are a lot of de Montefeltres scattered around the world." With a little less modesty he added: "My father, however, now bears the title."

The die was cast! Not only was Jane Belloc in love, she was entranced.

Robert Miles, who had witnessed the entire episode, was to tell me: "It all happened in a glance. It was obvious that he was exactly what she had been waiting for!"

It is probably true that Gaetano de Montefeltre's mixture of *savoir faire* and what Jane would have called "distinction" could not have helped but seduce—with the assistance of the train and its mystique—any sensitive, lonely, melancholy woman. And Jane was such a woman . . . although Mme. Dujardin and even Mme. Nagy, the attractive Hungarian widow, were both to be overcome by the same charm. Neither of them, however, was quite as vulnerable as Jane.

She was entranced with the lordly way he tipped the conductor of the car who seemed disturbed by the presence of the new arrival.

"Yes . . . I got on at the very last minute, but since I'm in the last car and I have no luggage, please don't concern yourself about me. I'll manage to find my compartment on my own."

His ease, his smiling, noble air—at the same time friendly—when speaking to that humble employee of the Compagnie Internationale des Wagons-Lits enraptured her. When he turned to her to remark on the conductor's respectful attitude—"Such people can be charming; it's all a matter of knowing how to talk to them"—she was hypnotized. So this was what real aristocrats were like, people whose origins were lost in the mists of time, people out of courts and legend . . . Gaetano did not seem to be in any hurry to find his compartment; on the contrary, he seemed to want to continue their conversation, and she found that, too, quite normal. At this, their first meeting, she did not for a moment find it surprising that someone should be interested in her.

When he asked her about herself and what she did, she shrugged charmingly, nonchalantly, and murmured: "I write a bit . . . that's all."

Robert Miles had given her the idea: Jane Belloc, the novelist.

Gaetano's expression was transformed. Now he seemed truly interested in her. "You write books?"

Jane gave the same offhand response: "Novels, yes. And a few poems . . ."

"Novels! Poetry! What luck, to jump onto a moving train and suddenly find myself with Jane Belloc, the novelist, the poetess! It's unbelievable. . . ."

Jane was in a dream, floating, soaring; she was carried away by her falsehood and because the aristocratic Italian, so like a knight in shining armor, had believed her so readily.

"Oh, it's not all that unbelievable. Lots of people write books . . . it's all a matter of describing one's own experiences, more or less."

And there it was: Jane Belloc had become another person. From now on she could say whatever she pleased, and she would end by believing it herself. As for Gaetano de Montefeltre, he soon began to pay court to her, but in a very light, almost joking, very Italian sense. As for Jane, her only wish was to be courted. They spoke about nothing and about everything, about everything in Gaetano that had attracted Jane Belloc, who was like some fragile moth attracted to a candle, its sole desire to perish in the flame.

"Ah, Urbino, the de Montefeltres . . ."

Courtly love, jousts between poets hungry for the beautiful gaze of a princess who would feed them the finest viands and extend her delicate hand for them to kiss.

"Ah, the d'Estes, the Malatestas, Ferrara and Vicenza . . ." Names of legend, the names of portraits, and over it all the dark glance of some noble highwayman and the ghost of Tasso . . .

"Did you know that the first code of love was drawn up in Urbino?" Gaetano asked her.

Jane blushed, and Gaetano put his hand on her shoulder.

"Yes, a code of love! For even love must have its rules. The right place, the right time . . ."

Jane shut her eyes and almost trembled when she felt his hand touch her so innocently; it seemed to burn.

"The time, the place," Gaetano went on, "because in love it's the moment that counts. What happens then, at the moment. My old tutors used to tell me so often in Urbino: 'You cannot swim twice in the same stream!' "

Their light conversation, their banter, outside time and space, could have gone on for the entire journey, but Gaetano suddenly looked up. "But what's happening? It seems that the train is slowing down."

Jane made a gesture that expressed how unimportant she found this. "Yes, one of the axles is overheating. They are supposed to change the car, but perhaps they have been unable to find another."

Gaetano's face grew serious; for a few seconds his good humor and glibness seemed to fade, like a cloud passing. Miles, leaning at the window at the other end of the car, had also noticed.

The train continued to slow down, and at last it came to a complete stop.

"I don't like it," Gaetano muttered.

The open countryside lay all around them; left and right, a series of hills extended along a valley through which a broad river flowed. Along the river were the roadbed and the double line of tracks.

For the first time since the train had stopped at Frankfurt and Gaetano de Montefeltre had come on board, Robert Miles approached Jane Belloc and spoke to her. "I'll go see what's happening."

He got out onto the track. Other passengers from other cars were beginning to do likewise. They were in the depths of the Franconian countryside, with valleys and forests as far as the eye could see. To the left, a castle that might have been Pommersfelden was just visible in the midst of a pine forest. The air was chill, but the day was growing warmer, and high above, as though set against the sky, a lark soared, singing. Miles took a few steps along the roadbed, but suddenly he was brought to a halt by a voice out of nowhere.

"Forbidden to leave the train! Get back on board at once!"

The command had been shouted in a guttural German with a northern accent. Miles took another step, and instantly three or four men emerged from the thick woods at the side of the embankment where they had been standing guard.

"Quick. *Schnell! Schnell!* Can't you understand an order?"

They were armed soldiers.

"Yes, I'd forgotten," Miles thought to himself.

Like Jane Belloc—who no longer remembered anything at all—he had forgotten after a night's sleep that in just a few hours Austria would be overrun. Other soldiers, who had been posted every twenty yards along the track, now appeared on the embankment. All the passengers were being ordered back onto the train.

"These fellows are overdoing it a bit," Robert Miles muttered as he passed Jane and her companion in the corridor.

As usual, M. Lenoir was complaining, standing in the door to his compartment in a grotesque pair of flowered pajamas. Mme. Nagy had also appeared, wearing a black silk dressing gown embroidered with red roses.

"I hope we won't be stopped for too long," Gaetano said.

For the first time, Jane noticed that the man with whom she had just fallen so madly in love looked worried.

In a few minutes, with a hellish noise, a train passed on the tracks parallel to theirs. It was a long convoy of military wagons packed with armed soldiers. There were also several flatbed cars carrying heavy weapons, machine guns and forms covered with tarpaulins and camouflage netting. Fifteen minutes after the military convoy had roared by, Jane and Gaetano felt their own train begin to move again.

"They're going to Austria, too," Robert Miles said.

Neither Jane nor Gaetano heard him. Yet with the convoy that had just disappeared toward the east, the hopes of all of us were to be destroyed.

Jane Belloc was filled with gaiety. In the bar car she drank champagne at Gaetano's invitation, and not once did she wonder why the handsome foreigner who had suddenly appeared in the corridor, a simple leather satchel on his shoulder, never left her for a second, not even to freshen up in his own compartment. To Jane Belloc, everything seemed normal. After all, she had set out on her journey dreaming of meeting a young, handsome man who would find her attractive, and now he had arrived.

Robert Miles was more down to earth. When he passed the Pullman table where Jane and de Montefeltre were sitting, he glanced at them, and the young woman could not avoid asking him to join them.

"Let me introduce Prince Gaetano de Montefeltre. . . ."

She could as easily have said duke or count, but prince seemed more magic to her, and since Gaetano did not protest, she realized she had done the right thing in avoiding the lesser titles.

"Prince Gaetano de Montefeltre, Mr. Miles, a professor in London . . ."

Robert Miles was in no mood to stop. "The Prince of Montefeltre?" he repeated, with a slight note of interrogation.

No less ironic, Gaetano bowed. "Yes, de Montefeltre," he said simply.

The train had picked up speed, but now again it began to slow. The hills had given way to mountains covered with pine trees, and de Montefeltre once again glanced at his watch.

"At this rate, we won't get to Austria before tomorrow!"

How could he know that Jane Belloc was thinking that, as far as she was concerned, they could take all the time in the world to get to Austria?

"You were saying that your father still lives in Urbino?"

Gaetano recovered himself and smiled. Why be bad-tempered, why reveal his concern that the train was slowing down? He made the best of it and launched into a detailed description of the palace in Urbino. "Oh, he lives a very secluded life now, but his library is still a marvel!"

He went on: books, faces, great halls in which large Danish hounds lay slumbering, books again and faces hanging on the walls of painted salons . . .

Shortly before lunchtime, the train stopped again, on either side were the same pine-covered mountains. Halfway up the slopes, they could see farmhouses and barns with flat slate roofs.

"Now what's the matter?" Gaetano muttered.

He seemed really concerned; he was obviously in a hurry. He had barely finished his sentence when the door to the bar car opened and the head conductor entered, followed by two armed policemen. Jane turned to look, and before she realized what had happened, Gaetano had gotten up and left the car. As he passed M. Lenoir, who was puffing on a cigar and perusing the previous day's *Wall Street Journal*, the Italian seemed to stumble; he regained his balance by catching hold of Lenoir.

"I beg your pardon."

M. Lenoir grumbled something about foreigners who didn't know how to behave on trains. He may have even mentioned Jews and Italians, whom he considered indistinguishable, but he certainly did not notice that at that very moment Gaetano had managed to lift his passport.

"I beg your pardon."

Gaetano de Montefeltre was gone, but the other passengers had also arisen when the soldiers and head conductor entered, milling about with exclamations of surprise, and no one had noticed. Over the noise, the head conductor signaled to the passengers to quiet down; he had an announcement to make.

"Ladies and gentlemen," he began, "please . . . please. . . The military authorities have just informed us that rail traffic between Munich and Linz has been halted. For an indefinite period of time."

There were expressions of indignation and discontent throughout the car.

Miles shrugged. "That's all we need!"

I cannot repeat often enough that Robert Miles was one of the few passengers on that train—one on which we were all traveling, a train that was not only the Orient Express—who realized toward what destination we were truly headed.

Mme. Dujardin's reaction was typical of her. "I've always said so! The day the trains stop being on time, the world will no longer be the same!"

The head conductor was trying to continue, and again he called for silence. "Ladies and gentlemen, please . . . the company regrets this incident and will do its best to see to it that the stop we have been forced to make will be the least disagreeable as possible. We will be stopping at the next station while we wait for the track to open again."

Arousing himself from the torpor that several glasses of Pernod had induced, M. Lenoir exclaimed: "It's unthinkable!"

As an administrator-director of the Compagnie Internationale des Wagons-Lits, he intended to write a letter of complaint to the board. As the sound of voices rose again, the head conductor and the armed policemen moved through the bar car to make their announcement throughout the train.

Somewhat taken aback at Gaetano's sudden disappearance, Jane stood up, confused. She did not understand.

Mme. Dujardin, although old, selfish and eccentric, had a heart of gold and came up to her. "He can't have gone far . . . I hope!"

Mme. Dujardin's concluding "I hope" was said to herself, as though she had sensed that something was afoot. Heavily, slowly, the train started to move again.

This time they stopped for good at a tiny station at the edge of the forest. A village lay a short distance away. The doors of the carriages opened, and the passengers, somewhat hesitantly, began to alight.

Jane, who was among the first, looked around. "Where can he have gone?" she was wondering.

Suddenly her worried expression relaxed; she glimpsed Gaetano standing alongside another car. He seemed to be involved in conversation with the short, willowy young man with the mustache who had been pacing along the platform in the station in Frankfurt. The young man quickly moved away when Gaetano, having caught sight of Jane, came toward her.

She felt an immense relief. "You frightened me! I didn't see you."

He smiled with that slightly mysterious air he had begun to cultivate, realizing that both the air and the smile made a great impression on Jane. "Believe me, in my vast experience it's not so easy to disappear, particularly on a train!" He flashed her a broader smile than ever. "I was looking for you."

Taking her arm, he led her toward the tiny waiting room where the passengers were gradually gathering. Behind them, a few yards away, the short man in black reentered his car. Their stop in Hetzel, which was the name of the village where they found themselves—so unfortunately for Gaetano, so fortunately for Jane Belloc—and where they were to spend nearly twenty-four hours had begun.

The passengers were at first shut up in the station for nearly an hour. By now, everyone had become fully aware that the trains had been halted all over that part of Germany in order that additional military convoys could be assembled on the Austrian border to bring that country into line. Gaetano had regained all of his sangfroid. He needed to get out of the country as soon as possible, but he managed to put up a magnificent front; he began to perform magic tricks for the few children who had accompanied their parents to the waiting room, among them the children of the attractive Mme. Nagy.

"What have I got in my hand . . . guess!"

He handed a piece of white cloth to a little blond girl with an Edwardian haircut.

"A handkerchief? So you think it's a handkerchief?" He smiled broadly, youthfully. "It looks more like a lighter, doesn't it? What do you think?"

With three passes of his hand, the handkerchief had indeed turned into a cigarette lighter. The parents applauded, Mme. Dujardin expressed amazement and Jane Belloc looked at him with an immense affection; he was not only handsome, he not only bore a great name—he also liked children! In less than an hour, Gaetano de Montefeltre had made conquests of every passenger on the train. Only Robert Miles remained wary. And, of course, the odious M. Lenoir did not even deign to glance his way.

"Of course," as Miles was to tell me, "there *was* something very sympathetic about him. But at the same time, I could detect beneath his polished exterior the touch of a mountebank."

Imperturbable, mountebank, con man or nobleman, Gaetano continued to produce tennis balls out of old ladies' pockets and goose feathers from behind the conductors' ears. Jane Belloc gazed at him, enraptured.

"Yes, it was that look of rapture that really irritated me!" Robert Miles was to admit to me.

After precisely an hour, the stationmaster of Hetzel entered the waiting room accompanied by an officer in SS uniform; he was the first of the death's head killers Robert Miles was to see, and the memory would remain with him.

"Ladies and gentlemen," the stationmaster began, "those of you who so desire may now leave the station. You can stroll in the village as far as the inn, where you may obtain a meal if you wish. However, you are requested to return to the train at nine o'clock this evening."

Miles's face froze. "In short, a curfew?"

The SS officer, his uniform as gaudily decorated as was the station-master's cap, merely stared at Miles with pale blue eyes.

"Not at all, merely a measure of security for all concerned. We would only ask that, as you go out, you leave your passports in the stationmaster's office; they will, of course, be returned to you when you reboard the train."

Miles did not pursue the matter; he knew the race to which the officer belonged. While most of the passengers prepared to set out for the village, a few of them—the thin young man and M. Lenoir in what was obviously a foul temper—preferred to return to the train which had been shunted onto a siding on the other side of the station.

As Gaetano was handing his papers to the corporal with round spectacles who was assisting the SS officer, Robert Miles noticed that the Italian was traveling with a Belgian passport.

Gaetano winked at him. "Yes, my mother was Belgian, and I have preferred to retain her nationality."

Once again, as though everything were perfectly normal, Gaetano de Montefeltre was playing double or nothing every second . . . up until now he had continued to win. Of course, Jane Belloc was making his task very easy for him.

"I don't want to go with them," she said, indicating the straggling group of passengers who were heading for the single village street. "What if we were to take a stroll?"

Gaetano glanced at her. "It's strange, the way you always seem to say just what I want to hear. . . ."

Jane Belloc trembled. That happened to be one of the sentences she had always dreamed of hearing herself. Gaetano had already taken her arm, and they began to climb a path that led up through the pine trees—like that stroll taken by Maria von Pallberg and her friends near that other village in the Tyrol, at the dawn of that other war. Slowly, in silence, the valley unfolded below them, and neither of them felt like disturbing such serenity.

After a moment, Jane stopped. "We seem so far from everything all at once. . . ."

She was out of breath; perhaps it was fatigue, perhaps the slope they had just climbed, but it was also emotion. As far back as she could remember, she could not recall a moment of equal happiness. She was surrounded by all she had ever dreamed off: the blue sky, the countryside, the scent of distant lands and a young and very handsome man beside her. What did it matter, when she had all that, that they had stopped in this place where the impossible seemed to be becoming real? What did it matter that the reason was an impending war? And although Gaetano sometimes glanced surreptitiously at his watch, she did not notice. She could not have grasped, let alone suspected, why he was preoccupied, worried, perhaps even anxious. She was living in her own dream world.

"Look down at the station and the train," she said suddenly, falling rather than sitting on the grass. "It's like a toy train, one of those little wooden toys children have! But you're not saying anything."

It was like a dialogue in a play. On the surface, it was all banter between a somewhat mature girl and an overly handsome young man: a final scene, like the one enacted by Helena and Damiens in Bucharest, of a first act.

The overly handsome young man tightened his grip on the arm of the somewhat mature girl. "What do you want me to say? You've guessed everything there is to know about me already. . . ."

Jane Belloc smiled, a smile that was as innocent and naive as even she could have wished. "You must be joking! I know your castle, your pictures, only because I have read about them in books, but I'd like to know so much more. To understand . . . To know, for example, what it must be like to live surrounded by all that!"

Gaetano once again glanced at his watch. Then, as though coming to the conclusion that there was nothing to be done and that he was truly marooned in the middle of the Franconian wilderness, that the train was not going to leave, he launched into an elaborate description of what Jane Belloc referred to as his ancestral home, his family, his life. He spoke almost idly, as though to pass the time.

"When I was a little boy, I had a nurse who taught me the entire genealogy of my family by heart. By the time I was seven, I could recite without any mistakes the names of all my forebears, back to the first de Montefeltre who conquered the Normans in Sicily. . . ."

Once again Jane was lulled by his words, by the names of cities and *condottieri,* principalities and painters. For that matter, it made very little difference whether a de Montefeltre had really fought against the Normans in Sicily or not. . . .

"Oh, Gaetano . . ."

She had not meant to interrupt him; she had spoken unthinkingly, and for a moment he felt that she was about to take his hand. It would have been the first time in Jane Belloc's life that she had held a man's hand in her own. For a second, she almost made that first gesture. But she recovered herself.

"Oh, Gaetano . . . it all seems so far away to me. . . ."

And then—perhaps because after all one of his professions was that of seduction—he lightly lay his hand on her shoulder.

"But I've talked enough about myself. It's your turn now to tell me something about yourself. . . ."

She closed her eyes. The light, bantering conversation, words flying by, the landscape and the station below, so small, and she herself, living a life that might have been hers . . . she closed her eyes and spoke. She related to him her invented life.

"I live in a large house that gives onto a garden whose every flower, every plant, every shrub I've chosen myself. I live there alone, with my cats and dogs. I live alone because I prefer solitude, and because words, poems, books are more easily created in solitude. . . ."

Indeed, it was her *true* life, the one she wanted.

"And then I live surrounded by books, which are my oldest and most faithful companions. Dickens and the Brontës, Jane Austen, Thackeray, George Eliot . . . I live as much with them, even more, as I live with my closest friends, friends who sometimes come for weekends and whom I put up in a wing far away from my own room and my library, so that I can continue to write in peace."

As she spoke, inventing the house of her dreams, her faithful friends and familiar animals and books, Jane Belloc was thinking that reality was far away. The portrait she was drawing of herself seemed so life-like to her that she suddenly felt she would never again be able to return to Acton Green, never again see the pharmacist, the rector, the grocer, the neo-Victorian dark house where she lived or the shelves of her real library with its complete collection of parish bulletins.

She stood up suddenly. "Let's go back down, shall we?"

She had broken off abruptly, and Gaetano noticed that there were tears in her eyes; suddenly he was moved.

."Jane!"

But she was already descending the path they had silently climbed together an hour before.

The village seemed to be asleep. In the street, in shop windows and on the doorsills of their houses, the inhabitants all seemed to have closed, somber expressions. It was as though what was happening—Hitler's imminent invasion of Austria—preoccupied them, as though all of them knew that it would, perhaps, seal their fate forever. And there were armed soldiers everywhere.

Jane and her companion reached the inn in a very few minutes.

In its single room, the same somber mood prevailed. The stolid innkeeper with her Valkyrie bosom was silently serving steins of beer, and one old man, laughing derisively, was crowing over the fact that on the next day the Reich was going to enter into a new era. Since they did not seem to share his certainty, the few villagers scattered about the room among the passengers listened without replying—but without daring to silence him.

"Ah, here are the . . ."

Mme. Dujardin had almost said "lovers" when she saw Jane Belloc and Gaetano enter. Jane's look told her that she could have said it, although the young woman would have blushed at hearing it.

"Well, and did you have a pleasant walk?" Mme. Dujardin went on.

Outside they could hear the distant sound of a train that must have been another military convoy, a reminder that what was to occur the following day had become by now inevitable. Answering with a smile, Jane Belloc sat down at the table presided over by the old lady, with Robert Miles at her right hand.

"I believe, despite the patroness' surly exterior, that you will enjoy a taste of this smoked ham."

Mme. Dujardin served the other passengers, then herself, and conversation around the table became general, general and political. Two attitudes quickly became evident among those present: that of Miles and that of Gaetano.

"Nobody realizes!" my English friend exclaimed. "No one really wants to! But what is happening right now is much more serious than even we imagine!"

Since Gaetano, to whom this speech—because he was Italian—seemed to have been directed, did not reply, Jane Belloc felt impelled to intervene. Naively.

"Oh, Professor! Don't you think you're overdramatizing the situation? After all, Austria is almost Germany already!"

For my friend Miles there were some things about which he could not talk lightly or naively.

"My dear young woman, there are in international law pieces of paper that are called treaties. And I like to think that those pieces of paper cannot be tossed into the wastepaper basket by one of the parties to them. Once the law has been violated, we expect the worst!"

Gaetano said nothing. At that moment, Mme. Dujardin noticed that he turned his head to cast a worried glance at the two or three policemen who were drinking beer and at the SS officers who had entered the room and were looking for a table.

"Perhaps it's all most complex. . . ." the Italian said, as if to change the tenor of the conversation.

Miles, an Englishman, was in possession of the facts, and—to defend both a certain notion of international law and his country's flag—he grew heated. "That's it! The end justifies the means, as one of your illustrious compatriots has said."

Gaetano hesitated, at a loss. "Mussolini?"

"No, Machiavelli. I'm surprised you do not know."

Miles's tone was cutting. All at once, Gaetano smiled; it was a smile that could have disarmed an entire regiment of doubters, policemen or even college professors.

"My dear professor, let me assure you that in the de Montefeltre family we know our Machiavelli, Tasso and Dante by heart before we reach the age of twelve. For that matter, we are able to recite Dante backwards and forwards and can read Tasso with a Roman accent. But you can understand that afterwards we prefer to draw the line and forget it all as soon as we can!"

It had not even been true combat: a few sentences, cleverly phrased, part of a conversation, and Jane Belloc's face lit up. Gaetano was so clever at having gotten the better of the pedantic professor!

As Robert Miles was to tell me later, shaking his head sadly: "She was so sure of him, and I don't know how I dared do what I did next."

He referred to the attempt he made to bring Jane back to reality, but we have not yet reached that point. The meal finished, Gaetano, who enjoyed being amusing and who was now relaxed, was playing with a handsome, solid-gold cigarette lighter.

"Let's just say that I don't share your optimism," Robert Miles concluded. He, too, was desirous of bringing the conversation to an end.

Mme. Dujardin proposed a toast, full of polite references to the hazards of train travel and the acquaintances one nevertheless made through that method of transportation, and an hour later the passengers were given permission to return to their compartments. Once again, before Jane Belloc had time to invite him to accompany her, Gaetano disappeared.

"You must forgive me. I'm dead tired."

The door to the inn had already closed behind him, and Jane Belloc's face mirrored her disappointment. She seemed about to go after him, but Robert Miles sensed that she refrained in order not to give him the impression that she was pursuing him.

"Won't you come with us?"

Robert Miles had extended the invitation. Mme. Dujardin, the widow Nagy and her children all moved toward the door to the street; the innkeeper and her assistants were already beginning to clear the tables. The odors of strong beer and steaming ham were giving way to the smell of stale wine dregs and cold ashes. The party was over; the candles were being snuffed out, one by one. . . .

"No, thank you. I think I'll stay here for a moment."

Suddenly Jane found the thought of her solitary compartment almost frightening after such a wonderful day filled with dreams.

Miles returned and sat down at the table, facing her. "You mustn't . . ."

He had begun to say something, perhaps a warning, perhaps a word of advice, but Jane Belloc's reaction was brusque and immediate: "I mustn't what?"

He stopped short. He knew what the young woman must be thinking: who was he, some professor she had met on a train who seemed to be taking pity on her, giving her lessons? For a few moments he was silent, but everything he had observed since that morning, all he had sensed about Gaetano, filled him with dire suspicion, and he wanted Jane to be warned, to understand. Finally, no longer able to restrain himself, he drew an object from his pocket.

"In his haste, I think your friend forgot something."

It was the Italian's gold cigarette lighter. Jane's expression hardened. "He's not my 'friend!' "

Robert Miles gave an ironic smile and continued. "Let's just say that our stowaway has forgotten his cigarette lighter, then."

His remark had its intended effect.

"Why do you call him a stowaway?"

Her claws were already out, ready to protect the man she thought she loved. . . . Then, very patiently, Miles attempted to tell her that he had seen Gaetano board the train in Frankfurt at the last minute, that he had given ample proof throughout their journey that he wished to avoid any contact with the authorities, both those on the train and those of the German state.

"What of it?" Jane interrupted. "Didn't you yourself say just a short while ago that Herr Hitler's Reich was a police state and that it meant a threat to the rest of Europe that none of us even suspected?"

Hoist by his own petard, Miles was fully aware that he was interfering in something that was none of his affair, but he had begun now, and he had to continue. He used the word "imposter."

"I wouldn't like to see you allow yourself to be taken in by an imposter."

Jane Belloc immediately rose to her feet. She was the very image of the woman in love, ready to fight for her man to the death.

"I was sure of it!" she said. "The typical arrogant Englishman abroad! Anyone else is either a half-breed or an imposter. Only we British know how to hold the flag of truth aloft! What if Signor de Montefeltre is only an ordinary passenger, just like you or me?"

Jane, at that moment, was superb, and Robert Miles felt all his tender feelings for her suddenly rise up within him. He wanted to take her into his arms and tell her that her only chance not to end up as a bitter, worn-out, lonely woman rested with him, not with some adventurer met by chance on a train, not with some fake Italian stage prince who was acting the part of a sleek-headed seducer . . . even if he did have the world's most charming smile. He restrained his impulse and merely stood up in his turn.

"If you are so sure of yourself, or of him—which seems to amount to the same thing—let us return this to him"—he held out the cigarette lighter—"and then we shall see whether he's just another passenger like you and me!"

It was a challenge, and he had dared make it; she accepted it. A few minutes later, under the drowsy gaze of a company employee who told them to hurry because it was almost curfew, they were back at the station, where an equally sleepy sentinel returned their passports to them. The train was standing in the dark on its siding; all the lights had been extinguished. As soon as they went on board, almost instinctively they began to speak in whispers, and Jane suddenly felt afraid. What had Miles said to her—so sure of yourself? She was no longer sure of anything. What was worse, she suddenly felt afraid of what she might find out. In the dark corridor of their car, she turned to him. Her eyes implored him to give up, to stop playing games with her and her love, and with that stupid cigarette lighter in his hand that had suddenly become a weapon to be used against her! But Miles returned her gaze unflinchingly.

"Let's go," he said. "Which car is he in?"

Jane remembered Gaetano's mentioning the last car. The die was cast, and they would have to play it out to the end.

"The last car."

They started down the train. One car, two, three: the entire train seemed to be asleep. It was obvious that, cowed by the orders they had been given to observe the blackout, the passengers had had no choice other than to go to bed immediately. Each car seemed to be like all the others.

"One more . . ." Miles murmured.

At that moment, the sound of another convoy rent the darkness. Jane jumped and caught Miles's arm, which she as quickly released; it was only another military convoy full of armed soldiers, headed east. As it sped by, they stopped where they stood, and they did not continue along the corridor until it was again quiet in the blue and white moonlight that was their only illumination. Jane was trembling all over now: what if Miles were right? What would she find in the last car? At last, they pushed open the door to the rear car, and everything else happened so swiftly. . . . At the end of the corridor, his back to the window, was the short, willowy young man with the sparse mustache, smoking a cigarette. As soon as he saw them, he threw down his cigarette and stepped on it; then he entered the compartment opposite to where he had been standing. A second later, Gaetano emerged, tying the cord of a luxurious print dressing gown around his waist.

"Jane, you've come all this way!" He was smiling, he oozed charm —and Jane's heart melted. He indicated the compartment from which he had just emerged.

"Alas, my secretary was only able to book a single, and I'm forced to share my compartment with him. And when there are so many young and beautiful women on the train . . . Isn't it a pity?"

Gaetano's smile was like the invitation to a dream, the answer to the lyrical longings of any shop girl or woman of the world.

But Robert Miles cut his sentimental effusions short: "Here's your lighter. You had forgotten it."

To forestall questions from the man she was devouring with her eyes, Jane explained: "Please forgive me for having disturbed you . . . I insisted. I thought you might need it."

The scene went on for a few more minutes, none of them knowing quite what to do and unable to take their leave. Finally, after a few more casual remarks, Gaetano gave one last smile, and the door of his compartment closed behind him.

Robert Miles turned to Jane; he gave up. "You were right. I'm an arrogant Englishman abroad, all I hate most in my compatriots. I must beg your pardon."

Jane's expression was chilly. "It's unimportant. But I'm glad that you can recognize it."

Back in her compartment ten minutes later, Jane Belloc looked at herself in the mirror above the washstand as she had the previous evening. And as then she could not tell whether she was beautiful or plain, sad or gay, young or old. . . . She made a grimace at her reflection.

"Jane Belloc, writer and poet . . ."

In the moonlight, the train began to move slowly forward. Continuously, endlessly, the death trains passed it with their noise of steel, wheels and iron rails. . . .

When Jane awoke with a start it was still dark, but the train had again come to a halt. As she looked out the window, she realized that they had pulled into a station. Signs in various languages indicated that they had reached the Austrian frontier, and there were armed soldiers patrolling the platform. Suddenly she jumped. A knock was heard at the door, and even before she had time to slip a robe on over her flimsy silk nightgown, the door opened and three policemen were standing before her.

"Border police. Passport control . . ."

The officer who extended his hand for her papers paid no attention whatsoever to her. His expression was suspicious; he turned the document over and over in his hands. Finally convinced that Jane Belloc was indeed Jane Belloc, he clicked his heels together and withdrew: for several minutes afterwards she could hear, from compartment to compartment, the same knocking, the same hoarse voices of the policemen, the same heel clicks. Then all was silent again.

The train did not get underway, and Jane began to wonder what could be happening. She lay down again, but she was unable to get back to sleep. Half-awake, images flew through her brain. When she had gone to bed exhausted a few hours before, she had fallen asleep at once. Now she daydreamed. She imagined herself in Urbino, some day. . . . She imagined Gaetano's father, a serious, gentle old man, and a vast library with miles upon miles of shelves. There she strolled, a book in her hand, Dante, Tasso, Manzoni. Gaetano, his Danish hound at his side, strolled through suites of rooms that opened onto other rooms, down marble corridors and antechambers, up noble staircases and through hidden passageways.

"But what can be going on?"

She got up again, completely awake now. Outside on the platform of the station, she could hear shouts and the sound of voices raised in argument—and the train did not leave.

She slipped on her robe finally and went out into the corridor, where she bumped into Miles, who was also seeking information. Indeed, the entire car was suddenly filled with people moving about.

"I don't understand it. We've been stopped here for forty-five minutes. Your friend M. Lenoir seems to be having some kind of argument with those gentlemen."

Miles got off the train, and he returned a few seconds later. Apparently M. Lenoir had lost his passport, and the German authorities were refusing to allow him to leave the country, whereas he, as an administrator-director for the train company, was loudly announcing his intention to refuse to allow the train to depart without him.

"That man's selfishness goes beyond the bounds of imagination," Miles remarked before he returned to his compartment.

Jane went back to lie down on her bunk, but she could not sleep. Then there was another knock at her door.

"What is it?" She jumped up.

Gaetano's voice came from the other side of the door, urgent and breathless. "It's me, Gaetano . . . open up!"

She did not have time to slip into her robe. Just as before, when the policeman checking papers had burst into her compartment, she barely had time to rise before Gaetano was in the narrow room, his leather satchel in his hand. He stopped short. He seemed surprised, almost astonished, to find himself face to face with her, nearly naked as she was beneath her flimsy nightgown. Jane's breath quickened. It lasted no more than a fraction of a second. Then they both recovered their composure, Gaetano because he was well aware of the danger that threatened him, and Jane because in the end she had all the presence of mind in the world.

"Tell me," Gaetano breathed into her ear, "the train is not leaving because of that man's passport, am I right?"

At once Jane understood. She stammered: "Yes, I think . . . He can't seem to find it."

For a second Gaetano appeared to be thinking. Then, seized with a sudden inspiration, he took her arm. "You will help me, won't you?"

It was an appeal from the depths of his soul, and he handed her his passport—rather, the one he had passed off as his: a Belgian passport which clearly bore M. Lenoir's name. Jane stood motionless, but her mouth fell open.

"Don't ask any questions," Gaetano said. "Just do as I ask. I'm being followed. I'm in hiding, and the train must leave as soon as possible. One more hour in Germany, and I'm dead. Take this passport, go out of your compartment and pretend you found it at the end of the corridor, on the floor. You can take it to its real owner then; that's all I ask . . . I beg you."

Gaetano clutched her arm. He had spoken in a soft voice, almost into her ear, and she had felt his breath against her mouth. She was seized with an emotion she had never known before.

"Why? Did you take his passport?"

He nodded. "Yes, but it's no use to me any longer. I'll explain later. I beg you, hurry!"

She was suddenly seized with a terrible suspicion, that awful sensation when one foresees the worst. "What have you done? Tell me . . ."

Gaetano suddenly let go her arm. "It's nothing wrong, you can be sure of that! Can a de Montefeltre do anything against his conscience?" His voice was full of challenge: once again he was playing at double or nothing. Then he held out the passport.

Jane took it from him. "I'm going. . . ."

Gaetano drew a deep breath. "I'll wait here for you. . . ."

There was a note of promise in his voice, complicity and a promise of everything. Without another word, Jane tied the belt of her robe and left the compartment.

On the platform, things went as well as could be expected. M. Lenoir looked dubiously at this woman with tousled hair who had handed him his passport, and the officer with whom he had been arguing turned his attention to Jane momentarily.

"But I told you—I found it in the corridor, and that's the truth!"

When M. Lenoir muttered something she did not catch, she turned to him with hauteur. "Consider yourself fortunate that I came out of my compartment at an opportune moment!"

Robert Miles, the eternal onlooker, had witnessed the entire incident. He was to tell me later that Jane was one of those women who will kill an enemy with her bare hands if it means saving a husband, a child or a lover who is in danger.

"There on that platform on that chilly night, she was magnificent!"

She stood there with her hair in disarray and her robe drawn tightly around her—and with a strange light in her eyes—for she knew that Gaetano was waiting for her in her compartment.

"It's all very odd," M. Lenoir grumbled.

The policeman decided he would have to put in a report, but nonetheless he gave permission for the train to depart.

When she returned to her compartment, Jane Belloc found Gaetano de Montefeltre waiting. He was leaning with his back to the window. She closed the door behind her and moved toward him, and then, very gently, he untied the knot in her belt.

"My love . . ." was all Jane said as she let him take her in his arms.

"My love," she repeated.

It was much later, two hours later, a lifetime later . . . The train was now proceeding through the Austrian countryside, and Jane

Belloc felt as she had never felt before. She felt all the emotions: happiness, joy, anguish, and perhaps something like disbelief. She was lying naked in a man's arms. The man was handsome, strong, and he had made her feel that she was beautiful and both very strong and very weak. . . .

"My love . . ."

She had waited thirty-seven years to say those two words to a man: "My love." It had been an entire lifetime. Gaetano's hand moved gently over her face, her shoulders, her breasts: he loved her, did he not? He could not help but love her, and therefore she was happy. "My love . . ."

The train was running alongside a river on the right. Then they began to talk. Gaetano explained everything to Jane, all the things she wanted to hear him say: that he was a political refugee, an outlaw, what we had not yet begun to refer to as a "resistant," but an opponent. He was wanted by the Axis police, since he had committed the crime of rejecting tyranny and the deprivation of freedom. He was a fighter.

"You're wonderful," she murmured. He was a hero. . . .

He drew her closer to him. "You are the one who is wonderful. And you really got me out of a tight spot."

She closed her eyes; a wave of warmth, tender and full of feeling, flowed over her. "When I think that you are risking your life at every moment."

He gave a shrug to signify that that was not important. "You can be sure that I'm not the only one and that in Germany, in Italy, there are thousands like me who reject any order that means death and dishonor. . . ."

There was a tremor in his voice as he spoke those somewhat pompous words, his voice that sounded so sweet in Jane's ears.

"You are a hero. . . ." she repeated.

She closed her eyes, and once more she was borne up on a wave of happiness.

The train began to slow down again. They were approaching Linz, and Gaetano sat up suddenly.

"I can't stay here!"

It was certain that the border police would have telephoned to Linz to report the matter of the lost passport. And since they were looking for him, there was sure to be another check. They would search the train from one end to the other.

"All the same, they won't bother me again!" Jane protested.

But Gaetano caressed the nape of her neck and smiled. "Come, my darling—who brought the passport to the police? Do you take them for total innocents?" Suddenly he seemed very depressed. "I've got to find some way out."

They were silent for perhaps no more than a minute, and then Jane Belloc stood up. "I've got it!"

I've told you that she was one of those women who will kill father and mother, rather than see a lover injured! In two minutes, she was ready to leave her compartment.

"Wait here, and, above all, don't move. I'll be back." She was already gone. . . .

When the train, which was falling increasingly behind schedule, pulled into the station in Linz, there were—as there had been in Frankfurt and at the border—armed soldiers patrolling the platform. And police. And SS officers, along with Austrian guards. No sooner had the train come to a stop than they all climbed on board and once again proceeded to make a systematic check of all passengers' passports. And the first compartment, which they searched with a fine-tooth comb, was that of Jane Belloc.

"Miss Belloc?"

But she had recovered all her aplomb. "I've already been through at least half a dozen identity checks since I boarded this train, and the last one was at the border."

However, the round, stern face of the inspector who was questioning her showed not a trace of a smile, even less any willingness to be lenient. With a snap of his fingers, he ordered the two soldiers accompanying him to search the compartment; lying in plain sight on the bunk was the leather satchel that Gaetano had left behind him.

Jane saw it at the very moment the officer gave his order to his men; it was too late to do anything about it. However, as Gaetano had been playing a game of chance from the very beginning, perhaps it had been a stroke of genius on his part to have left the satchel where it was. It was so obvious, there in full view, that no one—neither the officer nor the two soldiers—ever thought of looking through it. As for Gaetano, he of course was no longer in the compartment.

Nor was he to be found in any of the other compartments that the police searched with such meticulous care throughout the time the train remained in the Linz station. Having come up totally empty-handed, the officer in charge of the search was finally forced to allow the train to depart.

Just as they were about to pull out, a newspaper vendor came onto the platform with the latest editions, and Robert Miles hailed him. There, across four columns on the first page, was the announcement of the Anschluss—and now it was a *fait accompli*. Austria was henceforth part of the Reich.

"They don't know what's happening," the Englishman muttered to himself as he looked at his fellow passengers, all of whom seemed indifferent as they went about their morning occupations.

But Jane at least had finally come to understand. It was not until the train had regained its full speed that she went to Mme. Dujardin's compartment. Miles, looking up from his newspaper, saw her enter the compartment, her lips tight.

"Ah, my dear child," the old lady murmured when she came in, carefully shutting the door behind her, "you've given me some bad moments! To think that I had to show myself in my nightgown in front of those hoodlums before I could dissuade them from entering!"

Then, with a movement that was surprisingly supple for a woman of her age, she climbed onto her bunk and unlatched the closed upper berth. It fell open, and Gaetano rolled out onto the floor, entangled in sheets and blankets.

"Oof! For a minute there I thought I would smother!"

The whole thing was almost like a vaudeville sketch: Mme. Dujardin in her nightdress, Signor de Montefeltre rolling out of a closed-up berth with a pillowcase over his head; It was like a French farce, even though death stalked close behind. While Gaetano, overcome with gratitude by the old lady's action, was kissing her hand with feeling that was completely unsimulated, Jane Belloc, standing very straight and holding her lover's satchel in her hand, stared into space, repeating in her mind those two words: "My love!" Never had she been happier or prouder of herself!

In the end, when it was all over, even Mme. Dujardin became tender. "I'm so glad to have been able to do it for you! I'm sure my son would have been proud of me!"

Her son, killed in 1914, the peril they had brushed against, the excitement . . . Gaetano had put his arm around Jane's waist with a gesture that was completely natural. Jane, looking at Mme. Dujardin, suddenly felt that the two of them represented youth and struggle, in a way, the rejection of oppression. And she felt an even stronger emotion, too.

When they had all recovered somewhat from their excitement, Jane handed Gaetano the satchel he had left in her compartment. "You forgot this."

The young woman's expression was so serious that for a moment the Italian was frightened. "Did you open it?" he asked.

Jane Belloc gave him a smile that meant: "You know I would do anything for you."

"Of course not. That's your secret, not mine. . . ."

Gaetano's arm tightened around her waist. I think that at that moment, at that precise moment and if only for a few seconds, Gaetano de Montefeltre truly did love Jane Belloc. At least he felt towards her a great upsurge of tenderness that was perhaps his way of thanking her.

The following hours marked the high point of Jane's happiness. With the man she loved—as one can love at only one point in one's life—in a compartment locked behind them by a conductor whom they had finally had to take into their confidence—Mme. Dujardin knew the man and knew that as a hero of the Somme and the Marne he could be trusted—Jane Belloc abandoned herself to passion, to plans and projects for the future, to all those things we call hope.

In front of the door to his own compartment, Robert Miles smoked his pipe and waited. He was telling himself that he had no right to spoil their happiness. And yet . . . And yet, folded up in his pocket, was the newspaper he had purchased on the station platform in Linz.

"I want to go with you," Jane was saying fervently to the man who held her close against him. "I want to go with you, to struggle at your side. . . ."

Very tenderly, very gently, Gaetano explained to her how difficult that would be. He spoke of his life as a fugitive, of his fears, of how he was forced always to be on guard—as were all of his companions in their struggle—of how he felt condemned, but that he refused to lie down and die. He knew how to find the words to touch the proper chords, did Gaetano de Montefeltre in that locked train compartment that was taking him ever closer to his destiny!

"But we would be together. . . ." Jane sighed.

A second time, but with an ever greater tenderness, Gaetano undressed her. And Jane allowed him to do it, like some big, clumsy girl gradually discovering the pleasures of love. The first moments over, it was all intoxication, blind abandon: it was a giving of herself, a gift she was making to a man who told her in a low voice all she wanted to hear. When she stood naked before him in the compartment and he looked at her, when he said simply: "You're lovely . . ." she felt the tears rise to her eyes. She knew that she was not the sort of woman thought of as lovely. She knew she had bony hips and that her breasts were a bit flat and already beginning to sag. . . . But the things he said to her, the fact that he was saying them, made her feel once more like a little girl, and as the blood surged through her veins, she knew that her hips were round and full and that her breasts were firm.

"You're lovely . . ."

She clung to him.

Then, since that accursed axle had begun to heat up again and the train was going more slowly than ever, it became a journey that was like a stroll through a country at war, a journey that could have gone on for a lifetime.

Mme. Dujardin's was a large house in a dream landscape, with pine trees and green fields, known as Blächen. Each year, after stopping in Vienna, the train from Ostend or Paris would stop there especially for her. It paused just long enough for her two huge trunks to be unloaded from the baggage van and for her to descend, in her blue hat and veil, to the platform of the tiny station and into the arms of her closest friend, Violetta, who lived in Salzburg and who came to Blächen a few days earlier to open up the house. In Vienna everything had gone without incident; the last free government of Austria had just capitulated, German troops were everywhere and now the train was approaching Blächen.

Military trains and convoys had continued to pass them, all headed toward the east. . . .

A quarter of an hour before their arrival at Blächen, Mme. Dujardin, who was ready to leave the train, decided to warn Jane Belloc and

Gaetano of her departure. They would not be left entirely on their own; the old lady had taken care to inform Mme. Nagy of the presence of the clandestine passenger for whom the *Reichspolizei* were searching. As in the case of the conductor, the pretty Hungarian widow could be trusted, and the presence of her two children would make it even easier to mislead the enemy and to assist Gaetano in eluding his pursuers, if necessary. None of these comings and goings between various compartments on the train—her own, Jane's and Mme. Nagy's—had escaped the attention of Robert Miles, but he kept silent as before.

At last the moment of farewell arrived. Mme. Dujardin aroused the two lovers and informed them that there would probably be another search when the train arrived in Bratislava in less than an hour.

"Until then, you are safe. Blächen is a station where I've never seen a policeman. And at Bratislava, Mme. Nagy can provide you with a place to hide, as I did."

The conductor stood watch during these farewells.

"However, it would be better if you were to remain hidden during the stop in Blächen," he told Gaetano.

With a hiss of escaping steam and two hoots of the whistle like some kind of ritual announcement, the huge engine with its six cars pulled into the tiny station. Robert Miles watched as Jane Belloc accompanied Mme. Dujardin onto the platform; her friend Violetta, dressed in mauve with an antique pink veil, stood waiting. There was much hugging and kissing, and, as Jane was about to get back into the train, the old lady whispered once more into her ear: "Look after our hero. . . ."

He now seemed somehow to belong to each of them, and, as well, to Mme. Nagy, who was standing smiling from her compartment window. Gaetano de Montefeltre was idolized by every woman who crossed his path, all of whom trusted him completely.

Jane mounted the three steps to the train: one last good-bye through the lowered window, and Mme. Dujardin and the village of Blächen, with its onion-shaped steeple, its pine trees and its fields dotted with well-fed cattle, disappeared around a wide bend in the tracks. For Jane it was the end of twelve hours of happiness.

She was returning to her compartment when Robert Miles, who plays the role of messenger of fate in this drama, approached her.

"I must speak with you," he said.

He was serious. But since Jane Belloc feared nothing from this man who meant nothing to her—although for one day she herself had meant so much to him—she answered him almost distractedly. "Yes?"

He drew closer. "I wouldn't want you to do anything silly," he murmured.

Jane tossed her head indignantly. "I know what I'm doing!"

Robert Miles spoke in an even lower tone: "You know who he is, don't you?"

For the final time, her face glowed with that straightforward, proud look of women speaking about the men they love. "Of course. He's wanted by all the police in Europe!"

"Ah, so he's told you. . . ." Robert Miles's voice faltered.

"Yes. He is a hero. . . ."

Miles lowered his eyes. He knew that what he was about to do might very well seem ignoble, but he had too keen a sense of good and evil, of justice and injustice, to ignore his duty to speak out. And perhaps he was also a jealous man.

"At least read this." And he handed her the newspaper he held, the one announcing the Anschluss as a *fait accompli* on the front page in four columns. "The last page," he said.

Then, his despicable deed done, for it was a despicable deed, if not a jealous one, the noble and brilliant Robert Miles—as he himself would agree, years later—returned to his compartment.

Jane felt herself grow pale. She had not yet read a single word, but it was as though she had had a premonition.

On the last page, occupying only two columns of print, was a photograph of the miscreant and an account of one of the neatest swindles ever carried out. The Italian director of a German bank in Frankfurt had decamped with the money of some wealthy industrialists who had been overtrusting with regard to the overly courteous employee. Several important persons in the Nazi regime had taken advantage of his offers to be of service to them financially, and all the policemen in the Reich were now looking for him . . . although he had somehow managed to escape, along with his wife! Of course, the thief was Gaetano.

You can imagine the scene that ensued in compartment number one of car number two on the Ostend Orient Express. Jane Belloc must have returned to her compartment, her eyes filled with tears but filled equally with determination. She, too, like Robert Miles, had a keen sense of good and evil. That the man, the only man she had ever loved, had played fast and loose with all she held most dear was for her the most terrible trial she could have faced.

"I know everything," she said.

She was holding the newspaper; no explanation was necessary. Then Gaetano stood up and began to speak. At first, he spoke standing before her. He spoke hard, bitter words, words that only the son of Italian immigrants who had handled the money of other people all his life in order to send a monthly check to his mother, in some Neapolitan suburb, could have spoken.

"You cannot know what it is, the smell of cash that doesn't belong to you passing through your fingers."

Money, those marks that had, year after year, day after day, dropped ever lower in value during the Depression, making gigantic sums, thousands and thousands of millions.

"Whole suitcases full, they would carry whole suitcases full, my arms dealers, when they had to pay for a good meal in a restaurant! And I'd watch them leave, wanting it all!"

He faced Jane and spoke with brutal bitterness in a voice she no longer recognized, a voice she had not thought him capable of using.

"Then, when Hitler and his friends were able to make people forget the Depression, and the suitcases full of money began to dwindle to mere bundles, and then to a few banknotes, I decided that I, too, would carry some off, a whole satchelful. But the satchel would be full of notes that could buy me a million meals in all the restaurants in the world."

There was such sincerity in his story that Jane began to feel moved by it.

Gaetano understood this, and he dropped down beside her on the seat. "Oh, please don't tell anyone! Let me get away. . . ."

His face and his body pleaded together for her understanding. Jane Belloc looked at him: handsomer and more moving than ever, and so much in her power. Lost.

"And what about this woman?" she asked. "What about your wife, who is supposed to be with you?"

He began to weep softly.

"She's old and ugly. She means nothing to me. She helped me, that's all."

She looked at him. "Where is she?"

He had almost fallen to the floor at her feet. "She's hiding, too, in the last car. But I love you! Haven't you understood that?"

It was a cry from the heart. Overcome, Jane rose. "Come," she said.

She made him sit down beside her on the banquette and rocked him in her arms like a child.

"You won't turn me in, will you? Promise?"

At first she did not reply. Then, when he repeated his question, she murmured softly into his ear: "No."

And that was all.

As the train—more slowly than ever—drew near a small station somewhere between Vienna and Bratislava, Gaetano de Montefeltre almost succeeded in persuading Jane Belloc to follow him.

"As soon as we've left Austria, I'll be safe. And this time, you really will come with me. . . ."

She did not reply, but I think we can imagine what her answer would have been.

"You know," he added, "my name is really Montefeltre, but I'm no relation at all to the Duke of Urbino."

Jane smiled; he was telling her everything now. Like Helena on the train from Bucharest, his mask had fallen.

"And I'm neither a novelist nor a poet. . . ."

Where does a lie begin, and where does hope end?

"You are Jane," was all he said, in the same voice in which he had told her a few hours before: "You are lovely. . ."

"Aha!" Gaetano said. "It looks as though we were about to stop again."

He was leaning at the window; at the edge of the forest, he could see a small station up ahead—barely a shed at the end of a long, curving section of track. Like Blächen, it was a miniature village, with pine trees, a few houses with peaked slate roofs and a church with an onion-shaped steeple.

"Why? Does the train usually stop here?"

But Gaetano did not reply. Once again he seemed worried; yes, the train was slowing down, and finally it came to a stop beside what was not even really a platform but more like a sandy embankment. At the entrance to the station where the stationmaster was waving a red flag, six armed men were standing.

"I don't like it," Gaetano muttered, but it was too late for him to hide, and, for that matter, Mme. Nagy's compartment was too far away.

The six armed men paid no attention to car number two; they began running toward the last car on the train. Gaetano stood up, and Jane also rose to her feet; they waited together.

Soon they heard shouts, someone calling, a scream. And then the men returned: holding him by the arms—almost dragging him—they were bringing with them the short, willowy man in black whose mustache had come unglued. Neither Gaetano nor Jane said a word, but as the group passed their window, the man's black hat, which he had always worn pulled down firmly on his head, blew off, and a mass of blond hair fell down over his shoulders. Gaetano's wife—for, of course, it was she—was young and beautiful, twice as young, ten times more beautiful, than Jane.

Jane looked at Gaetano. She simply looked at him, but what ensued could only have happened between a Jane Belloc and a Gaetano Montefeltre, noble or not. The Italian looked into her eyes without flinching.

"They'll send her to prison, won't they?"

"Of course."

"And she'll pay for both of you?"

"If she goes to prison alone, yes. . . ."

Alone, he had said it. A spasm seemed to cross Jane's face. He was still staring at her, but a thin smile had begun to appear on his lips. Outside, the head conductor was having a discussion with the policemen. They could sense that soon he would be giving the signal to leave. Slowly, with a theatrical gesture that had been carefully planned and rehearsed a hundred times, Gaetano Montefeltre put on his jacket. He bent down, picked up the leather satchel that had slipped to the floor and opened it. It was full of banknotes—hundreds, thousands of pieces of green, pink and blue paper. He drew out a bundle and held it out to Jane.

"You'll see that my mother gets that. I told you, the suburbs of Naples. Care of the priest at San Luciano. They will know where to find her. . . . You will write to her. Tell her I've joined the resistance. . . ."

His face lit up; he was beginning to prepare for the role he was to play. The hero . . . He put his hand on Jane's shoulder. He tightened his grip slowly, more strongly; then, suddenly, he let her go.

"*Ciao*," he said.

And that was all.

Thirty seconds later, as the train was already beginning to move again, Gaetano could be seen running down the platform, his satchel in his hand.

From the window of her compartment, Jane Belloc watched him speak to the policemen; she also saw his wife—the short, willowy young man with the long blond hair!—throw herself into his arms. And as Jane's car drew abreast of them, Gaetano gave her a final farewell. Then the train picked up speed, there was another curve and Gaetano, the policemen, the village and its bulbous steeple all disappeared from view.

Standing at the window in her compartment, Jane Belloc wept. Two lines of tears ran down her cheeks, perfectly straight lines, completely regular. For a moment she stood there, weeping silently, and then she looked at herself in the mirror. For one final time, she made a grotesque face at herself in the glass. She was ugly and beautiful and sublime, happy and unhappy: she had loved a man.

From the window of his compartment, Robert Miles, his pipe between his teeth, had also seen Gaetano disappear, standing on the platform with the policemen. . . .

"In the end," he was to tell me, "Gaetano had been a hero in Jane Belloc's eyes. Perhaps he turned himself in to the police merely so that he could go on being one for a little longer. . . ."

MINA

Istanbul, 1939

When Lise Bergaud finished reading to the ambassador the last story she had transcribed for him, she laid the manuscript on the rattan table between them and poured herself a glass of the white wine—almost effervescent, very dry—that Paul de Morlay procured from a friend in the Friuli district. Then she reached out her hand and touched the photograph that was standing before her: it was of the face of a man, deeply lined, his mustache untrimmed, a pipe in his mouth. It was Robert Miles, taken some thirty years after the adventure on the Ostend Orient Express.

"He grew old, that's all," the ambassador murmured. "But people still come to consult him from all over the world. He is an expert on everything having to do with the deeds and actions—even the most intimate ones!—of Greek courtesans. He can tell you all their names, their specialties, their individual measurements as well as some people can discuss Victor Hugo!"

Paul de Morlay chuckled, and Lise Bergaud again marveled that, alongside this photograph taken of Miles more than ten years before, the ambassador had retained the look of an almost young man. But de Morlay's expression had darkened. He was remembering something else. . . .

"Gaetano never had the time to grow really old. . . ."

An American friend had told him that at the end of the war, in the winter of 1945, they had found in the camp he and his men had liberated north of Munich—in that green countryside!—a clever Italian who had performed innumerable services for his fellow inmates, all in exchange for signed pieces of paper that he had carefully preserved. For later . . . They had been checks, postdated six months, a year ahead, drawn on banks that had been destroyed, bombed out or failed for more than a year or two already. The man had died of exhaustion on the very day the American troops had entered the camp, but his friends had referred to him as the "Duke of Montefeltre," merely a duke, no longer a prince.

"There's nothing left of Jane Belloc."

After her trip to Greece, she had probably returned to her Kentish or Sussex countryside and just gone on living as before: the village primary school, the Misses Finchley or Jones, the doctor, the pharmacist . . .

"Would you have stopped Gaetano from getting off that train?" Paul de Morlay had suddenly spoken to Lise Bergaud in the familiar, saying "*tu.*"

She blushed. "Of course! If I had loved him, I would have kept him!"

Paul de Morlay put out his hand to hers and held it. "You can understand, then, why there's nothing left of Jane Belloc. . . . The love we manage to save when everything else is being destroyed . . ."

The old man's hand remained clasped around her own, and Lise realized that she was happy.

In the evening, Despinetta and Barberina brought out lamps, for Morlay had decided to dine out of doors. They also lit small sticks of incense to drive away the mosquitoes; neither Lise nor the ambassador felt like moving. She listened to the song of the cicadas and the crickets, the call of a nightbird, the distant ringing of a bell. The entire countryside, designed some three or four hundred years earlier for mankind's pleasure and which mankind's industry had irretrievably ruined in ten or twenty years, had suddenly regained all its magic. She felt the peace of lovely days when one's heart is calm: the smell of wood fires burning, piles of dead leaves going up in smoke, and Paul de Morlay's voice as he went on to tell her about the women, the countries, the journeys that no one but he could have invented.

Istanbul, 1939

"The last train is that of 1939. . . ."

He had shut his eyes, and, from the sound of his voice, Lise understood that there would be no need for her to turn on her small tape recorder this evening. Although the final adventure on this last train that he was about to relate to her was perhaps the most beautiful, it was also the most secret; he was about to reveal to her his innermost secret, and she wanted to share it with him alone.

"I am so happy with you," she murmured as he leaned toward her to inquire if she were bored, or cold, or if she would not prefer to go in. "I feel so happy with you, and it seems so normal, so obvious to me, that it must be abnormal!"

She meant: you must be a magician, a sorcerer, one who can easily cross the frontier between the normal and the abnormal, but he did not reply. He came around the table and sat down beside her on a long wicker couch. Paul de Morlay was ageless. Barberina and Despinetta, the little maids with their starched skirts, had settled in the shadows nearby, breathing in the silence, almost panting with emotion. The fact that the three of them—Lise, Barberina, Despinetta—together had fewer years than Paul de Morlay was unimportant; smiling, tender, gay, the ambassador had no age.

"The last train . . ." Lise murmured, encouraging him to continue. She felt a tenderness for the man who was speaking such as she had never known before.

"Yes, the last train . . ."

The moon rose over the Veneto which had become glorious and rich once more; it fell upon the faces of the four young people talking in the darkness.

"The last train left Istanbul on September 1, 1939."

For over twelve hours, panic—like that preceding some great cataclysm—had reigned in the lobby of the Hotel Pera. Everyone knew that only one more train would be crossing Bulgaria, and that afterwards nothing would be certain. And everyone wanted to leave, all those people Europe was emitting before the world came to an end through every pore, like some hot, unhealthy sweat . . . people who had been its life's blood, people who had made it live. Everyone . . . and that included Paul de Morlay, perhaps . . . was seized with panic and was trying to get away—to take the last train.

For what seemed like ages, those manning the ticket windows in the Stamboul station had not even bothered to respond to the waiting passengers. Now, in the lobby of the Pera, the few remaining tickets which had been purchased by people armed with foresight were selling at the price of gold. Gold? Platinum, diamonds! A short man who resembled Peter Lorre in *The Maltese Falcon* was doing a brisk business in the shelter of his capacious coat, under the affable but formidable gaze of his chief or bodyguard, who looked like Sidney Greenstreet in that same Bogart film. Indeed, everything about this final departure was like some black-and-white American film of the 1940s, with its parade of spies, easygoing but honest young women, Slavic barons, loose, foreign *femme fatales* and needy old couples. And it was all taking place beneath the copper chandeliers with a tumult that echoed off the mosaic and other Byzantine decorations on the walls—so authentic that they all looked fake—like the echo in an empty swimming pool. It was a heartrending scene: the model couple, office employees probably, fleeing the sinking ship—the wife had probably sold all her jewelry for the fare—and the Nazi officer disguised as a traveling salesman but given away by his black leather coat.

"And I was there, with my reserved seat booked, my first-class compartment, my ticket in my pocket. I was waiting, passing the time with a Giraudoux novel—I don't recall whether it was *Siegfried* or *Suzanne et la Pacifique*—in any case, a fateful title. I was waiting and watching."

Then Paul de Morlay noticed a woman. There were many of them in that hotel lobby, of course, and some who were perhaps more beautiful, richer, more luxuriously dressed. But this woman was not yet twenty years old, and she was the incarnation of all the ambassador's dreams as we have come to know them: a lost child with huge, waif-like eyes. After seeing her, Paul de Morlay paid no attention to any of the others. She was bargaining with Peter Lorre's double, and de Morlay saw her take a wad of banknotes from her handbag, and then another, then the entire contents of her bag, adding for good measure a few pieces of jewelry which she removed from her person. Her face was like the hunted face of some small, fragile animal, her full lips were red and her tired eyes had an expression to take the breath away from a stranger. That look alone had already captivated de Morlay. Forever. When she parted from the man, she held clutched in her hand a ticket on the last train; that was all she had left in the world. She was like that elderly couple whose name the ambassador had forgotten. He called them the Schleyers: Ernst Schleyer had been a professor of

Jewish history in Cracow and had fled with his wife to Berlin in the late 1920s, thinking to find refuge there. They had been fleeing ever since. Or like Lena, a prostitute who dreamed of getting back to Marseilles; or like that pale, haughty woman with a high forehead like Garbo's, who was accompanied by a man with receding hair, wearing a fur coat too heavy for that time of year—all of them had paid dearly for their passage on that last train!

De Morlay's attention had also been drawn to three men. One of them, who had a narrow, handsome Semitic face, wore gold eyeglasses; he was engaged in animated conversation with a short, oily individual in a black leather coat. More precisely, his companion appeared to be animated; the man in the gold eyeglasses, whom the other man was pushing, shoving, perhaps insulting, remained impassive. He seemed to be lost in a dream, smiling to himself. The third man who caught de Morlay's eye was—as the ambassador learned later—a former officer in the Imperial Russian Army, who hated the system the Axis powers were in the process of imposing on Europe even more than he hated the Bolsheviks who had taken away his land and his fortune —as well as hanged several of his ancestors from the chandelier in the main drawing room. At least they had been Russians. He was standing apart from the crowd with an ambiguous smile on his lips.

As the ambassador said, it was like a riot, a hubbub through which porters struggled with heavy bags or bore urgent letters that would never reach their destinations. Chauffeurs, kitchen help, interpreters, dragomen, even a young embassy attaché who had come to bid farewell to some mistress and had been unable to find her in the room where he had left her, since she had fled with someone who could be more generous: it was the confusion before the deluge. But among all those pitiable or brave or miserable or rascally people, only the face of the pale young girl with the dark eyes had absorbed Paul de Morlay's attention. Alas, it was a time when other people's misery had become commonplace. A minister plenipotentiary on a special mission, he was leaving Istanbul because there was no longer anyone there to listen to what he had to say. The ambassador was returning to Paris, and he had learned sorrow and bitterness, if not resignation. Then the young girl had been lost in a movement of the crowd, and he had returned to Giraudoux and had almost forgotten her.

Yet he was to see her soon again: along with the Schleyers, and the Russian officer, and the calm Jew and the couple of employees, all of whom had been the victims of the fake Peter Lorre, who had managed to sell at the price of diamonds seats in a car that did not exist on the train.

The Compagnie Internationale des Wagons-Lits looked the other way. In other words, the head conductor had allowed all those who had been victims of the hoax to board the train and crowd into the compartments of passengers who had tickets, such as Paul de Morlay, and who were willing to share their accommodations. Thus the ambassador had found himself in the company of Henry Wiesner—the phlegmatic man who had been insulted by the man in black—and all the other clandestine passengers had been scattered among the seven actual cars of the real train as it continued to stand at the platform without leaving. Its locomotive had broken down, and the mechanic who had been supposed to repair it had already left on the prior train, the next-to-last train. . . . So Paul de Morlay had made his way to the bar car, which had been transformed into a dormitory, and he had approached the dark young girl. . . .

"The last real journey of that old way of life was about to begin. Afterwards, we would hop around the world like fleas, crossing the Atlantic in airplanes. And although very little happened during that last journey from east to west across what was about to become a battlefield, it has remained in my heart and my memory almost as vividly as the first one I made so long ago on that same Orient Express, on my way to Budapest and my first post as vice-consul, when I was to meet Maria and Stephanie. Do you remember?"

Lise Bergaud's eyes glistened. As Paul de Morlay continued to speak, she sensed that his breathing, which had been somewhat rapid at first as though he were tired, began to grow calm, regular, peaceful. . . . It was as though the memory of this final adventure he was about to tell her were bringing him a new kind of solace. It was, in fact, to be the final note to all he had told her up until that evening. All the luxury trains that had crossed Europe in every direction for all those thirty years—from Maria's fixed smile on the platform of the Gare de l'Est to that of Jane Belloc, full of confusion and dismay, at the Austrian border—all were now in disorder, broken down, mingled in that final train that was to give way to those other loaded trains that would take the Schleyers, the Lenas and their companions in misfortune to another kind of slaughterhouse. . . .

It was not only that. Just as the ambassador had told Lise of her resemblance to Antonella with the vivid, overwhelming personality, so now, as he spoke of the dark young girl he came to know as Mina, Lise Bergaud sensed that there were signals, references, feelings that were almost appeals behind his words and that perhaps they were addressed to her. And she was deeply touched. As the ambassador's story continued, this feeling grew stronger and stronger, as though the young man talking for her benefit was also and above all talking about her. . . .

"We began to talk at once," de Morlay continued. "She was sharing the compartment of the woman with Greta Garbo's high, pale forehead, who was also standing at the bar, somewhat aloofly. As I had surmised, she had paid out her last cent for a ticket on a nonexistent train."

Mina Kransky's fingers were long and tapering, those of a pianist. She was, in fact, a pianist, and Jewish, and she was desperately trying to get to America where she had been told she would be safe. Her parents had disappeared when she was a child one night when the student officers in a military academy in the town had descended on the neighborhood where they lived, in a suburb of Lodz; Mina, like the Schleyers, had learned fear at an early age.

"It's only when I'm playing the piano that I can forget. . . ."

She had spoken at once of the things she loved: of Schubert and Liszt—"Who remade music!"—and expressed her indignation at the fact that the German National Socialist Party and its conductors and singers had adopted Wagner, whom she also adored. She introduced Paul de Morlay to the passenger who looked like Garbo—a Frenchwoman named Wanda D.—and he in turn had introduced them to his compartment mate, Henry Wiesner. The Russian officer, whose name was Boris Tukachevski, was drinking his first bottle of mineral water nearby; contrary to legend and stereotype, Boris Tukachevski drank only water. They invited him to join them, and thereby a quintet was formed that was to remain united—separated only by death—until the end of the journey. The Schleyer couple, of course, and the prostitute Lena, who sold herself to a Belgian banker in a poker game—he made a good profit from it—continued to cross their paths on the train. With rage in his heart, the ambassador was to see the Schleyers removed from the train when they crossed the Bulgarian border because the professor of Jewish history was missing a certain stamp in his passport—people were soon to die for one stamp too few, one star too many—but the five of them talked, ate together and grew fond of one another.

"But I don't want to bore you much longer. As I said, nothing—or nearly nothing—really happened on that final trip back. Ten hours late, the train left Istanbul, carrying twice as many passengers as it was meant to transport."

Around three in the morning in the restaurant car—where food was being served that would have disgraced a station fast-food stand—ah, the feasts in the old days!—Paul de Morlay and his friends were reduced to splitting one cold chicken five ways. The head chef had been called up to rejoin his regiment the day before; M. Paul, who had taught everyone how to eat on the Orient Express, had retired. And as they talked, Mina, Wanda, Boris, Wiesner and the ambassador tried to imagine what tomorrow's world would be like. They outdid themselves in lyric imaginings and in despair.

"Peace!" Mina exclaimed, having drunk all the vodka the Russian left untouched. "Peace! Suddenly I want to believe in it; I want to believe in peace! Is it still possible? Will you allow me to have that?"

She was drunk and desperate. She was beautiful, and her eyes were full of tears.

But Wiesner gave an imperceptible smile. "Yes, the peace of the grave . . ."

His expression was bitter, and Wanda D.'s face froze. She coughed, and at once a red spot appeared on her pale cheeks.

"You mustn't say that."

Wanda D.'s voice was hoarse. She glanced at Wiesner; it was in that instant—because she had heard him speak words that had touched the innermost depths of her being—that something occurred between them. It was as if both of them had sensed that a similar threat—a similar danger—was drawing them toward the abyss. But the train was drawing them all along too swiftly and in too much disorder for any of them to analyze their feelings.

Later, when most of the other passengers had returned to their compartments, the five chance acquaintances remained talking together for a long time. The regular motion of the train, the sound of the whistle in the night, the lights of the stations gave them a sense of time suspended. . . . Boris Tukachevski told them what he had heard about Hitler's Germany: Communists in camps, Jews already banned in a society that no longer existed, hatred, blind mobs, a synagogue in flames, conflagrations, blood . . .

"Someday," he muttered, "I'll start drinking again."

He meant to say: when this misery, this monstrous thing will have been wiped from the face of the earth, but not from our memories. As Mina raised another glass to her lips, her hand trembled. Again de Morlay saw glances exchanged. Then he retired to his compartment.

"I imagine that all along the track, standing on the embankments, there were already groups of men and women with pale faces, their backs bent beneath the load of their worldly goods, fleeing."

Henry Wiesner had come back to their compartment, and now he spoke. He told his story, perhaps, only because he, like the others, knew that the story was already over, that this was the end. He was a scientist, one of that handful of physicists and chemists who, perhaps without meaning to, had discovered in the secrecy of their laboratories one or another of those weapons that were to destroy the world. Wiesner's specialty had been what has come to be known as "heavy water."

"And then one day I said no," he explained very calmly. On the day when those who now ruled the world—no matter which side they happened to be on—had attempted to buy him off to bring closer the possibility of that great, final "boom," Wiesner had burned his papers, had left behind him in a hotel room—in Belgrade, in Varna, who knows?—the key to his safe and had departed. Since he had fled Vienna where he had been working, men had been on his trail, never letting him out of their sight.

"The man in the black leather coat who is on the train . . ."

For he was on the train, that Nazi or American agent—Wiesner pretended not to know which—increasing the surveillance because the scientist was Jewish, and there were a thousand and one subtle ways to blackmail him.

"And where will you go?" Paul de Morlay asked.

"I don't know. . . ."

He was lying above de Morlay in the upper berth, and de Morlay imagined him staring into the darkness. It was a time when there were people, like Robert Miles, for example, who never wanted to close their eyes. There was the loud noise of the wheels on the tracks, sparks shooting from the naked steel, and the train rushed on through the night.

"I can't repeat it often enough: it was the last train. We were together for so short a time!"

In their compartment, Mina and Wanda D. were also talking together. Wanda's secret would remain a secret until the journey's end, but she, too, was fleeing. She was moving on, not looking back, because what lay behind her was, simply, her life.

"She was pale when she went to bed," Mina told me later, "and she talked of a beach in the sun where she was going to live. As though it were some impossible dream but that she had to believe it."

She still coughed, Wanda D., and she was already spitting blood—a tiny drop of red in the fold of her handkerchief. . . .

"Our train—how impatient I am suddenly for it to arrive!—was, in the last analysis, transporting people who were dead, people living on borrowed time; those who survived would be lucky, like the winning players in Russian roulette."

In the night, at the stations along the track, stood the simple wooden huts of the Bulgarian plains and people whose last hope was that the train would stop for them, people who watched it flash by without slowing down.

"And just as she was falling asleep," Mina told me, "Wanda told me, very simply, that I was pretty. . . ."

The next morning, the Orient Express did stop. It stopped in the middle of an empty plain; the few hovels—almost like shacks—with their flat roofs built to withstand the fierce winter wind seemed to be part of the gray, yellowish earth in which they were half buried and showed no signs of life. When Paul de Morlay reached the bar car to try to find something resembling tea or coffee, the whole area was filled with sleeping gypsies. They lay strewn over armchairs and under tables, and had evidently boarded the train at an earlier stop when no one had been there to prevent them.

The exhausted bartender in charge looked at them with a shrug. "I can't force them off the train, after all."

He was a Swiss from Smyrna whose family had helped build the line from Adrianopolis to Sofia in happier days. But not he or the ambassador, not the gypsies themselves, had any idea where their caravan was bound. They had simply grabbed onto the polished copper of this luxury train that had turned into the last train out of hell, a train that moved through an endless chaos.

The man in the black leather coat who had been following Wiesner to persuade him to change his course and go to Berlin was smoking a thin cigar at the end of the car, cursing under his breath what he referred to as "these vermin."

"I'll complain to the company! I'll file a report!"

But who would have been there to listen? The Orient Express of the past had become a refugee train. A half hour later, when the train was once again underway, Morlay managed to obtain—by what miracle?— a cup of real coffee, and Boris Tukachevski, who had joined him, was already plotting to put a bullet through the head of the Nazi in the black leather coat simply because he reminded him of Goebbels or Ribbentrop, whichever. . . .

"It only takes the courage to do it," the Russian muttered as he drank still another glass of mineral water.

"Perhaps you might also find a revolver handy," de Morlay replied jokingly.

He laughed, but Boris did not. From the right pocket of his blazer with its crest of a British school that had trained six generations of prime ministers and as many czarist chamberlains, he drew a tiny, glittering chrome revolver with a mother-of-pearl handle.

"I haven't been without this little darling for thirty years."

The Vichy water flowed, and we were friends again.

At lunch, the train, making a noise like wood being scraped, was moving at no more than fifteen miles an hour. In the station where it finally came to a stop, hordes of fleeing men and women clung to the doors and windows begging for bread, for a piece of anything that could be eaten. In the mob of women wearing multicolored rags, the ambassador noticed a fifteen-year-old girl with a fierce expression who reminded him of Mina Kransky. The young pianist saw her, too, and then her eyes met de Morlay's.

"I think that that was when she understood what I had been all my life, and although I was ashamed as I reached over the heads of the crowd with a fistful of green and white banknotes in my hand, the child did not thank me. She did not even smile as she took them with both hands . . . but I knew it was something I had to do."

Tukachevski's hand was resting on Mina's shoulder, like a final reunion of old Russia and Jewish Poland; the man in the leather coat swore and spat on the floor. But when he returned to his attack on

Wiesner—"In Berlin you will have all the help you need, a laboratory
in the country . . . women"—it was Wiesner who swore at him,
without, however, spitting.

Already, in low tones, he was making plans for the future with
Wanda—she was as lost as he; the clinic that was expecting her was
little better than the camp that was waiting to receive him. So they
talked about that beach in the sun. Of some island . . . They clung
to each other because the train that was bearing them along was going
nowhere. The cities, the suspended lives, the blackened suburbs, the
gray plains, the borders so soon to crumble all sped by. The first
refugee trains sped by; as the coming disaster rose, the final moments
of freedom faded on the horizon—but at least those two had come
together.

At that point, Lise Bergaud interrupted the ambassador. She wanted
to know more about Wanda, who had crossed his path only for the
length of a train journey that had lasted for four days.

"Had you understood that she was ill?"

Could the ambassador tell her that with age he had become a philoso-
pher, that he had learned to read joy, life, health or disease and death
from a face?

"She said nothing to us. But although everything about her denoted
a wealthy, adored woman, the mistress or wife of a person of some
importance, there was something insane, improbable in the way she
had aroused the affections and tenderness and dreams of happiness of
a little Jewish sicentist bound for nowhere. Anyone could have guessed
that it was just her way of ending her life a bit less badly than she had
begun it."

"And he, did he know?"

The ambassador took Lise's hand and held it in his own. "Henry
Wiesner was one of those people who know everything but have never
learned anything. Like her, he simply refused to see."

He refused to see the Nazi in the leather coat who would probably
kill him at the end of the journey, rather than allow him to depart
with his secrets and to wait in America or in some isolated corner of
France or Portugal—where he was to be buried—for others to blow
up the world.

"No, I think that if neither of them told the other the truth, it was
just because truth no longer mattered."

Boris Tukachevski's hand had remained on Mina's shoulder, and the ambassador had felt an enormous rush of affection for these companions in misfortune who, in the end, were telling his final tale for him.

"But what about Mina?" Lise continued.

Paul de Morlay gave a tiny smile, lost in his own thoughts. "Wait . . ."

Suddenly everything changed. Men came on board wearing uniforms that were too new, carrying automatic weapons, when they reached what appeared to be a border station. Today it is called Dragoman, a large city with a marketplace filled with peasants with windburned faces, peaceful shopkeepers behind wooden shutters, fine officials. On that day in 1939, there was nothing fine about the militiamen who boarded the train. All the gypsies were taken off; it was a scene of total confusion. They also took the Schleyers and those other passengers who lacked the necessary stamps in their passports.

We had reached the border between Bulgaria and Yugoslavia.

It was then that the armed men had approached Mina. She did not have the necessary stamp in her passport, either. There was no discussion. The ambassador attempted to intervene; he displayed his diplomatic passport, but the cold look the officer of that advance guard of political police gave him was more than eloquent. All the pieces of papers produced by our moribund democracies were no longer worth even the trouble to examine.

Mina was taken off the train. Two men were leading her away with the Schleyers, the gypsies, the others . . . and she turned back to de Morlay, to her friends, to the train that was about to leave for some illusory freedom. . . . Her eyes had been like two black coals.

"Wait!"

Only one voice had been raised, a voice that was commanding and calm, full of self-assurance, with a Slavic accent. Boris Tukachevski jumped down onto the platform. He argued for a moment with the Bulgarian soldiers, who had been frozen where they stood by the tone of his voice alone. Without further ado, he drew from his pocket his papers and a note, a letter with red wax seals.

"I never knew," the ambassador murmured, "I never knew what that document might have been. But the men came to attention and saluted him."

Tukachevski strode after Mina, who had already disappeared from view around the corner of the station, and he returned with her, holding her by the arm.

"Come," was all he said.

The soldiers saluted as the couple got back on board. None of the other passengers dared question Boris Tukachevski, but they knew that this man who professed such hatred for the Nazis and all those who would one day be in power nevertheless possessed the means to make himself respected and saluted.

"Was Tukachevski his real name?" Lise Bergaud asked.

The ambassador released her hand for a moment, and before he took it again he made a vague gesture.

"Why bother to find out? He saved Mina. That was all."

The Schleyers and the rest, along with the gypsies, had been taken away, and the train departed. Who would ever see them again?

They had crossed into Yugoslavia, passing stations—Pirot, Bela, Nis—overrun with hopeful passengers who would never take a train. Boris stood motionless at Mina's side. It was as though somehow he had married her, so indissoluble a couple did they now seem. Wiesner and Wanda, too, were linked in a silence in which everything was being spoken between them.

"I know now that Wanda's husband had left her two years earlier and run off with a dancer, and that she herself had had an Italian lover who had been assiduous in frequenting every casino on the Riviera. But now, sittting beside a Jewish physicist who no longer believed in anything, she herself came to believe again in life."

Henry Wiesner began to reply to her with more conviction when she spoke to him of those sun-drenched islands she dreamed of, whose names she recited like a litany: Majorca, Ibiza, Sardinia . . .

"Of course I'll go with you. . . ."

Everyone knew—everyone on that train speeding like an arrow across Europe, among whom only the ambassador had a secure position awaiting him, soon to be in London where he would follow General de Gaulle—everyone knew that Henry Wiesner and Wanda D. were talking about the impossible, a dream. Málaga or Madeira, what difference could it make? The convent at Valdemosa that had sheltered Chopin and George Sand became their promised land, and Wiesner and Wanda were far away, on their island. The man in the leather coat might chafe at the bit all he liked, fondling the butt of his heavy revolver in his pocket, but he was powerless against them. For that matter, Boris had spoken to him, too. . . . But although the Nazi soon left the train—he was powerless against Wiesner, Tukachevski's words to him had made that quite clear—other men very like him would take his place in Paris, in Lausanne, even in Madeira or Ibiza, and everything would go on until that final "boom" that would bring all of it to an end. Until then, however, Henry Wiesner and Wanda D. were free, and they owed their freedom to Boris; such freedom—when death is reaching out its arms to enfold you—is worth living for at any price, even on a railroad line between Bela and Nis, Nis and Zitovak, in the middle of nowhere.

"But who was Boris? Did you ever find out?"

Lise Bergaud wanted to know because the face of the former czarist officer with the mysterious key that seemed to open every door suddenly seemed to have been drawn for her with too broad a stroke.

"I swear to you, I never knew. . . ."

There are such people—we meet them from time to time—people who with a simple gesture seem to be able to smooth out everything in their path, even though some unsuspected storm is raging inside them.

"And you just watched?"

"Yes, I watched. . . ."

The world had been divided between those who raised their hand, or a gun, and those who looked on, who "watched." For a long time, the ambassador merely looked on, merely watched, until he in turn joined the fray, perhaps because he had seen too bright a glow in the depths of frail, pale Mina Kransky's eyes. . . .

"Boris Tukachevski came to talk to me at dinner time." The Russian said nothing about himself, but Paul de Morlay detected the fact that the Byelorussian exile still had links, attachments, even in Prussia or Pomerania, that he had friends. And although his hatred for the men in power in Germany was boundless, nevertheless he still had influence in Berlin, in the very corridors of the Reich's chancellery itself.

What Tukachevski did not know was that the men stationed at the isolated outpost on the Bulgarian plains had telephoned to Sofia, and that from Sofia a call had been put through to Berlin. . . .

"For thirty years, I, too, have had the feeling that I am an unburied corpse," he said.

Then, and the ambassador did not show the least surprise since on this final train anything could happen, Boris Tukachevski exchanged his bottle of Vichy water for a carafe of vodka.

"Ah, well," he murmured, "I guess I will have to resign myself to the fact that I'll never see the day when they get theirs!"

He downed three glasses in a row: at the first, he made a face—he had not drunk for thirty years—but at the second, his face retained his frozen smile. He had rediscovered the taste of vodka; the third glass, he enjoyed.

Near him, her head resting on a cushion in the almost empty Pullman—the gypsies and the Schleyers were no longer on the train, and there were now only the regular passengers—Mina Kransky was sleeping, her lips slightly parted.

"It's because of young things like that that you want to put an end to everything, once and for all, or begin all over again. Whichever . . ."

He was now on his sixth glass of vodka, and Henry Wiesner and Wanda D. were still dreaming of the convent at Valdemosa. And as the names of nonexistent towns sped by on signs of phantom stations—Varvarin, Paradin—the ambassador was not aware that he was making this trip for the final time; the face of Mina Kransky, as it moved gently to the rocking of the car, reflected the image of all the distress of a world that was about to crumble. Why was this face so beautiful and sorrowful there in the darkest of all worlds? The land east of Belgrade is vast. . . . When Mina awoke, Boris Tukachevski had returned to his compartment, and for the first time the ambassador really spoke to her.

"I shall not repeat what we said to each other, for you have already guessed it. The words that are spoken between a man who is already past his prime—I mean fifty!—and a girl who is still almost a child . . ."

But they had been words in which all the emotions, the feelings, the longings that would soon become true tenderness could already be detected, like shadows.

"And she talked about her piano, her music . . ."

Paul de Morlay, in that Venetian night so far removed from the hell on wheels of that night on the last train, fell silent. He was silent long enough for Lise Bergaud to disengage her hand gently from his and—in an incomprehensible gesture—place it on the ambassador's shoulder.

"Don't say anything, Paul. Yes, I know. . . ."

He turned toward her. "Oh, you do?"

Once again he had said *tu*.

Paul de Morlay had been but a few years younger than Tukachevski, but he had had the vague feeling that the Russian had somehow entrusted the little Jewish pianist to his care. And he had suddenly felt a remarkably incestuous desire for her. Even had he tried to resist it, the impossible happiness that had sprung up in so few short hours, a thousand miles, between those other total strangers, Wiesner and Wanda, would have given him all the hope he needed. Three months later, six at the most, Wanda would be dying in a luxurious private clinic, her lungs destroyed by a disease with which she had learned to live so well that it had become like an old friend or distant relative whom one tolerates. As for Henry Wiesner, put in harness like a beast of burden to labor in some American or German laboratory—or dead in his turn with a bullet in his head because of his categorical refusal to create death—he, too, could be struck from the list of the so-called living, since those who mete death out to others have only found another way of dying. Still, both of them, with radiant smiles, lied to each other as the train crossed Yugoslavia toward the Italian border where it would all end. How could the ambassador refuse, having witnessed that encounter between those two suspended lives, to give way in his turn to the enchantment of one more encounter that had created sparks, that was like some kind of vertigo he had sought all his life, when Domodossola and Briga were at the end of the track?

Simplon Orient Express . . . journey's end . . .

On the platform at Mestre, the armed police who were waiting for Tukachevski—the telephone call from the border to Sofia, from Sofia to Berlin, from Berlin to Rome, from Rome to Venice and so on to Mestre, had borne fruit—knew what was on that paper with its seals and signatures that the Russian would show them. But they also knew that an order had been sent down from the highest level to ignore the paper, the seals, the signatures. Those who had affixed them to that magic *laissez-passer* had been gunned down twenty-four hours earlier, or tossed into a camp in Silesia. . . .

So when the Italian captain who had received those orders from Berlin passed Wiesner and Wanda, who were sleeping side by side in the Pullman car, he did not so much as glance at them. Nor did he look into the compartment where Mina Kransky was lying with her little girl's smile on her lips.

"I was already up, and I saw them go straight to Tukachevski's compartment. . . ."

The police had exchanged a few brief words with the conductor, and with that gesture typical of every policeman the world over, the officer knocked on the door. The shot rang out inside even before the captain had announced his identity.

In Boris Tukachevski's hand was the tiny chrome revolver. He had burned all his papers, including the document with its now useless seals, in the washbasin. Wiesner and Wanda had a few weeks of happiness still remaining to them. With Boris Tukachevski dead, Mina was alone. She was, in some way, a widow.

"So what would you have had me do?"

Paul de Morlay's face had the expression of an impenitent schoolboy caught in the act.

"You took her with you, did you not?"

Mina Kransky, that pale, fragile, doelike creature, the young widow, weeping, Mina whose fingers were those of a pianist and whose neck at the nape was like that of a little hunted animal . . .

"All the same, I could hardly leave her there alone on the train. For that matter, she had no idea where she was going. . . ."

Although the appeal he had first sensed in the girl's dark eyes with their burning gaze would have been addressed to anyone willing to take her by the hand, he quickly sensed that it was directed to him alone, and that it was for him she had smiled that smile, spoken those brief sentences, made those gestures with her fingers, caressing his arm.

"She was nineteen, and I was over fifty, and so we arrived together in Paris."

Stephanie de Morlay lived in a large apartment on the Avenue du Bois; she was waiting, and she was understanding. Like the ambassador, she welcomed Mina Kransky, and, in the ensuing days after the debacle while Paul de Morlay went off to London, it had been Stephanie who had insisted that Mina accompany her to that great house in Perigord where they were to live together throughout the war.

"Mina is not perhaps a great pianist, but she plays Liszt and Schubert divinely. And Stephanie, whose sight is beginning to fail, likes to listen to her play Schumann. So one evening Mina will play Liszt and

Schubert for herself, and on the next evening she plays Schumann for Stephanie, and both of them are happy."

The ambassador had spoken in the present tense. Lise looked at him. "And you?"

"Me? I return to Paris each winter and find them there together. For that matter, I'm going there soon, for we have finished our work, and it becomes damp early here in the Veneto. I shall listen to Mina and her piano, and Stephanie will tell me what she has been up to over the summer. She still sees many young people."

The Avenue du Bois is now the Avenue Foch, the walls of the apartment are lined with books and Stephanie is writing her memoirs, polishing them lovingly as if they were a gun she was about to fire—shooting to kill—at everything she has detested throughout her life.

"She lives with such intensity. Do you know that in May of 1968 she almost went out to man the barricades?"

An elderly woman of seventy-five waving a red flag? After all, she was the same impulsive Stephanie Kovaks who had so earnestly supported freedom on that first train to Budapest.

"I'm sure she would enjoy telling you her stories, for that matter. And you would not be bored."

Paul de Morlay had made his last remark with a glance to the side; there had been something ironic in his voice, a certain emphasis, as though he might have been issuing an invitation. But Lise Bergaud was too aware of all that had been exchanged between them that evening —for it had been a kind of exchange—not to have sensed it. But she said nothing. The entire night had fallen silent around them. Even the song of the cicadas and crickets in the huge plane trees on the lawn and in the cyprus above the trimmed box hedges had ceased. Even the tender, gentle breathing of Barberina and Despinetta, who were sitting nearby on the white stone balustrade of the gallery, was hushed. Only a large night moth flew around them, singing its wings in the lamp that lit the scene.

"I'm sure you would not be bored!"

It was an invitation. Lise Bergaud looked steadily at that very old man who had grown young, who had just told her four, five, six moments out of his life. In a few short words, he had proposed they continue. Lise accepted the invitation at its full value.

"And you, too, I imagine, you might have some stories left to tell me."

Paul de Morlay smiled. He was tired but happy, exhausted but serene. So many certainties . . .

"Yes, and I, too, may have some stories left to tell you."

Lise closed her eyes for a few moments. She imagined the life awaiting her in Paris. The man who had left her and who now seemed so unimportant. Her friends, the newspaper for which she sometimes wrote such useless articles. Her publisher. The long, empty evenings at the Closerie des Lilas or the Coupole, passing acquaintances. One-night stands, sleeping until morning in a strange bed. She saw all that and more. It was enough. She opened her eyes again.

"And might you not need a secretary? Someone to help you with your papers? To put those stories together for you?"

She meant: someone to live close to you, with you, with Stephanie and Mina, with Barberina and Despinetta—because, of course, Barberina and Despinetta would be there, too. It would last six months, a year, longer: it would last for life. And Paul de Morlay understood as well. Suddenly, and like the young man he had always been since their first meeting at the beginning of this book, he rose and stood before her.

"Why not?"

His voice was full of laughter, but his eyes were serious.

"Why not!"

Standing, too, she had answered him in the same voice. Then he kissed her forehead, held her close to him for a few seconds and released her.

"Upon these good resolutions, which I take to be a contract duly agreed upon, one whose details are not worth the trouble to discuss, I shall now go up to bed."

He had already left the veranda, followed by Barberina and Despinetta, and was halfway up the large staircase leading to the second floor when he turned back to her once more.

"Don't forget—all the same—that I was born in 1890!"

Lise Bergaud walked in the park the rest of the night.

Three days later the large white Bentley, driven by the same chauffeur with his fallen angel's face, took Lise and Paul de Morlay to Venice. The countryside was ablaze with the final glorious hues of autumn, and on the way, for one last time, the facades of the neo-Palladian villas outshone the oil storage tanks and factory chimneys.

On the train, which was only a common express with two sleeping cars, Lise and the ambassador occupied compartments fifteen and seventeen in the middle of the car. But through a miracle a real restaurant car had been added to the train with a real menu, one like those in the old days so many years before when the ambassador had traced and retraced his way across Europe in search of that youth that had refused to fade. Perhaps, like those millionaires who had once lit their cigars with twenty-dollar bills, he had merely had this last luxury car attached to the train for his own personal use, with its Galle crystal that had escaped all the breakage and the museums. The other passengers who were also to profit from it could not know that their journey was like a return to some lost time. Were they even at all surprised to find caviar and *foie gras* on the menu instead of the usual steak and french fries?

Padua, Vicenza, Verona: the way back. Frescoes by Giotto, white-pillared villas, the lovers on their balcony and night falling over the landscape, pink and mauve, scarlet and violet and soon deep blue. Brescia, Treviso: the train dashed past the brilliantly lit stations with a long hooting that was like a shout of joy.

Seated across from Paul de Morlay, Lise Bergaud had brought with her to the table a completed book—this book—but more than that, she brought with her her zest for living, discovering, seeking, which she had always hitherto ignored. She was smiling as she had never smiled before, another kind of smile.

"I telephoned to Stephanie and Mina, and they will be at the station," the ambassador remarked, before biting into a slice of toast carefully laden with *foie de canard*. And Lise, blond and unbelievably young, burst out laughing; she had become both of them, Stephanie and Mina, at once.

At the neighboring table—they had wanted to leave Lise and the ambassador alone together—Barberina and Despinetta were devouring with relish the same toast and *foie gras*, echoing her laughter. Soon that last remnant of the Orient Express would arrive at Domodossola; at Tonnerre or Joigny the sun would rise, and tomorrow would be a day unlike any other day.

"After all, all the stories I have to tell you are really just beginning. . . ." Paul de Morlay murmured.